SILVER KINGDOM

ARABELLA ROSIER

Silver Kingdom
Book Two

Find me at: www.arabellarosier.com
Instagram: @bookisharabella
Tik Tok: @rosierarabella

Printed in Australia.

First edition: June 2023

Paperback ISBN: 978-0-6453965-3-9
Hardback ISBN: 978-0-6453965-4-6

Special thanks and acknowledgement to:
Editor – Chloe's Chapters,
Cover artist – Gab Nao Designs,
Formatter – Author Services Australia.
This book is written in British English.

For the readers and dreamers who feel like
they're too big for this world...
Let's meet where the stars shine
and the nights are long.

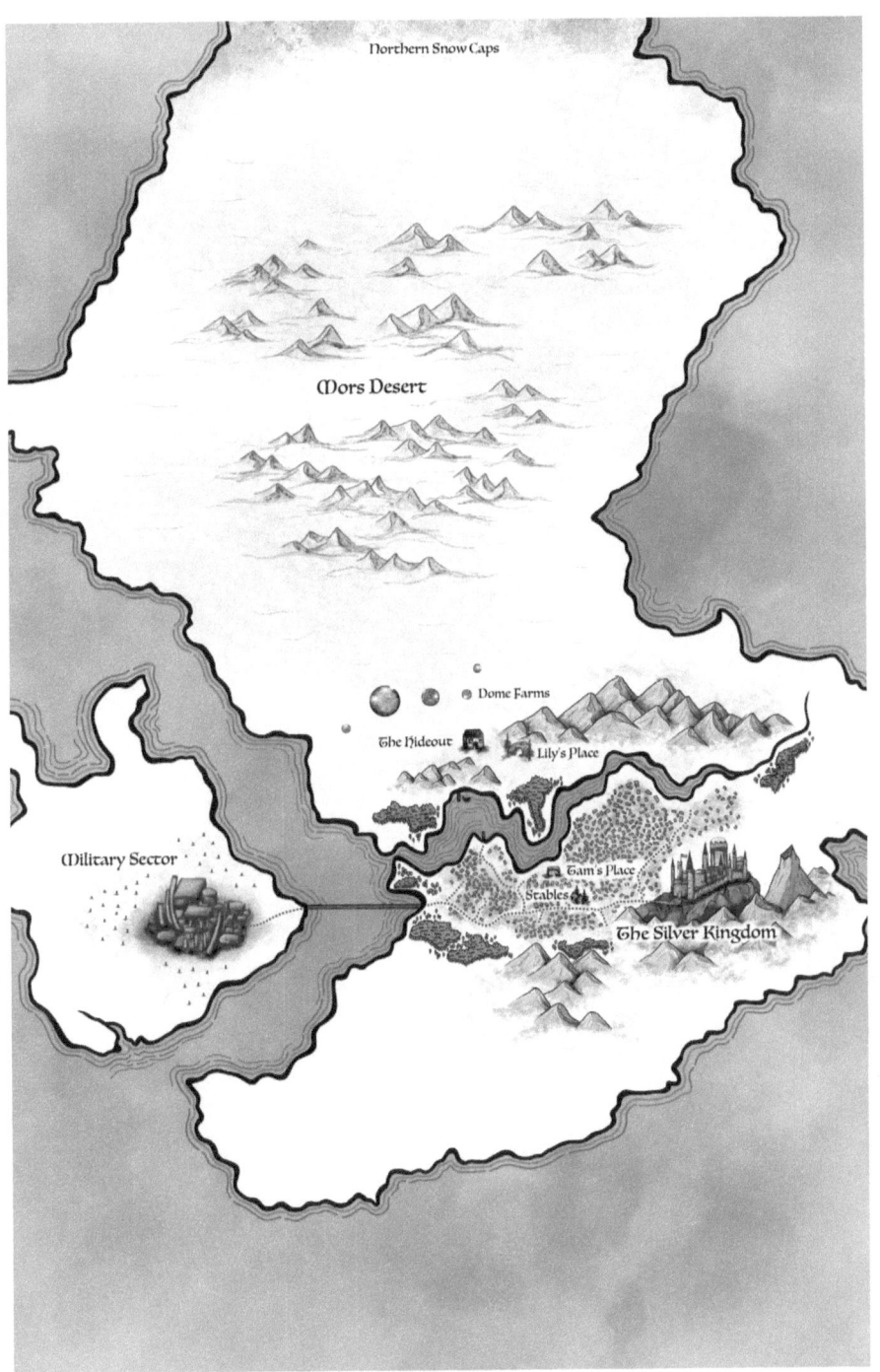

PROLOGUE

The scent of coffee will forever be haunting.

It mixes with the tang of blood that spreads over the metal floor—the same red hue as the Second Night lights and the handle of the dying man's blade.

His warm, familiar face strains as he reaches for that red handle, his fingers pushing past the white coffee cups that shattered on the ground in a storm of ceramic moments before.

Everyone—even the most trained guard—scrambles for their life as death approaches.

Especially when the murderer is their top pupil.

The student, nothing more than a pubescent teen, stands still as his hands drip with his mentor's blood. Under normal circumstances, he would wipe it away, but the scent of coffee pooling at his feet distracts him. It's stronger than the blood. Bitter and burnt.

"I'm very sorry, sir," the pupil utters. Storm clouds rage in his vision, but he doesn't temper them as he meets the soft eyes of the man he once knew. Once idolised.

But that was before the man took over his father's position.

It was before the Captain of Umbra's Guard—the pupil's own father—died.

The ache returns at the thought, pushing aside the smell of bad coffee and blood.

Pain. Emptiness. Nothingness.

The reason he is here tonight.

He is on the path to *escape* these feelings. Escape Umbra.

His mentor splutters his final breath. The light leaves his brown eyes.

He did not relish watching this, and the memory of his sword slicing deep into the wet parts of his mentor's chest will hang over him like a cloud for many nights to come.

It wasn't supposed to be like this.

His mentor wasn't supposed to be here.

The young guard had spent weeks memorising everyone's schedules and sectors.

But even he—a boy who had spent weeks of relentless planning, chest empty with nothing but the need to escape—did not foresee his mentor making a detour to get coffee this late at night.

He didn't have a choice. Killing his mentor was the only way to escape this cursed planet.

He sharply rounds a corner, forgetting to check for guards in his haste.

The flustered guard he bumps into draws his weapon.

I'm behind schedule. I missed the shift turnover.

"You there. Stop. What's the emergency?"

The pupil—a soldier in his own right—relaxes his face and calmly eases his blood-stained hands into his uniform pockets. A mask. One that every guard knows how to wear.

The one thing he *hated* doing.

It made him squirm. Feel unprofessional. Wrong in every way imaginable.

"No emergency, sir. I'm getting coffee for the men on the late shift." The lie slips easily from his lips, accompanied with a smile.

In truth, the blasted smell of coffee from the prior room still ails him.

"Well then, slow down. You're as red as a tomato."

The boy nods and heads back down the corridor toward the main hangar, head low as he tries to stay silent. His sword bounces against his calf, straining to be used.

Lights flash above him, illuminating the darkness—the blinding walls lining almost every hall in Umbra.

The boy shivers.

Cold dread surges into his heart.

The boy fears nothing these days. Nothing but the cold nights.

This will be the last one he will ever see, anyway.

He pulls his sword out of his belt and jams it under the control panel to the hangar. The panel blocks general access, but the lock can be disabled and removed if toggled.

Sweat beads his brow as he labours on it.

He has exactly five minutes until the next guard makes his rounds.

He could probably kill those ones too, but his legs are wobbling far too much. The scent of death usually doesn't make him so unsteady, but chills tickle his skin, and a small breath escapes him as the lights on the door blink rapidly.

Faster than expected.

The boy pushes the door open, leaving bloody fingerprints where skin touched metal.

And he bumps directly into yet another guard.

Stars, don't they have better things to do?

"Sir," the new guard almost shouts, turning his head from his post.

He smiles sweetly at him, his heart hammering, then beelines for the take-off port.

He doesn't even know where the shuttle is going to depart. That is the kind of knowledge only a hacker can discover. And he is anything but.

Whatever. He knows the guards on duty. He knows their whereabouts. And it's close to several ports.

Which reduces the number of ships he needs to check from 500 to four.

Someone yanks him back by his sleeve.

"Hey—"

He spins around and jams the butt of his knife into the stranger's head, throwing the questioning guard to the ground. The man who tried to stop him is old and grey and glares at the boy from the floor.

The only people with hair that colour have been to Terra. Many times.

"I've been sent by Liaison Stone to escort the prisoners to Terra," he tells the greying man hastily.

"Stone is already on the shuttle," the old man narrows his eyes. "He said nothing about another guard—"

"Those are my orders and if you were an elite, you would know what's going on."

"I'm Inner Circle—" he begins, not even questioning the blood on the hands pinning him to the ground.

He releases him. "Good for you."

And before the old man has time to collect himself, he spins on his heels and dashes away again. The sound of his own blood pounds in his ears.

Let's see if your old legs can catch me.

If the old man is smart, he won't say anything despite his reservations. Questioning the authority of the Liaison could be enough to get him kicked out of the Inner Circle.

It doesn't take long to find the ship leaving for Terra.

There's only one hangar swarming with guards—the usually

quiet section now alive with movement. The tall electric fence, temporarily disabled, is yawning wide open.

The boy's father was a pilot. Not him.

He's never been past these gates.

With a twisting gut, he sneaks past it, lowering himself into a storage area filled with wooden crates. They are being loaded into a different compartment than the prisoners, and the guards are nearly finished. The boy waits until none are looking his way, then ducks down and runs into the entrance.

It's almost too easy.

He wants to laugh, but his chest is too empty to allow the notion.

Once inside, he springs to action, his sword bumping against his thigh. What many people don't know—and he was only privy to because he listened for years in rapture when his father told him stories of flying—is that any part of the ship is accessible through mechanic hatches.

It takes him only a few heartbeats to find one.

Not a minute too soon, because the door to the storage unit slams shut behind him with a resounding crack, and his breathing grows laboured with panic.

Once the ship takes off, the passenger bay is the only place that will have oxygen, and his time is running out.

The shuttle starts to hum with the beginnings of take-off.

He squeezes through, hands jumbling through wires, his throat feeling tight. His heartbeat slams in his head as he navigates the tight space. Full of wires and metal and screens that pull out, jumbled with code.

He twists like a man dying, fingers arching for the small plate ahead. The hatch that will lead him to the passenger bay. The path to safety.

The ship locks into gear.

Air sucks out of his lungs.

He feels his foot tangle in a wire but the electricity pounding through his veins sends a fit of adrenaline to his legs and he tumbles free.

His fingers brush the exit.

His head feels like it's about to explode.

With a slam of his shoulder, the hatch to the passenger bay bursts open, breathing air into the tight space. He pulls it into his lungs, body sinking to the metal flooring under his stomach.

He waits a solid beat, coughing and gasping before dragging himself out of the small space.

He did it. He made it. He's leaving.

The space before him is cavernous. The prisoners stand locked in cuffs against the sterile metal walls, and the remaining lucky delinquents that are going to Terra roam among the centre of the ship, unsure what to do with themselves.

There aren't any seats in the shuttle. Only walls and windows.

This is not a joy ride.

He slowly sinks onto the floor and pushes the hatch quietly back into place, hiding it behind his back. His head rests on the metal, lungs still gulping in the scent of metallic air.

Everyone is too busy with the departure to notice him, but he feels watched regardless.

Despite the speed of take-off, he barely feels it, his mind not in sync with his body. If not for the dizzying blur of motion out of the window ahead of him, he wouldn't have noticed their departure at all. Umbra is already far behind them. The world flashes past in streaming colours, until it hurts to look at.

He squeezes his eyes shut.

"You're not as subtle as you think."

A soft voice. Sharp words.

He jolts, head spinning.

To his left, a girl sits hunched with her arms around her legs. She looks older than him, but not by much. Her light hair is soft and elegantly arranged. There are bruises around her eyes, on her arms, on her wrists.

"Were you watching me?"

The girl just looks at him, silver eyes piercing. "You know, there are easier ways to sneak onto a ship than crawling through the mechanic's hatch."

He tries not to react, but he can't help but smile a little.

She saw that?

"If you're a hacker, maybe."

The girl's hand spasms. Silk gloves run up her arms, the same colour as her white dress. She looks away from him as though he touched a nerve.

His heart hammers, the nerves in his body firing.

She's royal. A noblewoman at best, despite the bruising on her face.

At any moment she could tell the many guards swarming the ship that he's a stowaway. Her eyes drag past them, pausing on the Liaison at the helm of the ship, then travel back to him.

She pats the ground next to her.

Have a seat, her gaze conveys.

Her eyes are thin and silver, beautiful and terrifying all at once. He doesn't know why, but he feels like he has seen her before, perhaps among the upper classes. She looks like the kind of girl his father would've worked for.

Palms lined with sweat, he scurries across the floor, sitting so close to her that the heat of her body warms his arm.

Every muscle in his body stiffens.

"Oh, calm down," she mutters. "You officially snuck onto a shuttle that no one wants to be on. I won't announce you."

The heat in his veins turns to ice.

"So, you're a prisoner?" he asks.

Despite the bruises on her skin, her wrists aren't bound.

She merely huffs.

A passenger, then. An abused passenger, but a passenger, nonetheless.

"I am here with my uncle. I will probably never see Umbra again."

"Good riddance."

She shakes her head, unable to comprehend his contempt. "Are you on this shuttle to find the girl in the prophecy, then? You don't seem the type."

He tries to ignore her bluntness, not caring enough to snap back. Instead, he blows out a breath. "I'm here to escape."

She sucks in a deep lungful air. "We're all escaping from something."

There's more to her words then she lets on. But he doesn't pry.

Instead, he gives her a soft smile.

The first genuine smile he has made in a long, long while.

The girl extends her hand out to him. She seems determined. *Resolved.* If he had stayed on Umbra and made it to guard status, she might have been the kind of person he would've wanted to work for.

"My name is Melanie Beckett," she says.

He takes her hand and shakes it, the chills easing from his body. "Jesse Hayes."

PART ONE

THE ASHES

SAVANNAH

I hate Umbra.

I suppose I can't speak on the planet itself, but these days, I hate anything that reminds me of the people who bombed my home.

The island I knew is gone. Corpses are buried in the dirt beneath our feet, the absence of their liveliness a constant scream in my mind, reminding me of what I've done to them. They haunt my nightmares, my every waking moment.

I let them.

My thoughts are a riot of plans. My every breath counted, passing the time. Greenery has begun to climb back over the burnt trunks around us and the smell of smoke has long vanished.

Time is relative, but since the Elders blew up my home, every second goes into solidifying my plan to destroy them.

My fingers curl where they rest on Mason's chest, his Umbran cotton shirt fluttering around my hand.

I want to hold his tiny hands and never let him go. Ever.

The brother before me is no longer a child, and yet the innocence and awe that sweeps out of his searching eyes makes my heart squeeze.

It's been a couple months since the bombing.

Mason's eyes catch on the burnt landscape around us as if it isn't any less beautiful than what it had been a couple months ago.

I promised Mason I would take him to see the other side of the island, but without a Hover and with the massive clean-up needed in the Valley, it wasn't easy to make arrangements.

I release a soft breath, hands stilling in his curls.

It's a matter of fate that he is alive. On the night of the bombing, Mason and my father were out on a scouting party for me. It was late when they finished for the night, so they decided to spend the night at Mason's friends' house—the twins, Axel and Alexis—who live on the outskirts of town.

My father woke early that morning, as he regularly does, and saw the first bomb streaming from the sky.

Mark Shaw, a seemingly ordinary human, had made all the difference.

He had pulled survivors in various stages of pain and grief towards the northern finger of the island, using the untouched warehouse as a base.

If my brother hadn't been out so late that night, he would have gone home and my father would have woken only to see the first bomb sail down upon our home, right above where Mason would have been nestled in bed.

Fate, immediate action, and immaculate planning had all played a role in his survival.

I will do everything in my power to keep it so.

Jesse had offered to take us to the other side of the island the moment he had acquired a new Hover by rummaging through the excess wreckage.

I lean against the seatback of the vehicle, eyes glassing over. This Hover is much grander than Jesse's old one, all swooping angles and silver surfaces, a slightly uncomfortable but plush seat sprawling behind the driver's position, held in on either side by thin silver railings.

"I can't believe all of this is real," Mason murmurs, not for the first time.

I blink, giving him a soft smile.

"Wait until you see the base."

My heart compresses with those words, but Mason doesn't notice.

The base.

A wreck, now.

Smouldering, destroyed, and littered in bodies, I had urged Jesse to help clear it up before allowing my brother through the forest.

My hands shake, but I will it away, letting a steely calm overtake me. My arms cross over my chest, holding myself together.

The memory of the bombing is a distant ache, but one that never quite leaves.

The trees around us begin to lose their colouring, turning from green to brown, then to nothing but skeletons. Mason lifts his head up from my lap and watches as the edge of the base comes into sight.

My hands start to tremble a little, but I clench them into fists, jaw set.

Not your fault. The Elders' fault.

Those words have been a constant stream in my head since then.

Not. Your. Fault.

At the very least, it's a mess I can try and make right.

Jesse slows the Hover down, his back tensing.

Like a plague, death follows him—according to him, at least.

"Welcome to the Dome City," he says to my brother.

The same welcome he gave me in this city all those months ago, in the facility they first placed me in. I roll my eyes at the memory.

My brother, of course, doesn't pick up Jesse's sour expression and bounces in his seat, hands trailing the silver railings as if he can't wait to pull himself free.

"Ready to go look?" I ask him, already knowing the answer, but enjoying the way his face lights up at my words.

He pulls himself out of the Hover with an ease I never had. He's bouncing on the balls of his feet as he takes a step forward across the charred dirt, a dimpled smile stretching across his face.

"It's pretty ugly out there, kid," Jesse warns.

"Yeah, but it's probably just like Silver Valley. I'm used to that."

I grip my switchblade so tight I'm scared it'll break the bones in my hand. The small blade—its metal sourced from Umbra, the mahogany handle from Terra—had once belonged to my old friend, Jasmine Spark. It's become a part of me, a source of comfort.

I slowly release the death-grip on the handle, controlling my breath. Jesse turns to look at me, brow deepening.

My brother wanders towards the wreckage, but I wait a moment before following him. Jesse holds my gaze, the sapphire hue of his eyes piercing my own. I catch onto that look and the meaning he's trying to portray.

He doesn't want to explore his old home.

A small flush develops on his face and he starts to tap his fingers on his sword.

"How far have you been in?" I ask him.

"Outskirts, only looking for the things I need."

I want to take his hand, but he's too lost in his thoughts to notice me.

"Have you found anything useful, other than the Hover?"

His gaze deepens and he fingers the knives on his belt. "A few lower-class men of the Liaison have crept out. It doesn't usually take them long to talk."

Through torture.

I swallow the lump in my throat. "Right."

"I'll let you know if anything useful comes out of it."

"I know you will."

The fact he hasn't mentioned this before tells me what I need to know.

His fingers finally grasp his sword and his expression eases the way it always does when he murders an enemy. I take a step towards him, lifting my hand with shaking fingers to brush a lock of dark hair out of his eyes. The movement shocks him. His eyes blink rapidly, shaking away that calmness.

He turns away from me abruptly, mouth in a hard line.

For months, we have been training together, honing my muscles and teaching me how to hold a blade. I've felt the pressure of his hands on many parts of my body, showing me how to stand, how to fight. But this feels different. It feels uncharted, and when he continues to walk away from me, I want to scream.

I have absolutely no idea how to console him and feel even worse when he says, "I've never completely gotten used to death."

I want to ask him why. I've seen him wield miracles with those blades, but I don't dare utter a single word.

He stands before the wreckage like a pillar, the breeze ruffling his black shirt.

I take a deep breath and begin my search for Mason.

His animated frame wanders by the edges of destroyed buildings, his eyes wide, seeing past the wreckage, most likely wondering how it all looked before the trails of fire fell from the sky.

His whimsical eyes have no trouble seeking the glory of what had once been.

I trudge forward into the soot, making my way towards him. It cushions my footfalls, making my stride almost completely silent.

I don't have to turn to know that Jesse is following me. I feel him behind me, always silent to the ear.

Of course, an effort has been made to clear the debris, but with most of the Umbran population dead, progress was limited. The inhabitants kept to certain areas—resurrecting old facilities to turn them into apartments, burying who they could find and pushing aside imposing debris to make pathways. But still, the base is a maze, even more than it had been before. Everything is blackened—just chunks of ash, metal, wood and stone.

I can feel the souls compressing against me as we walk through the wreckage.

"Do you think Mum will come back to us now?" Mason asks as we sidle up beside him.

I take in his hopeful eyes.

"No offense, kid, but she doesn't seem the sentimental type," Jesse answers.

I've told Mason pretty much everything I've learnt, but when it came to our mother, the stories were significantly watered down.

Remember, the Elders always win.

"No, Mason. She won't."

He turns his head to me and I watch my younger brother's shoulders sink.

"You have enough family, kid. A whole bucket-load. Enough lovey-dovey to drive you to insanity and back again. You'll live," Jesse mutters.

I turn to him, my gaze wilting.

Mason kicks a bit of metal with the toe of his shoe. "I guess."

Jesse nudges his shoulder. "Here."

He leaps up onto the stone behind Mason, holding the butt of a knife out to him.

"Oh?" He handles it gently.

"To ward away the ghosts."

We watch as Jesse glides down the other side of the rock, disappearing into the abyss of debris.

His meaning is clear: enough moping.

Mason and I follow him clumsily, fingers clawing at the stone as we climb over. The other side is a mess of sharp metal and fallen branches.

I find tiny footholds within the fallen stone and metal, breathing heavily as I pull myself up. Mason follows me proudly, trying not to smile at the promise of an adventure.

I swing my leg over a beam and land somewhat awkwardly on the beaten path. The surviving Umbrans have cleared away a section of the medical facilities to continue storing and administering medicine.

The hair on my skin stands on end.

I recognise this area. Melanie kept me here the first time I came to the base.

I squint my eyes, leaning forward.

Thankfully, we don't stray that far into the wreckage. And as soon as I regain my footing, my breath catches.

My heart starts to hammer.

Blood roars in my ears.

"Mason, stay behind me."

I yank my brother behind a scrap of metal, too flustered to feel sympathy when he stumbles.

"Wha—"

"Shhh."

I pop my switchblade open. On the blade, in Jasmine Spark's handwriting, flashes the looping word *perseverance*.

Jesse's sword is out, his brow scrunched. If I didn't know him, I'd be scared of him. The man pulling himself from the wreckage certainly is.

A newcomer wobbles towards us down the cleared road, blood on his hands, a roughly spun bandage around his calf.

"Stop," Jesse growls.

The brute does, bloodstained teeth splitting his mouth when he realises who he has stumbled across. His eyes go directly past Jesse, landing on me and taking in my flimsy Umbran switchblade.

I stop breathing, staring at him.

The man I fought on the stage months ago in The Nook. The one that should still be locked up in the safeholds.

The one I stole my blade from.

"Excellent," he calls out to me. "I was hoping we'd bump into each other, Savannah Shaw."

And then Jesse slashes his sword at the brute's neck.

SAVANNAH

"Who is that?"

"Mason, get back. Now," I growl through my teeth.

The man shuffles backwards along the ground, one hand in the sky, palm out. Jesse's sword only nicked his shoulder, as he yanked himself away in time, probably anticipating the attack. Jesse can be somewhat predictable.

But the brute can't yet notice that he's planning another attack.

Not like I can.

Jesse has a tell.

Each time before he lunges, he braces his shoulders, as if in fear of inflicting pain on his opponent—he will kill if he has to, but that doesn't mean he always wants to.

The only time this tell dissolves is when Jesse melts into a state of red-hot fury, when all he can think about is survival or protecting someone.

This isn't one of those times.

"He doesn't have a weapon. Tell Jesse to stand down," Mason mumbles from behind me, face peering out from behind the scrap of metal.

"*I* have his weapon," I answer him, twisting my switchblade in the air.

Mason's mouth pops open as he makes the connection of who we're facing—probably remembering one of my stories.

Jesse's shoulders hunch as he twirls his sword in the air almost lazily, aiming it across the brute's throat once more. This time, lying on his back with nothing but his elbows to prop himself up, the brute won't be able to dodge.

He inhales deeply. Noticeably.

When I finally told Jesse about his tell, he just shrugged it off.

"Weakness only proves that you're human," he had said.

The furrow between his brows had told me that it bothered him.

Jesse isn't the kind of person who likes to be viewed as weak.

I walk slowly up to him now, placing my hand on his shoulder, reminding him of this—and in turn, his reluctance to kill the man.

"Your tell isn't a weakness, Jesse. It shows you have compassion." I had responded.

He lowers his sword slightly at my touch.

"I've been trying to find you," the brute mumbles from the ground, eyes landing on me.

I angle my body above him, switchblade hanging at my side, and remember what it felt like to once be in his position.

I'm stronger than this man now.

Training has forged my muscles, while this man has been rotting in a cell, growing weak. His skin looks ashen, dark bruises under his eyes, shoulders shaking from the trouble of supporting himself on the ground.

"Why?"

"Savannah." He purrs my name and I shiver angrily. "Savannah, our *wondrous* leader. We need you."

"Lose the attitude or I'll pike you to the dirt," Jesse warns.

To my shock, the man actually flinches.

"I'm willing to make a deal," he says.

Jesse scoffs. "You're in no position."

He pushes himself higher off the dirt, and Jesse brandishes his sword closer to him.

"Actually"—he smiles—"I am."

The swagger and peacocking I remember return to his features, the gratitude of being superior and praised.

"I have a large network," he continues.

"So do we," Jesse retaliates.

That's a lie.

We *had* a large network, before the bombs blew nearly everyone up.

The man simply raises a brow.

The sour expression on Jesse's face informs me he's about ready to kill him.

"How did you get out of your cell?" I butt in, easing my way in front of Jesse.

The brute licks his lips. "I have a friend. An old acquaintance. Jasmine-freaking-James. Can you believe it? The little girl still exists?" He starts to laugh. "You might want to give her back my switchblade, missy."

My stomach rolls, but I keep my nausea from showing on my face.

I haven't seen Jasmine since before the bombing. I knew she was still alive, only because she'd left messages. She'd leave little notes for me to find on my pillow, bound up in twine.

"I've been to the base today again, found more survivors."

"You haven't been in the forest for a while, hope you're okay."

"Has Melanie been practising her computer skills lately?"

She's still a part of my life, but her absence has left a sizable hole.

And, as usual, I've had the gut-wrenching feeling that her little notes were preparing me for something.

I suppose she has been.

Jesse raises his eyebrows.

From behind, I feel Mason crawl further out from behind the metal at hearing Jasmine's name.

"How?" I ask the brute.

"Electricity went down, but the bars remained in place. When the bombs hit, the rubble caved in. It dislodged my cell door, but I still couldn't pull myself through. Then the little girl came. She brought us food, stories of above, clothes that she likely stole from the dead for us to wear. Eventually, she got me out. Told me to find you. Apparently, you can get us all out."

He swallows deeply and my stomach twists further with his words.

Melanie and I made a promise to save them, but right now the thought terrifies me.

"I don't know how to," I admit.

"But you will, won't you, Savannah?" Mason asks from behind me, his wide eyes hopeful.

I peer down at the brute's rumpled clothes and sunken expression and remember the sight of that small child I met months ago in the cell.

To him, I was salvation.

To him, everyone down those cells are good people.

And I have the power to save them.

"Why did Jasmine send you, of all people?" I ask.

His eyes twinkle. "Because you'd recognise me, sugar."

I taste bile in my throat.

"What's your name?"

"Why does that matter?"

"What's. Your. Name?"

He squirms under my gaze. From the corner of my eye, I see Jesse trying not to smile. I don't need a weapon to gain power over someone and, apparently, he finds that entertaining. Jerk.

I try not to snicker at him.

"Samael."

My brother holds his hand out to the man, a smile on his face. "Nice to meet you, Samael. My name is Mason, and my sister promises that she will try and save your people."

Samael rolls his shoulders back and lifts his forehead to the sun.

The smile on the brute's face makes me want to smack Mason. But the endearing look on his face makes my heart warm. So instead, I wrap my fingers gently around my brother's shoulder.

"It's nice to see some people still have manners," Samael slurs.

Jesse kicks him lightly in the gut, earning a hiccough.

"That's rude!" Mason retaliates, pulling away from my grip.

"And he's a jerk who deserves it. Come on, kid, let's take a step back so the grown-ups can talk."

He pulls my brother towards the Hover, keeping half of his attention trained on me as I help the man up from the dirt.

"I'm not a kid," my brother mumbles.

"Yeah, you are."

"I'm fourteen."

Jesse nudges him forwards with a grin on his face.

I clasp my hand in Samael's. His large palm feels clammy and dry all at once. He stumbles to his feet and smirks at me.

I take a step back, refraining from wiping my hands off on my thigh.

"So, we have a deal?"

"On some conditions." I raise a finger. "No backstabbing. If I save your people, then we are on the same side. In return, when the time comes that we need help from you and your men, you *will* heed our call. No exceptions."

"Sounds like a diplomatic enough response from a wannabe-princess."

"I'm no wannabe."

"Oh, I'm sorry. Forgive the mistake, Your *Highness*."

I grit my teeth. "Don't call me that. I'm not royalty."

He grins deeply, enough that the dry skin on his face crinkles. "Whatever you say, Your Highness."

I kick the dirt and turn away from him, sights set on the Hover.

"See you tomorrow, then?" he calls out.

"Tomorrow," I shout out through gritted teeth.

We both retreat back to our respective corners of the base without another word.

SAVANNAH

E lijah Brooke stands hesitantly near the stream, a woven basket filled with citrus fruits balanced in front of him.

Melanie plunges her muddied hands into the salty water that streams directly from the ocean, washing away the dirt and sap from picking the fruit.

The villagers planted these trees years ago. A small farm, filled with citrus and small, elevated rows of vegetables planted some ways down from the salty water. They are watered via a filtration system that cleanses the salt out of the river, but the fresh water taps are farther away from where Melanie and Eli stand, down by the salty shore.

I stay by the edge of the forest, watching my friends hesitantly.

Winter has come to the Valley already; the blackened trees slick with rain and the ground beneath our feet muddied. I wind my coat tightly around me, making sure it blocks the thin sprinkle of rain from contacting my skin.

One of the survivors offered this farm behind the warehouse as a source of communal food, but the frigid temperatures offer a limited supply of fruit and vegetables. Money trade has ceased and everyone works together to keep warm and fed in the lingering effects of crisis. Word has slowly spread about the base across the island, but among the truth there are far more lies.

What surprised us all the most was how people stayed on-island after the bombs, despite that wobbly truth and the threat of otherness.

Twice a month, someone will sail to the mainland to get materials such as medicine, clothes, and food we can't source on the island, and the stiffness of my coat proves that it came from a recent shipment.

Other than those scant supplies, we fend for ourselves.

A pair of cows wanders over to the other side of the stream, wading by the salty currents and I watch Eli as he turns his head to me.

The loss of the Valley has been hard on him. He's worlds away from the boy I once knew. He is no longer Elijah Brookes, rich kid of the Valley and an annoying pain in Jesse's butt. Instead, he became the quiet kid in the corner, working constantly alongside Melanie to put food on the table for the survivors. At night, I hear him choking back sobs from behind the thin curtain separating our beds.

Even Melanie pretends to be less irritated by his presence, given everyone he's lost. To him, she is the girl that saved him from extinction in the safeholds. To her, he is her first loyal supporter in the quest to free Umbra.

Melanie comes back up from the stream, rubbing her hands on her pants.

"We need to fix a fence to keep the cattle in," Eli tells her.

"What's the point? They're trained enough to stay."

"The bombing scared them," he says quietly.

"I don't blame them, but there are more pressing concerns, Elijah."

She's right. He knows she is. But that doesn't mean he doesn't wish for an ounce of normalcy to return.

He lowers his eyes, and Melanie reaches out and touches his chin, bringing his gaze to hers.

"You'll be okay," she says quietly.

His eyes burn into hers and I bat my eyelashes against the moisture, glancing away from the intimacy of this moment. Their friendship has grown strong in the last few months, almost as much as mine has with Jesse.

Eli nods and Melanie drops her hand.

I clear my throat.

They both turn their heads to the forest, noticing me leaning against a tree facing the stream.

"Speaking of concerns," Melanie says, taking me in. "Savannah?"

I pick my way down towards them, sneakers squelching in the mud.

The sun twinkles between the clouds, casting a glare on the lake, and I avert my eyes as I approach them.

"What's wrong?" Melanie asks.

"Why would something be wrong?" I ask.

"It's your face," Eli grumbles. "You have this doomsday expression whenever you have to ask something horrible and revolutionary of us."

"When have I ever done that?" I rebut.

"Enough times for us to recognise the expression," Melanie says, trying not to laugh when I frown at them.

I resist the urge to roll my eyes, the muscles in my face twitching into a smile.

"Whatever. Looks like so-called leadership isn't exactly becoming of me these days."

"What happened, Savannah?" She fiddles with her wrist, fingers rubbing over the soft skin. Her glove has been stuffed into her pocket, revealing the wires from the still-open wound on her arm. Melanie Beckett lost her forearm in a fire when she lived on Umbra as a girl and had built herself a cyborg prosthetic. But months ago, before the bombing, she injured it. She absently attempts to shield it from view as she stands before me.

She won't be able to access any skin grafting until she gets to Umbra, and the way she always picks at the loose string of her glove when she wears it around the base tells me she isn't quite ready to tell the villagers about her arm.

Having it off now, after washing her hands, makes her fidgety.

She shoves her hands into her pockets and sways on her feet. Her strained silver eyes stare into my own.

And I explain to them what went down at the base.

They knew we were taking Mason there this morning. I hated the troubled look on Melanie's face that haunted her before we left. As we all suspected, she wanted to come with us; she probably wanted to turn it into a scouting trip to figure out how to get back at the Elders.

Her breathing turns short and sharp, small plumes of fog puffing out of her round lips in the cold. A small glint shines in her eyes, like stars during a new moon.

"He wants us to free the prisoners," she interrupts before I finish explaining.

"Excuse me, what?" Eli chimes in. "You want to go *back* to that prison place?"

"They're all like you, Elijah. Most of them are innocent."

She grabs an orange from his basket and starts bouncing it around her hands, her eyes glazing with the familiar look of someone contemplating a strategy.

I cross my arms. "I think Jasmine suspects you're the key to freeing them, Melanie. She sent me a note a week ago asking if you've been keeping up with your hacking... I hope you have been?"

My mind had been whirring with an idea the entire trip back to the base.

"Of course," Melanie mumbles. "I know how to override the main gates. It will be complicated, but manageable. But how do we get the bars open? And where will we put all these wounded people?"

"Don't worry about that yet," I say, grinning. "I'm... working on something. Meet me in my father's office in an hour, and bring a map of the base if you have one. Draw one if you don't. I'll meet you both there."

The orange stops bouncing from hand to hand, and she narrows her eyes at me.

Eli snatches the citrus from her grip. She doesn't even notice as she stands frozen, staring at me.

I turn back towards the forest, my brain whirring with the makings of a revolution.

ᔕ

I knew I would find Jasmine by the trees bordering the Valley, just off where my old house had been, only deeper. It doesn't take a genius to guess that she's been watching me this whole time anyway.

My only concern is that she took longer than an hour to make an appearance.

I lean against a tree, twirling my switchblade in my fingers.

The soot surrounding my street doesn't bother me as much as it used to. I haven't been living there long enough to really call it a home.

It's good to recognise that 'home' isn't supposed to be tangible. Family is what makes a home.

Because this place—my old house—is devoid of life.

My breathing is short and steady as I take it in, the fog from the mountains lapping at the base of the trees around me.

I twist my feet in the mud at my feet, sneaker tapping against a piece of wood.

My shoes are caked in the stuff from walking back and forth across the Valley all afternoon. First, I went to see my father, who is so busy with running the warehouse lately that he hardly had time to talk. He agreed to meet me later though, probably sensing the urgency in my expression.

Then I went to find Melanie and Eli.

After that, I wandered past the baker's quarters. Alongside the community, Bronson spent the last couple months rebuilding his bakery—providing the township with bread in return. I almost felt bad asking him to bake extra bread for tomorrow morning, knowing it isn't for any of the villagers.

The rain ceased but my hair still clings damply across my cheeks. I stand under a sheet of metal in the forest, trying to ignore how uncomfortable I feel.

Jesse has taken it upon himself to make watch posts around the Valley. I have no idea how many he's constructed, but so far I've only used two—and only when we've trained together outside.

He positioned them just above our heads, each scrap of metal a couple of metres long within the canopies. Any normal person would assume it's just a random piece of debris, which works both for the humans and those in the base, but their purpose serves as protection from the never-ending winter drizzle.

None of us trust that someone from Umbra won't return to check on us, especially now that we're nearing the optimal period when travel between Umbra and Terra is most direct.

I'm used to standing sweaty and shivering from the rain as the metal patters above me, but now all is silent, and I clearly hear the moment when my old friend announces herself from the forest.

I try to control my breathing, to keep my face even, but it feels like my chest is about to explode at the sight of her.

Her frizzy, blonde mane sits pulled back from her face, a brown coat covering her chest. Mud lines her ankles from her trek across the forest. She's dressed both for dexterity and warmth, and it surprises me. I've never seen Jasmine Spark dress so practically. She looks so mature.

"You're starting to look your age," I say in greeting.

Her forehead crinkles as she frowns at me. "Please try not to insult the help."

I roll my eyes, my heartbeat a deep throb in my chest. "Sure. I forget that Umbrans enjoy looking as smooth and unnatural as a boiled egg."

"You forget that you're one of them."

"Not really."

She snorts and wanders up to me, the matted grass squelching under her feet. Jesse has trained me how to walk quieter than that and her loudness makes me suck on my lips. She closes the distance between us slowly, her fingers shaking slightly. From cold or fear, I'm not sure.

There are so many unspoken words between us.

Gone are the days where we did everything by each other's side—when Jasmine Spark was my closest friend.

In the place of the girl I once knew stands a stranger, a person who manipulated my life since the moment I was born—Jasmine Spark lied about her age, her past, even fabricated herself into a new family by using Silver Magic. She is a liar, a cheater, a grand manipulator, and everything about her makes my hands shake.

I shove my hands against my chest, crossing my arms to hide the vibrations rocking up my body.

Her soft blue eyes take me in, bright against the gloomy day, analysing me like prey.

She's the only person I have ever met that has tricked an Elder.

Around the time I was born, she managed to escape from an Umbran prison cell and catch a shuttle to Terra to find me. No one else has managed to obtain such a feat, and if I accidently slip, she could fall back into the hands of the Elders.

She knows everything about me, all of my strengths and weaknesses, and right now she is a loose variable—she has no goal, no family, no life—it wouldn't take much for her to hijack a ship from the base and sail to Umbra, falling into the hands of the enemy with enough knowledge to undo everything.

Somewhere above us a bird starts chirping and startles me—it's taken a long while for the animals to return to the forest since the bombing of the island. I take a deep breath and take the last step towards my old friend. Jasmine pauses, then wraps her thin arms around me in a hug. I embrace her back, trying to forget about the extracted switchblade I have resting in one of my hands.

"It's nice to see you, Sav."

"You too." I pull back from her quickly, shivering.

She tucks a stray curl hesitantly behind her ear, unsure what else to say. Her face is flush from the cold, red brimming on her cheeks. Every few seconds her blue eyes dart to the trees, her body swaying, ready to flee.

I tentatively reposition my back against the tree behind me and school my expression. There's no easy way to approach this conversation, so I jump straight to the point.

"I have a proposition for you—a plan for Umbra."

The moment the words leave my mouth, I hold my breath.

Her eyes don't land on me, instead she continues to keep an eye on the trees around us. "Of course you do. I'm the one who brought you here. This is *my* plan."

I take a slow, deep breath, swinging my switchblade shut. My heart pounds long and steady in my chest, a drum in my ears.

She isn't ready to come back to me, the same way I'm not ready to accept her back.

But I need to do this—to let her back in.

Two weeks ago, Melanie taught me about negotiations. Niceties, a willingness to compromise and directness are all key components. It's something her upper-class parents excelled in. I'm not Melanie's parents, but I'll try my best.

I take another deep breath and casually cross my arms. She locks her eyes on the switchblade hanging from my fingers, sensing my reservation.

Jasmine isn't the enemy, not until she decides that I'm her enemy. She's definitely proven herself to be useful in many regards, and that can be utilised.

"Tell me where you're currently standing, Jas. What outcome do you want for Umbra?"

Will you betray me? Will you join the Elders, in the hope that I don't get the crown?

My pulse ticks in my ears as I wait, waiting for her to speak, or to flee.

She sucks on her lips, hands poised awkwardly in front of her. "I still don't want you on the throne. Not really."

My breathing stops for a beat.

She doesn't realise how close her ambitions line up with the Elders.

I straighten my back, picking at a hangnail on my thumb.

"You know I don't really care about the throne. What else?"

"I miss you."

I blink, my heart missing a beat. All the air rushes out of me. "You do?"

"I miss being close to you. I hate that I ruined it."

So, she wants to make amends? I nod slowly, trying not to smile, because I was praying for that possibility.

This is good.

"There's been times I've questioned whether we were ever truly close. I never *truly* knew the real you. But you'll always have a part of my heart, Jasmine—it's one of the reasons I'm here today."

Her shaking hands flutter by her side until she shoves them in her pockets. "So, what you're saying is…?"

"I want you back," I say through my teeth, barely hearing the words. "And maybe we can work to share a mutually beneficial outcome for Umbra."

"And work on rebuilding the past?"

I shake my head. "No, but maybe we can build a future."

She takes a step towards me, her shoulders hunched against the cold. It's strange, what we've become.

The sunlight briefly breaks through the clouds and touches her blonde curls, igniting her hair to look like a halo, an angel sent from the heavens.

"But we both know that you still don't really trust me," she says, her eyes darting back to the trees, her mind seemingly drifting far, far away. I pull myself off the tree, trying to catch her attention before I lose her focus entirely.

I need her spoken agreement. I need her to understand my terms.

I need her on my side.

I can't allow any loose ends.

Picking at the hangnail on my thumb furiously, I quickly speak the truth, "You're smart and you're crafty, Jasmine. You have a way of dealing with people, of knowing how to work situations to your advantage—"

She snaps back to reality. "That's unfair."

"I mean it as a compliment. I'm better at endurance, playing the long game. Together, we make a good team."

Please be on my side, Jasmine.

"So, you want me to paint you a pretty picture of what I want for the future?"

"For starters."

She raises an eyebrow. "And who's to say I have one?"

My lips twitch and I pull one of the many notes she has left me out of my pocket. I grabbed it after talking to my father. In the warehouse we all share close living quarters, but I've been stashing these notes in my father's office in the hope that no one except my family or friends are ballsy enough to go rummaging for them.

It doesn't matter which note I grabbed, any one would do the trick.

"A person without a hope for the future wouldn't bother leaving someone notes in the middle of the night."

She takes a shallow breath and rolls her eyes at me. I can practically hear her thoughts: *typical Savannah, always analysing the meaning of things.*

"Maybe all I wanted was to reach out to my friend. To help people."

My fluttering pulse stills.

She looks at me with her careful, wide eyes, and I feel the world slow.

She still wants to be on my side.

There's still hope for us.

I give her a look, trying not to look exhausted. Instead, I simply tell her, "The brute found me today."

"Oh. Finally."

"He said you freed him," I say slowly.

She nods steadily, eyes drifting to her old switchblade in my hands.

"It needed to be done," is all she says, swallowing deeply on the last word, her eyes drifting to the mud at her feet as if regretting the choice.

All these months, her mind has been ticking. But what she doesn't know is that I've been coming up with a plan too, and she may have just given me the final piece of the puzzle.

No one knows where my mind is at because, unlike Melanie, I haven't been going around complaining about the urgency to go up to Umbra.

Playing the long game…

"Why?" I ask her.

"Honestly?" She snorts. "It had nothing to do with you, Savannah. Maybe I was helping someone else out for once."

I backtrack for a moment, my mind whirring as I stumble over her words.

Helping someone else out for once.

I want to ask her if she's contacted the Elders, if she has picked them over me, but even mentioning them feels terrifying. Sweat licks down my back as I stare at Jasmine, dreading to speak for the fear of planting thoughts into her mind.

She takes a step towards me, tucks another loose lock behind her ears, and says, "I've been keeping an eye on you, sure. But it was an Umbran couple in the base who took me in after the bombing, not you. There's a community of survivors there.

"I've been telling them about the Valley and how you guys are staying afloat after the bombing, and they're using what I know to survive. They're good people, Savannah. They're *my people*, the ones taken and locked up by the Elders. I would've been with them in those cells if things had gone differently for me years ago."

My heart sinks. All the careful words I used—the planning—takes a hit. My thoughts whirl around my head like a storm, accompanying the pounding of my heart.

"I'm sorry. I didn't mean—"

"You didn't know." She brushes away my apology with her hand. "But yes, I want to save them. No one there cares about my past. To the people on this island, all I am now is Jasmine Spark. Just another survivor."

The empty space between us feels like static, yet neither of us bridge the gap.

We both stare at each other, feeling the emptiness as a cold gust whips us.

"I'm glad," I say, trying to smile, pretending that her statement doesn't hurt. "I'm happy you finally found a place in this universe."

She shrugs. "Maybe."

I lift my eyes up to the mountains and watch the drifting fog. And then I try not to smile. She watches the muscles in my cheeks twitch and tilts her head.

Her new family gives her incentive. And it's the same goal I have.

She isn't here for the Elders, she's here for herself.

My muscles tighten at the thought, but I steady my breathing and glance back at her.

"It still doesn't change my proposition."

"Which is what, exactly?"

"I want to take back Umbra—well, not just me, but this whole island. We all play a part in this. Let's shake this universe apart. Together. Would you like to help me?"

Jasmine smiles at me, trying not to show me her hand. Little does she know, she's already given me it.

She might not like me very much right now or want me on the throne, but at least I can offer her something to work for—a unified goal, a way to build a future for our families.

I offer her my hand and, as expected, she reaches out and takes it.

Almost sarcastically, she replies, "For you, Savannah, anything."

SAVANNAH

Everyone I care about is crammed into my father's office, ready to hash out our next steps. The only person missing is my brother, who I sent down to the food hall for dinner.

Elijah spreads the map of the base he and Melanie drew across my father's desk. The sharp scrawl tells me it was predominately drawn by Melanie, her brain moving too fast for her hand as she etched the spiked lines.

Jesse angles himself against the window panel, a fresh cup of coffee in his hands. My father walks around handing more cups out, a joyful bounce to his step.

It doesn't escape me that he's the only adult in the room, but I suppose age doesn't matter much when it comes to revolutions.

Melanie perks up as I enter the room. "What's the game plan, Savannah?"

I shrug off my wet coat and sling it over the chair's back, Jasmine trailing daintily in behind me.

My father misses a step, nearly sloshing coffee onto his jeans.

He knows everything—Jasmine's deception, her influence on our lives—and he doesn't quite know what to make of her anymore. If I had to guess, he hadn't properly addressed her involvement, given she hasn't been around for months. But now, the full severity of her actions seems to settle over him.

They lock eyes across the room and I swear I see Jasmine shrink under his gaze.

"Jasmine," he acknowledges, his eyes downcast.

She swallows a knot in her throat, "Mark."

Everyone turns to look at her and she lowers her eyes, her pale lashes closed into crescent moons above her reddened cheeks.

"Dad, she's on our side," I say, stepping towards my father.

My father's stare lands on me as soon as she turns away, his gaze sharp and full of intent. I can hear the meaning in that look: *So, she's back now? You forgive her? Because I don't think I do.*

"I don't trust her," he tells me, his voice deep.

"No one trusts me, but I can promise I won't get in the way," she says softly, "You won't even know I'm here."

Mark scoffs, "I'll believe that the day you die."

My stomach drops, mouth popping open as I reach over and slap my father. "Dad!"

He turns slowly, giving me a solemn expression, and without other word, turns back to his coffee. He glares down at the dark liquid, his jaw tense.

I release a long breath, turning with trepidation to face the rest of the people in the room. Most of them look amused as they meet my gaze, all but Eli, who's glaring at Jasmine with such a profound hatred I nearly stop breathing.

"Melanie, please show Jasmine the map," I say quietly, determined not to address the weird tension in the room.

The iciness in the air remains, but everyone turns to the task at hand.

Melanie pushes the paper across the desk, leaning towards us with fingers tapping against the heavy wood.

Jasmine wanders closer to the desk. "What about it?"

I hand her a pen out of my father's penholder and point at the map.

My father lifts his head from his coffee, long enough to stare at the pen in Jasmine's pale fingers. It shakes as she grips it, her eyes flashing back to the door behind her.

But my father takes a long breath and turns towards me, giving me the room.

"We're freeing the prisoners from the Safe Holds tomorrow," I announce.

Everyone stops breathing, looking at me with anxious gazes.

I quickly speak before anyone has the chance to comment, "Our biggest blind spot is available housing and large entry points across the base. Your job is to mark all the cleared roads and to identify which buildings are suitable to house, let's say, one hundred prisoners."

"There's one hundred and thirteen of them, last I checked," Jasmine mumbles, her eyes still partially downcast.

I nod, grateful that she knows.

Hardly anyone in the room breathes as the information sinks in.

"How do we know they're still alive?" Melanie enquires.

"I've been in there," Jasmine says quietly, "there's a gap in the building from the bombs. I've been bringing them food and *Sanitas*, but the pills are running out now."

Eli tilts his head, "*Sanitas*?"

"It's medicine, a condensed nourishment pill invented on Umbra post the Moon Blitz when people were struggling—those pills would be enough to keep the prisoner's bodies fighting and functioning. Jasmine, how did you get these? They haven't been regularly created on Umbra in years."

She shrugs half-heartedly, "just found some on the Base."

My heart flutters in my chest. I tap my fingers against the desk, a brief smile fluttering on my face.

This means we might be able to begin training with them immediately.

They won't need months to recover from malnutrition.

We might just have an army on our hands.

"Jasmine, this is great," I say.

She nods, chewing her lip.

"Okay, Jasmine, once you've mapped out the area around the Safe Holds, I want you to jot down all the possible routes towards the hangars, please. We'll need access to them within the next few days for prep, and all debris needs to be cleared by next month for our departure."

Melanie nearly chokes next to me, her eyes widening. "So, we're finally going to Umbra?"

I gnaw on my lips and nod. "It was always in the works, Melanie. When I said it was time the day we were bombed, I meant it."

I notice Jesse smirking next to me, his expression a touch suspicious.

He hasn't been training me for months for nothing.

My father snaps up his head, "Hang on... Savannah?" he asks.

"I'll make it as safe as possible," I assure him, not lifting my head.

"No offence, but your mother is there, and I know her well enough to know that nothing will truly keep you safe from her," he says gently.

My lip shakes, but I swallow sharply and try not to meet my father's eyes.

"I mean, it's obvious she would eventually... you know... go there," Jasmine says, trepidation marking her features.

Mark takes a long, long pull of his coffee.

Melanie clicks her tongue, rapidly changing the conversation back to what's important. "I have been saying we should go for months now, yet you said nothing," she says, looking at me.

"Plans take time and so does preparation," I say, giving her a knowing look. She is the girl who found the prophecy after all. "I planned to depart in June, but I didn't want to say anything until I knew it was possible. For the first time, I can nearly guarantee—"

"Nearly?" she hones in on the word, one brow raised in question.

Mark lowers his coffee down onto the table loudly, his gaze pointed, his body ridged as he prepares himself to also comment on the 'nearly'. I can feel swaths of frustration melting off his body in waves as I continue to speak, "It will happen in June, it was always going to happen in June. But there are still loose ends, and until we get into the hangar…"

Jesse sidles closer to me, his eyes on the window. "What ships will we need, and how many?"

His expression is gloomy, his eyes questioning. I sense distaste, but he knows the inevitability of going home. Despite the ghosts that are waiting for him, I know he will give me his all to get us there.

"As many as we can get."

It's not hard to ignore the light in Melanie's eyes. It's as if I've given her the greatest conceivable gift.

Jesse puts his coffee down and rubs his temples. I know he's already running through calculations about hijacking and the technicalities of space travel. It's obvious in the way his eyes flicker. But nothing is confirmed until we get to the hangers and assess what ships we have to work with.

Just the mention of it all has Melanie animated, her body tense as she paces the room.

"I assume we're all going?" Jesse asks.

"Anyone who is able and wants to." I try to not meet Eli's gaze as I say it. Tearing him away from the Valley might be incredibly painful for him.

So I startle when he immediately says, "I'm in."

Melanie blinks rapidly, turning to face him. "You are?"

He nods. "I'd be grateful for the change of scenery."

A heavy silence fills the room.

Jasmine's foot begins to tap against the floor impatiently.

Finally, my father speaks.

"Please tell me that you understand the risk of going there."

I'm going to my mother's homeland—a place where Argenti can actually use their Silver Magic. Use it *against* me. My father knows this as well as I do.

It's all he can see. His only daughter in danger.

My fingers drum against the handle of my switchblade and I smile through trembling teeth. "Completely."

Jesse grabs my wrist, stilling the nervous gesture, and I slide the tool back into my pocket.

I drift closer to him without thinking and I swear I can feel his reluctance as he releases my wrist.

Everyone turns to look at me as I take a deep breath.

"Before we can leave for Umbra, we have other tasks." I let my gaze rest on each of them, taking in the calamity of what I am about to ask. "We need to free the prisoners under the base. In a month, they could be our salvation."

Jasmine's face flickers with a satisfied smile and my pulse quickens.

Melanie starts to nod aggressively, down to do anything that will help us on our way to Umbra.

Jesse just lifts his coffee and takes another sip.

"Dad, I'll need you and Mason to arrange rations accordingly. Perhaps you can organise more frequent trips to the mainland. We need to unite with the people across the island, starting with food and clothes. In return, the Umbrans may give you better medicine."

My father nods as I speak, crossing his arms across his chest. He will do as I ask, without a doubt, but his face remains grave.

I think my father has forgotten how to speak.

"I have the baker working on more bread. If all goes well, the prisoners will be out of the safeholds by noon, washed and fed."

"If we cut back on getting first-aid supplies from the mainland, we can make more space on the ferry for food and clothes," my father mumbles absently. "Do you trust that they will uphold their end of it?"

"I'll work on it," I say, looking over at Jasmine with questioning eyes. She lifts her shoulder in a shrug, meaning that it's possible. Good.

"Jasmine, I want you to work with Jesse and show him everything you know," I continue.

She glances at him hesitantly. He lingers over my shoulder, dressed in dark clothes, his hair damp from the rain. As soon as they make eye contact, I notice Jasmine suppress a shiver. Next to me, Jesse shoots her a devilish smile.

I nudge him with my elbow, but it's hard not to smile.

Worlds are colliding.

"Don't worry, I'll behave, Princess," he whispers in my ear so only I register it. I try not to shiver.

"Melanie, you'll be with me. Your job is to figure out how to get the main gates open long enough for a hundred and thirteen prisoners to exit through. Once you've done that, I want you to stay by the gates and guide them to meet Jasmine on the other side. And Jesse"—I turn around and face him—"you're going to teach me how to pick the locks on the cells."

He doesn't bristle or say yes, but we both hold each other's gaze for a steady beat, and I nod gently, registering his acceptance.

As far as I know, Jesse was military on Umbra and has more than a hundred tricks up his sleeve when it comes to less lawful endeavours.

I hope I'm right.

"You better learn fast, Princess," he whispers again in my ear.

"Don't worry about me," I say back and a couple people turn to frown.

As long as everyone fulfils their duties, I can do mine.

"What about me?" Eli asks.

"You'll come with us to the base. We're all going to take Jesse's Hover and then you will drive it back to the Valley to get my dad. Together, you can distribute rations to each group of prisoners—"

"No way in hell," Jesse puts in, slightly breathless.

He let me finish most of my instructions before complaining, I'll give him that.

"If you have time after teaching me to lock pick and working on the map with Jasmine, you can show him and my dad how to drive," I say softly, feeling bad with every word I let out. "But it's not a priority, Jesse."

"I only just got a new Hover, Savannah."

His tone is flat and I hate it.

I grit my teeth as I say, "There's always others. I'll help you make a new one."

He clenches his jaw.

No one knows better than me how hard he worked on assembling his new vehicle. He took pride in it. Patience. Standing watch in the rain, training me daily and rebuilding the Hover at night had been his only joy over the last months. He, like me, enjoys keeping busy. Unlike me, he doesn't trust anyone else to carry out his roles.

"You're too busy to help me rebuild a Hover," he mumbles.

"No." I shake my head and take his hand in mine. His palm is warm and steady, and he grips mine back tightly. His thumb slides over the back of my hand. "No, I'm not."

I hate asking you to trust my old friends, but I don't really have a choice.

"I'm sorry," I whisper quietly.

He takes a deep breath. *I know.*

I watch as he turns and says slowly, "Elijah, if you break my freaking baby, I will make your life complete and utter hell."

I roll my eyes, but Eli only winks at him.

Melanie places a not-so-gentle hand on his chest, struggling to keep her composure.

"Talk to your princess about it, not me," Eli mutters. He makes a deep sound in the back of his throat. "She wouldn't ask this of me if there was another way."

"Jesse, please." I whip around, utterly done with this debate.

He takes a step back, puts his coffee loudly down onto the desk, and shrugs. "Sure thing, Princess."

I loop my fingers inside my shirt, a deep feeling of unsettlement trickling down and around my body. Suddenly, the urge to escape and get some fresh air overcomes me.

Melanie makes direct eye contact with me, her deep silver eyes almost hardened as she pushes her way around the desk.

"Okay everyone, you know what needs to be done. Scurry along now, time is wasting." When people don't respond, she waves her hands towards them. "Shoo."

But only Eli and my father leave.

My father practically storms out of the room, as if he cannot leave fast enough.

He needs time, and fresh air, maybe another coffee, before I can speak to him.

But I make a mental note to remember to.

There's no way I can get out of this without hearing a spiel from him.

I've spent too many years being the adult and taking care of Mason that I've almost forgotten to ask him permission to do certain things. Like leading a revolution.

Jasmine yanks out the chair behind my father's desk. She studiously ignores each of us as she picks out a pen from his cup holder and lowers it to the map in front of her.

"I need five minutes."

Jesse sucks in his lips, not moving from his position from beside me.

It's clear that he won't be leaving this room until Jasmine shows him everything he needs to know about the Umbran base.

Jasmine doesn't seem to care. At all.

She doesn't even flinch at the way he glares at her.

Melanie continues to watch me, her dazzling eyes piercing, and then proceeds to wander towards the exit like the rest of them. She hesitates in the doorway, her gaze suggesting that I follow.

I sigh deeply, reaching for a pen and scrawling a last-minute note down onto a piece of paper before indulging her.

It only causes her to glare at me harder.

"I'm coming, I'm coming."

Her lips curve up slightly as she floats down the hallway.

This hall has changed drastically since the first time I saw it, when I was searching for papers to figure out the mystery of the island. Looking back now, it makes me sad.

The walls have lost their colour, the bubble of voices has increased tenfold, and people scurry past me with their heads low and eyes hard. The place used to smell of newspaper and nature, but now it smells like mud and sweat, with the distant aromatic scents of dinner wafting from the food hall.

The simplicity of life has all but vanished, and I wonder if any of us will ever experience it again.

Melanie leads me past the cupboard that used to house the newspapers until we make it to a large window away from the main bustle. She heaves it open, letting in a gust of wind that breaks apart the dank smells. I gulp in the fresh scent of it, heaving my shoulder heavily against the wall in what I presume looks like a pretty pathetic stance.

"I've never thanked you, Savannah."

Oh? I expected a lecture from her, or a command on how to get to Umbra faster. Anything other than simple pleasantries.

"Uh… what for?"

She sinks against the wall next to me and closes her eyes. It's dark in this corner, hidden from prying eyes, so she lets go of herself completely. Her cheeks are flushed, hair a messy up-do—all the indictors of a busy afternoon.

Each word comes out slow and whispered. "I'm finally going home because of you. Of course I'm thankful."

I twist my arms in front of me, sucking in my lips. "It won't be easy, Melanie."

"Nothing about Umbra ever is." She tilts her head towards me, eyes opening slightly in a knowing look.

"I'm starting to see that."

She brushes a loose strand of hair from her eyes. I want to tell her that we should be working, that I should be consoling my father or scouring the warehouse for some acceptable lock picks, or that she should be analysing how to hack the main doors.

But Melanie knows when I need a moment to breathe.

"Do you think I'm ready to rule yet? You know I need to fight. But what happens after I have the crown?"

"*You* are the only one doubting your abilities."

I laugh a little at that. But I don't feel at ease. "Then, tell me, what will Umbra be like?"

"Like walking through a minefield. The shadows will be our best friend, the civilians with nothing to lose will be our allies, and every corner could spontaneously combust with Elders or Argenti ready to kill us."

I snort. "Sounds like a holiday."

Melanie smiles. "Home, sweet home."

I take a deep breath of the fresh winter air, crisp inside my lungs. "Thanks for this."

Her smile widens, and then she turns her head back and closes her eyes slowly. "The shadows have always been my friend."

I nod and don't say anything.

I can picture Melanie on Umbra. I can see her as a child, holding up layers of skirts as she tiptoes around a mansion.

She was made for high society, yet was conditioned to become something else entirely. I can see it in the way she holds her shoulders, so elegant and poised. I can see it in the way she leans against the wall—a quiet bird, well-practiced at hiding. But mostly I see it in her ambition, in her desire to climb her way to the top of any hierarchy.

I'm incredibly lucky to know Melanie Beckett.

"When we go to Umbra, I'll need you to stay with Eli. He calms you, but he will need your ambition to survive."

She snorts at that. "Don't tell him that. He'll have a field day."

"Wait, he also said that?" I inquire, laughing.

She turns to glance at me pointedly. "He seems to believe I've spent too much of my time around the reckless sort—Jesse and you—and that I need to curb my impulses."

"You're not really *that* impulsive, just fidgety," I argue.

"No?" She raises an eyebrow, then huffs. "I suppose you're right. Sitting still is difficult."

"You're doing it now," I offer sheepishly.

"I'm... standing," she says lamely, her mouth twisting into smirk.

"Whatever. Eli is good for you."

She doesn't respond to that. Her eyes drill into a far wall, her teeth nibbling her bottom lip.

After several moments, she says quietly, "If you ever say that I should marry Elijah once this is all over, then I'm going to push you out of that window."

I surrender both my hands in the air, trying not to smile. "I said nothing."

She grimaces. "He's like an annoying puppy I can't get rid of."

I know what that feels like. I smile and slouch against the wall.

It feels cold and hard against my back and, suddenly, standing around here makes me itch. I squirm, the cold breeze behind me lifting the hairs on my arms.

Melanie turns her head back to me, her face expressionless once more. "Ready to leave now?"

I nod. "Yeah. I am."

She pulls herself off the wall and I mimic her, trying to ignore the way my muscles ache.

"Thank you," I say gently. She's been showing me how to cope under the weight of leadership since the day I met her. It's nice.

Melanie smiles and reaches a pale hand around me to slam the window shut. It looks like more rain is brewing again and the sombre darkness makes me feel claustrophobic.

I wonder how the sky on Umbra looks in comparison. The thought sends shivers through me.

"Let's get this jailbreak on the road then, shall we?"

I stretch my arms above my head, arching my back. "Yes ma'am."

I take out my switchblade, twirling it around my fingers as I carry myself down the hallway, brain kicking back into gear.

Melanie leads me back out of the shadows, both our strides more purposeful.

Melanie does this coping thing well... better than me, at least.

I lean into her shoulder, slipping the small note I wrote earlier into her pocket.

"Rest time is over," I mumble to myself.

Melanie only sighs.

SAVANNAH

I t isn't long until Jesse finds me again.

Remarkably, he doesn't look as flustered as I expected after dealing with Jasmine for the past hour.

I'm sitting in the food hall, the seat still warm from where my father and Mason had sat just moments before I arrived. The buzz of society has dwindled with the setting sun. Most people have already left to attend their evening activities and the sound of rain fills the quiet as it batters the windows in heavy curtains.

In the warehouse, everyone starts their day early. People brew their coffees, then set to work farming or baking and, as a result, it gets pretty quiet around here at night, most people resting with a book or slowly making their way to bed.

Jesse glides across the room like a ghost, his feet seemingly not touching the floor. My heart does a little jump in my chest at the sight of him—as it always seems to nowadays—and I straighten my back in my chair.

His hair's in disarray, as if he's been yanking at the roots many times in the past hour. But his expression shows none of that. He smiles when he sees me, his posture relaxed, arms swinging gently past the sword that's always strapped to his waist.

I pull out the chair beside me and slide my bowl across the table.

"They were packing up dinner when I arrived. I added extra to my bowl."

He takes his seat quietly, the only sound he makes being the gentle scraping of the chair as he pulls himself towards the table.

"You sure?"

I nod, leaning my elbows against the table, waiting for him to take a bite.

He has a tendency to forget mealtimes, especially when tasked with a new assignment. He lifts his eyes to me, never missing a beat.

I've made it my mission to make sure he eats. Melanie too. They're both ridiculously neglectful.

"How was it with Jasmine?" He shrugs around a mouthful of the stew. Yep. They hate each other. "You done with her now?"

"I wouldn't be here if not," he says after swallowing.

I lean back a little, giving him room to eat. They might not like each other, but they would put their differences aside long enough to get the job done.

Jesse doesn't say another word, too busy finishing my dinner. There's only three other people in the food hall—the last person on dinner duty finishing the clear up, another person finishing a late dinner, and a child leaning over the counter, probably in search of something sweet.

We don't get dessert here. It's a sacrifice we've had to make for the sake of supply and demand.

The dim lights in the food hall flicker.

Once a staff room, it has since been renovated. Walls were

knocked down to extend the space and any undamaged appliances were moved in to form a kitchen, allowing 20 villagers to work in rotation.

Providing breakfast, lunch and dinner has become their only task here. It isn't a bad job. Some people got stuck with maintenance or cleaning duties.

The little girl finally leaves the counter, dragging her feet past the random assortment of table and chairs, her lips pouted as she sulks.

The man eating his meal across the room also watches her, a haunted expression on his face. When he notices me staring, he latches his eyes onto me, looking as if he wants to talk.

I pull away my attention.

I just really can't be bothered right now.

"You ready to go?" I ask Jesse.

He lowers the spoon. There's still some food left, but he doesn't argue. His chair scrapes as he stands, attention already on the door. I almost tell him that it's okay—that he should just finish his food—but he beats me to it.

"Forget the food, Savannah. We have a lot to do before midday tomorrow and I still expect to get some sleep tonight."

I grunt. "Fine. Come on."

The warehouse feels haunted at night, candles and camping lanterns covering every turn to replace the light fixtures that went out with some of the damaged structure. Our shadows look like ghosts, long and eerie, flickering ahead and behind us in the hallways.

A gaggle of children whisper to each other behind one of the doors to our right, a stereo plays softly from one on our left and I swear I hear soft crying from another doorway ahead of us.

Some people were allocated rooms—two to four families to a room—while the rest of us bunk down in the main sleeping hall. My father told me he organised people out of necessity, tallying up a fair protocol as to who gets what and when. I didn't argue, other than stating that I don't want any extra privileges.

Now, walking past the rooms, I almost feel sorry for those who would live in such a claustrophobic unit.

Why some people haven't left the island in pursuit of a better life is beyond me.

To my surprise, Jesse leads me outdoors to a smooth rock nestled by the stream. He perches lazily across it, pulling a knife out of his belt to clean the soot out from under his fingers.

The rain has softened once more to a drizzle, but we are still protected under the corrugated iron he salvaged from someone's garden—one of his preferred watch posts. It's not far from the warehouse and is close enough to the stream to practise swordplay on the bank. A mandarin tree sits nearby that provides a reason to stick around during mealtimes. It's not as conveniently placed as the one near my house, but Jesse likes it regardless. If I'm honest, it makes me more comfortable knowing he is out here, protecting us.

"Why are we here, Jesse?" I cross my arms over my chest, refusing to sit with him.

"Because let's face it, Princess, there's no way you can learn to pick a lock before sunrise. Especially not the ones at the base. It's not possible."

Shock and indignation cross my features before I turn my expression to stone. My stomach churns and, for all the questions I have for him, my mouth struggles to find the words.

"Sit down, Savannah. Before you have a stroke."

"I'm okay standing."

He flicks his knife against the rock, indicting where I should sit. I just stare at him.

"No one expects you to carry the weight of the universe on your shoulders. So, stars forbid, let me help you."

His words break me, and I sink down onto the rock.

Help.

That's what Jesse is good at, isn't it? Helping? It's all he does.

"Just show me how to free the prisoners and to open the cells." My voice comes out quiet, but he catches it.

He traces his knife down my arm, sending shivers down my skin. The metal is cold and sharp, but I don't move.

He points the tip into my wrist gently, piercing the skin. A small bead of blood runs down my wrist, yet I still don't move.

It looks as muddy as my hair in the darkness.

"You're only human, Savannah."

"So are you," I argue.

"This war is everyone's. Not just yours." He wipes the blood off my wrist. "It's been Melanie's since the day she was born, mine since the night my sister died, and the Argenti's since that blasted rock tore apart our soil. Everyone's."

Since the night my sister died.

My curiosity is thirsty, but I refrain from prying, and say instead: "You've been making your own plans, haven't you?"

He doesn't need to answer for me to know I'm right. The determined steel of his eyes confirms it, but he says it anyway.

"Since we freed your annoying human buddy, Elijah Brooke."

"He's not my buddy," I refute, although that isn't entirely true anymore. Eli is as much a part of this now as anyone else.

"Whatever."

"He's one of us," I grit out, the words forced.

"He *is* notoriously hard to shake."

Under better circumstances these thoughts would accompany laughter, a swish of a sword down by the stream, the taste of mandarin in our mouths as Jesse pushes my shoulders back to fix my posture before I take my strike.

But now, there's only hard glances, a distant clap of thunder, shaking fingers against the hard rock.

"Okay, I'll bite. What's your plan?"

He smirks at me. "You mean the one where I don't have to

teach you to lock pick?" He seems almost happy to have the prospect of a night off.

The rain increases and I cross my arms across my chest to keep the warmth in my body. "That'd be the one."

He notices the shivers wracking my body and scoots closer, the smile dropping from his face as he tries to trap his body heat to mine, not quite touching me. We both release a shaky breath at the effort.

"It might not work," he warns.

"Just spit it out, Jesse. Or take me inside to teach me to pick locks. I'm freezing out here."

Without taking his eyes off the trees, he finally lifts his arm over my shoulder. The leather of his jacket kisses mine and I shiver so deeply it rattles down into my soul.

It isn't enough to warm me, but it's a loud distraction from the cold.

"If we bring the power back, we can open the cells. I know a way that I can do it without Mel there. It'll keep the doors open long enough for you to pull the prisoners out."

"Is… is that even possible?"

It sounds almost too good to be true.

His arm shifts slightly off my back and I notice his spine tense.

"I grew up on a military base much like the space centre. Some soldiers and I used to play around with the power to send Morse codes to each other. It's possible. It's just hard."

So, if we do this, the entire plan will ride on Jesse's back and his schoolboy knowledge of Umbran power sources. Moments ago, I thought the entire base had been cut off and power wasn't an option. But now…

"What's the risk?" I ask slowly, scared to even voice my worries.

"The risk is that the Elders will know the moment we restore power. Even if it's just a flicker."

I pull my knees to my chest, my worst fears and the works of my nightmares becoming a harsh possibility.

"So we lose any element of surprise?"

"Maybe not. But we will lose the safety net of being in the dark. The Elders, your mother… they will know you're still alive."

I hadn't even thought about that.

They dropped bombs all over the island. Most villagers had died, and I was very nearly among them.

Is that why Umbra has been so quiet?

I stand up, inhale deeply, and push away any stirrings of doubt. "Okay," I say. "Mel will override the gates and get us inside first. I only want you to light the power for five minutes. No more, no less. It will have to be enough."

He almost gapes at me and, under better circumstances, I would have laughed.

If we don't do it his way, we might not get everyone out. We will lose allies. People will hate us.

This is the only way to start a revolution. Not with hesitancy, but with a full-blown electrical combustion. And maybe a couple of angry visitors.

"Are you sure you don't mind painting an extra target on your back?" Jesse says cautiously. His plan is better, but he doesn't like it any more than I do.

In truth, I don't mind the target if it means more lives are saved.

"It might be a stupid thing to do, but I couldn't live with myself if I didn't try."

He stands up from his spot on the rock to wrap his arms around me. The movement is so sudden and unexpected that I involuntarily gasp. Unsure how to respond, my hands flutter motionless in the air.

Jesse whispers into my hair. "That, Princess, is nothing to be ashamed of."

MELANIE

The beds here stink. *Bad.*

Which is exactly why I do not sleep.

Jesse finds me hunched over an old human computer, its screen flickering, codes ambling along the screen lazily.

He slides a glass down the desk towards me, eyes catching on the glove casually draped over the unit.

I turn and give him a long look, fighting the twitch in my jaw as he takes me in.

Papers are everywhere. Notes. Wires. Pieces of metal.

I can only imagine the state of my hair. But I straighten my shoulders, poising regally on my chair as I challenge his gaze.

My office survived the blistering inferno of the bombs, but remains inaccessible, thanks to my wonderful uncle.

A muscle ticks in my jaw at the thought of him. He all but

abandoned me. Hasn't sent a message. Hasn't uttered a single word since he left. If I'm lucky, he's dead.

Jesse picks up a seemingly random piece of paper off the desk and I snatch it from him before he can read it, my heart pounding. Out of all the papers, he chose *that one?*

Savannah's handwriting screams up at me from the paper and, in a huff, I jam it under the computer.

"What do you want?" I ask Jesse.

He slides a chair out from a neighbouring desk, dragging it towards me. The room is big, once set up to house many people's offices.

The computers dot the room, firmly planted on several desks. Some sort of dated PC room.

Well, dated for Umbrans. I suppose the screens are quite thin and the reception relatively fast for human standards.

"You look like you need a whiskey," Jesse says, plopping his feet on the desk and messing up some papers. "And you're being rude."

"Hey! Get off!" I exclaim, scrambling for the papers in a panic.

"Still rude."

"Go to sleep."

"When you do," he insists, pulling my glove off the unit and fiddling with it.

This is an old game of ours. He pretends to coddle me and I pretend to challenge him until we both fold and end up sleeping on my desk. Or my couch. Or behind a bar with a whiskey in hand.

"Tomorrow is a big day," he reminds me.

The moon is haunting as it spills blue light inside, the only illumination in the room other than the one from my screen. I rub my aching temples, my eyes straining with a throb that never seems to go away these days.

"You obviously want something from me."

He gives me a slow smile and my stomach trembles. Bloody charmer.

I flick my fingers against his shoe until he lowers his feet, never once taking his gaze off me. It is safe to keep our glances quick, to not let the purring cat in my stomach stir at every little smile, but I turn my eyes back to my computer out of habit.

Because he is Jesse. He is *family*.

And yet every time he looks at me a beat too long, old feelings surface.

No. I slap myself. He and Savannah—

"Did you just… hit yourself?"

"Shut up and go to sleep. I'm tired," I respond, locating an answer to a problem on my screen and pulling some mechanics from an old walkie talkie towards me in a rush.

"Oh, love. Listen to yourself." Jesse's voice is a gentle, stroking purr, but I don't think much of it because the bedroom talk of his tone is a guise. It means he is mad with me.

Instead of doing that, I reach over, take a swig of his whiskey, blink my eyes aggressively a few times and then continue working on my project.

We sit in silence for a few moments, Jesse watching the moon behind me while I tinker with the device in my hands. Finally, he clears his throat and asks the question that brought him here in the first place.

"I know enough about your workflow to understand how to restore power tomorrow, but I will need some tools," he utters.

My head whips up. "You're putting the power back on?"

He doesn't look at me as he nods. "Yes. To get you both out."

Savannah and me… his family. I swallow sharply and nod.

I could argue with him, ask him to stay somewhere safe—to follow Savannah's original plan. But I know she will never hurt him. So, if this is a secret string of her plan, then I trust it.

Even if it makes my stomach twist in ugly knots.

"Anything of mine is yours. You know this."

He nods again, his eyes dark as he stares out the window, not really seeing.

"I know," he says simply. "I just wanted to come in person so I could make sure you actually go to bed tonight."

"And bring me a whiskey," I tease, tilting my head to the side as I work, another small smile playing at my lips.

"Better than coffee, this late at night."

Yes, better than coffee.

My fingers slip on a small wire, causing a spark to zap my fingers. I feel it travel up my hand, tingling the wires in the prosthetic. But I just flick my wrist, bunching my eyebrows, and keep working.

Before me, scattered across the desk, are pieces of machinery—walkie talkies, radios, computer chips—the makings of a communication device.

We sit quietly for a few beats, then Jesse finally pushes back his seat.

"It won't be long before dawn, so I'm going to bed. Promise me you will try and get at least an hour of sleep tonight."

My fingers brush over the metal in my grip, twisting it to get a better look at it. I'm nearly done. An hour longer perhaps, then I can get some rest. After packing up of course. Which leaves about an hour, as he requested...

"Yes," I whisper, lifting my eyes to his. He holds them. Traps my gaze. "I promise."

He sucks in his bottom lip, shoving his hands in his pocket.

His shoulders slump low, his eyes rimmed with shadows, weapons out of sight. He keeps them under his bed and no one is brave enough to face his wrath to even go near them, but he always has at least one on him. Which just goes to show how tired he is and how nervous he is for what's to come.

Umbra.

Jesse Hayes will return to Umbra soon.

The thought makes me want to take back any wish I ever had

to return myself. My heart yearns for my home planet—for salvation—but if it means watching Jesse face his demons, then I would give it up in a heartbeat.

He sucks on his lips, nodding again.

Against my better judgement, I watch him as he grabs the tools he needs and hangs them from his weapons belt for tomorrow. Whatever he is to face, it haunts him in the same way Umbra does.

My heart drops in my stomach.

Plans within plans, I suddenly catch onto a new string. Something maybe even Jesse doesn't fully comprehend yet.

My heart pulls at the seams and I lower my project onto the desk, stabilising myself as I watch Jesse's departing back. My words are rough in my throat when I call, "Jesse, wait."

He stops, his hand clasped around the door. His deep blue eyes touch mine.

"I will love you, on any planet." The words are heavy as they leave my mouth. They sound strained, as if they hold way too many meanings, and I so I add roughly, "No matter what's required of you."

His gaze softens, shoulders loosening.

A small breeze sweeps past us from the open window, fluttering the curtains. It stands the hairs on my arms on end, but my skin still feels warm as he responds.

"I know, Mel. I know."

And with a smile, he disappears down the corridor.

SAVANNAH

I don't sleep at all.

Neither does Eli. I can hear him tossing and turning behind the thin curtain separating our beds. I rise before the sun to see his wide eyes plastered on the ceiling. I pause by the foot of his bed and our eyes meet.

He swallows sharply and I pause, my eyes imploring.

"I still dream about it," he admits quietly, face heating.

"What?" I whisper.

He has dark rims under his eyes, but this isn't new. He's been sporting the haunted look with easy acceptance for weeks now.

With a shrug, he turns onto his side, his back to me. When he finally settles, he utters, "The Safe Holds."

I release a shaky breath, but neither of us say anything else.

Beside him, Jasmine lies on a small cot with nothing more than a shawl as a blanket. But she, unlike the rest of us, sleeps blissfully.

My father and Mason occupy the spaces on my other side, followed by Melanie and Jesse three rows down. I'm sure they all had a mediocre sleep.

Except maybe Jesse. He sleeps like the dead.

Must be a soldier thing—part of sleeping just about anywhere and getting the most out of minimal hours of sleep a night.

I don't bother stirring him. As weird as it is to not have him wake this early with me, I'm grateful he is getting the rest he needs. Instead, I tiptoe past the many cots and exit out onto the main road towards the bakery, glad that I don't have the usual weaponry hanging off me to slow me down.

Jesse and I usually train at dawn.

Not today.

I bunch the furs of my new jacket around my ears, feeling the brisk morning air pinch at my cheeks.

It almost pains me, knowing that we might not have a chance to train anymore. I can only pray that I've learnt enough in the short time and that my small switchblade works to my advantage if anyone jumps me.

It's the only blade I like to carry when I'm not training.

The baker looks ridiculously cheery when I walk through the front door, rubbing my cold, red hands against each other. His countenance, mixed with the smell of fresh bread, almost knocks the frown off my face as well. It's remarkable, the smell—it fills every crevice of the small building like morning air.

"Bread's in the oven!" Bronson says upon my arrival.

I smile at his enthusiasm. "Thank you."

I settle down on the floor beside the fireplace and, shortly after, Bronson comes over to give me a bun filled with raisins. I grasp the warm roll in both hands and sigh.

"Thank you," I say again, my body inclined towards the fire.

"I must say I didn't expect anyone until later."

"I didn't either," I answer in turn.

I don't need to be here. I don't need to be anywhere. Not yet.

But doing nothing feels worse than being early.

He chuckles. Nothing bothers Bronson. His cheeks are always rosy and he whistles while he works. It eases my mind to watch him.

The roll steams when I open it, the raisins burning my tongue. I peel sections apart with my fingers, eating it slowly.

I lose track of time, but the sun has risen higher into the sky and blinds my eyes by the time Jesse comes in to the bakery, dressed in his usual pale Umbran tunic and leather pants. His dark hair is damp with rain and I watch him placidly as he discards his weapons belt on the coatrack by the entrance. He saunters towards me to warm his hands by the fire.

"Elijah Brookes is the worst driver I've ever had the displeasure of encountering in my entire life."

"You've been teaching him." It isn't a question.

"The idiot woke me the moment you left. He thinks it's a compromise."

I kick his foot to get his attention.

He spins towards me, barely batting an eye. The tunic is slightly too big for him, the sleeves dripping past his palms.

I smile, catching his dark blue eyes, noting the beads of rain dripping down his dark hair and pattering against his cheeks. "Ask Bronson for something to eat. It'll help with the anger."

"Good morning to you, too."

I wink at him. It hurt me to ask him to lend his new Hover. But he needs to get over it. And quickly.

Still, I try not to laugh at the scowl on his face.

Outside, the sun peers out from behind a cloud, spreading warmth through the windows. The image makes me feel heady.

I was counting on decent weather. We need clear skies today.

But even so, seeing it makes my palms slick with sweat, knowing it means one less excuse to not go ahead with the plan.

I wander over to Bronson, who sees me coming and reaches for my hands. I reluctantly give them to him and he dusts flour on my palms.

"I made 30 loaves, my dear. Is that enough?"

"More than enough. Thank you."

I let loose a soft smile, giving his hands a firm squeeze and he squeezes mine once back before releasing me.

He didn't lose his family in the bombing. He did, however, grasp the hands of many dying men. He helped retrieve bodies. He stitched up wounds.

He told me yesterday that the images haunt him.

Suffering is like a plague—it can engulf you.

So, I told him about the prisoners and what they'd need once freed. He'd immediately said yes to helping. Anything to fix. Anything to heal. Anything to banish the haunting images in his head.

Bronson smiles at me now, all happiness, but his gaze is heavy.

"My father will be around later," I remind him.

"Not a problem, dear. I'll do whatever I can to help fill the bellies of those in need."

My heart lightens at the sentiment, and I nod softly, shrugging my warm jacket higher around my face as I leave the warm enclosure of the bakery.

Jesse follows me out, the door chiming just as it always does. I make it halfway across the road before he grabs my wrist. "Talk to me."

"About?" My breath clouds between us, but disperses quickly under the winter sun.

"There's something you're not saying, but I can't pick it. What's going to happen to us on the base? What are you planning?"

I give him a weak smile. My heart pounds in my ears, bringing a small flush to my face. "You know what I'm planning."

I try not to wince as his fingers dig into my skin.

"Do I?"

I shake off his wrist and push forwards.

"Yes."

The barren trees rake their fingers against each other in the wind. I duck my head under them and disappear amongst the skeletons.

Jesse grunts, his footsteps unusually sloppy.

He's angry.

It isn't far to the warehouse, so each step forwards feels more pronounced.

I watch the trees go by with a feeling of unease. A part of me wishes that today would not come, that we could pause and rest and stay here forever.

I can already hear the bustle ahead of us, people roaming around the warehouse and Melanie's voice rising above the clamour. And so I stop. I take a step back, resting my shoulder against the tree. The bark is cold and harsh, catching onto my clothes.

"Talk," Jesse demands.

I resist the urge to grasp my switchblade, along with the incessant need to turn and face the beautiful man behind me. Instead, I reach out my hand.

My hand hovers there a moment, fingers cold from the wind, feeling lost.

And then I feel his calloused palm sink into mine, his fingers twisting around my own. His warmth seeps into my skin, filling an endless void.

My heart slows just as a nervous electricity pings up my body.

I breathe into my words, trembling as I say, "Promise me one thing."

I cannot hear him, but I can sense him. His presence looms above me, dark and steady, and I try not to laugh at the irony of speaking to each other behind the comfort of the tree.

Our clearing is gone, but we are not.

"I would promise a great many things to you, Savannah."

I gasp, my breath catching in my throat.

Of its own accord, my thumb roams over his palm, drawing a steady circle.

I hear more than see his breath clouding in long swirls by my ear, rapid in the chilled weather.

His presence feels like a looming cloud. I tremble slightly, almost unable to breathe. Without thinking it through, I spin around the tree, my gaze latching onto his deep emerald eyes, never-ending and heady. The emotion behind them heats something in my core and I force myself to remember to breathe.

Those eyes trap my body, looking at every detail, never missing a beat.

I tilt my chin up to him, gaze roaming over his face—marking that small freckle by his eye, the strong arch of his dark eyebrows. The way his dark hair brushes the curve of his ears.

With each slow, agonising second, I shift closer and closer to him until he is the one with his back to the tree. I move silently, except for the pounding of my heart in my ears.

"On the base, when the minutes are up, find me."

My words are all iron, despite the gentle warmth of our fingers.

I watch as my words cloud in the air between us, a fleeting fog.

His hand frees mine but, instead of leaving my body, it trails up my arm, drawing a line of fire until it rests on my collar. I gasp at the shock of heat, a flush rising to my skin.

He knots his other hand around my jacket, gripping a section of my waist as he leans his mouth down to my throat.

I don't dare move.

Probably couldn't even if I tried.

My breath gets lodged in my throat as he presses his lips against my skin, just under my ear, drawing warm, gentle circles against my flickering pulse.

I hold my breath as heat erupts within me and my skin begins to shiver like it's never seen the sun. I keep holding it until my lungs scream, not trusting myself to breathe in the earthy, metallic scent of him.

I feel him smile against my skin, his voice guttural as he murmurs, "As if I could ever abandon you."

The words undo me and I let go completely, the breath whooshing out of me. I reach up and push his head back against the tree, one hand on the bark, the other arm still trapped by his fingers.

He grips my chin, yanking my gaze onto his.

I push myself closer, but he holds firm.

"Now is not the time."

Like a bucket of ice thrown over my head, I swallow. Then nod.

The moron chuckles at the change in my expression, delighted in the way the heat on my face flickers as he moves his hand down my neck and across my bare skin once more.

"A promise," he whispers through a lazy smile, his fingers drawing circles over the place his lips met my throat.

"Promise," I mumble, unable to form any other words. The cold bites into my skin, bringing a flush to my cheeks once more.

He traces his thumb across my lips, sending a searing line of heat on my skin.

Unwillingly, my back arches, flattening me closer to him. He only chuckles, sliding free from his position against the tree. There's a bounce to his step as he heads towards the warehouse.

I shake my head. Stretch my fingers. Okay, Savannah. Okay.

He takes his time walking back, as if waiting for me, but I'm too lightheaded to be near him. I follow him at a distance, my steps nearly as silent as his. Every nerve in my body pops and fizzles.

I hardly notice the trees anymore.

The muddy ground.

The fog.

The way the wind smells like dirt.

But even in the highest state of distraction, I doubt I'd ever be able to stop smelling it—the difference in the air.

It smells like forest and mud, but it tastes thick in your throat. Whenever I breathe in, I can taste the motes of dirt and ash.

Under the Dome, across the island, the air tasted like metal.

The Umbrans cleansed the contaminated air on Terra into something breathable and non-toxic. So that everyone protected under the Dome would be immortal.

Just like it is on Umbra.

Each lungful of Terran air feels too heavy, too wrong.

Now that I know that it's killing us, I cannot forget. I cannot turn a blind eye.

So long as we remain here, we're all dying.

I grip my arms across my chest, so lost in my thoughts that I bump into Melanie.

I miss a step and curse, booted foot slipping in the mud.

The dainty girl grips my arm, yanking it free from my chest, holding tight.

She's dressed like the soldiers do on Umbra—fighting clothes for dexterity and warmth. Tight leather pants, a flowing shirt tucked in, and a thick belt wrapping around her waist. Boots make it nearly halfway up her thigh, laced and vintage-looking, made from the leather of an Umbran animal. The fluffy jacket around her shoulders slips as she slides her arm through mine. She's dressed exactly as I am, except for the old key card attached to her belt.

She's anticipating the power to be on—for Jesse to be successful.

I smile at that. At the million plans in play.

I blink a few times at her, trying to focus on the event at hand. She clings to me somewhat awkwardly, but neither of us slink away. Not as she slips something into my hand. I nod at her, fingers brushing metal, and slip the small device into my pocket.

Her warmth is comforting, and I wish to simply embrace it for a few precious moments, but we don't have the time to linger.

So I pat her arm in silent acknowledgement, smiling at her.

"Ready?" I ask.

She nods, pulling her jacket sleeve down her prosthetic, metal-plated arm, still hiding some exposed wires. "Of course."

We both simultaneously pull free from each other, taking steadying breaths.

Ahead of us, Jesse claps Eli on the back, who is sitting in the driver's seat of the Hover. He wears a hoodie and jeans, looking so human and normal that it makes my heart ache.

"Move," Jesse grunts.

Eli rolls his eyes and climbs into the back, his movements clumsy.

I clench my jaw at that thought and, instead of heading to the hover, I find my father in the gathering crowd and dart over, pulling him in for a long hug.

He grips me tighter than anticipated, but I don't push him away when it starts to hurt. He clears his throat and my heart dips.

"I really wish I knew where you got your hard-headedness from," he says.

"I'll be okay, Dad."

"You don't know that."

I finally pull away, raising my brows at him. His eyes glisten, reflective and unseeing. "I'm also friends with some of the most hardheaded people on this island," I assure him. "No one will get hurt."

He shakes his head numbly. "You're all still kids."

A corner of my lips lift. "Kids with a score to settle." A breath whooshes out of his chest and I swear I see his eyes roll. "I'll be okay, honestly. I'll send word when I can."

His jaw tightens and he shakes his head, as if trying to rid of his frustration. "You'll be back soon anyway. It's not like you're going to Umbra today."

I nod, giving him my warmest smile.

He pats my shoulder, his glasses sliding down his nose as he drops his gaze to the clothes I'm wearing. The otherness of them.

My switchblade is a comforting weight in my pocket, plastered against my thigh from the tight pants.

"Tell Mason I'll be back for him soon."

My father nods, his body tense. "He already knows that."

"Tell him anyway," I insist, bunching the furs up around my cheeks.

He mumbles that he will and I smile in encouragement. As he turns back to the warehouse, he misses a step.

Jasmine clambers out of the warehouse in that moment, keeping her head low.

They both tense as they pass each other and I swear I see my father mutter something under his breath.

She doesn't acknowledge any of us as she climbs into the Hover next to Eli. They both sit a breath apart, not touching, not meeting each other's glances. But while Eli sits awkwardly with his back straight, Jasmine calmly places her hands in her lap, entirely at ease.

"See you soon," I say to my father, whose lips are thin.

I yank myself up on the side of the Hover.

There isn't enough room to be seated, so I hang from the side of it, securing my foot in a lip on the floor and winding my hands around the seat railing.

On the other side of the Hover, Melanie does the same.

My father waves to us, then places his hands in his pockets, retreating into the warehouse almost gingerly.

"Have you ever driven with so much weight on a Hover?" Jasmine asks Jesse quietly, who slings a new leather jacket on over his cotton tunic. She doesn't show any ounce of concern on her face, but the darkness in her eyes says otherwise.

All of us look at her with wide eyes, not expecting her to really speak unless needed to.

"Nope," he answers.

Jasmine gives me a pointed look. *A flaw in your plan, or his?* she seems to ask.

I shrug. *Neither.*

"Were you planning on testing the weight first?" Eli adds on, voice catching.

Everyone looks at him.

I suck on my lip as Jesse turns, eyes crinkled with humour, his shoulders rolling as he finishes shrugging on the jacket.

He's the only one who manages to make Umbran clothes still look... Terran.

Eli lets out a drawn whoosh of breath, his brown cheeks pinked from the cold.

Little does Eli know, he's speaking to someone whose old Hover was obnoxiously decked out with no shortage of unnecessary supplies. They can handle weight.

Sure, human cargo is heavier, but none of us expect the Hover to last after this day.

"No time like the present." Jesse winks and guns the engine.

The sound of Melanie's and my own laugher follows us until the warehouse blinks away.

SAVANNAH

"Stars save me, I'm going to puke."

I don't tell Melanie, but I feel the same.

The reek of death and human waste cascades from the cracks of the half-obliterated gate. Knowing the stains beneath our feet were made from blood doesn't make it any easier to digest.

"Welcome to my hellhole, oh Mighty Saviour."

Samael. The big brute.

Jesse snarls from behind me and Melanie kicks him in the shin for emphasis.

Like a guard, Samael mans the main entrance to the Safe Holds, slouching on the ground, surrounded by old, rotting food and twisted sheets of metal.

Nothing about the entrance is familiar to me. The metal is black from the fire and dented in multiple places, like someone had hammered into it with a battering ram or a functioning Hover. Around it lies a swarm of debris and disaster.

Sure, there's a cleared pathway—probably due to Jasmine and the few she managed to save from the rubble so far—but there's no way in hell we are getting over a hundred people through here.

"Get up," I snap at Samael.

Cans are littered around him, half-eaten food that has gone to the flies. His fingers crawl through them, searching for a sharp bit.

"Get *up*," I just about yell.

I don't intend to, but my boot whips out, kicking his pathetic hand. Flesh meets my shoe with a hard *whack* and the poor man grumbles, holding his hand to his chest.

I wince at my outburst, but his hand isn't bleeding.

He'll deal.

I rack my fingers through my hair and wait for him to move his limp body aside. He's sitting right before the broken panel that Melanie needs access to.

On the ground, near the door, is a hole in the framework of the building. Sharp metal seems to have been pulled back, the ground underneath it smooth from use. Jasmine waves her hand towards the hole, her jaw tight. "I got in that way."

It's small. Much too small to fit over a hundred people through.

"I don't want to speak the obvious, but—" Eli begins.

"Then don't," Jesse cuts in.

I turn away from Samael, who is now noisily clambering to his feet, and watch Eli as his head whips in circles around us, taking in the broken buildings and dried stains of blood.

"Even if we get the main door open, it's still a small entrance—how are we going to fit everyone?" Eli asks anyway.

Jasmine, who hasn't left the Hover that Jesse parked several metres away from us, jumps down in a heavy leap and dances over to him, placing a hand on his shoulder. "I don't think we are. I found a better route, more gaps around the building."

Eli jumps at the contact of her hand and then brushes it off his shoulder, his body stiff.

"You found many routes. I picked the best one," Jesse confirms.

"And which one would that be?" She flutters her lashes at him, trying to put on a sweet smile that is instead filled with venom.

It didn't occur to me until now that Jesse never shared his plans with her. It must be eating her up. The way she shifts on her feet, fingers tapping, tells me as much.

"This switchboard is one of few left functioning on the entirety of the base, save for the ones in the Liaison's office." I lay out everything my friends have shared with me, turning towards my old best friend. "You'll be leaving Melanie and me here. I'll be going in this way, and you'll be taking Samael to the main entrance to the Space Centre, where we will lead people out."

Jasmine furrows her brows at me. "Do the Safe Holds connect to the Centre like that?"

Jesse crosses his arms over his chest. "Obviously."

She sucks on her lips, refusing to meet Jesse's eyes.

At my feet, Samael watches me like a fish and grumbles. "How do you know all that tech stuff?"

Beside me, Melanie raises her hand and wiggles her fingers.

He watches her longer than is comfortable, trying to place how he knows her face, probably. Melanie rolls her shoulders and shoves past him, seeking out the dead switchboard.

"But all the power is off," Samael tells her, as if this is news to us.

She rolls her head, her expression exasperated.

"You can't do anything, I've tried," Samael says with a huff.

Melanie's eyes twitch. "I can freaking-well try."

Eli chuckles, his laughter fading as I move away. I run my hands down my pants, trying to hide my fear in how much I'm relying on this first part working.

And worse still, trying not to think about what I must do if it does work.

First, I have to get through the door in front of me, which already reeks. It's a thick metal thing, but the edges of it have caved under the bombs. Samael has moved support beams around it, to prevent it from becoming inaccessible.

I curl my fingers inside my pocket, trying to hide the nervous tremor of my hands as I inspect the door, pretending to look important. Samael doesn't take his eyes off me for a second—not until Melanie hands me what looks to be a twisted piece of someone's Hover. The battering ram.

"Fast and smooth." I recite to myself the mantra Jesse told me earlier and slam the makeshift crowbar directly into the space between the door and the wall.

I peer between the gap I've made and see that the door has disconnected from the keypad needed to unlock the door. Disabled.

It's only possible to break if the power is down, Jesse had said. *And when power goes back up, who needs a key card if the door is broken?*

I had laughed at that. Something about Jesse sneaking into restricted areas on Umbra as a youth was oddly funny.

"Now what?" Samael clambers up beside me, poking his thumb into the sizeable gap I made between the door and the wall. He pats his stomach, emphasising how skinny he's become. "I may've lost my chub, but you're delirious if you think I could squeeze through *that.*"

I roll my eyes. "And now, you raging lunatic, we wait for the backup generator."

"There is no backup generator." He glares at me, shaking out the hand that I kicked earlier and shuffles his feet in the dirt like a child.

Behind him, Jasmine's tapping increases and she darts her head around behind her, the sound before we do.

The barest flicker—a small buzz coming from a fallen piece of machinery that is somehow still attached to a building. Without checking for clarification, I turn and face Eli's round, dark eyes, and nod towards the Hover parked a few paces back.

Eli furrows his brows, turning to find the original driver.

"Jasmine, take him away now please." I nod to Samael, watching her jump with my sudden address. Her eyes are still darting around her, searching for the source of the sudden sparks.

"Jasmine, NOW," I say louder, and she whimpers. "Space Centre. Go."

"It's dead. No power, it's dead…" Samael is muttering. I turn to pin him with a withering glare. I really, *really*, don't want to touch him, but I will shove him again if it gets his sorry ass moving.

Melanie takes over at the gate behind me, nails tapping on the pad, a small device already in hand as she connects a cable between it and the screen implanted in the wall.

A cloud of dust kicks up and Eli drives the Hover closer to Jasmine and Samael, one hand reached out for his old friend. She takes it without looking away from the ruins around her… searching…

Because no one noticed Jesse slip away. No one heard his near silent feet as he slipped between buildings, headed towards the hangar where the guards would stash small, portable generators. Devices pilots once carried with them on long trips before technology advanced and the generators grew dated and forgotten.

No one noticed him except Melanie, who turns and faces me with a massive grin the moment the Hover speeds off towards the Space Centre and the power flickers back on across the entire base.

"Got it," she tells me, and stands back from the door that hisses open.

I squeeze my friend's hand. "Five minutes."

She swallows, nodding once. "Five minutes," she repeats. Then we disappear into the Safe Holds.

SAVANNAH

"**G**O, GO, GO."

"Are you all *daft?*" Melanie barks after me. "Listen to her!"

The Safe Holds are open and Melanie stands by the torture station near the exit, he small device in her hand, her fingers tapping across it while periodically lifting her gaze to acknowledge my progress.

Which is slow.

They don't realise the power is back on—that Jesse is controlling it from inside the space centre, temporarily removing the electrical field on the cell bars.

Yesterday, before Jesse came and spoke to me about this alternate plan, Melanie told him how to redirect the electricity in their cells while pumping the power back into the rest of the Safe Holds.

Apparently, it's simple work, but I'm still surprised Jesse handled it so efficiently.

When the first person handles their bars, and nudge the door open without being electrocuted, I sigh in relief.

But it's not enough. They don't know it's safe.

"GO," I urge. "Hurry!"

Several prisoners risk escaping, but despite the *Sanitas* Jasmine has been giving them, their sprits have been drained, and most stare at me blankly.

They must think it's a trap.

I grit my teeth until slowly, more doors start opening, squealing as the rusty metal swings open months of disuse. Some captives hover near their open doors, fingers intertwined in the bars, sucking on their lips.

Others immediately move, but not towards me or the exit. They run into neighbouring cells.

Sobbing and shouts of joy follow, and I walk down the labyrinth, watching as the civilians heft their loved ones free from their cages—whether alive or dead.

Too many are gone.

The stench of their bodies wafts past us and it takes everything in me to not scrunch up my nose. Somewhere between the time of the bombing and now, this place has become a tomb. Many have died.

I squeeze the bridge of my nose, trying not to let a pained expression rise to my face. I never asked Jasmine when she found them.

The *Sanitas*, despite being a miracle, may have been delivered too late for a few.

Some bodies have had months to rot.

Others, only days—their waxen faces terrifyingly distorted.

The ones that have thoroughly decomposed don't have anyone coming into their cells. They're long gone, and their friends and families avert their eyes as they stumble past them.

"GO, EVERYONE OUT!" I repeatedly cry, voice spiralling down the labyrinth.

Near Melanie, I can vaguely see the stains of blood and vomit left the last time we were here. Most of it has all rotten by now, stinking up the entire area. The concept of having to wander further into the Safe Holds makes me want to empty up my stomach. The odour makes my eyes water and the breath catch in my throat. But we simply have no choice.

We herd them towards the rear exit with all the checkpoints.

Thanks to Jesse, they will stay open, giving us a clear path to the surface. But first we need to make it to the small staffroom in the back. Melanie needs to hack her way through the keypad before the power shuts down and, if we don't get there in time, no one is getting out.

I debate sending Melanie ahead, but I still need someone at our rear, checking cells.

Time is running out.

I turn around a bend, avoiding something fleshy on the floor that's writhing with maggots. Each corner exposes more rot. More decomposing body parts. More bodily fluids.

I try and keep my breathing shallow, but each time I open my mouth to call out to the captives, my lungs demand a deep steady breath. I try not to gag.

"Please! Jasmine sent us. We don't have much time, you need to follow!" I scream.

At the sound of Jasmine's name, more people stumble out from the safe haven of their cells, fingers clawing at the bars.

They all start mumbling her name.

Jasmine? Jasmine. Jasmine!

I wave them towards me, arms flailing.

They're so ridiculously *slow*.

"Three minutes, Savannah!" Melanie calls out to me from behind.

I spin, the light from her screen illuminating her face, highlighting the worry etched in her eyes. Around us, people begin moving to the exit, but it's painful to watch. Some of them carry dead bodies, slowing them down. Others simply struggle to stand after years of neglect.

"We have a way out! But we need to move NOW!" An old man beside me misses a step at the words, his eyes glazing at the sight of me, taking in my chocolate hair. "Leave your dead," I scream. "If you want to survive, save yourselves!"

My voice bounds down the labyrinth and soon hordes of people round the first corner.

Melanie shoulders someone forwards. I recognise her as the girl from The Nook—Samael's friend.

Thank the stars she's too far away to see me.

I usher people on, the entrance and torture table well and truly behind us.

I try not to flinch as the old man reaches a bony hand out to my arm. His finger trails my skin, cold and dry like bone. His skin is oddly smooth, clinging to the ribs over his sunken chest, and I realise it's the time spent being down here this long that gave him the appearance of age.

He opens his mouth, many of his teeth missing, and says loudly enough for everyone around us to hear: "Jasmine has sent us our queen."

The ones nearest me stop, depthless eyes snagging onto me. Their uttered words of Jasmine's name shifts.

Our Queen, our Queen…

I swallow deeply.

Our Queen, our Queen, our Queen.

I steady myself and cover my hand over that of the dying man next to me, my breathing shallow, as I call out into the tomb:

"My name is Savannah Shaw and I am the prophesised queen."

The man's hand slides out from under mine, his knees pounding into the ground. As he lowers his head, I watch as everyone around me copies him, falling to their knees.

They begin to chant my name. Over and over. Kneeling before me.

I try not to roll my eyes at them.

Tears prickle in my eyes at the scent of decay and I welcome the sensation, making it appear to those around me that I look moved by their gesture. Anything to get them moving.

I turn quickly to face Melanie, who holds up two fingers towards me.

We're running out of time.

But an idea forms in my head.

I wave a hand towards my friend and watch as she leaves the flank to come up towards me, brow furrowed in confusion. Her thin form slides between bodies, shaking hands holding her screen to her chest.

I reach down and lift the chin of the man, holding his gaze gently to mine, and then yell out into the crowd. "The Elders have finally taken up arms against us and I need your help to save our people. If the revolution has ever meant anything to you, now is the time to *fight*, to *live*. Please, leave your dead. Save yourselves! Every life matters! Get up and go. GO."

They listen.

Stars, they all scramble to their feet and head to the exit with an enthusiasm I wouldn't have thought possible.

Melanie crams people forward as she nears me. And they actually freaking listen to her, to *me*.

I grab her shoulder. "Go ahead. Open the door."

"But the people—"

"I'll do what I can. Just go! Otherwise we'll all be trapped."

She sucks in her lips, hands shaking faster, but nods at me. "One minute, Savannah," she reminds me.

Stars.

I take a deep breath. "Just go."

We can't save them all.

Only the ones who want to be saved.

I watch as people kiss the foreheads of their dead, mumble goodbyes, and crowd around me as I dash for the exit.

These are *my* people.

I am their cause.

Anyone who hesitates will rot.

"My name is Savannah Shaw, and I am here to save you!" I call out.

Melanie turns her back on us and runs, the sound of her feet echoing behind us. Some people take her panic as a reason to hurry, thank the stars. Others ignore her completely.

I usher people out from cells, coaxing them with my name, with freedom. Some of them glare at me, refusing to move, but others come freely.

You can't save them all.

I keep my gaze ahead, hands steady as I pull people forwards and take their frail fingers into mine. I almost miss a step when I notice the child who stopped me on the day we freed Eli coming up beside me.

I take the child's hand, holding tight.

"I knew you would come," he utters to me.

I give his small hand a gentle squeeze and then push him gently ahead of me. "Help me save them."

He nods determinedly and, despite the stumble to his step, he helps me pull open doors. The people flood out. Soon, there aren't many left in the cells. But I gnaw on my lip when I notice the crowd of cells still shut ahead of us.

The moment the power goes off, the closed doors will never open again.

"Open your cells!" I shout. My voice cracks, the desperation shuddering down the tunnels. In answer, the crowd around me begins to help, tearing open doors.

I stand entirely still, the invisible clock counting down in my head until we are almost out of time. I scan ahead, trying not to sob at the sight of people emerging from their cells.

And then, in a great flickering throb, a shockwave flares as Jesse releases his grip on the power. Electricity momentarily floods the bars of the dangerous captives, then in a great shuddering heave, the world erupts back into silence.

Someone behind me screams and I spin around and see Samael's friend was holding open a cell for someone she knew, far behind us. She lies on the ground, her yellow hair standing up, her fingers twitching.

The girl inside the cell is shaking. She looks so like Samael's friend on the floor, only her hair is a natural brown unlike the other's yellow dye.

Sisters, from the looks of it.

The girl inside the cell hadn't seemed inclined to come—she was so far behind the crowd—but her sister must've insisted. Must've reached out for her bars in the moment Jesse let the electricity run free when flicking the switch.

She kneels by her sister's body, checking her pulse.

"She's okay! Someone help me!" Samael's friend calls out, voice wobbling.

Two men next to her reach under the yellow-haired girl to get to her sister, holding her up in shaking hands.

I swallow deeply and spin on my heel, heading back to the exit.

The crowd behind me follows and soon we come up to even more empty cells, nearing the edge of the labyrinth.

The people left in these cells are all dead or close to it. But the ones who could've made it? The ones I sacrificed to leave behind so Melanie could open the door for us? They glare at me intensely, hatred and bitterness flaring in their eyes as they watch our group.

They chose this, I tell myself. *You saved as many as you could.*

There weren't many who didn't come. Even those who hate me

don't want to die. But even if there were only a handful of them left, it makes me want to scream.

I wouldn't wish this one anyone—dying down here, buried so far away from the stars.

But it was their choice, not mine.

I round the final corner, spotting Melanie ahead of us.

The door to the staff room is propped wide open and held in place by a chair. Beyond that, the first checkpoint is clear, opening the way through the endless tunnel into the space centre where Jasmine is making a home for the captives.

It's the largest safe space in the base, has leftover medicine and multiple offices that we can turn into bedrooms to house the captives.

I walk up to my friend and nod solemnly.

We did it. We actually did it.

We kept our promise.

There are tears in her eyes when she grabs me, her arm winding around my shoulders.

"Everyone through here! It's a long walk, but there's food and beds waiting for you on the other side. Just one more hurdle and then you're all free."

I smile, squeezing my friend, and repeat into the labyrinth.

"You're all free!"

MELANIE

I roll a mandarin around my fingers, my heart pounding like nightmare.

Free.

What an absurd joke.

My head hardly touches the wall behind me as I collect myself. Apparently, I'm 'resting' my body from our tedious 'rescue', as per instructed by Savannah's overly gentle brother, who has taken it upon himself to make sure everyone is okay.

Not a single person from the Safe Holds meets my eyes as I steer them around the bunker that has decidedly become the home of our dying—sorry, our soldiers.

This place reminds me of the warehouse, which shouldn't be a surprise because Savannah's father has now unofficially taken over the accommodations and aiding people who are little more than bones into beds. We're underneath an old apartment block—a hidden gem under the base that my uncle built many years ago.

People wheeze and choke as Mason hands them loaves of bread, the faithful hand of the sister who is currently... well, I wasn't quite sure.

I sigh.

They're lucky, I suppose. The fact that they can stand upright, talk fluently, and eat bread tells me that Jasmine wasn't lying about finding *Sanitas*.

Which, in turn, gives us a fighting chance to begin an army.

Savannah left another note in my lab at the warehouse.

What it said was simple:

June 15.

PS: Only comm me when you arrive. We operate under shadow.

Good luck.

I should have burnt it, but I couldn't bring myself to. I push my metal fingers into my pocket, glove meeting paper as I crunch the note in my fist.

In that same pocket sits my comm.

The comm I hope I will never have to use, because it will announce both our locations to the Elders and Umbran Argenti.

For now, it's just a backup.

I swallow deeply.

Until June 15, when we will embark to Umbra, we have our work cut out for us.

This group needs time to get healthy, to train and, finally, to unearth their ships from below the base. They need to become an army.

And we have just over a month to do it.

If it weren't for the *Sanitas* such a thing would never have been possible.

But it is. And Savannah has left me in charge of making it come to life.

I'm the commander for this army.

And I will bring them all home to Umbra.

A wave of emotion flutters in my chest and I lose my breath. I breath rapidly as I stare at them all, fidgeting with the glove on my wrist.

Savannah will organise us safe passage to Umbra, and we will bring her an army.

I let go of Savannah's note with shaking fingers.

I glare at the concrete walls. Somehow, we are here because of Jasmine.

Jasmine.

Her blonde curls are tied back into a braid as she slices loaves of bread and her head lifts as if she heard me. She glares at me and I smirk at her gleefully.

She takes in the way I'm sprawled across the floor, my body rigid despite our success.

Jasmine freaking James.

Her jaw clenches, head whipping to the exit. My heart lifts a little when panic floods her eyes and she races out of the room.

Goodbye, Jasmine. She's probably going back to the forest.

My fingers twist the mandarin.

Savannah is on the right path. She is an unmovable force.

A force that sends my body trembling.

Umbra deserves the retaliation we will bring. Deserves her.

But Jesse?

I clench my teeth.

From across the musty room, Elijah smiles at me. His lips are chapped and dappled with specs of dirt, his eyes wide and bright when he looks at me. I flick my eyes away, unable to take him in.

Juices leak down my wrist, the mandarin squashed between my

fingers. I stare at the concrete wall until I sense his presence, kneeling beside me.

"You okay?" he asks softly.

"No."

I clamber up from the spot I've taken on the floor. Enough rest. Now action.

"Where are you going?"

My head dips under a concrete doorway, past a disabled security camera that's perched in solitude in the far right corner.

"To find some tech."

My uncle didn't give me many things, but he did give me way too much access in the Space Centre. I can practically control the beast from the inside-out if I wanted to.

Suddenly, I feel the eyes of the bony captives on my back. I ignore them, tracing the creases along the roof where a thin vein dips down the concrete—a point that conceals the electricity.

A small girl huddles in the corner through the next door. All the eyes on me glance away when I pierce their gaze with my own, but she holds it. Her eyes are almost as silver as mine, and her hair is so pale…

Not quite a pure-blooded Argenti, but close.

My breath hitches, catching in my chest.

I stand by the doorway, body angled like a bird ready to make flight.

The dress hanging off the girl once looked regal, but it's now a tattered mess.

I blink rapidly, cheeks aching as my lips branch upwards in a smile.

The girl doesn't smile back, but she takes a deep breath, leaning deeper into her spot in the wall. A mini Melanie Beckett. A version of what I could have been in a different life.

Behind me, Elijah's hand touches my waist. Oddly enough,

I don't shy away from the touch. His warmth soaks through my clothes, filling me with a sense of belonging.

But I take flight, spinning down to the other end of the room.

Because this room once held computers. Tech.

All the desks have been moved elsewhere, the indents of them still marked on the floors. The space is vacant of everything except bodies and beds and the switchboard planted into the wall.

I reach out with my gloved hand, seconds from prying open the switchboard when Elijah's large fingers wrap around my wrist, skin sliding against the wires in my own.

I wince.

After we bombed the landing pads many months ago, I struggled to find any tech on the base to help add new skin grafting onto my prosthetic. Now, when Elijah runs his hand down my wrist and turns me, it causes the fabric to catch at the hastily applied metal.

The feel of any man so close to my injury awakens old aches. My uncle hated what I did to my arm—it reminded him of my parents, the very people who were most against everything he worked so hard to achieve. The day I came home with the mechanical addition on my arm, he beat me senseless.

I stayed in bed for two days.

On day three, I bought myself some gloves.

"Our priority is the survivors," Elijah utters in a smooth voice, his hazel eyes lowered deep into my own. I hold his stare, my heart a crescendo.

He doesn't move any closer to me, but I feel his heat. Gently, he wraps his fingers through my own. My skin itches and I fight the urge to pull away.

My uncle made me into this fearful mess. Even now, months after he left me, I fear his wrath. Is he watching me? Does he still have spies on the base? Are any of these people we saved loyal to him?

On my back, I can feel the weight of one hundred eyes, but I ignore them.

I cleanse my mind and it switches back to the two things I am certain of: *Jesse Hayes* and *going to Umbra*. And then Elijah begins to play with my fingers, fraying those thoughts piece by piece.

I swallow deeply, trying to latch onto those two things will all my strength.

"Our instructions were clear, unless you misunderstood the implications," I utter under my breath. "Jesse and Savannah are planning a move on Umbra. The humans are tasked with feeding and fixing our survivors, and I…"

"Will help them, too?" Elijah suggests, his dark brows rising.

I release a strained cough of amusement, but it threatens to make me giddy, so I reel any humour in and turn my eyes off him.

My lips twitch at the corners, nonetheless. "I'm their lifeline, dumbass."

I finally release his hand.

His gaze is heavy.

This is the face of a man who cries himself to sleep, who stares at the world through a grimace. Yet, when he looks at me, all I can ever see is wonder behind his eyes.

"What do you mean?"

The comm in my pocket is a heavy reminder. Mere metres from us, a man coughs. His chest is bare and riddled with bruises, but his grey eyes are intense as he watches us.

"Not here," I mutter.

Elijah places his hands in his pockets, his eyes focused on the switchboard before me as if it's our saving grace. Maybe I've been looking at it like that, too.

"Then where—when?" he asks, trying and failing to keep the urgency out of his tone.

I take in his smooth skin, so perfect despite the years breathing in Terra's air. Most humans across the island aren't so lucky, with the contamination on Terra ageing them.

"June," I say, my voice shallow. "We go in June."

It isn't quite what he asked, but when he meets my eyes again, I know he understands exactly what I mean.

I have a direct means of communicating with Savannah Shaw—even across the universe—except I cannot use it.

Neither of us will unless we plan to meet again.

I sink into the depths of Elijah's gaze and suddenly feel tired. So very tired.

"We go in June," he repeats.

And it's not the comm in my pocket that keeps me going. It's that statement.

SAVANNAH

The moment my eyes latch onto Jesse's, I feel my heart sink in the worst way possible.

I have known this was coming for months, but that doesn't reduce the racing of my heart or the sweating in my palms.

Pulse racing, my feet slap down the corridor, away from my family.

Away from the people we freed.

We got almost everyone out, I tell myself.

That's nearly a hundred civilians who despise the Umbran government.

Nearly a hundred people who can shift the tide of war favourably to me.

"You really sure about doing this now?" Jesse asks as he kicks down a door to a new corridor I've never been down.

"No, but it's our best bet."

Jesse grunts, as if he disagrees. Too much can go wrong, I know that. But we don't have time to debate it.

The world around us is dark as we dash towards the looming possibility of death. The civilians from the Safe Holds are currently being fed, clothed, and brought to beds.

They barely made it after the long trek underground, all overwhelmed by the long walk they were required to do. Hell, the journey freaked me out enough that I wouldn't want to do it again, hitting me with traumatising memories.

Jesse slams open the last door and I blink against the sudden familiarity of all the metal around us. It looks eerily familiar to the landing pad hangars, only larger.

Those hangars are now inaccessible, the tunnels connecting them to the main hangar flooded with water and barricaded by thick concrete gates that no one dares to touch.

I pause by the first ship, hands shaking as Jesse roams forward to select the one he matched in the systems earlier while flooding power back into the base. He left all doors to the space centres unlocked to allow our exit.

I cross my arms over my chest, staring at the gaping departure point ahead of us. It's dusk, and the stars are winking in greeting.

It's been months since the fated day we exploded the landing pads, but it feels like no time has passed at all.

"Are you coming or are you going to stand there gawking all night?" Jesse calls out from somewhere among the ships.

With a shake of my head, I follow him. Shiny metal ships and pods greet me from all sides, forming neat rows along the concrete. The sound of my footsteps echoes into the high chamber, which is why I don't see the blonde-haired girl until she steps out from behind one of the ships.

I hear her before she speaks. The pounding of her feet, her panting breath...

"I just *knew* it," Jasmine Spark declares.

With a frown, I turn and face my friend.

She stands in the doorway, her braid loose and her chest heaving as she pants.

My switchblade is out of my pocket and in my hand before I have time to think better of it, hidden behind the shadow of my body.

Wisely, Jesse stays ahead. I glimpse his shadow flattening against the body of the ship, feet firmly planted on the lowering ramp that leads inside the silver beast.

"Put your knife down," I tell Jasmine, looking pointedly at the blade she must have taken from the bunker.

I expect Jesse to barrel towards us at the sight of it in her small, pale grip but Jesse is quiet and well trained.

"I will if you come back to the space centre with me."

"No."

"You're going to Umbra," Jasmine notes, lips thinning.

"Obviously."

"I thought the plan was to depart in June?" my friend enquires, her chin trembling despite her tight grip on the knife.

"That's when Umbrans travel the most between planets, I need to make sure we have fail safes, that we aren't just relying on this squadron on Terra. I must go to Umbra first and build us another army," I explain.

She glances down at the knife in her hands and I use the distraction to take a glance back to the departing bay, noticing the sun dipping further below the horizon.

Resisting the urge to fidget, I sigh.

Her eyes flicker back up to me just as I hear a gentle whoosh from behind.

The ship engine.

"Let me go, Jasmine," I say gently.

The knife in her hand starts to tremble. She takes a tentative step towards me and I mimic her by taking a step back.

"You left me once already, went against my wishes to become the usurper Queen of Umbra. And I forgive you. I'm moving on from that. But if you leave now, I don't think I can ever forgive you."

"You were never going to forgive me at the end of this war anyway." The moment the words leave my mouth, I realise they are true. We can pretend to like each other, pretend to resurrect our friendship, but nothing will ever be the same.

The old Jasmine Spark is gone.

And soon, I will be too.

"You're starting this 'war', it's not some inevitable thing," she hisses at me.

"Maybe. But you still have to let me go."

I listen to how my voice echoes around the hangar, sensing the shift in the engine of the machine behind us. My body is angled and ready to flee at the slightest movement but, instead, all I take is another lazy step back, making a point of it.

I saved Jasmine's people, I promised to work with her. The latter wasn't a lie. Not really. But when Jasmine pulls her arm back it occurs to me that she doesn't believe any of it.

"I still had hope," she says.

I could move away. I could easily dodge the blade in her hand. Quite frankly, her aim is terrible.

But I don't move.

Jasmine Spark needs to know that I am on her side, despite everything. And instinct churns in my gut, telling me that if I flinch, she will see it as a small betrayal.

What I didn't expect was for Jasmine to actually throw it.

What I expected even less was for it to imbed into my leg.

The knife spins through the air, her body stumbling from the force of the throw, and then it impales directly into my thigh.

I gasp, stumbling back, pain screaming up my body.

Jasmine splutters, catching herself as she lands on her knees from the force of the throw. Her small lips pop open when she sees where her knife went, and with shaking hands, she lifts her hands to her mouth.

My own hands tremble slightly as I stare at her, not quite able to bring my eyes down to the knife inside my thigh.

"Savannah—"

I take a painful step back from her, stumbling as I put weight on my injured leg. I will take her judgement and harsh words and I will shoulder them. But I will not fight her.

I hold up a hand, still not looking at the knife in my thigh, gritting my teeth through the pain. Adrenaline kicks through my body, blood pumping hot and angry around the incision wound.

The urge to run away from Jasmine Spark overcomes me.

"The plan is still set for June. I'll see you in a month."

Nausea threatens to send me to my knees, but I stomach it, my nails digging into the handle of my switchblade.

The dark, scrawled word on the handle swims in my mind.

Perseverance.

I force myself to walk to the ship ahead of us, the ramp beginning to retract when I plant my feet on the surface. The world around me feels dazed, unsteady, as I blink through the adrenaline coursing through my body.

"It's a one-way trip without the landing pads intact!" Jasmine calls out, as if I don't already know.

It causes something in my heart to plummet.

Hell, I haven't been able to stop thinking about that since I came up with this plan many weeks ago.

I look down at my feet on the worn metal ramp, watching as the ship lifts off the ground and the ramp pulls me into the body of the ship, sucking me away.

I take her stupid knife with me, because I still can't bring myself to look down at it and pull it out.

I suppose medically, I shouldn't take it out anyway.

Jasmine's head is arched towards me, her shoulders set but heavy, hands hanging like weights at her side.

I didn't even get the chance to feel the forest floor under my feet or the Terra sun on my skin one last time. Instead, I'm hoisted up into the sky.

I try not to think of Mason and my father, who I didn't get to say goodbye to.

One day, we will meet again.

Just not on Terra.

I take in the heartbroken look of my old friend, her blonde mane knotting from the wind of our fleeing ship.

I smile sadly at her, not sure if she sees it. "Terra never wanted me anyway."

And then the ships swallows me up and I fall over, the force of super fuel propelling us away from the ground.

SAVANNAH

"*Trajectory set from Terra to Umbra: 134 hours, 2 minutes, and 31 seconds until arrival,*" the ship purrs around us, its voice metallic and echoing in the large chamber.

In a little over five days, my feet will touch Umbran soil.

The switchblade in my palm clatters onto the metal floor as I open my fist and slide onto my knees, hands flat on the cold metal.

The knife is beginning to burns, screaming at me as my muscles move around the metal, but I hardly notice it through the adrenaline as I stare at the night sky zooming past the window, clouds tickling the outside of the ship.

"Seatbelt! Now!" Jesse barks at me.

I groan and then crawl into a seat behind the captain's, trying to keep my expression neutral as I grip the buckles with shaking fingers. I ignore the fact that he isn't watching me.

My world spins, a haze covering my mind.

"As long as you don't mind blood on the upholstery," I mutter. Blood starts oozing from my thigh, spreading everywhere. I can feel my face go white.

The ship is near silent, so it's not surprising that Jesse hears, his head tilting back in his seat in frustration.

I watch the back of his head as he grips the steering wheel, lights blinking all around him. "What's new? You're always bleeding from something." He punches some buttons on the blinking dashboard before him. "Seatbelt!"

Leg jerking, I try not to focus on my thigh as I latch all the buckles together. "Alright, calm down. I'm doing it."

The window before us becomes a blur and my head gets smacked back onto the seat.

"Ouch!"

A throb works its way up my skull and my heart accelerates, pounding as I glance back at Jesse.

He hiccoughs in front me.

The ship is so *fast*.

I squeeze my eyes closed and listen as the ship announces, "*Preparing to exit the atmosphere.*"

I feel my head rolling, my arms going lax. "Now would be a great time to pass out," I say to myself, mind ticking back to the knife in my thigh. But of course, I don't.

Surprisingly, my ears don't pop. The ship must be stabilising the pressure. It's also a lot less shaky than I had imagined it would be when shooting into space.

Umbran technology? *Definitely.*

But that doesn't stop the way the world blurs. The way I see nothing at all as we shoot through the sky.

Stars. I squeeze my eyes shut.

Shoving my hand into my pocket, I grip the small communication device Melanie gave me this morning at the warehouse. To my shock, she never asked why I needed it. Never questioned when I asked if the comms could communicate between Umbra and Terra.

But Melanie Beckett knew. She *knew* the reason, the same way she knows most things.

Persevere, Savannah.

Melanie knows enough of my plan to keep the ball rolling on Terra. I will build an army for them to join with on Umbra, just as she will work on the one back home.

I squeeze the comm device until the skin on my knuckles strains and, suddenly, my chin drops forwards and I feel the ship level around us.

"*Atmosphere breached, engaging onto set path.*"

I blow out a heavy breath, sagging like a sack of grain into the seat.

Ahead of me, Jesse swallows deeply.

When I blink the stars from my vision, I find his sapphire eyes are latched on my thigh, mouth tight at the sight of the blood swimming in my seat.

With a small frown, he lifts his gaze to mine, then hiccoughs. "Did you have your eyes closed that whole time?"

I nod, inhaling a short breath, trying to find the words to speak. My heart slams in my chest.

The world around me feels too quiet. Too stable.

In contrast, my heart is an erratic mess.

"The take-off is the best bit. The only bit I like, actually."

My mouth twitches. I manage to croak out a word. "Debatable."

He tries to smile, but it doesn't quite meet his eyes as he surveys my leg.

I blink away the sight of him. The world around me spins and I can't tell if it's from the blood loss or from the stars dancing beyond the window.

Behind Jesse's head, the universe ebbs and flows, dark and

bright all at once. There is no up or down—just vast, endless space. I swallow and turn away from the window.

I don't see Terra anymore, but I'm hardly trying. Everything swims and sways. Too still. Too quiet.

I squeeze the edge of the seat with straining fingers, dumbfounded.

Jesse scrambles out of his seat towards me. I feel lightheaded, ghostly, as he reaches for my face.

His boot whacks on the edge of a chair as he nears me.

I blink at him.

He's so *noisy.* Jesse is never noisy.

He grabs my chin softly, tilting my head upright so I don't faint in my seat. Then he works at unbuckling me.

His hands are shaking, his eyes looking at anything but mine.

"Jasmine threw a knife at you," he says tightly.

I lick my lips to speak again, but can't seem to form words, so I mumble, "Mhmm."

His breath, warm and gentle, hits my cheek before he pulls away.

The spaceship we stole is quite small and fast, all smooth metal planes and long angles. The inside is pocketed with cupboards and hatches filled with what I can only assume are living necessities. Before us, the control panel is a jumble of lights and flashing interfaces across screens as paper thin as Melanie's computers.

Above it all, a holograph of Umbra rotates.

Round, and round, and round.

My throat thickens and I slacken in my seat.

It's hard to breathe. The world around me blurs, sleep threatening to take me.

A window coats the face of the ship, thick and heavy and so clear I can see my pale face reflected in it, brown hair in a jumble and grey eyes widened.

Jesse yanks open a metal latch off to the side of the ship. It's filled with bagged rations—water sachets in plentiful supply too.

He rips into one with his teeth, spitting the cap onto the floor before holding the pouch out to me.

I lift it slowly to my lips, tasting it hesitantly before gulping some down.

The water washes through my mouth, clearing away the thickness in my throat.

It tastes metallic and off, but it's water nonetheless.

Jesse grips my thigh in his large hands, blood leaking past his fingers, staining the seat below me. My leg is thrumming with pain, black spots covering my vision, but I focus on drinking the water, hands trembling, eyes darting across the swath of space before me.

With a trembling breath, he reaches for his knife and, very gently, cuts through the fabric of my pants to make a wider hole to examine the injury.

My heart stops as I take in his handsome face.

Long, graceful dark lashes, porcelain skin alight as he examines me, red creeping down his neck. His hair has grown since I first met him and a curl unravels itself around his ear, whispering over his skin.

"Why?" he asks in a gravelly tone.

"She was very angry," I say quietly, barely able to speak above the pain.

"No." His voice is clipped. With shaking hands, he storms back over to the edge of the ship and tears open another cabinet, pulling out a first aid box with urgency. "Why didn't you *move*?"

"I don't... I don't know." I mutter, and continue to pick at the skin around my thumb.

"Savannah," he warns. His voice is raw. Gravelly.

I take a shaky, steadying breath.

In one of his many trips to the base, I tasked Jesse with preparing a ship, filling it with supplies and, most importantly, accessing as much of the advanced Umbran medicine as possible.

"Can you please get it out of me, and maybe get some *Velox*?" I ask.

I left most of the medicinal supplies on Terra, in case my people need it. But it would've been stupid to not bring any with us, especially since we can't predict what we'll encounter on Umbra. It might not make sense to waste any now, but I don't want to spend my time on Umbra healing—not when Umbrans have *Velox*, a syringe that can increase your body's natural healing rate down to minutes.

"That girl is already broken, you don't need to get yourself hurt to prove it," he snarls, hands viciously tearing open the medicine cabinet.

"We have *medicine*," I utter, eyes trailing over his stormy features. He doesn't notice when I try and plaster a smile on my face, so it wavers immediately.

He slowly lifts his head. "If you insist on hurting yourself this entire mission to Umbra, I'm out. I'm *out*."

I stare at him, devouring the flustered state he's in with amusement. "But first, where's the medicine, Jesse?"

He stares at me as if he's stripping apart my soul, shattering his always-perfect disposition. His face swims before me as I lose focus, my breathing growing laboured.

"Stay here." He stands up, moving to the medicine cupboard.

I nod numbly because I'm not really listening. My head rolls and I squeeze my eyes shut. *Stars.*

Don't pass out.

One of his muscled hands grips my thigh, bringing me back to reality.

I crack open my eyes, narrowing them, trying to focus.

"Ready? I'm going to do it quick," Jesse says.

I look down at the knife in my thigh, the blood draining from my face. A long, deep breath pulls into my lungs as I tilt my head back and sharply nod.

My muscles stiffen and I squeeze my eyes shut.

I try and ready myself, but I don't have enough time.

Jesse grips the knife and yanks it from my thigh.

I wail, my scream battering around the ship.

And then a harsh ache spreads across my thigh, splintering my mind as Jesse drops the knife to the floor with a *clink*. Pain moves up my leg, encasing my body as Jesse releases a heavy breath.

Blood begins to pool around my seat, wet and sticky, so I slowly peel open my eyes. Before me, Jesse shrugs his jacket off, then places the tools on top, along with a bandage and a big bottle of some orange liquid.

Antiseptic. Absolutely not.

His eyes lock on me, heady and dark, urging me to look at him. So I do.

"Savannah," he demands, voice deep.

I'm here.

He holds me steady, then pours the orange liquid over my wound.

Pain rings up my leg, worse than before, burning over what feels like every nerve point. This time, my scream is guttural.

My head is pounding, brain melting into a puddle of nothing as I gasp at the agony heating my skin.

I disconnect, losing sight of him until finally, everything comes back into focus.

"*Jesse!*" I scream.

His hands are steady, working efficient as he reaches for the *Velox*.

My eyes lock on the swirling abyss of the stars beyond the window, finally remembering that they're still there.

"*Hurry up,*" I hiss.

The antiseptic moves through my wound. Unravelling me. Destroying me.

But eventually, it slows to a throb, then stops altogether.

I slacken in my seat but I don't move my leg. I don't dare move.

"*Velox.* Now." My voice is guttural.

Jesse grunts, holding the cylinder above my thigh and injecting the needle deep into my flesh.

A shaky shout explodes out of my mouth and my head tilts back in my seat.

The *Velox* may have been from an old batch, but it works fine.

The skin on my leg begins to pulse eerily, the blood flow gradually stopping, the angry wound turning to a soft pink.

The nausea bubbling up my chest begins to disperse, the pounding in my head depleting. Everything in my body begins to reset except for the clattering pound of my heart in my ears.

I hold my breath, vision focusing until I can marvel at the tidy smear of white across my thigh.

"No way," I utter.

The vicious injury reduces to nothing but a pale scar before absorbing into my body, vanishing entirely until there's nothing but drying blood splattered down my leg.

If someone were to look at me now, they would assume the blood wasn't mine.

I sink into my seat, an angry shiver convulsing my body.

"Thank you," I mumble into the emptiness before me, not sure what else to say. A chill bite from the ship engulfs me and I lean backwards, skin prickling.

Jesse releases a shaky breath. Twin bruises underline his dark eyes as he takes me in, his hair an absolute mess. "You should get some sleep. It's going to be a long trip."

I nod numbly at him as he walks down to the back of the ship, his shoulders hanging deep.

"*Passenger sleeping pod opening,*" the ship announces as Jesse slips his fingers into a metal panel against the wall. I turn to see a bed hinging open from before him, sheets stiffly covering it to keep the pillow and everything in place as it pulls to the ground.

Jesse dislodges the sheets from the edge of the bed, then comes back to scoop me into his arms. I'm too disassociated to feel much of anything, and even the warmth of his arms around my body feels distant. All I can focus on is the pounding of his heart, my own becoming one with his.

I don't feel the bed under me until he pulls the covers to my chin.

I groan, burrowing under the sheets, trying to ignore every thought threatening to invade the peaceful emptiness in my head.

They are all tomorrow's problem.

SAVANNAH

We're going to Umbra.

The thought lurches me awake.

I squeeze my eyes shut into my pillow, ears straining to hear Jesse above the humming of the ship. All is silent.

I push the hair out of my face and roll to the other side of the bed, turning my attention onto the sheet of stars dancing out the window.

My heart all but stops beating. *Stars*, this is impossible.

The lights, the colours, the endless depths of nothingness. My gut swirls, my pulse ticking behind my eyes.

We're going to goddamn Umbra.

"*Welcome back, Passenger Shaw.*" The ship's voice buzzes around me and I rub the sleep out of my eyes.

Everything around me feels slow. Muted.

Sleep still nags at me.

"Thanks...?" I stare up at the ceiling, wondering if the ship heard me.

My eyes travel down to the blood across my bare legs. Or rather, where there should be blood.

I rub my arms, blinking.

Everything feels fuzzy, like I'm still in a dream state.

I'm still in the same form-fitting shirt I wore on the base, the remains of my pants on the floor next to me. The blood, though, has been cleaned and a drip is now attached to my arm.

I yank it free with trembling fingers, then pull the blanket up higher as I turn to face Jesse, who is sitting in a seat at the front of the ship, mind lost to the stars as the ship runs on autopilot. The flight to get to Umbra is direct, and doesn't require much assistance from Jesse, and he doesn't seem to know what to do with himself because of it.

"How long have I been asleep for?" I say by way of greeting, blinking sleep out of my eyes.

He sits in one of the passenger seats, lazily stretched out to take in the view of space from the thick window before him. He slowly turns back to the window, hiding a sheepish grin.

"A bit over four days. We will near the wormhole in less than an hour and then it's another 28 hours until we reach Umbra."

My heart pounds in my ears.

"*Four days?* That's..."

"Impossible?" He tilts his head back, his blue eyes searing into my soul. "No. I kept injecting you with a sleep serum."

Heat rises to my face, my hands fisting in the blankets. Not caring about how bare my legs are anymore, I throw myself out of bed, stalking towards him.

Only to fall cleanly onto my face.

"Jesse!"

The ground is icy against my cheek.

Tingles ignite in my legs as feeling returns to my body.

"What did you inject me with? My legs are numb!"

He shrugs, turning back to face the stars before him.

Slowly, painfully, I force myself to move, practically crawling over to him.

Frustration builds in my chest as I will sensation into my limbs, but then I see what's out the window.

The sight of it all threatens to undo me—the swirling abyss of space cascading past the window, making me feel smaller, yet more powerful than I have ever felt. I pull myself towards it, hand aimlessly reaching for the glass and my breath hitches in my throat.

The wormhole is stationary—unmoving, unlike everything else.

In a month, Terra will have spun closer to the wormhole. It will take our friends hardly any time to reach Umbra.

In a way, it's reassuring, knowing they are so far away.

So unreachable.

I reach for the comm I share with Melanie, then recall it's in the pocket of my pants. My switchblade rests on the dashboard at the front of the ship, where Jesse left it.

A chill skitters down my back.

When we arrive, we will be utterly isolated, our fate entirely up to ourselves.

My hand begins to shake against the glass. *Persevere, Savannah. This is your plan.*

I take a long, uneven breath of air. We need to know what we are getting into and what awaits us. There was never a chance in hell that I would blindly let my friends and family step into unknown danger. That's my job.

I release my breath, mind spinning as rapidly as the blinking stars around us as I turn to face Jesse.

"You could've asked me before you knocked me out for days," I utter.

"You were busy sleeping."

I growl.

Jesse gives me a look and I can't be bothered arguing with him, so instead I work my way to the food cupboard, snatching up something squishy.

"It tastes gross," he warns.

"It's food." I shrug, ripping it open with my teeth. He was right. *Stars, it tastes bad.*

I swallow the food, giving him a shaky smile.

Pulling myself over to the captain's seat, I throw my legs up onto the dashboard next to my switchblade so that gravity can ease the blood back into my body. The stars dance over my skin—my perfectly healed leg.

Scientists be damned, I will never get used to this.

I toss the half-eaten food packet on the floor. Surely there are some that taste better.

"You can put your pants back on now."

"I could," I reply.

And soon I will.

For now, I reach for more food, eyes hungrily roaming for something that tastes half decent.

Outside of our window, a distant asteroid shower swarms past, vaguely unsettling. It's out of our trajectory, so I try not to let it worry me, but I cannot take my eyes off it.

This is the lifestyle—the universe my mother had always sought.

She was never fit for Terra. The same way I'm probably not. Not really.

But we are still both human. We can both die. Both vulnerable.

A screen in front of me shows our path, as well as the blip waiting ahead of us. We're nearly at the wormhole.

I remind myself that it's been done before—it's safe—so that my heartbeat remains steady.

Hell, I've never been in *space* before, let alone gone through a *wormhole*.

I choke back a mouthful of even more disgusting food.

Swallow.

Breathe deeply.

Jesse clears his throat, determinedly trying to make a point of not staring at my legs. I glance down at my switchblade on the dashboard of the ship, noticing how shiny the mahogany handle is. He's oiled it for me.

"Keep eating. Regain your strength. We will be there soon."

I give him a shaky smile.

"Have you eaten?" I enquire.

"Yep."

"Liar." I toss my half-eaten packet at him. He scowls, glaring at me. "And to think that I could've slept through this," I tease, staring down at my legs, trying not to imagine him injecting me with a sleeping serum.

"I debated it. But how could I resist your sunny personality?" he deflects.

I glower at him until he clears his throat.

"Considering how inept you were at handling the take-off, I almost let you sleep, but I figured everyone needs to see it—at least once," he elaborates.

I raise my eyebrows. "I handled take-off perfectly fine, thank you."

He makes a sound in the back of his throat and rises from his seat, heading to the food cabinet. I wonder if he slept at all these past few days, considering I had the bed.

No food or sleep... Some solider.

"Sure," he mumbles, rolling his eyes.

I resist the urge to throw something at him, but all I have is my switchblade and the flimsy food packets on the floor.

"Thank you for letting me see it," I say, pulling my arms across my chest and sinking further into the seat. "I want to see this. It's not every day you experience the universe folding itself in half." He throws my pants at me and I glower, but he's too busy searching for more food. "You shouldn't throw stuff at injured people."

"You're completely healthy," he mutters, head low in the cabinet.

I sulk, sinking deep into my chair.

I recall what I was taught about wormholes. They're a gateway between separate corners of the universe. I imagine the stars ahead of me as a paper map folded in half and picture a door between the folded pieces of the map, connecting the top and the bottom, allowing our ship to jump from galaxy to galaxy as quickly as you'd enter a doorway to your bathroom.

At least, that's the theory.

I zone out as Jesse eats, my mind ticking.

In the far distance, light spins across the universe—a star exploding perhaps—and I watch it in awe. As if allowing me a longer look, the ship slows down, putting a stopper on its fast, but steady pace.

"*Approaching wormhole entry point,*" the ship tells us.

I blink. Already?

"Oh," Jesse exclaims. "I asked the ship to stop counting down as it was driving me crazy. We're closer than I thought."

"I don't see anything."

He comes up behind me, hand resting on the back of the captain's seat behind my head. "You will."

We sit in silence for a moment, the supernova is utterly dazzling, until I register the sight of the anomaly before us and my breath hitches in my throat.

I don't recognise the constellations around us, but when my eyes catch the ripple in space ahead, my heart plummets.

The map of stars moves like water, bending around a dip in space as if falling down a waterfall. The wormhole appears stagnant, but the space around it moves constantly, rippling over the tiny hole ahead of us. Some stars twinkle further below, warped as they move across it.

I rub my eyes with my knuckles.

Impossible.

In my peripheral, the exploding star is blinding, as if clapping for our success. I swing my legs down off the dashboard, turning to face Jesse in confusion, but his face reveals nothing.

I rise out of the seat, moving for my own so that he can reoccupy the captain's position. He watches me rise, eyes darting to my legs.

"Savannah," he says with a sigh. "Pants."

"*Engaging entry point.*"

"Jesse. *Wormhole.*" I snatch my switchblade off the dashboard as I move past, spinning it in my fingers.

The window blurs in front of me and I squeeze my eyes for a moment to get rid of the residual sleep. The ship continues its leisurely pace, narrowing in on the hole ahead of us. It's very small and, if you squint, it just looks like a bright cluster of stars.

I know better though.

The ship enters the wormhole and a weird warping sensation grapples me. Stars compress in a distinctively different way than they had when we were floating around space.

The ship whirs as it pulls us forwards.

"Is it going to suck us in?" I ask Jesse.

"This isn't a black hole."

Our speed increases, faster than imaginable. Outside, the window blurs into a spiral of light, like the sun refracting against the ocean.

I squint back to look at the exploding star, but it's vanishing, as if melting away. Eyes wide, I turn back to the front of the window, but none of the stars make sense. Everything is just a mass of colour and light, compressed and knotting around itself.

"What—"

"We're in the fold of the wormhole," Jesse explains. "The blurred gap between the 2 portions of the universe."

The speed increases, but not enough to jerk me back in my seat. I grip the edges of the dashboard, twist my feet under my seat and gasp as the exploding star vanishes and we near the end of the waterfall, the tunnel of light spiralling open.

Bile tickles the back of my throat and I force myself back into my seat. The stars appear normal once again as the new corner of the universe peels into view and I exhale loudly as the ship breaches the wormhole.

Beside me, Jesse curses.

I turn to face him, my eyes blurry and overwhelmed at the sight of all the new constellations and galaxies.

"Asteroids," he says.

For a moment, he doesn't move. And then I see it.

Debris spirals around us, cascading across the sky.

Jesse dives for the controls and I squeeze the switchblade in my palm out of habit.

Centuries ago, one of Umbra's three moons exploded, throwing their planet into a state of natural disaster. The planet now has a perpetual ring of debris spiralling around it in memoriam of the havoc it reaped. But we aren't close enough to Umbra yet for that to be a problem with our ship. Are we?

The ship narrowly misses a chunk of space matter, sending my packet of food swinging into the air.

"Savannah!" Jesse shouts, head bent over the dashboard. "Seatbelt!"

Seatbelt. Yes. Obviously.

My fingers twiddle with the straps, my eyes burning in their sockets with the inability to force myself to blink. With an eagle's focus, I stare at the rocks tumbling around us.

On the screen before me, I can see a virtual image of the asteroids' trajectory, the ship still on autopilot.

Jesse's voice mumbles around me. "It's okay.... we're okay. This happens."

He says it more to himself than me. I don't answer.

I jerk my eyes from the asteroids to Jesse, noticing the sweat beading on his head and the way his fingers shake across the dashboard, hovering over a switch. A situation like this calls for taking a ship off autopilot. But he doesn't.

The ship jerks, rocking Jesse, and he exhales a shaky breath.

He's panicking. *Why* is he panicking? He's the best pilot I know.

"*Manual override suggested.*" The ship echoes my thoughts.

"Jesse," I quietly urge. My nails tap the wooden handle of my blade.

He runs a hand through his hair and grips the dashboard so hard his knuckles are white.

"Jesse, focus."

He turns to glare at me, the full venom of his emotions searing me. Unsteady, I pull myself up into my chair and glare back.

"Pull. Yourself. Together."

The ship wails around us, jostling us this way and that. I can see safety ahead. I can *see* where we need to go. But I can't fly a ship.

"*Manual override suggested,*" The ship repeats.

I point to the ceiling, jabbing my finger to the voice.

He watches my hand in vain, his focus half on the window and the world of death rising up to meet us.

The screen pings. Jesse's eyes dart to it, his breathing heavy.

"My father died doing this."

"*Manual override suggested.*"

My body won't stop shaking, and I know it's insensitive, but I can't help but snap back. "Then be better than him."

A large asteroid hurtles towards us and crashes into the ship. The collision vibrates along the hull, causing alerts to flash across the screen.

My head gets thrown back into my seat and I gasp heavily.

Ouch. Okay. I deserved that.

The ship narrowly misses another asteroid and I watch us dart around it through the window.

Jesse just has the audacity to say instead, "I won't be."

Oh, god. We're going to die.

"*Try!*" I scream.

His deep blue eyes flare.

Maybe it's something in my expression, or maybe it's one of the many more asteroids honing in on us, or because we both know the ship won't be able to dodge all of them, but he finally punches the button that switches the ship to manual.

It whirs.

"*Manual steering engaged.*"

Jesse grapples the steering in anger, his hands shaking as he tears his gaze sharply away from me. I sit next to him, plastered in place, my heart thumping at the sight of all the rocks hurtling towards us.

We're going to die.

I hold my switchblade to my chest, too scared to lose it as the ship swerves.

Jesse either doesn't realise I'm leaning forward or doesn't have time to chastise me, but he jerks the ship sideways and I hit my head on the back of my seat from the motion. I manage to straighten myself and control my breathing, head spinning as the ship dances around the asteroids like a freaking rollercoaster.

I want to squeeze my eyes shut, but I don't.

I wish I knew how to help Jesse, but I don't.

I lean forwards again, despite my better judgement, hands straining the edges of my seat. I know I should lean back, but I don't have the time to correct myself.

Instead, I scream and swing in my seat as the next asteroid hits us.

SAVANNAH

"We've been hit. *Twice.*"

"I know, shut up!" Jesse cries, pain tearing his words in two.

We're going to die, we're going to die, we're going to die.

The ship wobbles, narrowly missing the oncoming asteroids. An alarm screeches and whirs around us.

"Jesse!"

"*Minor damage to landing gears and exterior plating on left wing.*"

Landing gears?

"*Jesse!*" I repeat.

My pants slide past my seat from the impact and I reach for them, the communication device Melanie gave me digging into my palm as I clutch it in one hand, the switchblade in the other.

The temptation to call her pounds through my body.

What if we die, and this is my last chance to say goodbye?

What if we die, and Melanie doesn't know our end of the mission is over?

The thoughts wail in my head as I stare out the window.

Melanie would probably be able to refrain from messaging if she were in my position. She knew the implications since the day we left for the Safe Holds.

She knew.

Melanie knew.

But I will always need her help.

I need her now.

I make move to switch on the device, just as Jesse pounds his fist on the dashboard of the ship, startling me.

Jesse's hands are still shaking, and he takes a long deep breath. Cursing, he refocuses himself as he pulls us out of the danger zone and the cool quiet of nothingness greets us like a slap on the other side.

I nearly drop my comm.

I want to exhale, to restart my heart, but instead I breathe through pinched breaths and shakily make my way over to Jesse.

He's white as a ghost.

He turns hesitantly towards me, easing the ship back into auto-pilot. I watch the way he breathes rapidly out of parted lips and resist the temptation to shake him.

His father died piloting ships.

His fingers are clammy as I twine mine through his.

"We need to assess the ship," he says and yanks his hand out from under mine. I gnaw on my lip and nod. Of course we do.

I watch him fumble his way to the back of the ship, past the bed—which is now half on the floor—to the spot just behind the door. He yanks open a cabinet and I stand eerily still as he watches items tumble around his feet.

Rope. A bedroll. A tarp. Among other things.

"Wrong cabinet?" I ask.

He gives me an exasperated look. It's not like Jesse too be this uneasy.

He clambers past the items at his feet and pulls open another latch, this one hiding a control panel. None of the buttons or digits make sense to me, but after a moment of tapping, he inhales sharply.

"Landing will be fun," he mumbles, body swaying, his lips thinned.

I wrap my arms over my chest, fighting back the chills. "What does that mean?"

He pushes the latch closed with a click, resting his forehead on the metal cabinet and taking a few deep breaths before he answers. "I'll think of something. But we're probably going to land rough."

I tiptoe behind him still, fighting the urge to comm Melanie and let her know that we might not be okay.

I shake my head. "We'll manage."

"Yup." He pushes himself away from the cabinet, kicking the tarp that has fallen closest to him.

The ship hums around us, quiet for once instead of announcing its trajectory. We are about a day away from Umbra. One day to figure something out.

"Can the landing gear be fixed in time?" I enquire.

"Not from inside the ship."

"Can we climb outside of the ship?"

"Not without dying."

It seems stupid that we chose a ship without spacesuits to allow us outside. Stupid that I didn't think of it and stupider still that I let Jesse choose a ship for speed and not safety.

I pick at my nails, hands slightly shaking, as I stare at him.

"Then we crash land," I say, because what else *can* I say?

"We crash land," Jesse agrees.

What a mess.

I right the fallen bed and sit down, throwing the comm and my blade next to me. Jesse opens another secret panel in the ship and I sit there quietly as he briefly explains the rest of the damage to the ship.

I nod along dutifully, but my mind is not in the ship.

It's back in Silver Valley.

Terra has never felt entirely like home to me, but the past few months have become dangerously worse. Our dead are buried, our wounds are healed, and people are moving on, but I've never felt so out of place.

When I look in the mirror, my face has not changed. Dark hair just below my chest, skin as pale as cream, a smattering of freckles, and my eyes...

Silver. Not grey, like I once believed.

They're a symbol of Umbra. My mysterious heritage. The silvery sheen marks me as a relative of one of the most powerful creatures in the universe: the Argenti.

Venus Collins has never been a mother to me, but I will never be able to shed the glittering eyes she has given me.

I'm half Argenti.

And now, speeding across the stars, I have never felt more like it.

Will landing on Umbra fill me with serenity? Will I walk among the foreign forests and feel like I'm finally home?

I twist my arms across my chest, fighting off invisible chills.

Jesse doesn't look at me, so I don't feel pressured to hide the raging anxiety I know must be flashing across my features.

The last few months in the warehouse had been a wonderful dream. Some nights, Mason—all gangly now that he's fourteen—would venture to my bed and we would sit there for hours, talking.

I promised he would see Umbra and I intend to follow through on that promise.

We've set a date. Melanie knows what's to come and she will build an army—a fleet—then come home.

My heart rate increases as my fingers brush over the comm she gave me. "We should land close to civilisation, if we can help it," I tell Jesse.

I don't move my eyes from the window, but I hear him stir behind me.

"Your reason?"

"Simple, really," I say with a whisper of a smile. "We have minimal time to build a second army and to cause as much damage as possible to the Elders' power and influence before our Terran army steps foot on Umbra. The closer we get to civilisation, the more we can get done, meaning the less danger I bring my brother into."

Jesse scoffs behind me.

I turn to face him with a sigh.

He has his eyebrows raised, jaw set. "At some point, you're going to have to let Mason make his own sacrifices."

Heat pounds behind my eyes. I jump up from the bed, muscles clenched. "Absolutely not."

The window isn't far away. I go to stand by it, fingers inches away from touching the glass. Space twirls around me, making me dizzy. I let the cool serenity of it wash away the feelings burning in my chest.

"Fine. Shield him, I don't care. Just try not to get yourself hurt by extending yourself too far. As you said, we don't have much time."

I nod slightly, eyes locked on a point ahead of me. "We'll make it count," I utter softly.

The sounds of Jesse tinkering to fix the ship resume behind me.

"Ship, how long until landing?" I enquire, raising the volume of my voice.

"26 hours, 13 minutes and counting..."

I suck on the inside of my mouth, head pounding. Despite sleeping so long, I feel utterly exhausted. The moment we land on Umbra I can ransack a medical ward—and hopefully get some proper food while I'm at it.

In the meantime, I sink back into one of the seats at the front of the ship.

"Land near civilisation," I say to Jesse, leaning my head back.

"As close as I can, Princess."

My heart suddenly thumps in my chest. "But don't let us be seen."

"Two very different acts, Savannah."

"Just... try," I whisper.

"Yes, Princess," he sighs.

I shuffle in my seat.

I will see my family again.

The alternative is unacceptable.

Swallowing a lump in my throat, I nestle my chin lower into the chair and pray for sleep to carry the rest of the trip away from me.

SAVANNAH

"Can you see the broken moon?"

"It's a ring," I answer Jesse, my breath short and quick.

"The shards circulate the planet," he says from beside me, his fingers dangling above the ship's controls, hesitant to take it off autopilot for the landing.

Or should I say, crash-landing.

I swallow, easing moisture back into my dry throat, too stunned to reach for a water bottle from the food cabinet.

Umbra is beautiful.

The shadow of Terra. It is near-identical, save for the swirling ring around its edges, much like the planet Saturn in our solar system. But the planet itself is like Terra, covered in ocean and land, except the continents are few and large, and mostly a glistening red aside from stretches of green closer to the equator.

It's so similar to Terra, yet so otherworldly.

I release a long, pained breath.

It's incredibly small. Perhaps a quarter of the size of Terra. There's no way we could ever fit the entire population of humanity onto Umbra, there just isn't enough room.

We hover in orbit, ready to begin our descent.

"You must see the remaining moons from Umbra a lot," I remark, more to myself than anything.

Umbra's solar system is much smaller than I initially expected, consisting of one star—its sun—a small gas planet, the blitzed moon, and another two perfectly full moons which circle very close to Umbra, their rotation much faster than Terra's.

"Yes, it covers a large portion of the sky," Jesse says, his eyes downcast over the controls.

"Where will we land?" I ask him, turning in my seat. I wipe my sweaty palms down my pants.

I had Jesse pack us clean clothes and toiletries while the others worked on the prison break. The clothes now sit in a backpack in one of the storage cabinets, or already equipped.

"One of the desert sectors. Anywhere else is too noticeable. See the largest continent over there?" Jesse points to the dark, sandy one. In the middle of the southern desert sits a pocket of lush vegetation. "The forest is where the Kingdom is."

"How many days will it take to reach civilisation?" I ask him, my stomach churning at the thought of having to trek through the desert. *So much sand.*

My family grew up tight on money, so it wasn't often I went travelling. The desert is quite a foreign concept to me.

"Not many," he says, his expression stony.

"How many, Jesse?"

"Two days, maybe more."

I cast an exasperated glance towards him, but words get lodged in my throat when I make out the full depth of his expression. He sucks on his lips, his dark blue eyes unfocused. Hands jittering, he reaches for me.

"The nights here get cold. I'll land us as close as I can to try and cut our distance as much as possible. But"—he swallows sharply—"the asteroids impacted our oxygen supply. We don't have the luxury of waiting up here for long. If we can't avoid a Second Night…"

I furrow my brow, trying not to focus on his hands gripping on either seat of my seat. "Second Night?"

"It's what the Umbrans call the deadliest part of the night. The planet has a slow rotation speed, making the days and nights longer. The beginning of night reduces in temperature, but it's habitable, although since the Moon Blitz, Umbra's midnights became so cold, you freeze almost instantly—we call it the Second Night."

He pulls back, wrapping his shaking hands around the hilt of his sword, eyes glassy.

I take a deep breath, leaning towards him. "Have you been out during the Second Night before?"

His voice is barely an octave above a whisper when he answers. "Not me. Someone close to me."

I sit on my hands to stop from reaching for him and lean forward to catch his eye. "Was it a friend? Family?" I swallow the lump in my throat, before I utter quickly, "Lover?"

He jerks in his seat, eyebrows cast low over his eyes. "Ship, disengage autopilot. Engage landing sequence."

I lean backwards, clenching my jaw.

Hands still shaking, Jesse shifts his attention to the controls below him. Guilt crashes throughout my chest, heating the tempo of my heart. He is here, flying a ship towards a planet he wants nothing to do with, for me.

He takes a long breath, then urges the ship towards Umbra, taking us closer and closer towards the ring of a broken moon.

PART TWO

THE STARS

SAVANNAH

A fluttering panic evolves in my chest, threatening to combust my heart.

Jesse gasps involuntarily, his hands tight on the steering.

"*Caution. The landing gear is damaged. Repairs advised before engaging land mode.*"

"We *know*," Jesse growls, pulling his lips into a tight line as the ship enters the Umbran atmosphere.

I'm forced back into my seat, hands grasping the seatbelts with urgency. "Oh, we're going to die. We're definitely going to die."

"Savannah?" Jesse looks at me. "Shut up."

I swallow sharply, my mouth drier than the desert on the planet below as I look sideways at him.

We're going to die.

It's difficult to tear my gaze from the front of the ship, where the world is nothing but a haze before me as we speed towards the planet.

The Umbran ship is steady, built for smooth flying. In a quick blip, we pass the atmosphere and glide down among the clouds, the ship surging at a speed that makes my stomach tumble.

The man beside me has always been pale—the tell-tale skin of any Umbran—but now Jesse looks positively deathly; stark and haunted against the dark locks of hair on his head.

"You're okay. We'll be okay." My voice is surprisingly steady, and I notice a fragment of tension leave Jesse's jaw at the sound of it.

I steady my breathing and keep my eyes locked on him rather than the world zooming towards us.

"Savannah…" His fingers drag down a screen on the dash. It's much techier than the one I flew in the base, months ago. But Jesse navigates it like it's a second limb—something he's been born to do, despite the sheen of sweat on his brow and the sunken expression of his eyes.

My father died this way. The words echo in my head, and I swallow a knot, trying to bring moisture back into my dry mouth.

"Landing gear disabled."

Despite the flutter of panic in my chest, the ship's even, unbothered responses are a slight comfort. Jesse clears his throat besides me, taking a shaky breath, and instinct pulls me back to the window in front of us.

My breath catches in my throat at the sight.

Umbra.

The ripples of sand looks like an ocean from high above, but a million times more deadly.

My heart is a booming chorus in my chest, breath rattling in my throat as I lean towards it, eyes catching on the milky wisps of clouds as they fleetingly dip past our ship and open up to us entirely.

I fiddle with my switchblade in my pocket, knuckles brushing up against Melanie's comm, body straining against the seatbelt gripping me into my seat.

"It kinda looks like the Sahara Desert."

Between locked teeth, Jesse manages to sputter, "The shadow of Terra, Princess."

Of course.

Similarly, the forests look much like the ones in Silver Valley—at least from this distance.

"See that large section of desert above the green? That's where we're going—the *Mors* Desert—it's barren and just above the river to the Kingdom."

Jesse's face looks waxen as he drags a callused finger across a screen before him, changing the angle of the ship. Instead of heading down, he flies us almost parallel to the desert, tunnelling towards the sand in lazy circles.

"How's the landing gear looking?" I ask, hoping to get him out of his head despite already knowing the answer.

"Not good," he strains out between his teeth.

"Any plans?" I press.

The muscles in his arms strain as he answers. "To not die." He swallows deeply. "Ideally."

I grip my switchblade until it hurts. *We're going to die.*

The desert floor inches so close that sand sprays against the window. I hold my breath, watching as the metal underbelly of the ship sinks, nearly impacting with the ground.

"Warning, proximity to Umbran soil at dangerous levels. Repairs to landing gear required."

Jesse and I let the words of the ship ring out around us, eyes plastered on a cresting hill of red sand we are racing towards.

So close.

A whole new planet, so alike the one I'm used to, but honed to perfection. If we land safely, each lungful of air will set the course of my life back on track. I will never die. I will become an immortal.

That is, if the crashing ship doesn't take us out first.

My stomach churns, skin itching as I fight the urge to unbuckle myself. My seatbelt will do nothing if the ship reduces to rubble.

"Jesse." I gasp involuntarily as the base of the ship clips the top of a dune, kicking up half a metre of sand from the tip and spurting it around us. It almost slows us entirely, but Jesse pulls the ship up higher at the last minute, as if losing his nerve.

We hit the tip of another dune.

And then another.

Another.

Each time it impacts, my heart stops, but the more we hit, the more the ship slows.

With a grunt, Jesse jabs his finger into the screen. The engine powers off.

I can't breathe. *I can't breathe.*

Anxiety shreds apart my chest, nerves sputtering throughout my body, making my limbs feel leaden.

Jesse covers his head with his forearms, seat belt loose at his feet.

"Power disabled. Brace for immediate impact."

I ignore the ship's directions and stare out the window unblinking, breath lodged in my throat as the ship collides into a sand dune, the angle of the slope propelling the ship's nose into the air, then sending us tumbling down the other side.

Jesse crashes into me, fingers pulling my seat belt free.

I stare out the window with wide eyes, just as a strong hand grips my wrist and yanks me out of my seat, Jesse yelling, "SHIP, open the hatch!"

Even with the main engine down, the ship hums in answer, a distant hiss echoing in my ears as the exit unravels before me, the ramp cascading into the sand.

The heat of the *Mors* Desert swarms into the ship.

I turn to gape at Jesse, understanding making me go numb with shock. But the man before me doesn't hesitate; he circles his strong arms around my chest, cradling my head against his shoulder, then falls backwards into the abyss.

I breathe in the heady scent of him, gasping against the fabric of his shirt as sand and heat clambers down my throat. We fall through the air—me face first, Jesse backwards—and the breath gets knocked out of the man intertwined with me as his spine contacts the sand, taking the impact as we tumble down a dune.

He takes the brunt of the fall on his shoulder, the weight of my body on top of him sending us spiralling down the sand. His arms slacken and I fumble to grab him, chin tucked into his shirt as I strain my muscles, nails digging into his back.

We roll down the sand, gritty granules getting into our clothes, my hair, my mouth.

And still I don't let go.

The Umbran sun pounds down on us, making the sand warm, a stark juxtaposition to the cool, placid temperature of our ship. I exhale deeply, trying not to spit the sand out of my mouth with Jesse so close to me.

Eventually, we slow until his arms hang limp around me.

When we stop rolling, I release him, watching as he slides down the sand, his face to the sun.

"Jesse?" I croak. My throat feels hoarse, the word chafing as it climbs out of my mouth.

I scramble towards him, ignoring the sand rubbing under my clothes, the hair hanging dirty in my face. Red sand crusts the corners of my mouth and I spit it out in disgust. My fingers pry into his clothing, my other hand drifting up towards his throat, searching for a pulse.

It *must* beat.

A shaky breath rattles out of my chest as I feel the familiar rhythm of his heart against the tip of my fingers and I rock back onto my heels, my heart a much more chaotic tick in my chest than his as I stare at his face.

A slow grin slowly merges onto his face. He peels his eyes open, deep blue and sparkling, red sand peppered across his dark lashes.

I slap his arm hard enough that he winces and glares at me.

"Jesse, what the *hell*!"

That bloody smile spreads wider. "Would you prefer to get thrown around in an exploding box of metal, Princess?"

He tries to stand. Fails. His body crumples back down.

"I would prefer if you *told me* your plan to jump ship!" I grumble, tossing a handful of red sand at him angrily, trying not to let a matching smile ease onto my face as he watches me with amusement.

He rolls his eyes and winces as he props himself onto his elbows.

Lines mark the corners of his eyes, caked in dirt. My chest seems to swell at the sight. I love those creases, the subtle hints of aging marking his otherwise supple skin. They are proof of his ventures, proof that he was one of few people that came to Terra and found me.

"You gave me the idea, you hypocrite. Stop tossing sand at me," Jesse growls.

I furrow my brows at him, hands splaying in the warm sand. The sun hangs relatively low in the sky but the heat is already rising. It'll be hell once the sun is in the middle of the sky, which is a problem, given Jesse is too hurt to get up.

"Me?" I elaborate.

"Yes, you. As the ship was hurtling to the ground, all I could see in my mind was that goddamn day you jumped out of your pod to crash the landing pads."

A short breath huffs out of my mouth. I almost died the day we blew up the landing pads in the base. "So you thought *recreating* that was a good idea?"

He tries and fails to hold back a smirk. "Surprised you didn't come up with the idea yourself, Princess."

I jump up, kicking red sand around me as I do. He groans and I give him a withering glance. "Screw you."

Turning abruptly on my heels, I begin the trek up the sand dune, ignoring the ache in my chest at leaving Jesse in the sand. The fact that I'm standing at all is because he took the brunt of the fall for me. And the fact that we're both alive is because he slowed the ship down. He saved us, but my chest still feels filled with venom.

He groans some more from behind me, and I whip around to face him, feet scooting in the loose sand. He's too battered to move but he tries anyway.

"Stay there!"

He angles his head backwards, slumping into the sand in defeat. Rolling his eyes at me, probably. I huff and continue my trek up the dune.

The sun thrums against my skin, not a shadow in sight. I breathe shakily, choking down the dry air.

I'm no stranger to blistering summers. Perhaps not the harshness of the desert, but the Australian sun is merciless, nonetheless. Still, the warm gust of wind feels like a death sentence to me.

I have a good idea what awaits us here. The moment the sun reaches its peak, the heat will be our greatest enemy.

My head throbs as I tick through answers to questions. We will need extra clothes—thin ones, but full coverage for the heat—as well as medicine, shelter, food, and water. Especially water.

My feet lug like a dead weight as I pull myself up the never-ending dune, sweat already tickling down my back. There will be many hours of walking over the hills and dips of this place.

Hopefully we have enough time to get to the forest before the *Mors* Desert takes us.

The very thought of being exposed to Umbra's deadly nights makes my blood run cold. I drag my fingers through my hair, skin meeting sand, my breathing laboured.

It mustn't come to that.

My feet finally hit the top of the dune and I release a long drag of air.

I cannot see the ship. The only thing in my gaze is the deep graze into the sand it made, clipping dunes and wreaking havoc.

But I have no choice but to find it. Clothes, medicine, food, water—I need to salvage what I can.

My hand slips into the tight pocket of my pants, wrapping around the mahogany handle of my small switchblade, my mind on the small engraving in Jasmine Spark's handwriting.

Perseverance.

With a steadying breath filled with the gritty desert air, I push my feet onwards.

MELANIE

"Okay, this just hurts to watch."

Rain smears my vision, splattering droplets through the forest.

Silver Valley is freezing today. Fog touches every tree and nook in the mountain, swaying against the persistent downpour.

My grey jumper grates against the rough bark of a tree, a scrap of metal above my head twisted into its limbs. Jesse's watch post has become incredibly useful, separating us from the rain.

The cows that occupied the farm before us have crawled into the far back corner, only visible as a dark stain against the otherwise green landscape. The rest of the farm has been converted into a training ground.

The first step to building our army.

It's been close to a week and the training has only just started.

Stars, my veins feel like they're on fire. Agitated. No one on Umbra—notably my uncle—has appeared to have attempted contact or identify how many survived the bombings.

They don't know how many we have or what we're capable of.

Besides me, Elijah chuckles at my comment.

I suck on my lips and turn to him. "Laugh all you want, but you're no better at this than they are," I insist, trying to keep my face from looking sour.

The rows of soldiers drop their planks like flies into the mud, panting in the crisp mountain air, mud staining their gym clothes. It's like a line of dominos—each person's arms wobbling until their body fails under them.

Elijah grins. "Speak for yourself, Melanie."

I *am* better than them. Jesse has shown me how to wield a weapon. These people are either weakened from malnourishment or just ill-trained.

I glare at my companion. His dark hair is damp from the rain, eyes lit as if the sun is striking me from behind his pupils. His hair has grown out in the last few months and a curl dangles in his eye as he stands beside me, a smile cracking his face.

He soft, green jacket rustles as he crosses his arms and legs and leans against the tree beside me. He always looks so... happy, next to me.

Stars.

My stomach churns and I turn away. It feels wrong to laugh or feel happy when somewhere out there Jesse might be fighting for his life. I've become a ghost of a person, thinking of them—of *him*—every god damn night.

My Jesse.

I rub my fingers against my forehead. Life has been surprisingly straightforward while we wait for our new army to regain their strength. Hell, I've actually been sleeping for once.

And yet, all I can think of is how badly I miss those sleep-deprived nights, the nights I spent fighting alongside Jesse, and then later too with Savannah.

Building an army is thrilling but tedious work.

"Where's Jasmine?" I say, changing the conversation.

The little blonde cockroach is nowhere to be seen despite the fact she was scheduled to train this morning. I took it upon myself to make a voluntary sign-up sheet for what Elijah has been calling 'our little guerrilla war against the Silver People' and, with that, allocated sessions where people can train. To our favour, many of the revolutionaries from the Safe Holds are old Umbran guards. They've converted our little derelict group into something that makes me shiver to look at.

They're weak, but they're determined. Although today, our group is peppered with villagers.

Shockingly, most villagers from Silver Valley weren't surprised by the concept of the base across the island. Over the years, many had unknowingly made the journey across to the base—not unlike Elijah—only others were a lot better at not getting caught.

Elijah is a little broken in that regard. He lacks common sense.

My lips twitch at the thought.

A leaf falls from the tree above our heads, resting on his shoulder, and I fight the urge to pick it off. I'm so focused on that blasted leaf that my soul leaves my body when Elijah whips his arm up and points across the field.

"There," he exclaims.

I blink. Heart skittering, I take a long drawn of breath. And then I see her.

"Is Jasmine fighting the guy who took her switchblade?"

About a hundred metres from where we stand, Jasmine swings her fist into the jaw of the big guy, her muddied curls swinging in the rain. His right-hand crony kneels in the mud, her yellow hair pulled back from her face, the long length of brown regrowth stark against her skin. She's yelling at Jasmine as the brute stumbles and falls.

From behind a tree, her sister is cowering, still thin and sickly from the years spent in the Safe Holds.

Without thinking, Elijah and I both push ourselves across the field and run over to the fight.

The villagers on the training field twist in the grass to turn and face the action, their panting breaths a chorus around us as we run.

From the end of the line, somehow still holding his plank, Mason lifts his head. His curls stick to his forehead, dark against his skin, and he pulls himself up from the mud. His navy gym clothes are splattered with dirt as he follows us, a young girl with red hair calling out for him.

I slow as we near the treeline, watching as Jasmine wipes her mouth, blood seeping from her lip. The brute groans as he struggles to stand and she smirks at him victoriously.

The man was strong once, but the Safe Holds have broken him. Not physically, like many of the other bony and emaciated captives, but in the way he has simply given up. On everything.

His female crony turns to face me, her eyes bright with tears.

Jasmine slowly lifts her head to me, her expression blank. "I'm done now," she says in a monotone, turning so that her shoulder brushes me as she walks past.

"Jasmine?" I exclaim, my breaths short from running.

She doesn't turn as she responds, her voice half muffled in the rain. "Go to hell, Beckett."

Elijah's mouth thins and I catch his shoulder as he surges towards her.

"Leave her," I say. "People are watching."

The female stands up when I turn and glance at them, her arms crossing over her chest, shivering from the rain. She stands by her sister. Protecting her.

My heart lurches for a split second. I may not know or like them, but I respect that kind of loyalty. That kind of protectiveness.

My mind drifts back to the day we freed them—how the yellow-haired female had practically torn her sibling from that cell. Her sister had all but given up.

Seeing her now, shivering in the rain, pink blooming on her thin face from the chill, makes me feel proud.

Mason catches up to Jasmine and I blink when he leans forwards to plant his hands on Jasmine's shoulders, nearly pushing her back into the mud.

"Mason, what the hell?" she yells, her pitch reaching us.

Elijah immediately brushes past me, dashing over to them without a moment's hesitation. There is nothing but pure, unyielding friendship in his soul as he dashes forwards and grabs Jasmine, protecting her from Savannah's brother.

Savannah's 14-year-old brother, trying to throw her in the mud.

Something like pride fills my chest, but I pause. What has this world become? With a long sigh, I step towards them.

"You didn't have to *hurt* him," Mason says, the words catching in his throat. Ever since his sister left, the poor boy has a wounded look about him. The usually gentle boy is now a raucous teenager, constantly irritated. He's the best of us, yet he is breaking.

Savannah would say that he's simply mad she didn't take him to Umbra with her, but if I were to guess, I'd say he's madder she didn't tell him about it.

"Well, he hurt me," Jasmine says, pushing Elijah away from her.

I purse my lips.

"That doesn't give you an excuse to hurt him back, I thought you guys were friends?" Mason continues, his ears and cheeks red from the cold.

"Just because I helped him out of the safe holds doesn't mean we're friends," Jasmine sneers.

"You promised you would stay out of trouble, Jasmine," I

remind her. "That day we planned their escape in Mark's office, remember?"

Jasmine shoves past him, her head down. "I know. I'm working on it."

"Clearly," I muse.

"Melanie," Elijah warns.

I flash him a look. Mason cracks a small smile.

If Savannah was here, she would console her brother.

I reach for him, but he jerks back, sucking in his lips. "Don't touch me. You're not my sister."

I don't miss the way his eyes drift longingly to the sky. My eyebrows arch, the comm in my pocket a heavy weight. "'Course not, kid," I reply.

I mean, fair enough. I wouldn't want a near-stranger to replace Jesse either.

"Come on, Mel. Let's get to cover before we all freeze," Elijah utters.

That's not my name.

The clouds mock me. My body feels so wet. So itchy. But I give him a shaky smile.

Elijah's warm hand brushes my gloveless wrist, fingers knotting around my jumper. My heart turns to stone at the touch and I nod my head, allowing him to tug me back to Jesse's watch post

Back to doing nothing.

I allow him to keep my wrist in his hand simply for the show of unity in front of our army. Our pathetic army.

But hey, we're trying. We'll get there, and we'll bring hell back to Umbra with us.

"Screw the rain. I'm going inside," I say, turning away from Jesse's watch post.

The world quietens.

No one stops me.

SAVANNAH

My booted feet pound against sand-crusted metal.

Our ship is *trashed*.

I wipe the sheen of sweat off my brow, take a long, laboured breath, and collapse onto the sand beside it.

The vessel is surprisingly intact, bar the trail of broken metal that led me here. A slab of the door, a strip of panel, a handle from the exit ramp—all sprinkled over the sand dunes on the way.

I drag my legs through the sand covering the ship and pull myself to my feet, heading deeper into the helm. Everything in my body screams at me to rest.

But the image of Jesse collapsed in the sand is a constant ticking clock in my mind.

The temperature inside the ship is significantly higher than outside. The heat thrums against my skull as I note the swirling motes floating in beams of sunlight.

I lick my lips, easing moisture into my mouth as I track the sand that fills the interior of the ship, the steam hissing from exposed plating.

"In and out," I tell myself.

My priority is finding medicine and water, but when I stumble over a folded tarp that was previously in the storage cabinet, I bundle it in my arms, placing it near the exit to grab on the way out.

It could be vital during our trek to build shelter, catch rainwater... my mind ticks through all the survival shows Mason used to enjoy watching. I laugh at the irony of me telling him we would never be placed in a situation where those skills were needed.

I reach the helm and wrench open the cabinet storing water, my chest tight. I pray none of the pouches were ruptured during landing.

My head pounds angrily and I release a long, measured breath when I find the cabinet lined with all the sachets I remembered. Jostled from landing, but still intact.

Thank the goddamn stars.

I grab a pack of *Velox* vials and some soothing balms, filling my leather pockets with as many as I can carry.

My hands shake as I yank upon the cupboard next to it and begin piling water into my arms, as well as a few packets of food.

Water is more important than food.

I pack as much as I can carry.

Gut churning at the food left behind, I turn, my mind set on the storage cupboard in the rear that fell open during the crash. I rummage for a backpack, spare clothes, a rope, and rip open the zipper of the pack with my shaking fingers.

The backpack bulges with the copious amounts of water I stuffed inside.

There's only one backpack, so Jesse and I will have to alternate carrying it once I've healed him.

I nudge the collapsing cabinet shut with my hip just as a pale white ribbon flutters to the floor at my feet. I watch it drift in the breeze, swirling like a breath of air before settling by my feet.

Whoever owned this spaceship before us must've been close to our age—perhaps a young girl who had grown up in court. I blink at the pure beauty of the ribbon against the harsh metal and red sand.

Heat crawls under my skin, raw and dry, and I rub my gritty eyes in irritation.

Reluctantly, I twist open a lid from one of the water sachets and dribble a few drops over my face, clearing the sand from my eyes before lapping a bit into my mouth.

Despite the weird taste of the water, it's the best thing in the entire universe right now.

I wish I could justify drinking more.

Lucky for us, I was asleep for most of the flight, reduced to medicinal means of hydration, so the physical water consumption was reduced to one person. One very stubborn person who, for some reason, rationed his water intake already.

There are only four empty sachets of water.

It's as if Jesse expected the worse.

I exhale sharply, snatching the pretty ribbon off the floor and using it to wind my comm around my wrist. As Melanie had explained to me several weeks ago when she enabled the comm, a small clock ticks on the upper corner. An Umbran clock, counting down our daylight hours.

I roll my shoulders back to ease all the unpleasant kinks and take a deep, steadying breath.

Beyond the ship, red sand whirls towards me, drifting around my feet. The sun pounds down on the rolling dunes outside and, with a silent prayer to the stars, I make my way back into the desert.

"Perseverance," I utter, steeling myself.

The *Mors* Desert waits silently in return.

ᔐ

I didn't realise that immortality would feel this *hot*.

Umbra is a death wish. The air may be clean, but the land is deadly and endlessly, awfully bright. How the Umbrans survived for so long is beyond me. Each inhale swirling through my chest is clean and pure but tastes gritty and so damn hot.

It's awful.

When I finally reach Jesse again, I grip his hand, my calluses sliding up against his. In his stupor, his hand tightens as he senses my touch, squeezing my fingers until they turn white. A warm flush that has nothing to do with the heat creeps across my skin. I study him, at his pale skin glowing red from an angry sunburn.

I wonder how the Umbran race manages to maintain their pale skin, under all sun exposure. No matter how much they mixed their DNA with the Occupants, tanning would eventually be inevitable—unless they spend their entire shielded from the *Mors* Desert.

"Drink," I say gently, squeezing a water pouch over his lips.

His sand-crusted eyelids flutter and his dark eyes pin mine, squinting against the bright sky.

"You were gone for ages," he groans, words scraping as viciously as the sand underfoot.

"Shut up and drink," I say, tipping more water into his mouth until he chokes.

He fumbles upright, clenching his throat. "Relentless," he says around a chafing cough.

I bite my lip, pulling back from him to rummage within the backpack.

He props himself up on one elbow and watches me with glazed eyes. His large hands grip the water sachet I left for him, but despite swallowing roughly against the grit, he doesn't raise it to his lips.

I sigh. "Drink, Jesse."

"We need to ration everything," is all he says in response.

I don't know the last time he drank on the spaceship, and as much as I want to argue with him, I don't. If he wants to suffer, fine, he can suffer. So long as he takes a sip every half hour or so, I won't complain.

I make this resolution with a deep sigh, to which he gives me a steady look.

My fingers brush the cool cylinders of the capped *Velox*, half a dozen of them all bound together with strapping.

I pop a syringe free from its casing with a small snap and yank the cap off with my teeth, extracting the tool.

So unlike the clumsy things doctors use on Terra. This thing is the size of a finger and blunt on both ends, until I press the release button.

I shuffle closer to Jesse, ignoring the way the dunes swell and shift under me, and I hold the end that extracts the syringe over his upper thigh.

"Count me down?" he asks sweetly, his eyes lifting slowly to mine. He wraps a hand around my waist, angling me close to his body, and I hold my breath.

"Three—"

I press the release button, eyes pinned on him as the needle pierces through his clothing and into his skin.

"OUCH, SAV—"

I stand up abruptly, brushing sand off my pants and watching his hand fall from my waist to clutch the spot on his leg.

"You have 2 minutes to lie here and cry before I'm kicking you to your feet," I interrupt, holding the small comm Melanie gave me up to my face, squinting at the screen under the sun. "I'm hopeful we can find some sort of shelter to rest and ride out the heat before the sun is at it's peak."

"We're nearly smack bang in the middle of the *Mors* Desert,

Princess," Jesse grunts, wiping his hands over the incision point like a little baby.

"I'm being optimistic."

I lean towards him, holding my hand out across the space between us, watching it waver slightly.

He sucks on his lips and nods, clasping his large hand over mine, letting me yank him to his feet. He clambers upwards—already steadier with the medicine in his system—and grips my shoulders. His body still sags, though, and he hisses through his teeth.

The *Velox* hasn't entirely run its course yet.

A chill drifts through my body as I stand and watch him sway before me. Automatically, he holds his hand out for the backpack around my shoulders.

I glare at him. "I'm carrying it. You can barely stand."

"You're such a wonderful little adventurer," he says, finger trailing over my face to wipe a trail of dirt off my cheek. My heart clatters in my chest, heat blazing across my skin. "How far away was the ship?"

His breath is a caress against my skin, as warm and ticklish as the gentle breeze swirling across the dunes.

I reach for his hand, grasping it. My palm is clammy in his, but I squeeze it tighter. He slides his other hand down to my waist, holding me close—as if he's terrified of the walk ahead of us. As if he just wants to touch me and know I'm okay.

I shudder slightly at his touch, leaning into it.

"About eight dunes this way," I say, pointing to my tracks up the side of the dune. I chew my lip, eyes locked on his as he looks down on me, a slight smile on his face.

"I think that's heading south," Jesse muses, his face thoughtful.

I scrunch my eyebrows, taking in the dunes around us. They all look the same to me.

"How do you know what's north or south?" I ask.

His brows furrow. I can see every small detail on his face—the sand gripping his skin, the small freckle by his eye, the tilt of his dark curls brushing his neck.

He takes in the sky, his face taunt.

The beautiful thing about Umbra is how close all the stars and moons are to the surface, shattering the skyline with whispers of space. From our vicinity, the remaining moon covers a wide section of the sky—pale and more distant from the exposed sun, but beautiful in all its glory. Cutting through it is a perpetual ring, the remains of its fallen sibling.

"I don't, I got disoriented when we crashed. But we were facing south when we initiated landing," he observes, shaking his head.

"Okay, then," I say, "let's give it a go. We have to try and find shelter before nightfall."

He licks his lips and squints at the lingering moon and the slashing ring of the other. "We won't make it. We need the night stars to navigate, but by then we will be dead."

I swallow, his hands suddenly hot on me. I take a step back. "Oh," I gasp. "The heart and the hat constellations!"

Realisation strikes through my body, causing the hair on my arms to stand on end. I pick at the skin around my thumb, blinking away the distant memory.

"How do you know this?" he utters.

"My mother." My words come out unsteady. "Indirectly, she taught me everything." He lowers his eyes, wild and stormy. I give him a strained smile and turn my back. "Come on, I said two minutes. We have a long walk ahead of us."

He chuckles quietly to himself, the sound of swishing sand following up behind me. His movements are dragged. Still healing.

"I wouldn't want to do it with anyone else," he purrs.

I lug myself up the dune, trying not to roll my eyes. "Don't get your panties wet."

His laughter splits around me, coating me in honey. And the feeling of his eyes on my back follows me the entire way up the first dune.

SAVANNAH

I roll my switchblade around my fingers, not able to stand the feeling of it trapped against my leg in my sweaty pants.

We had a sip from a water sachet less than one dune ago—staggering our intakes to approximately every tenth dune—but already my mouth feels as dry as the sand under our feet.

I twist that mahogany handle around my fingers, the blade glinting in the sun whenever I flip open the switch. *Perseverance.*

The moment we make it to the Silver Kingdom, I plan to drink the entire Umbran water supply.

The burning of my limbs and the scratchy sand covering every inch of my body is nothing in comparison to the dry sensation in my mouth.

Jesse and I hardly speak.

Our exchanges consist of grunts and rapid breathing, pants and dry coughs against the sandy gusts that reach us at every peak of every dune.

It's endless.

Perse-freaking-verance.

Instead of running my tongue over my dried lips every few seconds and ingesting nothing but sand, I work on the makings of a plan.

Before she came to Terra, Jasmine was a 15-year-old child on this planet, arrested for conspiring against the coalition of Elders and thrown into a cell by the very guards whose swords were still slick with her father's blood.

But one of the Elders freed her. *She got out.*

And so my first order of business is to learn all I can about the Elders. Spy, sneak and gather as much intelligence as I can. Hopefully, I will find the Elder who helped her along the way.

From what I understand, he is a crack in the system. A crevice to worm my way in.

Find him. Use him. And then corrupt their entire government.

Of course, there are also the commoners to address. Which is why I brought Jesse with me on this mission. Not just for protection, but for his knowledge of the working class.

We need backup—to find the people rallied to my cause—and we need them fast. That'll be Jesse's job.

I glance over at my protector and shadow. He exposed skin is reddened from the grating sand, his beautifully soft curls a matted mess against his head as he wraps a clean tunic I snatched from the ship around his face, blocking out the heat.

I nearly followed his lead with the head covering, but the extra fabric made my neck glisten with sweat. Something I'm very rapidly regretting, as I wipe my hand across my forehead and feel it ache.

Sunburn, worse than I've ever had.

A part of me wants to stop and get a tunic from the backpack, but I know if I stop walking now, I won't be able to continue.

So I keep going.
And going.
Until my muscles ache and the world blurs into swirling red.
Perseverance.

SAVANNAH

O
h, stars. This *sun.*

My knees slam into the sand, my entire body nearly convulsing with fatigue.

Is it midday yet?

My face is a tapestry of blisters as I crawl my way towards a piece of scrap metal.

Blood pounds in my ears, blocking out every thought, every feeling, as my fingers finally touch the ground under the wreckage.

I collapse onto my side in the shade, eyes plastered on the metal above me. A crashed spaceship like ours, but much older.

A massive ache sets around my shoulders from the back-pack—I've had it the entire walk, so Jesse will take the next turn after we ride out the heat.

The metal wreckage looks banged up but sturdy, planted deep

into the sand. It's nearly vertical, slashing up into the sky, barely covering us in shade.

Good thing I packed the tarp.

The blue plastic washes over my vision as Jesse attaches it to the top of the metal, holding the other side down by the weight of the backpack. When finished, he collapses next to me with a sachet of water in his hands.

"You first," he rasps.

I clasp my fingers around the sachet and drink half. A small relief. The stale liquid washes around in my mouth and I shudder, my body sinking into the sand.

I pass the rest of the sachet to Jesse, wrapping his fingers around it and stabbing him with a sharp look. *Drink every freaking drop.*

He does. He actually does. I'm transfixed as I watch him tilt his head back and squeeze every excess of it past his chapped, flaking lips.

All gone.

My head meets the sand, my pale skin hot and blistered from the scorching heat. I just lie there, in a star position, too exhausted to do much else. The shadow of the tarp does nothing to relieve the heat that had been absorbed into the sand prior. Despite the slip of shade the ship wreck left behind, it still feels hot, branding through my clothing, eating at my skin.

But I do not move.

My muscles feel trapped, oozing away from me and into the burning sand. Head pounding with the makings of a relentless headache, I force my mouth to gulp down the dry air, lips permanently parted to get as much oxygen into my lungs as possible.

The heat is never-ending.

We could take some *Velox*, but that would be a waste of resources. The drug only aids in your body's natural healing cycle— healing tissue, muscles, cartilage, bones. It does not heal dehydration, high temperatures or an empty stomach. My head clears some, my muscles relaxing, but my mouth still feels as dry as the desert, the heat of the world around me like a branding blanket.

My muscles are exhausted.

I take deep, drawn-out breaths, my body plastered to the coals underneath me as it fights for energy. As I do, a small bug comes to rest upon my exposed palm.

I zero in on it, my eyes widening but my muscles too exhausted to flick it away. It's only a centimetre long, but its armoured skin is covered in reddish-white fur. Small fluffy wings fold down its back like a bird and the antennae on it look like a blackened leaf stripped down to its veins. It studies my hand with increased fascination, clicking away as it roams its large black eyes down my palm.

My hand is clammy, draining me of precious water, but drying quickly in this heat.

It's as if the bug sensed the moisture.

"Drink," Jesse demands, peeling another sachet of water and holding it over my chest. The small bug flutters its wings in fright, humming away from my hand and disappearing.

With shaking fingers, I grasp the water Jesse offers me, take the smallest sip, and then pass it back.

Jesse glowers at me.

"How much do we have left?" I ask, knowing my body can take more than the drop I just had, but not being able to sacrifice it. "Maybe we should—"

"Keep sipping at that water, otherwise I will leave you right here under this tarp."

With a frown that hurts my lingering headache, I lift the water to my flaking lips. He watches every movement. I sip no more than a teaspoon, but my body sags as though I fed it ambrosia instead of stale spaceship water.

I clear my throat. "Says the busybody who rationed the entire flight over—"

"Savannah, please, or I'll—"

"You'll what? Abandon the prophesied queen in the middle of the desert?" I sneer.

He blinks at me.

I'm the girl who will bring peace back to Umbra. Who will usurp the Umbran throne and end an extended period of social and political unrest. A period manifested in the 1800s after the effects of the Moon Blitz and loss of the original Occupants of this planet.

Without me, who's to say what will become of Umbra? The Elders have become immortal barbarians, sinking back into their Georgian roots, bombing the bases on Terra, killing innocents, and restricting a nation just to appease their power.

It doesn't help that they have the Argenti—immortal, silver beings derived from the consummation of human and Occupant intermingling—who have access to Silver Magic. The Elders are nearly untouchable.

From everyone but me, supposedly. I suck on my lips, staring at Jesse.

He's quite beautiful when speechless. His dark blue eyes are stark against his pale Umbran skin, looking so bright and out of place in this world of red sand. He runs a large, callused hand through his dark hair and sighs.

"We're approaching midday." He says it quietly, matter-of-factly.

My body quivers, and I clench my jaw, forcing down a large swig of water before answering. "You mean... this isn't midday yet?"

My words fall flat around us.

"Not yet."

"The sand is nearly hot enough to cook a steak!"

He stands up abruptly, wavering on his feet slightly. His eyes keep dancing between me and the backpack, knowing full well it's the reason why I'm much worse off right now than he. That, and the fact I've only had a few months to strengthen my body.

Jesse has been a fighter his entire life.

"We need to keep moving."

I take a raspy breath, lowering the empty water packet onto the searing ground and wincing as my fingers brush past the shade of the tarp, slipping over the heat from the sun.

It's not midday, but it damn well feels like it.

I watch the canopy of the tarp. "This shade—"

"Will make little difference at midday. Come."

I take a deep breath and get up. The sand moves under my body, shifting against my weight as I stand. It's awful, that shifting feeling. The back of my thighs protest the movement until the *Velox* works its way further through my system.

Mere minutes. That's how long Jesse let me rest for. He bundles the tarp back into the backpack and I stifle a gasp of pain as the sun flares above us once more.

Lovely.

Jesse hands me a spare slip of clothing and I place it over my head, fingers shaking against the heat. It feels as though I'm back in Silver Valley on the morning of the bombing, combing my way through a burning forest. The sand under my feet feels close enough to the embers, the sun above us like the lick of flame.

And just like that morning, a blistering need blooms in my chest.

Not a need to kill the Elders for what they did to my friends and my home, but a need to survive so that I can enact that wish.

The need to set wrongs to rights whispers past my fingertips, burning with the sand under my feet.

Right now, nothing matters but surviving this hellhole of a desert so that I can fix every damn wrong in this entire messed-up universe.

Jesse comes up next to me, his fingers dancing across my arms, his eyebrows low. His sharp, beautiful face is etched with concern.

I grip his hand, my calluses brushing against his lightly. I'm a nervous hummingbird at his touch. At the way his fingers fumble for my own, his knuckles bending against mine. Squeezing.

Melanie's comm brands into my wrist from where it's looped with ribbon. Reminding me of what's back on Terra. Reminding me of why I am here.

"We can do this," I tell Jesse. "A few more steps."

The muscles in his arm spasms. His dark blue eyes lock on mine. So human. Nothing like the Elders or the Argenti.

Just Jesse.

"We can do this," he repeats, his voice deep and gravelly. His words tendril down my body, causing a riot of feelings.

I may be facing heat and death in the face, but at least I have Jesse.

I shiver, sinking into the crook of his arm and hunching forwards. Then we scale the next set of dunes.

SAVANNAH

"Run."

The word is whispered against my neck, my fingers slipping against the cloth I have over my head, hands dry and flaking.

Jesse tightens his grip on me until my eyes frantically meet his.

Ahead, a shadow of a distant forest lines the desert—tall, bony trees, pale swaths of leaves dribbling around them. If we squint, they look to be about 500 metres away, but I almost wonder if it's a mirage.

Jesse's body turns stiff as my eyes meet his. He yanks me forwards, spurring our feet faster than I believed manageable after the day's trek. Aches travel up my thighs, cascading around my back, from my pores. Everything hurts, and like a rusted piece of machinery, I feel hot and creaking as he gathers his arm across my back and hurtles me down the next dune.

Pure, primal fear swims in those eyes. It ignites something in my chest, causing my heart to erupt.

The crests around us are dwindling somewhat as we gradually enter a new domain of land. More stones. More shrubs to dance around. More foreign animals skittering at our feet.

Moments before, I saw what looked like a small lizard, only it didn't have a face. Or scales. It looked like a long rock, slithering away from us.

My feet dance over a slippery patch of sand, heading down the small dune we crested. Jesse's breath still lingers on my throat, soft and humid against the rest of the world.

I loosen my hands around the cloth mostly covering my head, trying to quell the way the fabric blocks off the edges of my vision to see what startled him. Until now, there wasn't much point in evaluating the desert around me. I had simply immersed myself into the repetitive motion of dragging my feet forwards.

Until now.

"No." Jesse yanks the cloth back over my head. The skin on his face is blistering, his lips flaking. I must look the same to him.

"What?" I wonder, flabbergasted. "I can't see."

"We're being tracked."

The words settle between us and, for a moment, we both pause. He releases my back, fist bunching in the fabric around my face, tugging it closed like a curtain.

"Keep your face covered," he grunts. "At all costs."

We pick up the pace. I miss a step and stumble, heat and exhaustion getting the better of me.

"How. Do. You. Know?" I ask between pants, each word punctuated with a heavy footfall.

He glares ahead, his expression unreadable. "I can hear a Hover."

He pushes me ahead, making it hard to talk. My fingers ache with the pressure of keeping the fabric squashed around my face.

"How do you know it's tracking *us*?" I ask, words barely scraping past my dry lips.

"It's been humming in the distance since we left the last shipwreck. Whoever it is must've noticed our tracks in the sand."

My feet skid over some loose needles from a desert shrub. Somehow, we pick up the speed even more. Fear drenches my skin, coating me like sweat. In my panic, I almost don't feel the heat and the pain, pushing myself even harder.

"That's speculation," I insist.

"A speculation that, if not acted on, could get us killed." He winces as he speaks, brow deep over his eyes.

I miss another step as I flicker my eyes worriedly over him.

The backpack thumps against him as he jogs behind me, a furrow in his brow sending a spiralling pang down my chest.

That was me earlier today. The backpack is hell.

I slow my gait, reaching back for him, but he glares at me, ushering me forwards. I don't let go of his arm though. I grip him so tightly I almost tug him up the next small incline. Not quite a dune anymore. Just a swell.

He moans as the path tilts up slightly and I sympathise with the pain I know he's feeling. The world feels lighter for me than before.

The sand and stones still tug at my feet, causing a small landslide, but the pressure on my body feels less demanding.

But not for the man next to me. He grunts, mouth opened wide as he takes each painful breath. For his sake, I try to not let my own struggle show.

Each drawn-out breath sears my mouth, stinging with dry heat and sand. My lungs explode, scattering a ripple of torture across my body as I struggle for air.

If we don't die in this desert, that air will keep us alive forever— free from the dying agent that makes humanity age and deteriorate.

And so, I don't hold qualms with sucking in that air. It may taste like garbage, but it's salvation—so long as we survive the desert.

Ahead of us, the trees loom ever closer. Not a mirage then, thank the stars.

And yet, they don't look like desert vegetation.

"Are trees like that possible in the *Mors* Desert?" My breath clambers around us as we jog, nearly inaudible.

"Yes," he says.

One word that makes all the difference.

Pain lances up my body, but I can hear it now, beyond our slapping feet. The sound of a vehicle. It gets louder, even as we approach the trees.

"Nearly there," I urge. As much for Jesse as it is for me.

Just the promise of shade makes me want to melt. *Shade. Trees. A moment to rest.* My dry throat clenches as I try to swallow.

Jesse grunts beside me, beyond saying anything else. Beneath the slip of his clothing, his arm feels hot. I squeeze it until my muscles ache, coaxing his warmth into mine. The sensation of merely touching him makes my breathing hitch, my thoughts a whirlpool in my head.

But now is not the time to think about the feeling of his body against mine.

The forest looms closer. No, not a forest.

The desert heat is a living thing, rippling and oozing across the sand, hazing everything. The forest outline looks like its dipped in lacquered oil.

The sun is nearly peaking in the sky and my body can barely function.

We need shade. Now.

My vision dissolves as I attempt to focus my eyes ahead of me. Nothing makes sense. We are nearly ten metres away from the trees by the time I finally realise what we are running towards.

An orchard.

It's eerily similar to the farms I remember seeing spotted around the old Umbran base on Silver Valley. Hundreds of fruit trees, lined up in neat little rows next to each other, with small, glittering robotic farmers buzzing around the aisles and collecting fruit.

My body bangs into something that feels like a window. The sound ricochets around me, muffling the whirring sound of the Hover searching for us in the distance.

"A Dome," Jesse explains. "It protects the fruit."

Shakily, I take a step back, rubbing my ringing skull. Every nerve in my body is firing with pain, my head thumping with the effects of dehydration. Now that we've stopped, I can barely stand, so I lean forward and rest my head against the cool surface of the Dome. There's an imposing metal entrance off to our left. It glimmers under the sun, coaxing me forwards. The heat is so suffocating, I can barely breathe.

"Entrance?" I ask. It's the only word I can manage.

Jesse dumps the backpack on the ground and collapses against the Dome beside me, his body shuddering with every rasping breath.

My blood feels like it's boiling inside my body. I don't know how much longer we can stay out here and survive.

"Entrance," I say again.

Jesse doesn't move. Doesn't speak. His whole body jerks, rebelling from what we've just endured.

I take a dry, painful swallow of the crisp air around us and try not to choke on granules of sand as a warm wind picks up around our feet.

It's an effort to focus, but I drag myself off the Dome and woozily edge towards the entrance.

My hand fumbles across Jesse's chest, fingers tangling in the dirty fabric of his shirt. He realises what I want and utters a deep groan as he peels himself upright and follows me.

The Hover sounds disperse, melting into the distance.

We are safe. For now.

As soon the driver sees this farm, however, I'm sure our destination will become clear. We have to hide.

"Entrance," I confirm to Jesse, yanking him with me.

We both stumble towards it, using the Dome as a crutch on our right. I've never been through the entrance to the Dome near Silver Valley—at least, not while I was conscious. But I don't imagine it being as small as this one.

"The Dome regulates the outside temperature so that the fruit can grow. We can wait out the heat," Jesse murmurs, barely able to speak through his laboured breaths.

I nod shakily. Wait out the heat *and* our pursuer if we're lucky.

Two metal doors enter into a tunnel, kind of like a zoo enclosure. I'm not surprised that it's locked, but it still takes my brain a moment of pause to address the situation. I inhale deeply through my nose and turn to Jesse.

"Sword, please."

His fingers tremble as he reaches for his belt.

Melanie taught me a few things about machinery in Umbra, including certain ways to hack through doorways. Lucky for me, the control panel on the farm looks basic, much like those in the base on the village. Still, it isn't what Melanie taught me that gets me through this door.

I rotate the sword, holding the hilt out to Jesse. "I can attempt what you taught me, but you know it better than I."

He's taken to leaning on the edge of the Dome where the door melts into the foreign Umbran substance, and peels himself upright to come closer to me.

I close my eyes for a moment, taking deep breaths, trying to stop my body from falling over and failing on me.

Jesse angles the sword just so, lodging it at the precise spot to intercept the currents working the lock. It takes him approximately five minutes to deactivate it.

The metal door swings open silently and a surge of cool air fans across our faces, licking our clothing and soothing the heat slamming over our pores.

My body shivers, wilting as if gravity is hefting its mighty hands down my body.

I make a small noise in the back of my throat and Jesse groans in pleasure at the wafts of cool air brushing our faces.

We don't move immediately. Not as a spasm rocks my body at the sound of the Hover.

It's loud now, as if it's right behind us.

Bones creaking with the effort, I take one small glance behind me. And there. A few hundred metres back, on top of a small dune.

Jesse sees it too, his whole body stiffening. "In, Princess. In!"

He yanks me through the door so hard I nearly trip.

As the cool air wraps around my entire body, I want to collapse and never rise again. The grit in my eyes aches, my arms and legs still leaden from running. But Jesse wraps a large hand around my arm and pulls me with him.

The metal door chimes closed.

We're inside a small room covered in silver plating and shelving lining every wall. Farm clothes hang from a rack to my right, a plough laid forgotten on the floor to my left.

There's another control panel ahead of us, which presumably operates the door leading to the peach farm. There's no time to reach it.

Not as the sound of the Hover drifts closer. Jesse stumbles as he attempts to keep me upright, too stubborn to let me fall.

If we can get to the peaches, we can climb a tree. Maybe. But would that even hide us?

The Hover sounds only metres away now.

Jesse silently coaxes his sword under a lip of metal plating at our feet—a hidden compartment beneath the metal floorboards. It's like a coffin, but it's just a thin hole used for storage. Ropes. Tree cutters. Things you'd use for harvest.

Jesse pushes me down, easing his sword into the space while he holds the lid up. I slink around the items, legs twisting in some rope as I struggle.

Outside, the sound of the Hover quietens.

Jesse slides in after me, near silent even when his movements are choppy and sluggish. We cram in together, tangled among the tools. The handle of a tree cutter prods into my back and I squeeze my eyes shut, trying to calm my racing heart.

Jesse slides the panel closed over our heads just as I hear our pursuer prod outside at the control panel.

Our footsteps probably line the sand all around the entrance.

It's just a matter of whether the Umbran outside believes us to still be inside the Dome or not.

I press my head into Jesse's shirt, breathing in the pungent scent of desert and dried sweat clinging to his body. My stomach clenches and I run my hands down my arms, noting the puckered skin from a heat rash.

Above us, a door creaks open and footsteps sound above our heads.

Together, Jesse and I hold our breath.

SAVANNAH

"**A**re you hiding in *here*, little mouse?"

A man. His voice makes my blood run cold, my pain forgotten as fear takes over.

"Oh, how the instinct to survive triumphs rational judgement." The man clicks his tongue and mumbles to himself, his voice deep, smooth, and flush with pleasure—as if nothing is more exciting than tracking us down. "If you were smart, you would avoid the obvious safe haven. It makes you so easy to pursue. Come out, little mouse."

I can hardly breathe. Jesse's hands circle around me, one coming to rest behind my neck and the other on my waist, pulling me to him. His muscles are taut, tension rippling out of him in waves.

Jesse, the once unmovable rock in my life, is slowly unravelling.

The metal coffin we are in seems to compress into me, cold

and dark and causing my nerves to catch flame. Adrenaline pumps through my body, but I still my heart.

Our pursuer circles above our hiding spot, rummaging around in nooks and crannies. It's only a matter of time before he finds ours.

Jesse's chest heaves from behind around me.

I place a hand on his chest, urging him to quiet down.

We just need to wait him out, and then we'll be okay.

I recall how he dropped our backpack outside and scratch my stomach uneasily, fingernails raking over the heat rash on my skin.

Maybe it was that and not our footmarks in the sand that told the man above where we are. Maybe it's a confusing enough lead that he will grow bored and leave us be.

We just need to persevere.

I bunch my fingers in his shirt, the movement pushing the small veil of clothing further off my head. It slips off my shoulders and onto the metal flooring beneath us.

The man above clicks open the next door to the farm, roams outside, and vanishes for a moment.

Jesse still doesn't say anything.

I can hear our pursuer calling my name among the trees.

"Savannah, my darling. Where are you, little mouse? Show yourself, Savannah."

I gasp, my eyes widening. *He knows my name.* I try to rein in my quickening breaths.

Jesse grips my hand, stroking soothing circles with his thumb.

My name on the man's lips is a purr, deep and husky as he wraps emotion around the vowels. Taunting me. I squeeze my eyes shut, trying not to shiver.

"Savannahhh," he sings.

My heart pounds in my head, the headache intensifying. I fold into Jesse, breathing into his shirt until the pursuer and my name vanish deeper within the farm. It's not until the sound is gone that

I fully slump against Jesse, my fingers shaking as they grip the gritty fabric on his chest.

He's gone, he's gone, he's gone.

I fight the pain lancing my body and the utter fatigue gripping my shoulders. I fight it with every damn breath in my body.

But when the pursuer is too far away to hear and Jesse begins tracing careful circles into my back, my eyes roll back into my head.

And all at once, my body fades into oblivion.

৲

Cold, followed by a humming noise. Air-conditioning?

Air blasts into my face and the smell of fruit chokes my nostrils. The rope is still at my feet, trapping me within this metal coffin.

It's stupid, but the first thought I have is that I don't remember the storage compartment having air-conditioning.

I lie in a numb haze, letting the outside world wash over me. My eyes remain closed, the grittiness of the desert sand and air still aching.

Death didn't claim me and, for a small moment, I allow myself to be surprised.

I'm here. Still alive. Still trapped in the metal coffin. But *here*.

I reach for the familiar feel of Jesse's shirt, but it's gone. A small gasp rattles up my throat and I reach around me, fingers brushing against tools.

No, no, no.

Our pursuer got him. I lost him. My hand brushes over something sharp and I flinch at the small nipping pain, followed by hot, wet drips down my finger. I hold my hand there, eyes still closed, unsure what to do.

Drip.

My blood taps the metal ground. I must've cut myself on one of the gardening tools.

Drip.

I rub my other hand over my eyes, picking sand out from the corners until I can squint them open.

Light pours in. Someone has removed the flooring off our heads—off my head.

My heart wages war inside my chest, threatening to explode out of my body.

Jesse is gone.

I shakily pull myself upright. Surprisingly, my body obeys, albeit slowly.

Someone must've given me *Velox*, because the heat rash is gone, the stinging and aching all gone.

If only I had some water too.

Drip, drip.

Blood has coated a few of my fingers, trailing down my palm and over my wrist until it patters in a crimson trail where Jesse had been laying.

I tuck my fingers into a fist, which sends a shooting pain down my arm. Momentarily, the blood stops dripping.

"Jesse?" I try, my voice hoarse.

"Out here, Princess."

My body shudders. He's safe.

I yank my legs out from the rope, kicking and flailing until I wriggle free, then reach down with my good hand and toss it into the corner, the rope thick and heavy.

My other hand isn't bleeding so much anymore.

Before lifting myself out of the metal coffin, I pull my hand close to my face and frown. Right before my eyes, the *Velox* works at knitting my skin together, working furiously on all my injuries.

I watch it with trembling hands, utterly fascinated by the drug.

First, the bleeding stops, then begins to clot. It goes through multiple stages of colouration before the skin begins to smooth out, turning into a soft scar, and then easing back into my normal skin.

I open and close my fist. It's still sore, but not from the cut.

My whole body is a wreck and there's only so much Velox can heal. Fatigue is not it.

I scramble out of the hole in the floor and pull myself into the room that has been blasting me with air conditioning. The second door to the farms hangs open.

Not by Jesse, whose sword is still strapped to his belt, but likely our pursuer.

Only, his Hover isn't outside and I can't hear him on the property. *He's gone?*

I strain my eyes, but beyond the Dome there's nothing but sand, which must mean he left.

A shudder runs down my body and a soft smile lights my face.

I wander outside and try not to sigh as the cool air of the farm encompasses my body.

Jesse kneels by a lone water tap in the middle of the farm. Water trickles down his arms, his muscled back shirtless.

My breath hitches, my eyes slightly teary. I bunch my hands into fists, trying not to reveal my emotions and failing. Beneath the grime on my face, I can feel my cheeks flushing.

His pale skin is a chiselled sculpture—years and years of hard work screaming at me with every twist of his body. As the sun catches on his back, liquid gold pours down every crevice, revealing a broad upper back and defined arms.

His dark blue eyes catch on me as he leans back. Sunlight ripples across his body, outlining his strong arms, peaked skin and the small tuft of dark hair that trails down into his waistband.

I clear my throat.

"My eyesight is awful right now," I croak.

"Is that why you're staring?"

I lower my gaze, jaw set. Every step towards the water tap feels clumsy, as if I've forgotten to walk, but I cross my arms over my chest and squeeze, my chest feeling tight.

The silence is oppressive as I approach him, kick off my shoes and kneel next to him in the mud.

We watch each other for a moment and then I unwrap my arms and grip the tap, lowering my head under the surge of water.

It pours over my eyes, across my forehead, into my mouth. I open my lips, gasping in the water like it's a nectar from the gods.

Stars, it tastes good.

Jesse remains still, watching as the water trickles over my face, through my hair, catching over my shoulders.

When I'm done, I come back up gasping, a clumsy grin on my face.

"Want me to help you undress?" he suggests, a twisted tilt to his mouth.

I give him a long look.

He pulls his weapons belt off, lowering it in the grass forming around the base of a tree. The leaves hang low. The branches long, spindly things that arch into the air. Fruit is just starting to form on them. Most of them are green, but a few are ripe with colour. The beginning of harvest season.

"Peaches," I say, my head tilted to the leaves.

"Not exactly my favourite fruit, but beggars can't be choosers," Jesse replies. "Here."

He reaches towards me, hands brushing my clothing. I abandoned my belt somewhere in the desert, feeling suffocated and itchy from the extra material. Without it, my once white cotton shirt hangs as I lean forwards. Water stains the fabric, plastering it to my skin.

Jesse averts his gaze from me, but his fingers fumble as they work at freeing my shirt from my pants.

He doesn't meet my eyes when he nudges my arms and says, "Up."

Like a child, I lift my hands. He bundles the fabric upwards, sliding it over my skin. I let him take the top layer of my clothes off, until I'm shivering in my underwear.

The air is chill under the Dome. I can feel my skin puckering as Jesse takes a deep breath, struggling not to gaze at my exposed stomach and the way my skin glistens with water.

Now the air suddenly feels warm. Swallowing, I move forwards under the tap.

My back is to Jesse, but I can hear each sharp inhale as he watches me. The water pounds against my back, biting into my neck.

Slowly, as if unsure how to proceed, Jesse lays his hands on my shoulders. I gasp as he runs his hands down my arms.

And then Jesse Hayes begins to wash me. I tremble like a child, my eyelids fluttering closed as I let him.

Gently, he shifts my thighs down into the mud, hands running down my leg, washing away the sand. Then his hand is in my hair, detangling it. A finger brushes my lips, coaxing a stain away.

Every touch makes my skin tremble, my heart a soft thrum under my chest, causing a flush to rise to my cheeks. Everywhere feels warm where he rests his hand, his touch like fire on my skin.

I remain under the tap until the stillness begins to make me itch and I pull myself up from the mud. My underwear is soaked, and we don't have a towel to dry ourselves, so I lay down across the grass under the peach tree. I watch the sky, the leaves fluttering above my head. It reminds me of our secret clearing in Silver Valley, the way the trees sway above us forming a soft canopy. Except here, the sky isn't grey and turbulent. It's blue and scattered with shards of the broken moon, a faint film from the Dome separating it from us. I inhale deeply, letting the clean air around us travel through my exhausted body.

The tap continues to pound next to me, the water a crescendo as Jesse hastily washes himself. I can feel his eyes pinned on me, as if washing himself hardly matters.

I matter. The girl in soaked underwear lying under a tree.

It takes a moment, but eventually Jesse joins me, his pants now with mine in the mud.

He pads towards me on silent feet, the grass sighing as he lowers himself down onto it.

He doesn't look at me, but my self-control is way less than his. My eyes roam, then my body stills, the air seeming to halt around me.

He isn't. Wearing. *Anything.*

Warmth floods my face, but I don't look away. I take in every inch of him. His torso. His legs...

"You're naked, Jesse."

My words hang between us. A small grin flickers on his face, but he works at hiding the amusement from me. His heavy gaze traps me.

And—and he isn't wearing anything.

I stare back at him, a tingling trailing my body.

"I don't particularly like bathing with clothes on."

My words are hushed when I reply, "I can see that."

"Would you like me to bathe again? You were busy watching the sky."

The corner of my mouth twitches and I abandon looking into his eyes. I roam my gaze down his body, taking in every inch of him. "No. But the sky can wait."

He cups his hand across my cheek, bringing my gaze back to his. "As you wish, Princess."

He tilts his body towards me and his hand runs down my arm, holding the exposed area of my stomach, fingertips brushing my ribs.

I inhale deeply, words beyond me as he lowers his head and brushes his lips against my neck. My world shatters. Exhaustion doesn't matter. Food doesn't matter. Fighting the Elders doesn't matter.

Nothing matters except Jesse.

His lips caress lazy circles across my skin, travelling down my neck and across my shoulder until the strap of my bra gently slides down one arm.

I feel him shudder against me as I spin to face him.

The urge to have those lips on mine consumes me and I twine my fingers through his hair, hands pulling his face up to mine.

He stops me. Holds me still. I pull away, frowning.

"Are you ever going to kiss me?" I ask softly.

He swallows, his breath catching. Every time, he avoids doing it. Every time, we miss the chance. His body towers over mine—a large, imposing sculpture, trapping me in him.

"Didn't realise you were keeping track," he says.

I stare into his eyes, a flush spreading down my chest. Stars, *he's beautiful.*

I get lost in his intense, sapphire eyes. And I shiver.

"If you want me to stop, say so," I whisper, my hand twisting in his dark hair, his soft curls wrapping around my fingers.

"*Stars*, no."

And, finally, his lips crash into mine.

Finally.

I groan, my eyes fluttering closed. He's gentle. More than expected as he coaxes me onto the soft blanket of grass, one hand on my back and the other planted beside my head.

His lips press into my own, warm and slow as he works at my bottom lip. I arch into him, both of my bra straps hanging down off my shoulders as I press my chest into his. He moans and his breath spills into my lungs.

He tastes like the desert—warm and coarse—but underneath it all there's the soft taste of peaches. He must've found some on a tree and ate them before I woke.

I thought he hated peaches.

I pry his mouth open, desperate to taste more of the fruit, but he pulls himself from me, roaming kisses down my face, my neck, my chest. His lips touch the sensitive spots along my collar bone, trailing a line of heat on my skin.

And then silence rips me apart.

The sound of the tap disappears—the absence of pounding water rupturing us into silence. All I can hear is Jesse's breathing. My breathing.

At this point, it's one and the same.

My legs twist in the grass, toes digging into the ground. I try and lift my head to see why the world went quiet but Jesse has angled himself above me.

His kisses make it down to my stomach and then he rises back up. I wrap one leg around his own, pulling him to me.

"Jesse," I mutter against his mouth.

He shudders, his muscles trembling, his restraint slipping as he lowers himself down.

"You could have turned the water off first," a foreign voice says, making us jump. "So very wasteful."

Jesse freezes above me, his dark eyes flooding with fear. His mouth is pink as he pulls his lips from mine, the body covering me now rigid.

I tilt my head sideways in the grass.

Our pursuer is an Argenti. And he's watching us.

He's tall and rippling with power, with a shock of silver hair the colour of a glittering pendant. Wisps of that hair curl against his forehead, slightly longer at the front. He's so beautiful, it's enough to make my breath catch.

Our eyes crash, his gaze seeming to bore into my soul.

I freeze entirely as fear nudges down my spine, pricking my skin.

His silver eyes shine with amusement as he tilts his head at me. Soft angles meet sharp ones as those sculpted brows arch while he watches us.

He never left, I think, my heart sinking. *He was just waiting for us to come out.*

The juice of the peach he's holding drips down his palm and I watch as he lifts the fruit, holding it up in the air and framing it around Jesse's exposed buttocks.

"Nice view."

It's the last thing the Argenti man says before Jesse yanks himself off me, scrambling for the weapons he abandoned in the mud.

SAVANNAH

"Nice try, but we can't have that."

The Argenti tosses the peach lazily and, before it has time to land, Jesse's weapons belt surges off the ground. I watch in awe as the weapons swing through the air and into the man's hands.

Silver Magic.

Jesse freezes mid-step, his jaw tight as the man removes one of the knives and holds it up against the sun, watching the shards of light reflect off the clean surface and beam onto me.

I clamber to my feet, uncaring that I'm half naked, and stride directly up to the man. Up close, he smells like cinders and a heady cologne.

I peer up to look at him. He's a whole head taller them me.

"Hello, little mouse." He smiles, a cocky sneer slashing his face.

I reach over to slap him, but my hand jerks mid-air, not quite touching his smooth Argentian flesh. I struggle with the invisible power, my palm at a complete standstill mere inches from his face. He analyses my hand as if it's the strangest specimen on this planet, his silver eyes twinkling.

"Get away from her," Jesse growls, his arms twitching.

I turn my head to see him standing entirely still, feet planted in mud. This Argenti has the ability to manipulate both inanimate objects and living organisms, it seems. Telekinesis?

I angle my head towards the man, eyes wide as I take in every corner of his amused expression. He must see a switch light in my brain the moment I discover his magic, because he releases my hand in a whoosh.

"You know, I never really left." He studies me, then tilts his chin as he takes in my companion. "You're getting sloppy, Hayes."

They know each other? A small shiver scuttles down my spine and tingles down my legs.

"You were watching us? This whole time?" Jesse's tone is indignant. Offended.

"Well, you've got to admit, it was quiet fascinating."

He's nearly laughing at this point.

I glare at him. Hatred pours out every one of my pores. "You're disgusting."

"I'm not the naked one here," he says, not bothering to look at me.

Jesse spits a few choice curses at him.

While the man is distracted, I dart my hand out and grasp Jesse's weapons belt, still dangling from the man's hand. My skin brushes the leather, grazing across my fingertips, before the man whisks it away.

"Uh, uh, let's play nice for a moment, Savannah. Don't get all flustered on me."

I blink at him, frustration brewing in my chest. I have nothing to say, so I stand utterly still. Among all our training, Jesse always made one thing completely clear to me: if ever in danger, distract the attacker—don't let him know you have a switchblade in your pocket unless absolutely necessary, and wait until help comes.

Well, my help is currently trapped in the mud.

My fingers itch towards my weapon but, despite my instincts to flee, a different strategy enters my mind.

I plaster on a sweet smile and widen my eyes at the man before me. "You know our names, yet we know nothing about you. Your name, if you will? Before you kill us."

The corner of his mouth quirks and the man leans towards me. His scent spirals up my nose as he whispers against my hair. "Oh, honey, I have much greater things in mind for you than death."

I don't for one second let him fool me that he's on our side. Not one second.

"Who are you?"

He pulls away from me, amusement never once fading from his face. Not even as I hiss at him.

He swings Jesse's belt over one shoulder, repositioning himself before extending a hand. "Marcellus Hart. It will be my pleasure to be the one to bring you to the Elders, my dear Savannah. Shall we get a move on then?"

I let his hand hang between us, but he holds it adamantly until the silence stretches to a breaking point. I stare deep into his eyes, my gaze burning holes in him until he drops it.

"Sorry, but that doesn't work for me."

Instincts override my common sense and I spin, kicking him clean in the groin, scrambling for my switchblade and resting it on the fallen man's throat.

It takes me a moment to get to him, but he seems to be waiting for me. Marcellus lets himself fall, practically smiling as I kneel on top of him, one knee between his legs. He reaches down and grabs my waist, and his eyelids begin to flicker. Rapidly.

My fingers tremble, but I squeeze my blade deeper into his neck.

My waist feels hot beneath his hand. Behind me, Jesse begins to scream.

"Ahh," Marcellus moans. Energy whisks out of me until my head spins. "Lovely. Your mother gave you a taste of her Silver Magic. How adorable."

A warmth seems to radiate out of Marcellus's pores. This is *wrong*.

He grips me sharply, his fingers digging into my flesh. My heart is pounding rapidly now and, in my panic, I scramble off him.

Jesse moves sluggishly towards us. He's yelling something at me, but all I can focus on is the silver man at my feet. Slowly, Jesse reaches me. As if the Magic is wearing off.

Can Silver Magic do that? No one ever said anything about Magic fading. On Umbra, the Argenti draw energy from the planet. Magic can be applied in all shapes and forms, depending on the individual Argenti. But once the Magic is cast, it sticks. At least, according to what I've heard. In Silver Valley, Jasmine had a pendant that could even traverse space and time and still be used.

So why...

"You were wrong about my powers, little mouse. I don't have my own special Magic—I suck the abilities from others. Versatility can be quite handy, you know." He shrugs, as if stealing is as natural as running his mouth. His voice is soft and gentle, but humour underlies ever word. He props himself up on an elbow, watching me lean back into Jesse. "Lucky for me, your mother's Silver Magic is telepathy. If she speaks often enough into someone's head, she can read them in a crowded room—farther, even. Yours, however, seems to be a lot sweeter than that. You can feel people's minds, little mouse... and when you touch their mind, you can find that person anywhere. A human compass, if you will."

Jesse's hands tighten on me as I begin to shake.

Marcellus pulls himself off the ground, brushing his hands

down his pants. "Now scurry away, little mouse. Do what you do best—run away from me. I want a chance to test your Magic before we lock you away."

I had every incentive to squeeze his brain for information. To knock him down, steal his Hover and never see the man again.

It's like he's spoon-feeding my plan back to me. Which can only mean I will never escape him. Not as long as my supposed Silver Magic runs through his veins.

And so, I laugh. Giddiness overcomes me and I rub my temple with my knuckles. "I definitely do not have Magic, but I'll be more than happy to oblige you."

As I turn to go, Jesse squeezes my shoulders. "Savannah."

"What?" I lean into him. "Want to stay with him? Be my guest."

He clenches his jaw, but eventually he drops his hands, seemingly at a loss.

"I don't have Silver Magic," I assure him, giving him my best shot at a gentle, reassuring smile. "See? My hair is brown. I'm not an Argenti."

I twist a finger around a wet lock of hair, feeling Marcellus's eyes on me.

"You are a beautiful anomaly."

I inhale deeply and roll my eyes at him.

He pins his eyes on me, one eyebrow quirking. We watch each other for a moment, both daring the other to speak first.

I break first. "Well, thanks for the info. I'm leaving." I yank my clothes off the ground and pull Jesse with me, his naked skin glistening in the sunlight. "And I'm stealing your Hover."

Marcellus runs his finger down Jesse's sword, gently caressing it. That sword belonged to Jesse's father.

My gut twists at the thought. But Marcellus isn't watching me, his eyes are on Jesse as he stiffens and sucks on his cheek.

I can feel the pain radiating off him and I know in my bones that Jesse will kill him for this. Slowly.

He collects our clothes and a few peaches, piling them in his arms as he follows me, leaving his sword behind. Covering the shame.

Our footfalls are near silent as we leave, but I feel Marcellus watching our every step—can feel his eyes dance between Jesse's naked body and my fleeing back.

"See you later, little mouse."

I yank open the exit door he left ajar, my blood boiling. "Don't call me that!" My flustered voice echoes both through the orchard and the small metal exit.

I slam the door after Jesse and, in the distance, Marcellus's laughter fills the air.

MELANIE

"I hate you," I utter into the dark.

The computer room is void of life as the sun sets, the many blank screens mocking me. My face flashes on every single one I look at.

Dark blonde hair, eyes like silver death, and skin so waxen and bruised it makes me smile.

If Jesse was here, he'd be proud of me.

I've never been very good with my hands when it comes to combat. But today, I planted Jasmine face-first into the mud.

They shouldn't have teamed us together for drills. The way she kept smirking at me, convinced she could beat me… it made my muscles itch.

After all her peacocking, she's just as untrained as I am. And I beat her. It took a while, but I beat her.

"You're an awful human being," I tell my reflection, flexing my aching muscles. "You should *not* be enjoying this,"

I may have beat her and pushed her down into the mud, but I can feel the effort of it lining my body. We both put everything we had into that fight.

The memory of grappling with Jasmine and tripping her forwards flashes in my brain. Our training arena was majestically backed by the brown, boneless branches of the nearby trees arching into the field. She didn't even glare at me. Not a single bat of her eye. She just got up, brushed the mud off her hands, and strode off the field with a vacant expression.

I know it hurt her pride. The girl is in mourning—in utter agony—but I can't really bring myself to care.

Mason gasped when he saw it, eyes flashing to me. Elijah bit his lip, held his breath, then glared at me when he saw me snicker.

The villagers all carried on.

No one cared. No one except the brute, Samael, who seems to respect Jasmine more since she freed him and then beat his sorry ass, putting him in his place. I cannot quite understand how his mind works, but I do know that he admires her. In a weird, twisted sort of way.

Watching her go down hurt his pride, too. He's been avoiding me all day, choosing to spend his time with the sisters who shadow him.

A smile cracks onto my lips and I'm so focused on my reflection that I hardly notice when an outside light splinters through the doorway.

"You *are* an awful human being," Elijah says.

He's a silhouette in the entrance, leaning on the doorframe with his arms crossed, a crimson sweater pushed up to his elbows.

He comes here a lot. Sometimes to visit me, sometimes to find some peace.

I stop breathing as I look at him, fancying the way the light filters through his messy hair. We both pause for a moment, staring.

It's not uncommon for us to share this space, but it is uncommon to watch him look so…

I shudder. It's difficult to keep my eyes from roaming, so I lower my head, hiding the warmth flooding my face by analysing the papers in front of me.

I can feel his heated gaze trace the bruises on my face, dissecting each one. I've had worse injuries in the past. Broken bones, hair yanked out of my skull and scars on my back from the tail of a belt.

But Elijah doesn't know that. He only knows the pretty pieces of me—the silken image of a courtier turned hacker.

I push the scattered plans on my desk aside, making room should Elijah wish to join me. Amid training and readying our small coup, I've been mapping the Silver Kingdom from memory.

My head aches when I glance at the many holes in my map and anxiety tickles out of my chest. I could ask some of the people from the Safe Holds what they remember of Umbra, but that involves talking to people I don't know and I'm never really in the mood for that.

"We have some Velox now," Elijah says, deadpan. He knows I know, I just don't really mind the bruises. I never really cared to look pretty.

I rest my head in my hands, drooping. Immediately, Elijah starts across the room. He yanks a chair forwards, sitting beside me, and my chest aches.

Jesse's chair.

I glance up abruptly, catching Elijah's smile. Or at least, his attempt at one. His eyes are still darkened, especially as he traces the bruises on my cheeks from up close.

I maintain his gaze, our faces closer than I'd like. The pad of his finger brushes a hairsbreadth from my cheekbone and I wince slightly.

Oh yes, that one is nasty. I hold my breath. It doesn't look like he is breathing either.

His chest is tense, his eyes downcast to look at me. The only movement from him is a small muscle twitching in his eyebrow. He's so tall compared to me—taller than Jesse, but less muscled. The veins in his arms pulse as he tenses further and drops his hand ever so gently onto the table.

"You're incredible," he says on an exhale. "You're good at everything you do. Even if that is slamming a broken girl into the ground."

"Why, thank you," I whisper.

The corner of his lip twitches, but he doesn't say more. I pull back from him, rustling the papers across my desk. *My* desk. The people in the warehouse have begun to see the computer room as my hole. Whenever someone needs access to a computer, they linger at the entrance, visibly nervous.

But not Elijah. He leans back in the chair, arms crossed, completely at ease. He toes off his shoes, crosses his ankles, and then shuts his eyes. This place is his solitude as well.

My throat becomes thick as I watch him gradually succumb to sleep.

Like me, he doesn't often sleep. Not because his heart is a pulsing thrum of nervous energy like my own, but because he simply can't. I suspect the night of the bombings plagues his every moment.

The only place these thoughts don't seem to shroud him is in this office.

I don't even have to be present. He just likes it here.

I slump down in my chair, my lids growing heavy at the sight of him. Around the room, the setting sun leaves streaks of gold across the floor. It's always so dark when I'm here, but when it hits a certain time of day, it's magical.

As the sun hits the horizon out by the ocean, reds and golds crack apart the sky, and I spin my chair around to look at it.

The warehouse is positioned away from the wreckage of Silver Valley by a point close to the ocean, intersected by rivers for our cattle and produce. From the vantage of the computer room up high in the warehouse, I can spot both a sliver of the ocean and one of the small river channels. This place is such a lush section of the island, full of vibrant life, and yet so lonely and excluded from the rest.

I turn towards Elijah, sensing movement at my back and hoping to share the beautiful image with him, but my chest falls when I find Mason instead.

He has grown so much. It makes me blink whenever I see him.

I can't tell whether it is his elongated limbs that strike me first or if it's the way he carries himself—the experience he has gained.

The soft-hearted boy stares at me, then Elijah. Then he takes a shaky breath.

He moves one foot into my computer room, pushing his shoulders back. Whatever he intends to say, it appears to be important. At least, important to him.

I sigh deeply, leaning further back into my chair. "Hello, little Shaw."

He plants himself in front of my desk, eyes skimming the plans as if he already expected to find them there. Unintentionally, I glare at him and cross my arms until he looks away.

The sun's rays gild his gentle face. He takes a deep breath and says with conviction, "I know you have a way to talk to Savannah and I want to send a message to her."

I maintain my casual posture, assuming a friendly disposition. Years of hiding my true emotions around the snakes in the Umbran court make the mask easy to find, but my heart batters in my chest, forcing the uneasiness out. I think I feel a muscle in my face twitch.

"Before we get into figuring out how you know this, may I ask what message would be important enough to jeopardise your sister's position on Umbra?" I say calmly, my voice strong but steady.

Mason doesn't meet my gaze, instead staring at the sunset behind me. I watch his throat wobble as he swallows deeply. "Savannah wants us to build an army. That's why we saved the people in the base, right?"

I don't say anything as I watch him wring his fingers in front of his chest, his bare arms exposed in the chilly room.

It doesn't take long until the thoughts spill from his head.

"I've been looking into guerrilla warfare," he says, then waits a beat, his eyes flashing to my face. My eye subtlety twitches, but I keep my face even. He mustn't see the way my heart is pounding out of my chest, so he continues, eyes drifting back to the golden sun.

"It's about stealth. Which is good. Not as violent. But then I spoke to some of our new people and lots of them lost family that way. The Umbrans are nice people. Happy here, like us. If we take them to war, more people will die. So I"—he swallows again, knotting his hands across his chest—"I have a better idea of how we can get into the castle."

I finally deign to speak, softening my gaze so he feels comfortable. It works, and he watches my every word when I ask him casually, "Who ever said about getting into the castle?"

Between us, Elijah mumbles in his sleep, so dead to the world that our hushed conversation goes straight over his head. We both glance at him, our strained postures softening. Mason's shoulders loosen and, while my posture doesn't change, my heartrate calms.

Mason doesn't sway from my question when he looks down at me, and he explains quickly, "The castle is where my mum lives. Savannah can bring her to our side, if she is powerful enough, which I think she is. I am betting Savannah will go to the castle, which is where we should probably go as well if we are to help her. And I *want* to help. I know you do, too."

I pick at the edge of my glove, absently gazing at him now. "You know too much, kid," I say, knowing the boy before me is no child. Not anymore.

"I've been talking to people, connecting dots. Will you listen to my plan or not?"

If I don't listen to him, he will keep talking until the group is divided.

It's too early. We aren't ready. Savannah isn't ready. For the sake of everyone, this needs to stop.

"Sure." I shrug, dropping my hands into my lap. The wires on my arm feel like they're spurting through my body, but I know it's just nerves. "Just know, we need to stay on schedule and time ourselves with Savannah and Jesse. If we change anything too drastically, they will be in the dark about it and, ultimately, be at risk. So, I hate to say it, but no matter what you tell me, it probably won't happen."

He takes a quiet step before me, placing his hands on the back of Elijah's chair.

"That's why I want to contact Savannah about it. I already spoke to Jasmine and she agrees that my plan is much better."

Oh, stars. Did mud get into her curly-headed brain?

I clamp my jaw, settling the warmth bubbling in my head.

Mason watches me with increased fascination, but through the soft tilt of my lips, I know he sees none of it. His wide eyes explore me, eyebrows slightly furrowing.

"Jasmine needs to stay out of everyone's business," I breathe, the words coming out a little sharper than I intended.

"It's her business too."

I cock my head, unable to stop one of my eyebrows from raising slightly. "Is it?"

Mason says nothing.

I stiffen my jaw, twisting the glove around my fingers. Elijah is still dead to the world, so I point towards an empty chair off to the side of my computer desk. While Mason retrieves it, I stack more of the plans to make space and lean onto the desk, chin cupped in my palms.

The poor kid seems to be trembling slightly. I don't blame him. Most people see power and anger in my gaze—most people fear both those things.

I may not be pure-blooded Argenti, but the silver fire in my eyes served me in court better than any powers ever did.

He crosses his ankles and reluctantly leans forwards. It looks as if he is debating whether to fly off his seat or settle casually like Elijah.

"Can you please just listen to my plan?" he asks me quietly.

The sun has faded behind us, casting the room in eerie shadows.

One thing I've always had in common with Jesse is the way we both find comfort in shadows. There's something safe about hiding from the fray, observing and calculating the moves of others. I once navigated the castle in shadows and all the back doors and loopholes have been permanently engraved in my brain.

Mason is a child of light, not yet ready for a war.

Frustrating as it is, I take a long breath and nod. I do not go back on my word.

His breath is shaky, his voice quiet. "Jasmine said the bombs wrecked some firewalls, and we think you might now be able to access Umbran security cameras. Can I show you?"

My prosthetic arm spasms and we both stare at each other.

Stars.

SAVANNAH

"He's going to follow us," Jesse's voice mutters from the front of the Hover.

"I don't have Silver Magic," I say with clarity, my lips smacking around the flesh of a peach, legs sprawled in front of me.

I'll give Marcellus one thing—his Hover is incredibly comfortable.

It's both stylish and more efficient than any Hover I've seen on Terra. The curvature of the model is slick, the dusty red metal arching towards the front of the machine in an elegant arc. The world beyond the vehicle is blocked off by a roof. The magnetic machine floats across the desert like a car, protecting us from the elements.

Below the sand, much like Silver Island, I suspect magnets are planted to keep the machine hovering above ground. Either that, or it's run by some unique alien fuel. I don't have the chance to ask Jesse before he pounds me with more logic.

"He's going to track us with your Magic and bring us to the Silver Kingdom. We have to head somewhere he won't suspect, make a trail somehow…" His brows furrow, his knuckles white as he steers. "If you can test your Silver Magic, we can understand how it works and—"

"I *don't* have Silver Magic," I repeat. "My hair is brown."

I squirm in my seat behind Jesse. It's made of leather and insanely comfortable, sprawling in a crescent moon to allow room for 3 passengers. Damn Marcellus for having good taste.

I prop my legs up on the other end of the lounge-like seat, eyes unfocused on the *Mors* Desert brushing past us. On the floor is a brown satchel in which Marcellus had stored some supplies among a single knife. We've been drinking his water supply slowly, the sun slinking down the sky like a ticking time bomb.

"What did he steal from you then, when you touched him?" Jesse rebuts.

"Beats me." I shrug. "Everything that came out of his mouth could've been lies."

My fingers trail over the pocket holding my switchblade. I'm grateful I didn't lose it in the same way Jesse lost all his weapons. The permanent cinch between his brows tells me he's going to be eternally troubled by it.

At least we have Marcellus's knife.

"Then why did he let us go, Savannah?" His words are flat, a deadly calm brushing over the anger in his tone.

Hairs rise on my arms, but irritation floods my chest and I swing my legs off the seat, no longer comforted by the plush leather. "I don't know Jesse! But I wasn't about to just let him drag me by my collar to the Elders."

I stare at Jesse's back as he makes a point of focusing on the terrain ahead of us. He drives fast. Terrifyingly fast. I should be used to the sensation of it by now, but I'm not.

I grip the edges of the seat, my thoughts muddled as I focus on the rough Umbran landscape ahead. The *Mors* Desert fades gradually away, softening out around more shrubs and trees, taking us ever closer to the lush forest in the middle of the planet.

Umbra is much smaller than Terra. Granted, we didn't land at the apex of the planet, where it's cold even during the day, but we still made it across a large chunk of the planet in less than the whole Umbran day cycle.

After a moment of tense silence, Jesse finally speaks. "So, what's our plan now?"

"We find allies," I say, as if it's as simple as that. My churning stomach knows otherwise. "The Elder who helped Jasmine is our way into the Kingdom. I hope. I'm also assuming some Elders lost family in the bombing of Silver Family. We find them and rally them to our cause. We cannot fight this alone."

"Tear the Elders' dynasty apart by the roots. I like it."

I flex my fingers, peering down at them as shade ripples over us when we tunnel under a patch of trees, skimming past the edges of a Dome harbouring another farm. Beyond it, even more trees begin to circle the *Mors* Desert. I squint, trying to make out the faded blip in the distance. The trees look vibrant—so at odds with the harsh terrain around us.

I take a deep breath, stilling the anxiety running through my chest and down my arms. Peppered between us and the forest is the occasional roughly hewn house, having been nestled within the sand so long their wooden walls are stained red. Jesse avoids them, preventing me from getting a clearer look or any indication of how the small homes can survive such intense heat.

Umbrans prize their immortality. They are afraid of death. Surely having houses among the sandy landscape would threaten their longevity? And yet, there they stay.

"How do they withstand the heat?"

Jesse turns his head and blinks, taking in a small bundle of houses closest to us. Despite the dirty nature of them, the houses are surrounded by small vegetable gardens, lush and thriving, and clothes lines with Umbran garbs swishing in the wind. One even has a small swing set for a child, the sand underneath scuffed from play.

"You know the Dome around the farm?" he answers softly, turning his head back to focus on our direction. "It's different to the one on the Terran bases. Same material, but instead of filtering out the air, it filters out the climate. These houses have them, but nothing compares to the Dome around the Silver Kingdom."

"Is that why the forest looks so green?"

Jesse nods curtly. "Pretty much."

I turn my eyes back to the houses and the forest stretching ahead, my breath slowly dragging out of my lips. "Amazing."

We ease across the desert in silence for some time, Jesse's posture slowly losing its tension the farther we drift away from Marcellus. My skin prickles at the very thought of him, his irritating voice following me even as we put lengths of desert between us.

After an hour or so of silence, when the forest sprawls around us and the desert floor has faded into a tangle of knotted grass and stones, Jesse finally speaks.

"I don't like being here."

I sit upright, my heart kicking up its rhythm. "Should I be looking out for something?"

"I came here a lot when I was younger. Umbra has two main continents. This is the main one, but I came from the military island. I used to sneak across on the Ocean Train, pretending to be a noble with my friends. It brings back happy memories."

"And that's... bad?" I ask.

His voice sounds pained when he responds. "Yes."

Sunlight flickers through the dappled trees, peppering our

stolen Hover in a patchwork of sun and shade. The forest isn't unlike the ones on Terra, though it does seem more barren. We haven't entered Jesse's so-called Dome yet and the trees dotting throughout look like pines and cacti. The stones and shrubs around us are muted little things, harsh and dried out from the sun.

The sand spirals in the wind behind us, kicked up by the breeze the Hover leaves in its wake. I lift my eyes to the canopy just as Jesse slows on a hill. Below, a river wraps and bends around the trees and a wide, iridescent Dome stretches out to a thicker forest beyond. The trees there look unnatural. Pine trees and oaks, among others that look foreign and way too green.

Civilisation.

Thank the stars, we've been travelling in the right direction. I smile softly and glance at Jesse animatedly. The river means we're getting close to the Kingdom.

But still, not close enough.

If I didn't know the Dome was there, I may have missed it, and it's only because it travels so tall into the sky that I can see it at all.

"Do you know any nomads?" I ask Jesse.

He slows the Hover further as we near the river. "Not anymore. I grew up on the space centre, surrounded by metal walls and strict protocols. I escaped to be with them sometimes."

I blink. Jesse has friends in the *Mors* Desert?

I scan over the sun, which has dipped down from its position in the apex of the sky. We've been driving for what feels like hours. I lick my lips, feeling my stomach rattle with the desire for more food and water. The peaches and Marcellus's water supply ran out.

"Well, why don't we go stay with them? Their houses would be safe, right?"

The cool air in the Hover makes me shiver, pinpricks running up my arm.

"I suppose so. If we can find them."

I rub my arm, staring in wonder at the now ever-changing

landscape. I keep my eyes peeled for animals, curious to see how they differ. But even with our slower speed, we still traverse too fast for me to make any out.

A few of the muted green trees flutter in the breeze. My eyes snag on a dangling branch as we glide under it, its leaves looking like giant pods instead of the flimsy green wings I'm used to seeing on trees.

Once I notice this tree, I see many others like it. Their pods appear to be open, soaking in the sky. The ones in the shade seem to remain closed.

Photosynthesis at its finest. Like squirrels hoarding nuts in preparation for hibernation. The image makes me feel even colder in the Hover, a small trickle of fear settling in my gut at the very thought of Umbra's cold nights.

"You never told me," I begin, unsure how to breach the subject. I swallow deeply and try again. "You never said who you lost on the Second Night."

Jesse stiffens, the Hover slowing, and I wonder if I've crossed a line.

I see the glittering of the river, the soft iridescent film of the Dome not quite covering this side of it as it slashes deep into the middle of the river. Further down, the Dome manages to cut into our side of the desert. But not here.

My brain struggles to understand why Jesse is stopping until I notice us approaching a small cabin. It bleeds into one of the pod trees beside it, the wood it's made from matching the dark hue of the tree. Out front is a small garden, untamed and dangling down into the sand. It looks neglected, but not dead.

"My older sister, Lily. I was only five at the time." The Hover grinds to a halt, but Jesse makes no move to get out. He stares ahead, his body tense. "There was a snow cat outside of the military base, causing a scene among all my peers—snow cats aren't commonly seen so far south, but it was injured and trying to find help." He takes a deep, rattling breath and the next words come out strained. "Lily went out to the cat. The blizzard took her life."

I rise off my seat, arms wrapping around his back, my heart melting as tears flood his eyes.

His muscles are tense, only stiffening further under my touch.

The back of his hand whips across his cheek and he pushes me away, pounding a hand on the section of the Hover that lowers the protective Dome down over our heads. The warm air hits me instantly and I inhale sharply. With the sun lower in the sky, it's nowhere near as bad as it was. But, after hours of sitting in regulated temperature, it's enough to steal the breath out of me.

"Jesse." My voice follows him as he jumps out of the vehicle, his hands wrapping around the back of his head. "Her death wasn't anyone's fault."

I climb down, grabbing Marcellus's knife from his satchel as I do so, my eyes locked on Jesse's back.

"Tell that to the mother who took her own life a week after. In the same way."

I freeze, my hand inches away from touching Jesse's wrist. Shivers convulse down his spine. The world is so quiet for a moment that I can hear every tree creak as the wind wraps itself around the landscape. The soft buzz of insects fills my ears, muffling the sound of flowing water.

I finally take that last step towards Jesse, and he turns and faces me sharply.

"This is why I hate Umbra. I hate the memories. I hate the Second Night which stole half of my family. I *hate* the ship that stole my father's life years after, leaving me alone, nothing but a half-trained guard in the wake of his shadow. I hate it here, Savannah."

Another tear dances down his cheek, pooling around his chapped lips. His dark blue eyes seem to glow, a melting pool of sapphire as I reach for his hand and wrap Marcellus's knife inside his grip.

"Then let's make Umbra pay," I say, resting my head against his chest.

He takes a deep breath and pulls me closer into him. I breathe in his scent, so warm and familiar, and sigh as a tingle eases down my chest.

Savannah Shaw and Jesse Hayes. Just us against the world.

After what feels like hours, he finally pulls away.

The forest feels muted now, all sounds a distant ambience as he points to the cabin before us. "This is where me and my friends used to come and hide."

I squint at it, unable to find the familiar bubble of a Dome around it. A fuzzy insect rests on my cheek as I move forwards and I bat it away, brows furrowed.

I look at Jesse. "No Dome?"

He blinks, eyes narrowing as if noticing that for the first time, too. He strides ahead, hands slashing the air, trying to find it.

I wander around a small metal generator almost hidden behind a shrub where Jesse had stopped, staring down at it with vacant eyes.

It's dead.

Jesse kicks it with his shoe. "This used to work. Used to power the Dome."

"What happened to it?" I wonder.

Jesse shrugs.

One of the bugs I saw during my delirium in the desert rests on my shoulder. I flinch when I see it, flicking it away. The furry thing climbs into the sky to join a swarm.

A small breath escapes my lungs. They circle above our heads, growing in number as more come from deep within the forest. Thousands of them.

"We can't stay here without the Dome. We have enough time to find someone to stay with—"

"But is it enough time to escape that?" I ask, pointing.

Suddenly, I can see what the bugs are escaping. I cover my face as they zip past us, trying not to breathe one in.

They swarm towards the river, slapping our skin like little needles as flee. Because in the distance, a large red cloud tumbles our way.

Jesse curses. "Inside. INSIDE."

I turn towards the direction of the Hover. "We can pull the Hover's Dome up around us in there!"

He clamps his hand down onto my arm and I squint, struggling to see his face through the cloud of bugs. "No time!"

He pushes me towards the cabin. The unregulated, hole-filled cabin. I lower my head, feeling for his arm as he leads me towards it.

It's impossible to see. Our feet sink in the sand as we stumble over vines from the overgrown garden. I pull the thin material of my Umbran garb over my head, blocking out the tiny wings clipping my face and the incessant buzzing in my ears.

Jesse coughs.

I try not to laugh at the idea of him swallowing a bug and risk a peek from behind the fabric as the sound of the bugs dwindle, just in time to see the cloud completely engulf the trees. The pods hanging from the branches above the cabin close instinctively, protecting itself from the anomaly.

"Stars," I mutter under my breath.

Behind me, Jesse gets the door to the cabin open and screams my name. Heart pounding in my chest, I fall inside, just as the sandstorm crashes into the building.

SAVANNAH

I slam the door closed with the force of my body, gasping as I choke on plumes of sand.

Gusts swing under the door, prying through the cracks in the window and battering the tree above the roof.

"Chair!" Jesse shouts, his voice barely audible over the gale.

I catch the wooden chair he slides across the floor to me and prop it up under the handle. It keeps it closed, but wind still surges through all the cracks. The door is made of roughly hewn planks so dark they are almost black. Sturdy, but pocketed with holes.

I know a Dome would stop these sorts of things from touching people's homes. Everything—everyone—beyond the river will be safe.

My breathing is rapid as I spin around the small house, eyes raking for anything to jam the holes.

The cabin is cosy, but dusty from neglect—the fireplace a hollow, forgotten thing and the blankets threadbare and bug-eaten.

We never should've stopped the Hover to stay in this place.

"Here." Jesse appears from the back of the cabin, tossing blankets at me. The one on the small bed remains untouched.

I immediately work at jamming it under the door while he works on the windows. My muscles ache, but we don't stop. We persevere.

We always persevere.

The winds howls outside, the sand ripping against the trees.

The sandstorm appeared so suddenly, so peculiarly, it was almost as if an Argenti summoned it. Hell, maybe one did. Maybe Marcellus got another Hover and finally found us. I doubt he'd be in the desert without reinforcements nearby.

My heartbeat explodes against my eardrums. Knuckles white from tearing strips of cloth from the blanket, I jam the last piece into the final gap in the door.

Jesse pants beside me, face unreadable as he watches the storm through a tear in the blanket he just covered the window with.

"We're going to have to camp here until the storm stops."

Obviously, I refrain from saying. "Would we be okay in here during the Second Night?" I ask, already dreading the answer.

"No. We'd likely die without some form of heat."

My eyes snag on the fireplace. It's barren, not a log in sight. We could always break apart the wooden dining table.

I know nothing about sandstorms, how long they last or where they come from, but I immediately prepare for a long night in this cabin.

It creaks in the wind, the small foyer dark and eerie. My body shakes, instincts coming naturally to seek out Jesse in the gloom. His large hands fumble over the mantle of the fireplace.

I drag my feet forwards him, a silent wraith as I venture into the cabin.

There's a small dining table, some chairs sprawled across the ground, and a shattered vase splintered across the wooden flooring. A kitchen sits tucked to the side of the cabin. It's not much—a wooden benchtop riddled with old knife wounds from chopping food and cluttered with jar upon jar of fermented food, old grains and herbs. No fridge. No sink. There's a rack for hanging meats to dry and a dusty crevice fashioned into an oven—although the oven looks more like a fireplace. Utterly dated and Georgian.

I don't go near it, my body flinching when what looks like a small rat darts under the meat rack.

Around the old fireplace, the wooden décor peels paint. Agitated, Jesse picks at it as he takes a deep breath, eyes catching mine.

"No matches."

A small table with a lace cloth hangs precariously beside him with its drawers open. Needles and thread, an old scarf, a rusted candleholder that once shone gold and a smattering of dusty candles line its stomach.

But nothing to start a fire.

I pick one of the candles up, rolling it around my fingers.

"Can we make some flint?" I stare down at the cold candle, my breathing slow. "Or rub some wood together? Isn't that how boy scouts do it?"

"You mistake me for a Terran," Jesse grumbles, taking the candle from my fingers and placing it back inside the drawer. "And your fidgeting is making me nervous."

I take a deep breath and then move towards Marcellus's pack, our last resort.

Jesse watches me with his jaw taunt as I rummage through it.

"A flint!" I exclaim.

Jesse swallows sharply. "I don't know if we should trust anything from in there."

I hold the flint up towards him, grinning. "As long as it helps me make a fire, I don't care."

His hand brushes my wrist, skin meeting skin. My cheeks heat as I stare into his eyes, my heart missing a beat and my body wilting.

I almost drop the flint.

He moves his hand, trailing his fingers around my wrist, soaking in the heat from my pulse. Everything around me feels warm and I want to sink into it, despite the erratic pounding of both our hearts. Outside, the world is alive with death, but inside, the world is deathly alive. I'm hyper aware of every moment he makes as he releases a shaky breath, feeling my skin prickle under his touch.

His muscles are taut, every line in his body hard. I want to trace my fingers down his chest, up his throat, across his back. I want to breathe him in, soak in his warmth and never let go.

We could die at any moment. Death clouds us from every corner. We haven't even made it to the Silver Kingdom or contacted any allies, yet each breath swirling out of my lungs feel like a ticking clock.

I might never feel the heavy press of his bare chest against mine again. That very thought heats every sore, aching part of me.

I want to utterly consume him, but instead I let him drop my hand.

"I'll start a fire. You make us something to eat." My voice is decisive and when I pin Jesse with a steady gaze, he sighs and nods.

"You have no idea how to make a fire, Savannah," he says as he walks towards the kitchen, as silent as a ghost.

The absence of his body is gruelling. A cold wind slaps me in the face and I suck in a painful breath. A small cottage between us, but it feels like the whole goddamn world.

"And you're a horrible cook," I retort. "Get chopping."

He snorts, but he doesn't argue when I turn back to the fireplace.

I stare down at the old, blackened pieces of wood and take a deep breath.

Let's get this going before we freeze.

My hands are red and raw—even hotter than the gentle licks of the fire before me.

I'm no boy scout, and starting this fire took me hours. *Hours.* Jesse had offered to help, but from the way he kept frowning at Marcellus's pack, I ignored him. My shivering and teeth clattering accompanied my work until *finally* a spark from the kindling in my grasp finally held. I cupped my fingers around it, urging it into the fireplace. It caught the threads Jesse ripped from an old potato sack as he held it near the sparks, casting his fingers in an ember glow.

Not even the sour tang of the fermented cabbage Jesse found was enough to tempt me from my task of getting that damn fire started. I glared at him when he offered it to me, my nostrils flaring with the bitter smell of the stuff.

It was all Jesse could find in the cabin. At least, it was the only edible thing until I mentioned Marcellus's pack.

A pack which Jesse is still utterly reluctant to touch.

Thankfully, sitting inside, wrapped carefully in brown paper, sat a handful of nuts. It didn't take much convincing to get Jesse to unwrap and begin eating them and, more excitably, feeding me.

He places his fingers against my lips, his calluses gently brushing my skin as I suck a nut out of his hand, shivering from something other than the chill in the cabin.

It's officially cold now as the day eases into night. The wind is dying, but still too dangerous to withstand outside.

The cabin is warmer, but not by much. Now we sit, shoulders pressed together, staring at the pathetic excuse of a fire with all the bug-eaten dusty blankets we could find piled around us.

Jesse places another nut into my mouth.

I stopped making the fire an hour ago, but he continues to feed me as if my fingers have wholly stopped working. I bunch them into fists, palms raw and shivering, and think to myself they may as well have.

All the better, because each time his fingers near my mouth, my stomach flutters and I warm from the inside out, cheeks heating.

"What kind of nut is this?" I ask him, my body shaking in the cold hitting my back. He trails a gentle arm around me, pulling me against his shoulder.

I shiver at that, too.

"It comes from a polly tree. They grow by the sea, under starlight in the Silver Kingdom. They kinda look like macadamia shells, but are white as milk."

"They're nice," I say, rolling it around my mouth.

My head starts to thrum, fatigue battling against my skull as I watch Jesse roll a small nut around his fingers, looking reflective.

"They're a bit too sweet for my taste."

"Do you like *anything*?" I tease. Hates polly nuts. Hates peaches. Hates Umbra.

The corner of his lip quirks as he meets my eye. "I like you."

I lean further into him, head pounding but my heart swelling. Jesse.

My Jesse.

The muscles in his arm tighten as he grips me against him. Every inch of my body pounds—my head, my heart, the small creeping warmth flushing my skin. I sink my head against his chest, burrowing myself in him.

His heart is speeding faster than mine.

A small smile curls on my lips, easing out the pattering of nerves blooming across my skin.

"Have you ever dated someone—on Umbra?"

Jesse shrugs. I don't know what that means. I want to lift my eyes to his, but I'm comfortable and tired. So tired.

He circles his arms around me, cushioning me. "Not really," he finally admits. "It was all surface stuff."

"Surface stuff?" I mumble. The scent of him envelops me, over-powering and all-consuming.

Outside, the world is still roaring. Endless winds batter against our small house, making the world feel like it's tilting.

Or maybe that's me. Maybe my head is making me dizzy.

"I've always been... too caught up. In becoming a pilot like my father. Losing my father. My sister. My mother. Everything." He swallows deeply, his breathing sounding hollow. "Everything always hurt. And there were girls who temporality took away that hurt. But..."

I rustle around in his lap, one of my hands moving to steady myself on his thigh.

Heat rises up my chest again, but I don't move that hand. Fingers wrapped around his upper thigh, I hold my breath and say, "But?"

"But when and if I settle down, I want someone I have a deep con-nection with. Someone who knows every part of me, heart and soul."

I sit upright, my fingers reaching for his. He stares straight ahead, dark eyes reflecting the flickering fire. We should go to sleep and rest while the storm passes, but the shivers wracking our bodies make us reluctant to leave the fire.

"You're like me, then," I whisper against him, snuggling closer to steal some of his warmth. "Family above all else."

He nods. "Family."

Am I like family to him, or something more?

He releases my hand and pulls me closer still, so we're fully wrapped in the blanket.

We stare for a few long beats at the fire, the warm tendrils lick-ing our faces as we lean towards it, the creeping night at our backs. The cabin is dark, cold, void. The only section of comfort is the place we have made a home of on the floor.

My voice breaks apart the darkness, uttered on a single breath. "Do you think the storm is enough to keep Marcellus off our trail for a bit?"

"Unless he's some sort of indestructible force, then yes."

"He's only human," I mumble to myself.

"He's Argenti," Jesse clarifies. "Not human."

He's still glaring at the fire. I shiver, my body convulsing against the cold.

"Get some sleep, Princess. It might still be a long night, yet."

A branch slams against the house, making me jump as the wind temporarily changes course. "I don't know if I can," I admit.

"Try."

I squeeze my eyes tightly shut, fighting the burning behind my lashes.

Somewhere above, past the storm and the clouds and the peppered moon streaking across the sky, is the wormhole that takes me back to my family.

So far away, it feels almost entirely unreachable.

And, as always, the comm Melanie gave me digs into my thighs.

If we take too long—if anything happens to us and I don't give Melanie an update by our agreed-upon date in June, they will come.

I must not let that happen. Not until we are ready. Not until I have built a safety net for them on Umbra. And here, stuck in this cabin, I'm doing anything but.

"Savannah," Jesse croaks, his voice low. "Sleep."

I release a heavy breath. "And you?"

"I'm taking the first watch. But I'll wake you up when the world is too freezing to bear, don't you worry."

"We need to be out of here before that," I say, eyes still closed.

I can feel his body turning, possibly to take in the way I clamp my jaw set in a determined frown. Every muscle in my body feels taut and too itchy to sleep. I force my body to stay comatose anyway, bullying my brain to turn sluggish. To clear of all my thoughts and simply persevere through the monstrosity of waiting.

"Okay," is all he says in response. It doesn't feel genuine.

I rake in a heavy breath, tossing around in his grasp, head lowered against his collar bone. I feel warm enough to sleep, but not warm enough to ease my mind.

My fingers shake as I brush them against my switchblade. Melanie's comm. Those items feel like a lifeline, in more ways than one.

"Stars, Savannah. Stop wriggling and sleep, otherwise I'm knocking you out."

"With what weapon?" I enquire, my lips twitching.

"A piece of firewood. That chair. Whatever."

"So brutal." I smirk, my eyelids fluttering.

He sighs.

I pull my fingers up against my face and ease my brain into a slumber. My body is so exhausted, it doesn't take long until the world around me begins to grow sluggish.

His breathing slowing beside me, Jesse repeats so quietly I almost don't hear it, "I'll watch over you."

I don't know why, but it doesn't entirely feel true.

SAVANNAH

I snap my eyes open at the sound of shattering glass.

It feels like my soul gets sucked out of me when I wake, eyes rapidly scanning the dark house around me. I gulp in air as cold as ice, so brutal it sears my lungs. Beside me, Jesse is immobile on the ground.

Sleeping or dead?

Fingers shaking, I poke his cheek. His eyes twitch and I sag in relief. Sleeping.

"Who's there?" I yell out into the dimness. Like a fool, announcing her location.

So stupid.

I slip my switchblade out of my pocket, hiding the open blade under my sleeve. The tip of the sharp blade brushes the centre of my palm while the rest of the small weapon remains hidden.

The world is eerily quiet. My whole body feels stiff as I move.

Outside the shattered window, the forest remains still. Cold winds blast into our small area of solitude and, slinking towards me on massive paws—its freckled white coat stark in the dark room—is the biggest cat I have ever seen.

I crouch in front of Jesse, my switchblade ready, my free hand fumbling behind me. I find his face and start pawing at it, trying to wake him up.

My pinkie accidently goes into his ear and he grunts.

"Shut up and stay still," I say on a lone breath, my words clouding in a fog before me.

The sounds from the sandstorm has ceased, and through the window, the stars are shattering across an inky black sky and the remaining moon bathing the world in opalescent light. Illuminating the cat before me.

The cat that's looking at me like I'm its dinner.

Cold fear licks down my spine as I stare at the thing, the fire glimmering softly and casting our small area in the cabin in orange. The cat flicks its eyes towards it. Then towards me.

Its sharp ears are perked, its squashed snout pushing back into a growl. It would be beautiful if it weren't so bloody terrifying.

Its coat is thick and shiny, curling over its muscled body.

Quietly, Jesse pushes the blanket off himself and makes direct eye contact with the beast. A gasp escapes his mouth. "No." I swallow, my fingers trembling, heart pounding in my skull. "There is absolutely no way," he continues.

"*Stop talking*," I hiss through gritted teeth, aware of the cat turning its head towards him, his loud words piercing the silence of the cabin.

Jesse suddenly stands and walks up to it, not an ounce of fear in his movements. My body stills. I let my small switchblade sink more comfortably into my palm, wrapping my blue, shaking fingers around the handle.

Stars, it's so cold.

Jesse is still walking towards that freaking cat.

I clamber to my feet, heart racing in my chest. Jesse reaches a hand towards its snout, fingers brushing through the cloud from its hot breath.

Adrenaline spikes through my limbs and I arch my arm back, hefting my switchblade into the air. I don't want to kill the cat. I want to distract it.

"Don't—"

Jesse's words get lost in my ears. Blood courses through my veins, numbing the chill of the night.

My switchblade lands deep in the cat's muscled shoulder and the thing squeals in shock, its bared teeth unleashing a howl. I clap my hands over my ears, panic flooding me as the cat turns towards the window, *taking my switchblade with it.*

"No," I breathe, lowering my hands. The cat slinks through the window and into the night. "No!"

I race for the window, fingers slipping over the shards of glass, the cold numbing the sensation of the glass biting into my skin. On shaky legs, I throw myself out into the night.

"Savannah!"

The sandstorm is gone, but there is still an icy gale in its wake. It rips into me, shredding my senses. I gasp at the finality of it, this icy harbinger of death. It's so cold that my body instantly falls numb. It's an effort to move my limbs, to coax them towards the cat.

The dirt below my feet is crusted over, any moisture that was within it hardening. It crunches under my feet, too loud for my sanity.

But there is no rain—no snow—just the Umbran sea of stars, cracking through an opening in the trees.

A galaxy winks down at me, a never-ending vortex. The ring of the shredded moon is a hazy riot of swirling colour, slashing through constellations and its sister moon.

Constellations.

My mind stills, freezing with my body. The moment my gaze stills on a constellation shaped like a five-pointed-star I recall what my mother had once told me.

"The one shaped like a heart points north, and the one shaped like a hat points south."

My mother always followed these constellations—which meant she was going home. To the Silver Kingdom. I whirl towards the river, which I assume to be south. And there, branded into the inky sky, is a glistering hat-shaped constellation, a smattering of lights pointing Umbrans on their way to the Kingdom.

"Stars, Savannah. Are you mad?"

Jesse stumbles behind me in the darkness. Jesse. Stumbling.

His shaking hands grasp an icy branch as he hovers metres behind me, his lips blue.

"It's so cold, Jesse."

"We need to get back inside."

With my body beyond trembling, a frozen hunk nearly completely unable to move, I stare at him. "That house is freezing too. It will kill us."

"What do you propose then, Your Highness?" he enquires, voice positively dripping with distaste at our circumstance.

"The cat must have a den." Speaking is hard. Words are hard. It's like the cold has sucked all basic human functions from me. My heart beats slowly, nerves thrumming in my stomach.

"Those '*cats*' come from the north and south poles of Umbra. They don't feel cold like we do."

"Do we have any other options?" I manage to squeeze out of my frozen lips, the words heavy and broken from the effort of speaking.

But Jesse doesn't respond, so I turn to see what he's staring at.

The cat has returned, blood soaking its leg as it peers at us from behind a brush of desert firs. I don't know how these plants survive the cold, but in thinking that, the plants don't look entirely normal—not like the ones that pepper Terran deserts.

The cat perks its ears, staring intently at us. There's a faint grey mark behind its ear, jarring against the angelic beauty of its snowy coat.

And behind me, Jesse pants with distress, his gaze wholly locked on the beast. He makes no aggressive move towards it. No move at all. He just… stands there, looking at it.

I wrap my arms around my body. I can't feel my fingers or toes. And I sure as hell don't want to lose them.

"Where do you live?" I ask the cat, my eyes on the blade in its body instead of meeting its gaze.

"With me." A slender woman winds her way around the firs, a coat bunched so tight around her face that only her reddened cheeks and dark eyes peer through. Her gloves slide through the coat of the cat and she bunches her hand around its ears, covering the grey smear.

We stand completely still and stare, both unsure what to make of the other.

Behind me, Jesse has all but stopped breathing.

I don't turn, but I expect his hand is instinctively shifting towards his absent weapons belt and coming up short.

The wind plays around the fir covering the woman and the beast, then crashes into me, so cold I can hardly feel it.

"Who are you?" My voice is almost inaudible, but somehow the woman hears me.

"An old girl whose entire life revolves around adopting cats."

"That's…"

"A joke. Come on."

She turns, disappearing behind the brush just as the wind picks up. I stand there dumbly and watch the leaves flutter before coaxing my muscles to move—they operate like a rusty machine, creaking at the smallest of movements.

"If you throw another blade into my cat's shoulder again, that's the last move you'll ever make." Her voice drifts from ahead, nearly lost on the wind.

Jesse stands immobile, watching where she disappeared, his brow furrowed. I quickly turn and face him as I move onwards, waving my hand for him to follow. He bites down hard on his lip, his troubled eyes flashing to mine.

For the first time since I met him, I don't know what he's thinking.

I swallow deeply and wave a little more animatedly. *Come.*

My heart shudders when he finally lifts a foot forward, body slinking towards me. Our feet crunch into the ground, the fir peeling at my clothing as I trudge past it.

The woman keeps walking ahead, not once glancing back at us as we struggle to follow. I distinctively register that her coat is made from animal furs before a cold wind slaps my face and I let out a deep moan.

Jesse clutches me from behind, wrapping an arm around my torso. His warm breath musses my hair, staining my cheeks.

Still, the woman doesn't slow.

With hands frozen beyond feeling, I grasp Jesse's hand and urge him forwards. Thankfully, we don't walk long.

The closer we get to the river, the rockier the terrain becomes, until there's a smattering of stones clanging with every footfall we make. Trees twist and bend into the stone, arching over a large boulder before us.

No, not a boulder. A cave. It's almost impossible to decipher.

The trees here are denser, many of them alien to me. One tree has deep purple leaves. Another looks like reddish bamboo, but with a cascade of dried wispy leaves coming off it.

There's a tree much like the one near our cottage, pods hanging low into the night, concealing the entrance to the woman's cave.

It's a slit between the rocks, only visible if you approach it from the right angle as the entrance is horizontal to the stone.

The woman shoulders her way through, walking sideways towards her right to enter the small gap. I take a steadying breath and plant my hands on the stone, my breathing coming up short.

"I can go first," Jesse offers.

I give him a long look. Then, on a deep inhale, I dip sideways into the cave. The woman's cat still has my switchblade, after all.

The rocks from the cave must be cold, but I am beyond feeling as I fumble my way through, numb fingers scraping over the harsh texture. The rock feels like it compresses me from both sides and I habitually hold my breath until my shoulder hits a familiar slimy substance. A forcefield.

The stranger must have flicked a switch because it's gone instantaneously and I gasp as my shoulder falls sideways through empty air the moment it vanishes.

Warmth hits me so abruptly it feels like being thrown into a steaming bath. Steady hands grasp me and lower me onto the cave floor just as the entrance closes again. The moment Jesse touches that forcefield with his fingers, it slinks away from him too.

The woman doesn't take her eyes off me, head tilting as she takes in my still trembling form. Jesse has taken to staring at her cat again. They lock eyes, both fighting for dominance in their stares.

I breathe in the heady air of the cave, ripe with the smell of a fire and roasting meat, hay and the scent of animals.

The woman releases me, her soft braid tickling my arm. She is majestic—one with the animals. Her black hair winds down her shoulder in a thick braid tied with leathers. Her cheeks are rosy and peppered with dirt-like freckles, a small, faint scar marring the corner of her lip as she quirks it at me.

"Oh," she says, dark brows furrowing.

The nomad stands determinedly—a fighter in her own right— body half angled towards the entrance of the cave as if possessed.

Those deep blue eyes sparkle as she makes a connection in her mind. "You're the girl everyone talks about—the one prophesied to revolutionise Umbra."

I slouch against the cave wall, shoulders digging into the rough stone. Dust kicks up around my feet, fighting its way into my nostrils as I take a deep breath.

"That's me."

There isn't much to see in the cave. It's relatively dark, save for some lit lanterns along the wall, but the cat guards a tunnel behind the woman—one which glows a deep flickering orange. Their den.

My eyes trail over the stranger's coat, weather-worn and white. She's one of them. The leader of the pack.

She holds her hand out to me to help me stand. "Well, best of luck with that," she responds, her voice slightly husky from the cold.

My lip twitches, but I don't say anything. In my mind, I recall the direction we have walked in. We're much closer to the river here. To civilisation and the beginnings of a revolution. We need only wait out the rest of the night.

My hand slips into hers and she helps pull me to my feet. Her grip is solid, rough from calluses and marred in tinted scars, as if her cats have scratched her multiple times over the years.

My body still feels numb—the clothes clinging to it chill to the touch—but I take a deep breath of the warm air around me and step farther into the cave.

She drops my hand and turns to face Jesse, their sapphire eyes crashing together. Both simultaneously freeze.

Jesse takes a shaky step forward.

She takes a step back.

The cat angles its head, watching them both in amusement. As if it already knows what is happening.

My hands flutter for my switchblade, but it's still in the shoulder of the cat. Instead, my fingers grasp around the comm, my last connection to home.

Jesse's eyebrows lower and, just as the woman opens her mouth to speak, Jesse blurts, "Lily?"

He sags against the wall, struggling to keep himself upright. Pain lashes his features, choking him. Not for one second does he lift his eyes from her face.

My heart misses a beat. The comm drops back into my pocket as I lean back against the cave wall, eyes moving rapidly between the two.

They have the same hair colour, the same eyes and the same determined stance. Both fighters. Both protective of their families—or rather, their packs.

My tired mind filters through Jesse's stories. His sister died saving a cat. Could it be the same? Could this woman actually be his sister?

Air rushes out of my lungs as I stare at her.

My stomach lurches. I may have just thrown my switchblade at his sister's cat. The cat she tried to save on that fated Second Night.

A muscle in my face twitches.

The nomad woman—Lily—takes another step back from her brother.

His hands are shaking, eyes as wide as the moon outside. He gapes, his mouth opening and closing like a fish.

Her lips shake and she pushes them into a hard line. It's an effort for the woman to answer him, but when she does, Jesse falls to the ground.

"Yes," she breathes. "Hello, little brother."

SAVANNAH

ily takes us deeper into her cave, feeds us a bowl of stew from an animal I've never heard of in my life and offers me a blanket made of animal hide.

The cave is warm, both in temperature and homeliness. A grated fireplace slumbers quietly, with some sort of engine built in to aerate it and diffuse the smoke—an Umbran invention, Lily assures me. Soft carpet layers the ground and hay stacked in piles against the cave walls gives the cats a place to doze and lick their paws. Jesse perches on the edge of one of these hay bales, too unsure of himself to join us where Lily has decorated the place with furs and pillows.

She hovers around the edge of the cave near an exit leading to a stream for bathing and watering the cats, and an inbuilt latrine I used upon arrival.

The walls and shelves around us are covered in food, spices and plants, breathing life into the small cave. Lily plucks leaves from one of these plants, her lip between her teeth.

My heart swells in misery as the cat with the grey smear behind its ear rests its head beside me. Its injured shoulder is now free of my switchblade, but it whimpers quietly against my thigh, making me feel sorry for it.

"Absolute baby," Lily croons, grabbing a mortar she smashed leaves into and kneeling beside it.

I tell her we have some Velox at our crash zone that she's more than welcome to, but she shakes her head. "No thanks, little friend of Jesse."

Despite the words bubbling up my throat, I don't say any more on the issue.

My knee bounces up and down as I trace my eyes over the cats lounging around us. Periodically, they come and go, enjoying the biting temperatures outside unlike the lost humans inside the cave. A small cub tumbles in from the entrance, its white fur puffed instead of sleek and elegant. Its mother nudges it with her nose, sliding it forwards across the dirt floor.

They give us a wide birth, eyes wary around us newcomers.

Jesse leans forwards, feet digging into the hay bale under him, arms supporting his face as he stares at his sister. Not long ago, he'd presumed her dead.

They both occasionally glance at each other, but quickly look away. Neither know what to say. I still my bouncing knee with a fist, fingers latched around my closed switchblade. The silence in the cave is deafening.

Instinct makes me want to interfere in their business by speaking up and bridging the gap, but the words remain lodged in my throat.

After what feels like hours, when my eyes are beginning to droop from fatigue by the warm fire, Jesse finally speaks. I startle, a soft gasp exiting my lips as I clutch the animal hide around me. Neither he nor Lily notice, too busy studying each other.

"How?" is all Jesse asks. The word seems to echo through the cave.

One of the cats lifts its head, teeth slightly visible as it assesses Jesse.

"I would've reached out to you," Lily answers, not entirely circling back to his question about how she isn't dead. Perhaps it's been too long and she's forgotten how to read him. Perhaps she simply doesn't care to answer. "After I went out into the Second Night, I was near dead. The cat—I call him Cerberus—took me to Faye's cave."

I blink, eyes locked on the wispy tendrils of fire sending smoke into the chute arching into the ceiling. "Cerberus? As in the dog that prevented the dead from leaving hell?"

She pokes her tongue against the inside of her cheek, shifting those dark blue eyes down onto Cerberus. "Yep, and from the living getting in."

Jesse releases a shaky breath.

I pick at my nails as I stare the cat down.

All of my muscles feel taunt.

But the cat just huffs and lowers its snout onto its paws. Lily snorts at our reaction to the cat, kicking her legs up on a pillow.

Comparatively, Jesse hunches deeper into himself, more guarded than I've ever seen him. He flicks his eyes onto me—the exact shape and colour of Lily's—then darts them away.

"Who is Faye?" I whisper.

Lily picks at a hangnail, her body splayed against the cushions. "You mean, who *was* Faye?"

Jaw tight, Jesse locks her in his gaze.

A small smile twitches at the corner of Lily's lips, then falls away as she drops her hands to the dirt. "I hated her. Then I loved her. She was everything to me—we were going to spend eternity together, living forever here in our cave. But she got on the wrong side of an S.P. gun and, just like that, *poof*, she was gone."

Despite the steady tone of her voice, her hands clench around a pillow beneath her. I know better than to ask more about Faye. So, I open my eyes further, taking in new hints peppered around the cave. There are two sets of cutlery by the herbs, two plates, two chipped mugs and, by the wall, a space that resembles a bed with pillows and blankets big enough for two people. It's set aside from the cats for privacy and a personable space, but close enough to the fire for warmth. My eyes flicker away from it immediately, but I can tell Lily saw in the way her lips pucker. The bed is casually unmade, but looks as if it hasn't been used in a while. A place of memories.

"Lily," I whisper, the woman's name soft on my tongue, "I'm so sorry—"

"What's an S.P. gun?" Jesse interrupts, his eyes burning into Lily's own, who meets his stare with an equally sharp glare.

I swallow and sit back. It's like watching the same person combat themselves.

Lily clicks her tongue then rolls her head back onto a pillow. "*Sanguis Pulvis* gun, like as in 'blood dust'. A dumb name for a cute little Elder contraption known for 'poofing' away the existence of people standing on the wrong end of it."

Jesse's eyebrows scrunch together. "Poofing?"

Lily mimes holding a large gun. "Aim, fire, *poof*." Cerberus lets out a loud breath as Lily mines an explosion with her fingers. "Whole body turns to dust."

"It vaporises people?" I inhale sharply, my eyes darting to Jesse.

As far as we've been told, Umbrans haven't advanced their weaponry in years. It's the reason they still carry blades around.

"How?" Jesse asks.

Lily shrugs. "I'm not a scientist, Jesse. That was always your job."

Jesse physically recoils, his back straightening. "Father planned—"

"Unlimited greatness at every turn," she says, as if it was spoken in their household many times before. Lily traces her tongue around her cheek, hiding her frustration. "He wanted you to be him. If you plan to crash yourself into a planet, Jesse, then by all means, idolise him."

Jesse stands, his body jerking off the hay bail. He swallows deeply, redness creeping up his face. "Father didn't kill himself."

"He certainly beelined for the biggest asteroid field he could find."

"By technical default—"

"And who was the technician, Jesse?"

Jesse's hands move towards his face, then slap back down to his side.

"He was an exceptional pilot."

"*Who* was the technician, Jesse?" Lily repeats.

He storms closer to her, his face flush. "People make mistakes!"

"Did Father ever?"

He spins on his heel, turning down the end of the cave. I blink, watching as he stands near the exit, hand slapping against the rock.

I glance down at my feet, my throat feeling thick. To Lily, I say softly, "Maybe I should—"

"Oh no, please stay here, little usurper. You're the buffer we always needed."

Jesse slams his fist into the rock, then rests his head gently on the wall. My instincts fight to pull me towards him—to touch and console him. But I don't move. I hardly even blink. Especially not as Lily sighs and stands, navigating stray pillows and wayward cat paws towards a small cupboard against the far wall of the cave. She moves with the ease of knowing her cave inside-out.

Helplessly, I look between them both, twisting against the animal hide and shoving my switchblade back into my pocket, where it clatters against my comm.

I miss home. I miss my family, the smell of the forest and the scent of fresh coffee in the morning. Slowly, I take a steady breath, inhaling the scent of hay and animal.

Jesse pulls himself from the wall, eyes narrowed as Lily moves up to him, a worn knife in her palm. He stiffens, but she holds it out to him.

"See that girl over there?" She nods her head to me.

I tighten my jaw, eyes wavering as I watch the scene before me, blood pumping around my entire body in anticipation.

She wraps Jesse's rigid fingers around the handle of the knife and says, "Don't do to her what Father did to Mother."

Then, with a curt nod to herself and a small smile, Lily dances back around the pillows and plops back onto the cushions. "I'm tired. I'm going to sleep now." She falls back beside me, letting out a deep sigh. Cerberus huffs, rolling into her and placing his head on her thigh.

Jesse furrows his brows at her, knife balanced in his hands. "We're going to wait out the night, then head to the village."

Lily shrugs, fluffing a pillow around her head. As I assumed, she doesn't use the bed in the corner. That bed holds the memories—maybe even the scent—of her partner.

"Night," Lily says, rolling over. Then she kicks Cerberus, who nuzzles into her. "If you drool on me, I'm cutting off your tongue."

The cat bares his teeth, but settles in closer to her.

I make eye contact with Jesse, who looks unsure what to do with himself. I shrug in response to his silent question. Pulling one of the cat-smelling pillows towards me, I make myself comfortable.

My lips twitch as I take in the sight of Jesse looking so lost, the bubble of amusement coating the nervousness in my bones.

A part of me believes I should coax Jesse to bed, but against my better judgement, I let him figure it out himself. So long as he doesn't shove that blade into Lily's heart, I guess it's safe enough.

I suck on my lips, head sinking into the pillow. The last thing I see is him standing poised in the centre of the cave, the knife dangling from his fingers as he glares down one of the cats around us.

My internal laughter carries me to sleep, faster than a draught.

SAVANNAH

"Every single god forsaken fool in that village will know who you are," Lily advises me, tightening the leather around her braid.

When we woke, she told us she would take us to the docks along the river, where we can enter the castle. But she will go no further.

"Unless the Elders printed a wanted poster, they have never seen my face before," I argue.

We stand by the river, obscured by a tree bending in the wind. Ahead of us, a Dome glitters like an opal in the soft flush of dawn. I pass a water skin down to Jesse, who stands behind Lily and me. He takes it, sniffs it, then lifts it to his lips.

"Savannah doesn't always care about risk," he says after taking a sip.

"Alas, I do," she comments. "So I won't be going with you."

Behind us, Cerberus stands in the shade of a tree, his tale hissing against the ground. Lily keeps darting her eyes back to him, ready to flee at any moment.

"Are you still in touch with some of your old friends in the Kingdom?" Jesse asks her, eyes focused on the Dome.

"Yeah, we're in touch," she mumbles, her eyes softening as Cerberus yawns.

"Then we need you," Jesse responds from behind me, the shadow at my back as he scans our perimeter.

She whips her head to him. "Ha, no. Sorry. I'm staying here."

"Can you at least direct us to some of these people?" I ask softly, talking my eyes off the water. "We need supporters."

She shakes her head, slowly stepping backwards, almost bumping into Jesse. "I only go into the Kingdom for food, supplies, things like that."

He grips her shoulders, chuckling quietly, "well, today feels like a beautiful day for a supply run."

she turns and glares at him.

"Just one day, that's all we're asking," I offer. "Point us to some of your friends, and then you can leave. You don't even need to talk to anyone."

Cerberus gets up from his spot behind us, stretching his back. Lily watches him with a sad expression. "You're a little bit hard to say no to, Savannah Shaw."

Jesse winks. "You used to say the same about me, dear sister."

She rolls her eyes, the corner of her lip quirking. "Must be why you're so in love with her."

My lips pop open. Then I snap them closed. A small breeze gusts past, tumbling my dark hair around my face and I furrow my brows, lips bending in amusement.

I turn and face the shadow at my back and stage whisper. "You're in *love* with me?"

Jesse doesn't meet my eyes. His face is flushed as he studies the Dome, frustration etched in every crevice of his expression.

Lily shrugs again and turns back to the water, hands twisting around a rope securing a small boat. I don't fail to see the small smirk hanging from her lips.

Our group remains poised by a dock, the worn wood groaning under our feet as the waves from the river push against it. Everyone is deathly silent as we whisper over the planks, taking the form of a hunting pack.

Realising Jesse isn't going to reply, I turn and help Lily.

"I don't suppose you have a plan for after you find your army?" she asks.

Jesse snorts and says, "kill some Argenti," just as I answer, "probably cause a scene."

Her eyes widen. "Not very discreet."

I look over the open expanse of water. There is nothing hiding our arrival. Enemies at our forefront and a tracker on our back now makes the idea of subtle kind of humorous.

I respond, "I guess we will see."

Lily frees the boat from the dock. It's nothing grand, but it's our only passage under the Dome, because straight ahead, in line with the dock, is a small gate within the shiny surface. Much to my surprise, the gate remains unmanned.

"You're a wild one, aren't you?" she enquires. I raise my brows, pointedly looking at her furs. She cackles. "Fair play."

"Says the one with a cat following her," I point out.

"Good point," she turns to the snow cat, "Cerberus, go home. Wait for me to come back."

I don't know how, but the cat understands. With a deep yawn, it turns around and slinks back the way we came.

Lily turns away with a smile on her face, failing to notice the slight shiver down my back and the way my sweaty palms keep brushing my pants. With a pang in my chest, I realise I miss Melanie. She should be here with us.

I gaze up at the sky, ignoring the deep pang in my heart. My chest squeezes and I release a slow breath, belatedly realising my hand had found my comm.

Perseverance.

As much as I want to use the comm to message Mel, I don't.

"Alright, in you get," Lily says.

Tentatively, I step into the boat, which dips and sways under my weight. I slink into the small vessel like one of Lily's cats, the months I spent training and honing my muscles moving me like a wraith.

Jesse doesn't say anything, but he shadows me into the boat with a stillness of his own. Lily, on the other hand, leaps right in.

I gasp, hands immediately slamming into the metal railing on the boat, body tossing with the sudden sway as her feet slam into the deck. Jesse swears under his breath and his new blade goes spinning somewhere under his seat.

"You guys are as cold and stiff as the Second Night," Lily snorts, eyes raking over our straight backs as we steady ourselves. She towers above, not taking a seat, and lets the rope hiss between her fingers to curl like a snake on the boat floor.

Jesse finds his blade and sighs, just as Lily punches a finger into a navigation panel and the boat churns us forwards, a silent blip slicing through the clear water.

I marvel at the lacy white patterns the boat leaves in its wake and the fish swimming away from us underneath. I can't quite make out the bottom of the river, but it's clear enough that a whole new world is visible below.

My pulse quickens as something like a small shark swirls with a group of others and follows the boat for a time. Lily finally takes a seat and dips her hand among the crystalline water, fingers playing with the currents. I hold my breath when the small pod comes close enough to touch.

Sunshine basks her face, painting it in soft pinks and reds, and her grin splits her face.

Jasmine Spark.

My Jasmine.

That's what Lily looks like, right now, in this moment—the Jasmine from my memories. I flick my head away from her faster than I can catch my breath, a lump lodging in my throat.

No matter what my future holds, one thing is for certain: I will never get my best friend back.

I lean back against the boat, faced turned up to the sky as I count the stars instead of counting my memories, head lost in space for the duration of our trip.

It isn't until our boat taps the lip of the Dome that I raise my head, neck stiff from leaning against the rough wood.

My eyes trail up the height of the Dome, heart pattering in my chest as Lily slows the boat and eases us gently through. It doesn't disappear or open, but sucks us through—the thick compound momentarily pasting to my skin like slime. It's only a finger thick, but I shudder as it pushes me free.

Jesse's eyes are wide as his side of the boat enters, yanking him through with it.

"How does that work at keeping anything out if we can enter so—"

"Easily?" Lily answers for me, her word half obscured by the Dome as it pulls her through. "Argenti blood does the trick. Those without silver blood—like the Elders—are stuck like a bird in their toasty cage."

Even the Commons must have just a small drop of Argenti blood, surely.

It *is* warm in here. The wind is softer, carrying gentle motes of pine and fruit along it from the mainland.

A brown bird with streaks of purple feathers coos above our

heads, circling the entrance of the Dome. I swallow deeply, wondering if the rule applies to animals and if the poor thing has ever seen the other side.

My eyes begin to water at the sight of so much beauty. I flick my gaze this way and that, trying to take in every detail of the mountains, the rolling hills, the fruit trees and pines, and the peak of a distant volcano. The border of the Silver Kingdom meets at the river where a quaint little Georgian village made of stone houses with low resting roofs and chimneys sits. The succulent green grass winds around them, hugging flowerbeds and pens for farm animals.

A few common folk stand by the water where a lady in a long brown dress is bathing a child. Her skirts are tied at her waist and she wipes her hands on her apron donned over her top when she spots us. Her hair tumbles down her body, unlike the Georgian updos I had expected to see. I suppose they've had centuries to adapt to it.

Her naked babe wades out of the river, joining a group of other ladies with children of their own. Each commoner wears simple skirts or flowing cotton pants—different to the tight-fighting clothes of the military—and have varying shades of brown hair. All from different races and ethnicities. They have all descended from either the pale skinned Argenti, or from the Elders who discovered the planet centuries ago. It occurs to me with a jolt that I have no idea how the Elders could look like—they aren't Argenti, they could walk among and blend in to this crowd without me being any wiser.

My fingers wrap around the edge of the boat, the wooden railing cutting into my palms. I can hardly breathe as Jesse comes closer to me, his presence a soft warmth as we take in the world before us.

"It feels dangerous, to build the Kingdom near a volcano," I murmur.

"It's regulated by a power plant, and they have machinery tracking the volcano so we will get ample warning if it ever explodes.

Besides, we need the volcano, it's vital to power the Dome," Jesse says.

I scan the translucent surface above our heads, stretching so far I cannot make out the end of it. I wonder where the palace is—the towering spires I know the Elders reside in.

The boat rocks as a soft current drags us gently down the shore away from the Umbran women and children. There are multiple docks along the shore, some large and others small, all dotted with wooden boats of various shapes.

Lily directs us to one farther down the shore, away from onlookers.

"Is this where you lived when you were younger?" I ask quietly, turning to face Jesse. He's already watching me and I realise he hasn't been looking at the Silver Kingdom at all.

Static bounces between us and suddenly I'm all too aware of his knee brushing the back of my thigh.

"No, my family were military."

My hands fall free from the railing, whispering by his as the water sways and the impact makes me rock against his chest. I swallow, my eyes roaming over him. His gaze clashes into mine and we hold still, my nerves screaming as I drown inside his blue eyes.

Lily clears her throat aggressively.

"So, when you guys are done making eyes at each other, let me know where you wish to stay in this god forsaken place."

Jesse immediately pulls away and I suck in a breath, my eyes blurring as I take in Lily's form before me. Wisps of hair stroke her cheeks as the warm summer air manufactured from under the Dome brushes against us.

"I hadn't thought about accommodation," I admit.

"Don't go expecting a holiday inn, my lady. Anyone who comes and goes from Umbra has family to stay with, or their own house."

"Do you? Have a house I mean."

Her mouth twists up in the corners, just as the boat gently taps a dock and makes us sway in our seats. She moves her braid over her shoulder and tries not to laugh.

"Do I look like I own a house in the Silver Kingdom?"

With her animal furs and faded cotton, she looks more like a cat than she does an Umbran.

I sigh. "It's fine. I doubt we will get much time for sleep."

A small school of fish swim around the orange reeds under the surface of the river as Lily bounces up and secures the boat to the cleat.

"Remind me, what *exactly* are you planning?"

I don't miss the sarcasm in her tone, nor the civilians keeping a close eye on us by the shore. Both make my skin tickle.

"If we can find dissenters among the commoners, that would be ideal. We'll need them to take on the Elders."

My words are so low they're almost swallowed by the breeze. The wind isn't as harsh this side of the Dome, but it still dances in my ears.

I feel Jesse's eyes boring into my back, as if he suspects that I'm relying on him for this job. I fully intend on tracking down the Elder that brought Jasmine to Terra many years ago. He's my key into the Kingdom. I fix a strained smile on my face, but Lily buys it, smiling back.

"Yeah, I might know of a few," she says quietly.

I roll my shoulders, pulling myself out of the boat and onto the Umbran shore. The dock is a lot grander than the other, the wood a soft, reddish brown.

The beach before us is eerily silent and nerves tingle down my spine as I turn, helping the others from the boat. I was wrong before—no one is watching us anymore. The beach is empty, but the sensation of being watched lingers.

"We need to go," I whisper, turning back to them.

Jesse doesn't ask why, but his new blade is already in hand at the sight of my agitation.

"What is it?" Lily asks, clambering onto the wooden planking.

I swallow deeply. I don't know how to answer that.

Jesse jumps by me and grabs my elbow, pulling me down the dock towards the beach. Towards shelter.

"Marcellus?" I ask, so quietly only he can hear.

"Wouldn't have caught up with us yet, unless he found a Hover and rode it through the storm," Jesse mutters back.

We clear the beach, sand tracking up under our feet, and I duck under a low hanging branch. My instincts warn me to flatten myself against the tree, but Jesse pulls me towards the sprawl of houses. They arch into the landscape, stone meeting grass as flowers and vines crawl up their bodies.

Smoke wafts from several chimneys, but it's the eyes peering out of windows that make my heart skip a beat. Every single soul watches us as we dash past.

"I don't like this," I gasp between breaths.

Jesse grunts his agreement.

I'm not sure if Lily follows us. I would bet my life on it that she doesn't.

I groan.

Jesse spins me around a small home, hiding us among a smattering of wildflowers at its rear. I plaster my head back against the wall and attempt to calm my laboured breaths as Jesse slips his hand into my pocket and hands me my switchblade. I pop it open into my hand, hiding it up my sleeve.

Suddenly, Jesse freezes beside me.

The world is utterly quiet but nothing can mistake the distant words breaching the buildings from afar.

My heart stills and goes cold as ice.

"Come out, come out, little mouse!"

And just as he says it, a message pings through my comm from Melanie.

MELANIE

I stumble down a path from the warehouse, my body shaking, unable to breathe.

I broke through the Umbran firewall today. Twice.

I gained full access to Umbran security. Twice.

Mason Shaw is slightly unhinged, his plan an unruly mess, but I will give him one thing: the idea to focus our cyber efforts on Umbra was ingenious.

"They know," I say softly to myself, tripping over a branch. "They know."

I ran outside the moment I lost connection to Umbra, scrambling for my comm.

The Elders know Savannah is on Umbra.

I lower my head into my palms. The Elders know they're,

gleaned from footage of Jesse and Savannah's ship crashing into the desert.

Old footage they have likely watched and speculated over a hundred times by now. The Elders will be chasing them. Could already have them. Could be *torturing* or killing them.

And I'm still stuck on Terra.

I don't stop walking until I splash into the river, freezing water pushing against my legs.

Teeth chattering, I hold my finger down onto the comm, my fingers trembling so much that I nearly drop it. Voice rough, I speak into the device, "the Elders have found you, they saw your crash and have been tracking you since—they have cameras hiding in trees, following your movements, be careful and try and blend in as much as you can."

My finger lifts from the button.

Unable to hold it any longer, I let the comm drown in the river. It won't die from water damage—I made sure to make them resilient—but it feels good to suffocate it right now.

Savannah asked me to make the comms for emergencies, just in case it gets tracked, which is unlikely, but a possibility.

But that doesn't matter now, considering they already know Savannah's whereabouts. We haven't had a single Umbran come to the Island's base since the bombs, which means we are much more safe.

And besides, I'm beyond caring about my safety.

We're building an army, if they come for us here, we can fight them.

I dare them to track my message.

Slowly, I sink below the water gushing at my feet. I don't realise Elijah is near me until he pulls my head up from the stream.

I splutter, teeth chattering, eyes wildly taking him in.

Elijah's hand strokes through my hair and I wilt ever so slightly. I haven't bathed in days. Haven't had a proper sleep in weeks.

I don't let him pull me out of the water, relishing the way the cold clears my head, pushing away all my panicked thoughts.

The water eases unholy scents from my skin, reminding me of the neglect I've surrendered onto my body. He stands above me, fully outfitted in Umbran clothes. A brown linen shirt covers his torso, the pants—rolled up to his knees—held in place by a leather belt equipped with a knife.

One of the Umbrans gave that knife to him. They've begun scouting for old weapons in the wreckage on the base, handing them out among their people. Even the clothes on Elijah's back came from one of them.

My teeth chatter, lips feeling frozen as I attempt to speak or move, but nothing comes out except a forced sob. One long sob. Nothing more.

Elijah finally pulls me from the water, and this time I let him, his hands circling my back as he holds me to his chest. My wet hair matts under his chin, my breaths coming long and sharp.

I reel back my tears, forcing the biting pain out of my eyelids by rubbing them clean with his shirt. He smells of pines and home, the ocean scent of the warehouse mingled in his pores. I breathe deeply, trying to patch over the building crescendo of fear in my chest. Normally, I wouldn't panic this way, but I'm just so damn tired.

Stars.

I sink against him, a heaviness clouding my body that never quite seems to go away these days.

"One more minute," Elijah says into my hair.

The husky sound of his voice brings me back to reality. I blink, each movement feeling raw and red against my eyelids. Around us, the trees are singing in the wind, the ocean churning in the distance. And, warm and smiling and still holding me, is Elijah Brooke.

Home. This feels like home.

The bird calls around the Silver Kingdom, the soft fountain

bubbling out the front of our manor house, the smell of apple trees, the warm tang of summer air.

Happy, peaceful, and full of unyielding love. It's like a vacant whisper, but it's not this place. Not this planet.

I let the sunshine of Elijah's heart win over the darkness in my soul and drink in his smile like it's a drug. It sobers me, refocusing my mind.

Either I get to Umbra and help my friends, or I die trying from Terra.

We've made a connection to them now. We have a way to worm in. There must be something else I can do.

"Ten seconds. Maybe less."

"What?" I breathe, squinting against the bright daylight to focus on Elijah's mouth.

"Until Mason comes down here."

I have to compose myself. I can't explain why I'm fully clothed and saturated, but I don my courtier mask and take a deep breath. On shaking legs, I walk back to the water and fetch my comm from where it's lodged itself between some stones on the bottom of the water.

And sure enough, Mason ambles down to the stream. His curls are mussed from stroking them—stress, no doubt. He also wears Umbran clothes, but they make him look more foreign than they do on Elijah.

A girl follows behind him, a hand to her chest as if she's chasing a stitch. Her red hair is like a flame, burning in the sunlight.

"Alexis, it's okay. Please." Mason softens his eyes as he turns to the girl, supple skin twisting as he gives her a deep look.

She crosses her arms, tightens her mouth and stays put.

I smirk, immediately liking her for it.

Her brown eyes glimmer as she lifts them to me, seeing my expression. I raise an eyebrow at her.

"You're wet," she observes.

"An astute observation," Elijah provokes. He crosses his arms besides me and the two appear to stand off.

Surely they must know each other. I take a step towards Mason, whose imploring eyes roam my wet clothing.

"Melanie, I—"

"I'm going to make the connection to Umbra again," I interrupt, storming up the bank. Umbran techs discovered me and pushed me out of the system. They know I'm prying around their defences now, but it won't be difficult to override them. Not for me.

Mason whirls as I pass him, chasing me through the trees. "Your system is on default, still searching for holes."

I fiddle with the glove on my left hand. "I can do it better manually."

The hairs on my arms raise as the wind kisses my wet skin. I reel in my shiver as I beeline for the warehouse. Ideas are already ticking through my mind—new ways to worm myself past their defences.

They know someone is weaselling around.

My father used to aid the techs charged with security. Upon his death, his employer must have promoted one of his trainees. Handy for me, as I know how they work.

My system is currently searching for gaps in their network, but they are too small and too many. I can worm my way around better than any AI can.

Mason grabs my right elbow, yanking me back. I gasp, feet slipping on the wet ground.

His stormy blue eyes appear urgent and imploring as he practically glares at me. It gives me pause for a moment, unused to seeing such a determined look on his face. I took him as a sweet, unsuspecting boy, but he continues to surprise me every day.

"Eli spoke to Dad yesterday. He's worried about how tired you're getting. You're getting chaotic. You need sleep—"

"I'm fine." I yank my arm back from him, regaining my feet and spinning back towards the entrance to the warehouse.

"I wasn't finished," Mason says.

I stop and release a breath as my hand brushes the wall of the warehouse. Slowly, I spin and face him, lifting my eyebrows at him to continue.

"Show me the basics of what you do so you can sleep. When you wake up you can take over from me again. That way we will have someone working around the clock to help Savannah and Jesse."

It takes a moment to process his words. I feel a crease form between my eyes as I glance at him. His hands are knotted in front of him, thumbs twiddling.

He really wants this, I realise.

He swallows. "I want to do what you do. I want to help."

I pick at the edge of my glove, beginning to shiver as the wind batters me. "It took me years to learn what I know," I say plainly.

"We have time."

"No." I take a step towards him. "We don't."

His chest rises and falls quickly, a breath away from me now. His expressions twist, then his eyes seem to dull, losing that sharp edge.

Elijah and Alexis emerge from the treeline at that moment. Both look sheepish, as if they were both in on Mason's intentions. The boy watches me with anticipation and hope, leaning forwards like he's about to either hug me or run away.

I manage a sigh and some of the anxiety lifts from my chest as I nod at him. "Okay, I'll show you the basics until nightfall. When I wake, you can watch me work."

"Thank you." His face brightens, his shoulders elevating. "Thanks, Melanie."

"Don't thank me yet, you have a lot of work ahead of you."

He nods quickly, swinging his arms as he follows me into the warehouse. I don't think I've ever seen Mason as happy as he looks right now—not even when he was with his sister.

The thought sits with me for the rest of the afternoon.

SAVANNAH

"*Stars*," I curse. "The Argenti. He must have had backup in the desert."

Jesse swallows sharply, his eyes unfocused.

I shakily place my comm back into my pocket, my breathing uneven. Melanie's static voice still spins around the small space between us.

The Elders have found you, they saw your crash and have been tracking you since—they have cameras hiding in trees, following your movements, be careful and try and blend in as much as you can.

For Melanie to have risk sending that, to risk alerting the Elders of her position on Terra, our situation must be bad. Really, really bad.

My chest shudders, but I can't find it in myself to respond to her.

Melanie will be okay, she knows what she is doing.

We have our own problems to deal with.

"It was idealistic to think he'd be stranded after we stole his Hover, there would've been other trackers chasing us down that he met up with," Jesse muses.

"We don't know that," I gasp. "But we do know that we're not safe in the Kingdom."

The Elders know about us and have been sending out trackers after us this whole time, and not only that, but tracking all of our movements via CCTV. My heart plummets.

"How else would he have caught up?" Jesse asks.

He tightens his hand around his knife as he watches me. His mouth opens and closes, as if he is lost for words.

The only thing we can do right now is hide or run, but neither option will help me rally the people to our cause. We have a job to do and it's not hiding in the shadows.

"I wish I knew how many trees have cameras in them," Jesse manages, his teeth gritted.

A tree groans above us, as if in answer. I sink further to the ground, nearly flat against the wildflowers.

Jesse's brows scrunch together as he watches me, his mind working through the problem. My own stretches for a solution and I give up, dropping my hands with my switchblade into my lap.

"Can you use your Silver Magic?" Jesse asks.

I chew on my lip.

"You have *Magic*?" a female voice screeches.

My heart shudders and I knock my head back against the wall of the house. Even Jesse flinches, nearly dropping his knife.

Above us, Lily is perched in the tree, making the wood groan in the wind. The tree is small but wildly green, almost entirely obscuring her.

"You're still here?" I ask, gasping.

My heart misses a beat, just as I sense movement in the house behind us. Footsteps shuffle around, voices whispering.

I brush my sweaty hands down my pants, hands shaking.

Lily continues to watch me, her head tilted.

She doesn't answer me.

But her eyes dart away from me, as if realising for the first time that she *should* have fled.

"Where did you come from?" Jesse spits.

"I'm a good climber, little brother."

"We need to go," I whisper, rising off the grass.

The people in the house stir closer to our window. Lily senses my irritation and attempts a shaky smile, then dissolves back into the branches.

With a shudder, I turn to Jesse. "Want to climb a tree?"

He frowns at me. "Absolutely not."

"Scared of the cameras?" I tease.

"Scared of slipping and falling on my face," he responds.

I don't even have the energy in me to laugh.

I continue to wipe my clammy hands down my pants, trying to get the dirt off them.

"Then let's try not to get caught on foot," I say, ducking my head under the window and making a run for the next home.

I don't turn to make sure he's following, too focused on trying not to be heard as I dance across the lush grass, feet slipping on the loose soil underneath.

The civilians have trampled most of the grass, but I keep off the main footpath, heading uphill.

The next house is smaller than the last, the stone brighter under the reflection of the sun. I flatten my back to the wall, facing the trees away from the village and attempt to collect my breath.

I can't hear Marcellus anymore, but that doesn't mean he isn't near. Not to mention the fact that we are on his home turf and he could have a million sentries pouring down from the Kingdom to find us.

"Maybe you're right," I tell Jesse as he ducks under a low garden awning and flattens himself by the wall next to me. Vegetables sprawl around our feet and I try not to stand on the tomato bush by my right.

"I tend to be. But about what this time?" he asks, hardly out of breath. He steadies himself next to me, voice whispering on the wind.

My body isn't accustomed to the long days and physical strain, and it hurts my ego as I struggle to breathe evenly. "If Marcellus says I have Silver Magic, it wouldn't hurt to try? I just don't know..."

"How to do it?"

"Pretty much."

Nausea bubbles in my stomach and I slouch against the wall as a chorus of sounds gradually rise in volume. Villagers. And Marcellus.

I attempt to banish the worry from my mind, but it feels as if I've chugged many cups of coffee, my body tingling in flighty anticipation, itching and shaking.

I close my eyes, breathing in the scents of wildflowers and baking bread around me. I try and pluck at the root of my soul, searching for any scraps that might resemble a tingle of Silver Magic, but all I find is nerves, making the hairs on my arms stand on end.

At some point, my hands wrap around my small blade, popping it open and closed as I struggle.

"Either he sapped me dry, or he was lying," I spurt. Loudly.

Jesse slaps a dirty hand over my mouth as a group of villagers wander down the street near us. I frown, but he holds it there as he leans around the corner.

I breathe heavily, casing his hand in my wet breath, and he frowns at me.

"Your hand is *dirty*."

His hand drops to his side and he pulls me to him. "Do you see Lily?"

I flatten my gaze, giving him an exasperated look. "My eyes were closed. How could I have seen her?"

"I don't know where she went," he mutters, pulling back from me and leaning around the corner. I let out a heavy breath, accidentally stepping on the tomato bush and squashing a fruit. "I know a friend from way back who lives near the beach. If we go to his house, he *might* hide us."

Jesse's words tumble around my head, and I think them over. "Might?"

"A strong emphasis on the might. I killed someone he liked."

"Jesse," I sigh.

He shrugs. "We need allies, and he's the best ally you'll get. He's incredible and he knows the Kingdom. Knows its people. It might be a long shot, but we can try."

His eyes are bright and full of restless anticipation. Jesse, restless. Who would've thought?

I snicker. "Got a crush on him?"

He shrugs. "Only a little."

I snort and then gesture in front of me. *Lead the way, it's not like I have any better ideas.*

He surges forward and slips his hand into mine, gently ushering me along. My skin heats at the gesture, the hairs rising on my arms at the casual familiarity.

The trees sway around us, brushing in the breeze, and my mind drifts towards Silver Valley as we quietly slink through the village.

My heart is a heavy weight in my chest as I picture my family walking among these streets and living in this beautiful village. Mason's awe would be never-ending and my father would take in every facet of the environment.

My gaze snags upon a house made of brick, the white stone

melting into the brown earth. My heart shudders. In a grander life, this would be my home.

Instead, I spent my childhood squatting inside a small apartment, pointing out the stars outside my window to my brother, who always longed to be where I stand.

My boots sink into the sidewalk, the rich soil moulding into a footpath.

I remind myself that the village is based on beings who spent their days of origin as Georgians on Terra—people used to glamour and death going hand in hand. But this world... it's too beautiful for death.

"There's a mob ahead," Jesse says.

"A mob? Wow."

Jesse's eyebrows lower as he casts a quick look behind him, not missing a step. "Wow?"

I grin. "We raised a mob."

"You sound happy about it."

"How many people can claim to have raised a mob over them?"

"Well, you can't. Because Marcellus raised that mob."

"Don't burst my bubble."

He gives me a pointed look. Rolling my eyes, I grin at him.

I begin to make out their voices. The mob. The anger.

We head towards them with no intention of stopping. My freaking heart is a chorus in my ears with every step.

"Not much farther, I promise. I swear he lived around here," Jesse says between breaths.

The ground is slightly crusted with sand, wildflowers squashing under our feet in a way that makes me wince. There are hundreds of them, all popping up around the village in a way that's almost unnatural. The heady scent of salt and florals battles down my throat as I pant for air. Squat little homes peak out from the landscape, each as inviting as the next.

Jesse slows as we near a portion of closely-packed, ancient

houses, most of them adorned in flowers and vegetables, made of slated stone and too small for a larger family to inhabit. He aims for one in the middle, the dust underfoot merging into stone as he wanders towards the entry.

Sweat clings on his brow and he hisses through his teeth as he tries to school his breathing. We lost Lily somewhere in the trees, so it's just the two of us now. I give him some space as he lifts his hand to knock on the door, then hesitates.

I'm about to ask what's wrong, but then he pulls himself together and knocks quietly, so as not to alert the houses surrounding us.

Sounds scuffle from within, followed by a quick conversation muffled by the thick stones.

Jesse holds his breath as the door gently creaks open. I try and plaster on a smile, but it's hard to put on a chirpy disposition when the distant sounds of the mob echoes down the streets.

"Hayes," the man before us says.

His eyes are amber and his olive skin is pocked with burn marks. The glare he gives us rages like fire, too. His thin lips roll into a sneer, the Umbran cottons on his body fluttering in the wind as he stares down at us.

"Get off my doorstep."

A muscle in Jesse's jaw twitches. "Hi, Tam."

"In case I wasn't clear—get the hell off my doorstep."

I attempt to step forwards, my mouth popping open, but Jesse holds his hand back and stops me. "We need a place to stay. One night. Then we'll be out of your hair."

"And why the hell would I do that for you, Hayes?"

Behind him, an elder lady holds onto the wall, her eyes sinking into Tam's back, her gaze as strong and steady as a lion's. Her pale shawl hides most of her face, but wisps of greying hair brush her chin, looping in gentle curls. The silver hairs trickled through the black give her an air of wisdom, rather than making her appear old.

She could almost pass as an Argenti, if it wasn't for the time she must have spent on Terra. I wave to her and her strong eyes immediately latch onto mine.

"Your grandmother's been to Terra?" I say to the man, breaking the showdown between him and Jesse. Tam startles, his eyes narrowing as he looks at me.

That was probably a rude assumption to make.

"My *daughter* has been through a great deal," he corrects. "Who the hell are you?"

Fighting the rising nausea cresting up my chest, I shoot him a smile.

Screw it. There's only one way this man might let us through his door.

"I'm the future queen of Umbra. Nice to meet you, Tam."

SAVANNAH

"Savannah Shaw?" Lucille gasps. "Father, your contacts have been asking about her."

"Yeah, hell no. Not a chance. I'm not doing this," he responds, wide as he takes me in. Tam goes to close the door, but Jesse shoves his knife into it, stopping it from clicking shut.

"Hayes, I swear on the stars, if you bring your mess back into my house, I'm turning both of you in."

"One night just to ride out the mob, then we'll be out of your hair."

Your contacts have been asking about her.

I pick at the edges of my thumb, hands slightly shaking.

These people could be the link we need. The way to form an army.

"Please," I say softly.

Tam tackles the door, trying to close it, but Jesse swings it open and shoves his way into the house. Tam's daughter takes a step back, shaking, and the shawl falls from her face.

While Tam doesn't look a day over 25, this woman looks like she is approaching 70. Her hair is elegantly styled in an updo, the clothes she wears hugging her frame with careful precision. A soft blush highlights her cheeks, but her amber eyes look dull and lines crease between her brow, marking her old age.

Tam's daughter.

She watches as her father unhands Jesse and slams him into the wall, locking his arms behind his back and jamming his knife under his throat.

Jesse squirms in his grip, trying to get me in sight, but he isn't quite strong enough. Blood roars in my ears and I take a step back from the door.

"You responsible for the mob?" Tam asks Jesse.

"Nah," he grunts. "She is."

Both their eyes flash to me. I wave.

Tam's daughter hobbles towards me and fixes her eyes on my face, my hair, my eyes.

"Let him go, Father. They just need a place to sleep. We don't have to tell your people about this, either. We can just cater for them for one night, in and out."

"Over my dead body."

Jesse moans as Tam throws him out of the door. I sidestep to avoid getting knocked out and trot into their lettuce patch.

"You have an army for us, Lucille?" Jesse coos, his tone gentle.

She smiles at him, but doesn't say anything.

Jesse grins, wiping his forehead. "Nice to finally meet you, sweetheart. You make ageing look good."

Lucille swallows, her throat bobbing. She doesn't say anything, but her gaze is strong enough to make me shiver.

"I'm surprised you made it back from Terra," Jesse says. "Who helped you?"

"Absolutely not," Tam repeats, then goes to slam the door. This time, Lucille is in the way.

"Come inside, Jesse. It's too loud outside." Her voice is as gentle as the buzzing bees fluttering around their garden, but there is a bite to it that leaves little room for argument.

Her father tries anyway. "No—"

"It's fine, Father. It might be nice for Amadea to have some more people listening to her music, too."

Jesse's face remains blank, but it's the lack of reaction that tells me he has no idea who this Amadea is. The sound of the mob draws nearer, so neither of us hesitates when Lucille opens the door for us.

Tam mutters to himself as I step into the foyer, holding my breath. The place looks similar to the house we crashed in outside of the Dome, but clean and modern, with hints of tech peeping around the corners. A sheet of glass is standing upright along the kitchen bench displaying a high-definition video of the mob out in the village and the sound of humming fills the space, coming from an appliance I cannot see.

Far down the hall, a singing voice is playing from some speakers and, as we enter the kitchen, a gentle piano begins to accompany it.

"That's Dea. I'm a youth carer for the Elders and Amadea sometimes visits me at my home. She has a beautiful voice. I cook her dinner and she sings for me. It reminds me of a singer I met on Terra," Lucille mutters, as if trying to excuse the sound, worried it is annoying us.

It isn't.

My chest lightens at the sound of it, easing the nerves I hadn't realised were tapping through my body. At some point, I tuck away my switchblade and sigh.

"The stain of seeing you in my house unnerves me, Hayes," Tam says, quietly seething. His fingers wrap around an amber-filled bottle in the kitchen and he swigs directly from it. His hooded eyes are narrowed on Jesse, muscles twitching. The burn scars on his face don't move, but the rest of his face does.

"It's Lucille's choice," Jesse counters, coming up to him and wrestling the bottle from Tam's grip. He holds on tight, knuckles white under his skin, but the man is visibly sweating and the bottle slips from his grip.

Jesse's eyebrows quirk as he drinks victoriously.

Lucille takes a deep breath, her lip thinning as she turns to face me. Softly, she explains to me, "My father was best friends with Jesse's grandfather, until I had an on-going affair with his son, Jeremy—Jesse's father. I didn't know Jer was engaged until it was too late, then one night we got caught and I was sent to Terra."

I swallow deeply.

"Stars, Lucille," Tam grouses, reaching back for the bottle in Jesse's grasp.

"And to answer your question, Jesse, I was never sent to the Safe Holds." Her lashes flutter as she turns her gaze from me, dropping them to the wall behind us, as if she can't quite bring herself to look into Jesse's eyes. "I was sent to the base in Africa, where they hadn't built a Dome for us yet. As you can see, I did okay." She offers a strained smile, but her chin remains high. "It took many years until I found a shuttle that could take me home—at which point Jeremy was already dead. And then Jeremy's son killed his mentor to hitch a ride to Silver Island."

I cough. "Jesse did *what?*"

"Killed his mentor to hitch a ride to the Silver Island," Tam repeats, staring at Jesse blankly as he pours himself a tall glass of whiskey.

I watch Jesse inhale softly, his eyes focused on the glass screen on the kitchen table, the rowdy crowd at odds with the tranquil music drifting down the hall. "He didn't give up. He kept trying to stop me, but I was..." A slight tremor shocks his face before he continues. "I really needed to leave."

"Carter was a good guy," Tam says with deadly quiet. "He was my friend. Your father's friend."

"I *know* that, Tamaz."

Without warning, Tam smashes the whiskey bottle into the side of Jesse's head, spraying amber liquid all throughout the kitchen.

My breath lodges in my throat. It takes me a second to move.

The switchblade slides back into my hand as I leap towards the kitchen, blinking as Jesse loses consciousness and collapses onto the hard floor. I've never seen someone beat Jesse so easily and it makes me hesitate a moment more. Jesse isn't himself—being back on Umbra is affecting him. Or, stars forbid, the man before me is better than Jesse.

Tam shakes his hands, flicking the liquid off.

"Damn it, Father!" Lucille cries. "This mess!"

I stare him down, but Tam takes one look at me and laughs. "Give it up, little queen. He'll come around."

I blink.

Jesse is sprawled on the floor, shards of glass sprayed around his body like the exploded moon in the sky above us. I swallow deeply, unsure what to do.

I can't access my supposed Silver Magic, I can't beat this man in combat and goddamn Marcellus is sniffing around for me outside.

Lucille gets to her knees, not once batting an eye at Jesse as she plucks the glass from around his head.

Down the hall, the music has stopped.

Tam grunts, swinging around and plunging his hands into a basin of water to the side of the kitchen. He lifts a rag, dragging it down his fingers, watching me carefully as he does so.

On the glass screen, I recognise the homes we were at earlier. Many feet are now stamping down vegetable gardens as they track us. Marcellus isn't visible, but several people appear to be Argenti— or at the very least, have strong Argenti genes. One girl with a long silver braid crouches where I sat by the tomato bush.

"The talk on the street is that the Terran girl planned to land in the Silver Kingdom to assassinate all our Argenti, but the Elders hijacked your ship and crashed you into the desert. A team was dispatched to get you," Tam says in a flat, slightly accusatory voice.

My gut twists and words get stuck in my throat as I lift my eyes to his.

The piano music starts up again and Lucille clears her throat, head bowed low as she cleans up the glass.

"That girl playing music is Argenti," Tam continues, his eyes not once moving from my face.

Lucille freezes, her hand hovering over a large shard of glass.

"She plays beautifully," I say.

"Are you here to kill her?" Tam injects.

"No, why would I do that?"

There's no volume on the glass interface in the kitchen, but the sounds of the Argenti mob trickle through the house, filling the space outside.

Neither Lucille nor Tamaz answer me, so I swallow deeply and look down at Lucille's back. "If it weren't already clear to you, the Elders are lying," I say.

Slowly, Lucille continues her work of picking up the glass. Something in me believes the lady already knew this, but Tam doesn't budge. He crosses his arms, eyes baring into mine.

"I'm here to… I…" I clear my throat.

The past few months, my head has been lost to a haze of planning and revenge and, suddenly, every thought leaks from me. I was so certain that coming to Umbra would be simple, that people would see my face and instantly move from the Elders to my side.

My side. I don't even fully understand what that is. I just want a place to bring Mason. Somewhere my father will never work another day in his life and a place where I can be surrounded by warmth and trees and never have to smell the scent of blood again.

That has not been the case. Umbra, as Melanie had warned, is a mess.

"I just want a place to call home," I finally offer.

"And you'll achieve that by killing the people who help run this planet?" Tam snaps.

"I don't know what I've done to give you that impression."

Lucille suddenly straightens, throwing the shards of glass in a waste bucket with a resounding clink. "I, for one, believe you're exactly what this planet needs."

The sound of the crowd outside fills my ears and my nerves trace through my veins. Their windows are covered, but it feels as if Marcellus could walk into this house at any given moment.

Amongst the spiralling in my head, I push my luck. "And what do you think this planet needs?"

Lucille smiles. "Someone who will stop the fear and bloodshed."

The Argenti girl begins to sing again, at war with the crowd outside.

"Do you think I can do that, Lucille? Even now?" I ask, focusing back on the screen.

Her eyes twinkle. "I don't know, can you?"

With Melanie, yes. With a conscious Jesse, yes.

My eyes flutter closed for a moment and I breathe deeply, letting the music ease my rising fear. With my eyes closed, I can sense Tam staring at me, drilling a hole into my face, but it's Lucille's energy I succumb to the most. It feels the same as the music. Gentle. Trusting.

My veins feel like they've been injected with coffee. Stars, I miss coffee.

I open my eyes. "Can I meet her?"

The girl playing the piano misses a key, pauses, then starts over.

Tam says "No" the same time as Lucille says "Alright."

I raise an eyebrow and brush past Tam. He could probably catch me if he wanted to, but he doesn't.

A gentle euphoric energy sweeps through my body with each step I take towards her room, rampaging through my body like a gust of birds trailing a summer breeze. From the kitchen, I can sense Jesse mumbling my name, coming to, but I don't stop. I follow the energy, the lilt of the music, until my fingers brush a wooden door-frame down the back of the house.

The window in the room has been swung open, letting in the warm air. The cotton curtains flutter as if they are dancing to the music. The room looks like it's made of starlight, with a deep navy carpet underfoot, floating lights like fireflies drifting around the ceiling, and floor-to-ceiling drapes made of blue and silver lining the walls. The drapes are star maps—directions to travel the cosmos. My eyes find my mother's familiar heart and star constellations, then skip over to meet the piano in the centre of the room.

The girl doesn't stop her playing, but I know she senses I'm there. I lean against the doorframe, letting her finish her song.

Her milky hands are small and slender, and a constellation of orange freckles trail up her arm. Her white dress drapes down her seat to the carpet, at odds with the shock of ginger hair on her head.

Not a silver bone is in this girl's body, but I trust that she's an Argenti. I can feel it.

Her euphoria is magnetic, there's no other word for it.

Something stirs deep within me, igniting my nerves. I have no words for it, but it feels like I'm drowning on starlight, unable to breathe from the weight of it. The girl's presence makes my skin feel like it's glowing, my pulse shuddering, and I take another step forward without thinking.

It feels like magic.

The song comes to a soft close and her hands drift to her side, as gentle as a bird. "Our Magic is speaking like the music," she says after, as if in mourning as the sound vanishes, leaving only the shouts and stamping of the mob in its wake.

I blink. "Huh?"

She spins in her seat. She couldn't be more than seven and looks so… human.

Her smile is shy as her light brown eyes meet mine. She crosses her arms, short fingers twisting in her dress. How those small, young fingers can play so well is jarring.

"I'm not supposed to be talking to you," she says.

"Yeah, feels like that's the general take around here," I answer.

The euphoric feeling begins to leak from my bones and I back away.

Amadea tilts her head. "I don't think I'm happy to see you yet, either."

"Yet?"

We both look at each other and she blinks. Moisture buds in her brown eyes. "We'll pretend better next time we see each other," she says in the tone of a child hiding from her parents. Like she's playing the long game.

A game with me.

I dash back to the kitchen, one foot after the after, as a sense of fear sweeps back into my chest. I don't know why, but what Amadea said feels like a stone in my gut.

"Jesse," I say, coming to a halt in front of the man frantically sweeping his eyes across the kitchen for me. "I think we need to leave."

33

SAVANNAH

"She's just a child," Lucille says after I've voiced my concerns. "She's just here to use my piano."

Jesse pulls himself from the ground, rubbing at his jaw in mock anger. Honestly, if his role were reversed with Tam, he would've done the same thing.

Tam scoffs, but doesn't take his eyes off us.

"What she said suggests otherwise," I argue.

"What did she say?" Jesse enquires.

"I can't explain it..."

The mob moves on from outside, but the sounds still travel the village. I rub my eyes, fighting chills. The room feels tight and full of energy.

"You're an Argenti," Tam suddenly says.

I blink, struggling to pay attention over the roaring in my head. "Huh?"

"An Argenti," he confirms, eyes narrowing at me.

"Oh," Lucille utters, cocking her head.

"What?"

Tension strains my neck and I take a deep, painful breath. From the back of the house, I can feel eyes watching me.

Amadea stands in the hallway, chest plastered to the wall, eyes peering around the corner. Her vibrant red hair looks dull in the darkness, causing me to momentarily believe her hair is brown. But I blink and the light catches her hair to flames again.

Jesse brings his hand to his neck, rubbing under his ear, eyes flickering between everyone in the room.

The sky outside slowly bleeds into dusk. Vibrant orange cuts through the house, then starts to fade.

"Your mother is a mind reader. I have felt you messing with my head since you stepped foot into my house, so it figures," Tam says.

"You're swelling the electric pull around the house," Lucille offers after, like I'm supposed to understand any of that.

Amadea's lips brush into a knowing smile. Jesse's eyebrows tighten. And I turn and blink at Lucille.

"Excuse me, what?"

In the back of my mind, a memory resurfaces.

Melanie's uncle, Liaison Banks, staring at me in his sterile office.

Jesse comes up behind me and thumps a book in my arms. It has a brown cover and appears to be some sort of journal.

The handwritten script in the book looks extremely old.

It's dated from 1845. A journal entry from one of the original scientists.

It was this journal that taught me about the Argenti—silver-haired, silver-eyed beings who can perform wonders on Umbra. They were Umbra's salvation and the only thing standing against annihilation. They were—are—the offspring of Elders and Occupants.

My mother is one.

I shiver, and a paragraph from the journal flashes in my mind:

They can pick up the electric energies surrounding the core of the planet and manipulate it to their will.

"Not that I care," Tam remarks, moving about the kitchen with his drink in hand, "but if you get enough Argenti on your side, overruling the Elders might—with a strong emphasis on the *might*—be a piece of cake."

I take a deep breath, breathing in the pull of power. Raw, strong, and mouldable Magic crashes around the room.

Terra also has an energy of sorts—fate, coincidence, déjà vu, a higher power that humanity relies on in the form of religion or in other underground practises.

On Umbra, such a thing is even more real. More intense.

I cross my arms over my chest, reigning in the foreign feeling forking through my veins. "From what I can tell, the Argenti are just dangerous lap dogs."

"Which is just Sav's way of saying they're a lost cause," Jesse clarifies.

From behind us, I swear Amadea snorts at us. Tam raises his brows and takes a long pull of drink from what's left in his glass.

No one says anything. It's even quiet outside now, but Marcellus's proximity hangs over me like a shroud.

I wonder how much of my Silver Magic is still coursing through his veins—considering how mine feel like they're on fire, I'd wager not much. It seems to be returning.

But that doesn't matter. He knows I'm in the Silver Kingdom, which means I'm a sitting duck.

"I promised friends I would gather some semblance of an army," I say, so quietly the words feel as haunting as ghosts in the darkening kitchen. "I won't allow them to come here until it's safe and we have some sort of foundation in place."

"You want a way into the Silver Kingdom?" Amadea finally says from the hallway. The way she looks at me, it's almost like she's offering. Tempting me.

My fingers shake, but I hide it beneath my clothing before anyone notices. I don't go to her, but Lucille does.

"It's getting late. I should take you home before your brother murders me. Stars, help me," she says, throat bobbing as she crosses the kitchen, snatching a quill from the counter.

"You'll need the Elders and Argenti on your side to win," Amadea says, her chin slightly lifted.

"And then that will be the day I join you—the only way I'll join you—because then we'll have a chance," Tam's words bounce around us.

The colour drains from Amadea's face, but Lucille quickly snatches her focus.

If you get enough Argenti on your side, overruling the Elders might be a piece of cake.

"What if you promised to help me make that happen?" I urge.

"No promises, sugar. You don't get it yet—how it works here. Nothing is ever black and white. You aren't the only saviour that walked this planet and you won't be the last," he continues, eyes plastered to my face.

The whiskey begins to bleed colour into his cheeks, but he looks more composed than I've seen him so far. His eyes are hard, jaw set. Something cold travels down my neck, pinpricking my nerves. The high of the Silver Magic withers away.

"All I want is a place people can call home," I repeat, my voice weak.

"We're working on it," he rebuts.

"And I'm fighting for it," I argue.

He's closer to me than I'd like, but I'm too frozen to move.

Jesse's fingers tighten around the edge of the counter. I can basically see a vein pumping in his forehead. His eyes scream, *touch her and you die.*

Considering this man is two Jesses rolled into one, I don't like our odds.

The darkness leaves his eyes for a moment and he takes a small sip from his drink before responding. "Alright, then."

"Join me."

"Eventually," he slurs.

Lucille tugs on Amadea's hand, pulling her away, but the girl walks over to me. I don't know how to act when her small hand reaches for me. No one does except Lucille, who glares at Tam.

The way Amadea looks at me, her brown eyes wide, sends a hot tang of pain down my throat. Hopeful, happy, dreamer eyes, like Mason's.

"My family isn't all bad," she says and hands me a piece of paper.

I don't open it—I crunch it into my fist.

By the doorway, Lucille waits patiently, hands trembling. Amadea skips towards her, her arms swinging slightly before Lucille wraps her in a coat.

"Just promise me one thing, Your Highness," Lucille breathes.

My body stills at the words—once mocking on Jesse's tongue, but full of meaning as they now swirl around the room. I give a curt nod, unable to speak.

"Leave the children out of it." Then she pushes the door open, taking the child with her.

The kitchen feels cold, my hands aching too much to open the letter. So Jesse reaches over and does it for me, his movements assured.

I don't even glance at Tam when Jesse mutters, "Argenti names."

I immediately flick my eyes onto the paper in Jesse's grasp.

Evaline
Alexsandre

Roman

Celestine

Marcellus

And somewhere, deep within me, an inferno ricochets in my soul.

SAVANNAH

The next morning, we wake to Lily rapping on our window.

Lucille let us sleep in the room with the piano, on thin cots that hurt my back to rest on, and as I turn towards the window to ease a pain from my neck, Lily slaps a note against it, rapping the glass to get my attention. The note says one word: *stables*. One long, puzzled look with Jesse as his head lifts from his cot confirms that he has no idea how the girl found us.

We exchange a look, my heart pattering, as Lily dips away and runs from sight.

Jesse doesn't speak, but his eyes look decided. We're going to the stables.

With a long, steadying breath, I pull myself from bed.

Tam doesn't speak to us the entirety of the morning, he simply watches me with dark eyes over a cup of coffee, his posture stiff, but

Lucille is the epitome of sunshine as she sails around the kitchen. She brings us each a bowl of porridge that tastes like glue and a dark coffee that leaves me reeling. After an hour, we leave the small house with clean clothes from Lucille and a not-so-subtle threat from Tam to never come back.

I rub my forehead, head instinctively ducked as we depart the small house, Jesse shadowing me from behind.

The cotton dress cinching at my waist and flowing down to my feet is long and impractical, but it breathes against my skin like a summer breeze, covering my clean, raw-from-the-sun, skin.

"Wait!"

My body stills, freezing by the edge of the road, close enough to the entrance to another house that a hydrangea tickles my shin.

Lucille dashes down to meet us, her cheeks flushed. I can hardly breathe as she stops before me, hand over her heart. "One second," she urges, eyes imploring my face.

Jesse clears his throat, eyes scanning for threats around us, but the mob from yesterday is nowhere to be seen.

Lucille pushes a letter into Jesse's hand, her dainty fingers crunching his around it insistently. "An address. Meet us there tonight, and I'll convince my father."

I fiddle with the edge of my dress, holding my breath as I step forward and ask, "what for?"

"I can get a few people together to build your army," she whispers. Her eyes dart to the edge of the street, her lip breathing shallow, "just… try your best to arrive discreetly, my father won't come if there's a mob."

Jesse nods sharply, stuffing the letter into his pocket.

"We can do that," I breathe. "I promise."

Lucille ushes a soft smile, creasing the skin around her cheeks. With a gentle nod, she dips her head and makes haste back to her house.

Jesse releases a long, long breath.

My stomach flutters, and I wipe my sweaty palms down my new dress before turning back up the street. Maybe, hopefully, Lily has a plan to get rid of the mob.

And if not, I'll make one.

Without another word, we continue, our heads low as we navigate our way through the Kingdom.

I continue to fiddle with my dress, eyes darting around me.

The dress is beautiful, but it feels so exposing in comparison to the fighting clothes I've worn since we arrived.

My hair is pinned up, leaving a few loose strands tickling my skin. Jesse's eyes keep flashing over me before he looks shyly away.

Dressed like this, I feel like Melanie.

Or at least, how I imagine Melanie would have been when she lived on Umbra.

While the Elders originally came to Umbra during the 1700s and departed from the history and life they knew, they kept contact with Terra post-Moon Blitz in the 1800s. Many Umbrans travelled between the two planets, sometimes bringing families with them. As a result, their fashion blossomed into a hybrid of regency fashion and more practical daywear.

Corsets have long since been abandoned, but the dress still hugs my chest tightly, pressing around my curves. Thankfully, people don't wear those annoying silk or lace regency gloves, so my hands remain free to brush the flowers lining the path.

If it weren't for the comforting presence of my switchblade and Melanie's comm bouncing in the deep pockets of my dress, I'd look at myself and almost question whether I belonged to Terra at all.

Jesse was lucky enough to be given pants and a cotton shirt, but with the way my dress billows in the breeze, I can't help but enjoy my choice of clothing more. It feels magical and I choke back a ball of emotion each time I pass a reflective surface.

Lily's message told us to meet her by the outlying palace stables. I don't know where that is, but Jesse's jaw is tight as he heads towards it.

The homes we pass progressively become grander the closer we head to the centre of the Silver Kingdom. Trees line our path, but my eyes keep drifting to the skyline, aching for a view of the castle that sits on the mountain peak.

Jesse clears his throat, gripping my hand to help me sidestep a Hover. The ones near the Palace are green, blending into the foliage around us.

"How do they source the electricity to run them here?" I ask. A few options have been tickling in my mind—the sun, the river behind us, Silver Magic—but nothing seems quite powerful enough to maintain that and a Dome.

The Hover's slick body zooms past, causing a gust of wind to slap against my cheeks.

"The Palace was built on an active volcano," Jesse reminds me.

"A dangerous choice," I remind him in turn.

"It's just science, and if the science fails, we have the Argenti." Jesse's voice is sombre, as if remembering the list of names we were given last night.

I burnt the paper with a match not long after, but the names hover in my memory like a curse. Thoughts whirl around in my head, a plan attempting to form. Somehow, I need to divert the Argenti's attention away from us, long enough for us to meet up with Tam and his people later today.

Evaline, Alexsandre, Roman, Celestine, Marcellus.

I swallow against the dryness in my throat. Enemies or allies? No one gave any indication, or any hints at how to get that information.

"What can the Argenti do, if the science fails?" My voice wavers slightly. That sounds like using it as a weapon.

"They can do anything—they can protect us in the village," Jesse says with a furrow in his brow.

"Is that what they told you?"

Our eyes lock, unspoken words tumbling between us.

Power is an array of carefully selected words and guided actions, twisting and turning every single one of your intentions until it becomes a game. Planning a way to get to Umbra these past few months has shown me that, though I'm incredibly ill-versed in the matter—unlike the Elders.

"According to Mel—" Jesse begins, stopping at my raised brow. He tries again. "According to Mel, the Elders aren't inherently good or bad. Wielding power doesn't equal destruction. We aren't here to compete with them."

No one is ever good or bad, light or dark, but when the choices you make hurt others, you need to learn how to stop.

"Who ever thought you'd became an Elder sympathiser?" I tease.

"Melanie," he reiterates.

His stony gaze cuts into me and I laugh. My hands brush the comm in my pocket as we wander back onto the now empty road. Jesse doesn't know I have it, but his eyes drop to my fidgeting.

It takes us nearly an hour to cut through the village, tramping up the steady incline until the housing becomes sparser, the cottages transforming into manor homes and the Hovers zipping past us becoming more frequent.

Each time we pass an Argenti, static bubbles in my veins. Their energy hits me like a wave, each one feeling different, but no less powerful. Most of them notice me, but no one stops to talk, thank the stars.

A white manor glints in my eyes as I turn my gaze up to the top of the mountain, searching for the stone turrets that should appear above us any moment. Instead, my eyes catch onto a clear pool along the edge of the home. The turquoise water sits as still as a mirror, bordered by white rock. A gentle wave of steam floats along its surface, glistening in the heat. Hot springs.

I grasp Jesse's hand, leaning into him to sidestep another Hover. A muscle quivers in his hand, but he doesn't say anything. Eventually, even the manors fall away, leaving us to the forest.

Umbrans float past us, some on foot, others in Hovers. Some dressed in higher class garments, others in fighting clothes.

I hold my breath as a guard approaches us, turning my gaze to the trees bordering the path. He doesn't bother us.

Jesse squeezes my hand and that's when I notice the guard's weapon.

Not a sword but a gun of sorts.

Dread swarms in my gut. I don't look at it very long, but the image of it lingers in my mind. It's compact—all smooth edges and looping metals. It swings on the man's belt, reflecting the sunlight. On it, shinning in the sun, the Umbran symbol. I could recognise that U shape, sword slashing down into it, anywhere.

I'd bet on Mason's life that it's an S.P. gun.

The guard was no Argenti—none of them are—so the Elders must have fashioned a weapon to give them their own power.

I can't stop the quivering in my nerves and it takes every drop of concentration to focus on my breathing. Before long, we make it to a fork in the road and Jesse leads us down it and into the oncoming bustle. No one looks at me, but I feel so exposed.

My breathing hitches and sweat slides down my back. Jesse's fingers twitch momentarily as I try to drop his hand, but he lets me go.

The pathway is well worn. Puffs of dirt circle the air, but wildflowers and plush grass still stand off to the side, leading all the way up to the stables ahead of us.

It's a sturdy structure, made of the same dark wood as all the other houses, a garage made to hold Hovers, except it looks much like a refurbished horse stable. We approach it with our heads held high, but my mask slips when I puzzle over the odd structure.

People roam in and out of the building, some pulling their vehicles with them as they go. Everyone looks upper class.

"Stables?" I question, unsure what else to say.

On a breath, Jesse responds, "it used to be for horses back when the Kingdom was formed, but we use Hovers now."

I chew on my lip, eyes raking the tall wooden pillars, leaves hissing against it as the tall trees around the stables sway in the breeze.

I'm about to enter the large threshold when someone brushes my elbow and yanks me. The breath leaves my lungs as I'm whisked to the side, pulled into a dark canopy next to the stables.

Heart hammering in my throat, I blink and stand face to face with Lily.

A satisfied little smile sits on her face, so at odds with the streaks of mud staining her cheeks. She does nothing to brush the clumped hair out of her face before she shoves some brown paper into my hands.

"Took you long enough," she says.

Jesse's boots are silent as he joins us beside the vehicle bay, his jaw clenched and eyes flat.

I unfold the paper Lily gave me, quickly scan its contents, then give a curt nod. After the list of names Amadea gave me, I'm unsure how to proceed with my original plans. My stomach churns, threatening to bring up my breakfast.

"What is that?" Jesse asks.

Lily raises her eyebrows in amusement.

"A list of her friend's names, and locations," I say, eyes focused on a crowd of people busy with loading themselves into a dirt-brown Hover.

"I'm going home and won't be back until everything dies down." Her face is hard, words steady. Her cheeks are red, hair twisted and untamed.

Neither of us ask why she is covered in mud, but we both give her a withering look. I stare at her thoughtfully.

"Jesse knows an old guard, we're meeting with him tonight, along with his people," I say simply, "would it be rude to ask your friends to join?"

Lily shrugs, her eyes half on us, and half on the people coming and going from the stables.

I hand the paper to Jesse, but he doesn't open it.

"How about the mob?" Jesse's words hang between us.

"It's died down," Lily breaths, "but the Argenti tracking you has friends all over the Kingdom, all over the desert, and perhaps everywhere else, too. You won't get far while they are all on your trail."

Lily leans back against the stables, picking dirt from under her nails.

She needs a bath, but I'm too agitated and full of energy to care.

I already know what I came here to do.

There's only one thing I can do.

Amadea's list of names sits heavy in my mind. It's the only thing I have no answer for—no plan. Everything else, while a risk, has an ultimate outcome.

Her list can mean anything. I itch to unearth it from my pocket and ask Lily who these people are, but I don't, because I already know one person on the list. And whether he is a friend or a foe, I can count on him to draw in the Argenti.

Marcellus.

"We need someone to distract the Argenti tonight," I whisper, "so that this meeting can take place."

"Huh?" Lily mumbles, pushing herself off the stables.

"What do you mean by that?" Jesse whips his head to me, his blue eyes searing. He doesn't say it, but a part of him knows exactly what I mean.

Lily blinks, her breathing growing rapid as she attempts to put her thoughts together, "If you want me to distract them, then no. I have nothing to protect me."

"How about your darling wittle kittens?" Jesse mocks, his eyes glinting as he rubs her head.

"My kittens will tear your throat out if you don't watch it."

"Is that a bet?"

"It's a threat."

"You're adorable," he says, hand touching his heart.

"Will you both just shut up?" I inject.

"Bully," she spits at him.

"Loser," he says back.

"Guys!" I shout.

A group of Umbrans turn and face us. I lift my hand, mouthing apologies. They frown but turn away, already forgetting us.

Lily snorts from behind me and Jesse elbows her.

I bite my bottom lip, reeling in my heart. The familiar presence of Jesse dances over my skin as he peels away from his sister, blocking me from onlookers.

"There's only one certain way to get every single Argenti off our trail," I say helplessly.

Jesse furrows his brows, his lips opening and closing. Instinctively, he takes a step closer to me. I control my breathing, struggling to meet his gaze.

They both stare at me, and my mind whirs. I list ideas in my mind, but each one has a fault, a possibility of capture. We need the meeting tonight to happen, no matter what.

And I can't be there to witness it.

Not unless we have a way to fight off a whole squadron of Argenti.

Jesse's lip shakes as he struggles to compose himself, a weak mask dropping over his face as he stares at me. He knows my plan. He knows what I need to do.

But he can't bring himself to say the words out loud.

We've been standing here too long. To anyone passing, we could just look like a group of friends catching up, but the mud lining Lily's face looks suspicious and the way we all keep glancing over our shoulders...

"I'm going to announce myself to the Argenti." The words come out blunt but quiet.

Lily's mouth pops open, her face going white, as she connects the dots, "ahhh."

"You're not serious?" Jesse demands.

I look over at him slowly, hands shaking as I struggle to meet his eyes. "Marcellus won't stop until he has me. With me in his sights, he won't be looking to you guys."

"I can't form an army without my Queen," Jesse growls.

I swallow a knot in my throat.

"You were trained for this, Jesse."

I gasp as he pulls me to him. His arm twists around my waist, stronger than a steel band, pinning me to his torso.

I huff, fingers scraping over his arm. I don't have it in me to actually hurt him, but I pull all my strength into prying myself free.

"Let me go," I grumble. Then I stomp on his foot.

He grunts, but doesn't relent. His chest is warm, and the nerves flutter away as he tightens his grip on me. Always my protector. I stomp on his foot again.

"This is amusing," Lily comments, her face expressionless from where she still lounges against the stables. She doesn't side with Jesse, because she knows I'm right.

This is the only way.

I huff, flopping my arms to my side.

He repositions himself by wrapping his arms around my shoulders and pinning my arms to my side. I could get my switchblade from here, but it's not like I'd ever use it on him.

A soft breeze brushes past us, tickling my cheeks. Jesse's scent of fresh linen and metal flows over me, causing the skin on my arms to prickle. He feels so comforting—a familiarity in this harsh new world.

He doesn't release me when I stop fighting, which I expected. He doesn't trust me to not run.

"Let me go, please."

"No."

Lily scoffs. "Hilarious."

The only way to free myself from his hold is to convince him with words, but we don't have time for this. I need to find Marcellus. Now.

I twist a little more, my butt pressed right up against him as he squeezes me into his chest. I can feel every line of him branding into my body, claiming me from the rest of the world. It's almost enough to get me to stop fighting him. Almost.

Frustration mounts in my chest, heating my chest. "Jesse, I love you, but if I need to hurt you to do this, I will."

He releases me, his muscles suddenly taut but pliant at the same time.

I turn and face him. He doesn't say it back. Shock covers his beautiful features.

I love you.

"I…" He stumbles over the words.

I smile at him gently, not wanting to force a response out of him. I meant what I said, but I said it now to startle him. Apparently, it worked.

"I'll see you soon," I say. And I dip into the forest.

SAVANNAH

I release a rattling breath out of my lungs as I see him.

Marcellus, with Jesse's sword still strapped to his back. Venom twists in my gut, making my nerves itch. It only took a few hours to find him. The noisy bustle surrounding him helped, but a part of me just had an odd feeling.

Refusing to admit that it has anything to do with my untrained, unruly Argenti blood, I labelled it down to instinct. I feel like I *know* my enemy, in a way. He's unpredictable, but there's an odd pattern to it.

The ugly truth is that he likes to play games. Unpredictability, keeping your opponents on edge, making them feel trapped and in a state of constant fear and confusion… I swallow sharply. There's still a lot to learn about Marcellus, but every bit helps.

He sits out the front of someone's manor, his face stony and a glass of clear liquid in his hand. He doesn't drink it or engage in conversation. He just sits there.

People seem magnetically drawn to him. They whisper by his shoulder, talking to him. A lady with soft blonde hair and a dress that pushes her breasts sky-high parks herself on his lap.

He doesn't touch her, even as she smiles at him with red lips and gleaming white teeth. He hands her his drink, then promptly pushes her off his lap.

She stumbles onto the lawn, trying to save the liquid from sloshing over her. She brushes her hands down her skirts and struts over to where the Argenti put on an array of afternoon canapés. She pops what looks like salmon between her teeth and scans the crowd, making sure no one saw her rejection.

No one did but me.

I lower myself behind the hedges at the perimeter of the home, losing my spot where I can see between the leaves. After a beat, I peer back through the small hole and refocus on Marcellus.

I don't know what I expect to discover sitting here, but I watch anyway. I bide my time before announcing myself. Somehow, I need to give myself an edge, to keep the upper hand. Dirt rakes the front of my dress from where I kneel on the footpath, the sun beating down on the back of my neck. I'm not as dishevelled as I have been in the days prior to this, but I feel a lingering sense of disarray.

He sits stoically on his seat. People drift around him, chattering, laughing, slowly becoming drunken fools. I don't know who any of these people are or whether they are Elders or Argenti, but I'm surprised to see a few among them that don't have the classic Argenti white hair and skin.

A man with olive skin and thick, dark hair that spills down his back in a ponytail approaches Marcellus. They exchange a blank look until the man squints at him.

I'm too far away to tell if he has silver eyes, but I don't need to see them to know he comes from wealth. His clothing, while casual, fits him like a glove and glitters in the sunlight, with silver jewels adorning his wrists and the beads of his cotton shirt.

Marcellus must have said something to him, because the man's armour cracks and he smirks, eyebrows lifting. He walks away, ushering people inside the manor house.

Everyone but Marcellus leaves.

He reaches for Jesse's sword and strokes it slowly.

I clench my teeth, face growing hot.

I could walk up to him now, while the lawn is empty. But it feels like suicide.

A lady with short silver hair walks over to him and places her hand on his shoulder. She doesn't say anything, and he doesn't say anything back, but his chest quickly heaves before she withdraws, sucking on her lips.

Then he is utterly alone.

And yet, it still feels too dangerous to approach him.

A soft breeze plays with his silver hair, pushing the silken strands around his head. He slowly lifts himself from his chair, stretching his arms before him like a cat.

My breaths lodge in my throat, quickening my heart as he turns and faces me. I don't dare move away from my peep hole, afraid the movement will catch his eye.

With a leisurely smile, he sweeps his gaze across the perimeter of the manor. "I know you're there, little mouse."

My body freezes.

His voice carries around me, causing my skin to pucker. I watch with wide eyes as he makes his way over to the spread of food and pops a grape into his mouth, sheathing the sword onto his back so I can see it.

I can barely breathe as I watch him.

The urge to flee overcomes me. Ideas spiral around my head, ways to keep him on my lead yet keep him away from my friends.

But neither of us makes any move towards each other as he

proceeds to pluck bits off the table. He chews slowly, eyes raking around the garden. In the distance, a hot spring slumbers by the trees and two Argenti dip out of the back of the manor in their swimwear, silver hair on fire under the sun.

I take a deep breath and stand up behind the hedge, ready to run.

My head appears around a hole in the hedge and Marcellus's eyes immediately catch mine.

Run, run, run.

My stomach churns, and I freeze, unable to breathe, to think.

We both stand motionless, watching each other, before I swallow deeply and walk towards the gate, my legs shaking with each step.

This isn't the official entrance to the manor house. No, the grand, swooping iron entrance around the other side of the house opens up to white gravel and a sprawling garden where Hovers are parked between the rose bushes.

This is a side gate.

Run, run, run.

For some reason, I don't. Not yet.

Amadea's list nags at me, and the question of why his name is on it.

There's no one on this lawn except him, and against my better judgement, I take my chances to learn what I can about him.

Marcellus's lips twitch when I slam the gate closed—the first dent in this expression all evening—before his face converts back into a stone mask.

Slowly, without taking his eyes off me, he begins to butter what appears to be a savoury scone.

I brush past the white chairs the Argenti had scattered throughout the garden and track over what looks like an incredibly expensive blanket to stop out of reach in front of him by the food table.

The most exquisite food I have seen since coming to Umbra lines the table. Berries of all kinds, even strawberries and pomegranates like on Terra. Cold meats, soft cheeses, pancakes with cream cheese and honey, pickled vegetables and dips—so many dips—cover the entire table.

It's been picked at for hours, some of the food sweating from the heat. A jug of pink lemonade by the end of the table is nearly empty, the ice in it long melted. My stomach still grumbles loudly.

Marcellus doesn't smile, but the edge of his lip twitches.

It should strike me as odd that he doesn't seem startled by my arrival, but considering he's an Argenti with friends in high places, I don't bother questioning it.

"Hello, little mouse."

His words spiral in my head, invoking a weird sense of irritation. I fight the urge to squirm under his gaze, ignoring the way my skin crawls.

"Want something to eat?" he coaxes gently as he studies me.

"No."

The corner of his mouth twitches again. I watch with increasing anger as he lifts his food to his lips.

I didn't come here to play stupid little games with him.

"What do you want from me, Hart?"

Electricity buzzes in my veins—a response to Silver Magic, I've now come to realise. It quickens in my pulse, causing my heart to pound. He watches as I struggle to maintain composure, but mustn't see anything on my face because he appears stoic when he finally answers.

"You sought me out, little mouse. Why don't you answer your own question first?"

A muscle ticks in my jaw and I clamp my teeth down to stop from frowning. He notices the small reaction, his eyes twinkling with quiet amusement.

One of the Argenti in the pool accidentally makes eye contact with me, then quickly looks away. My pulse buzzes. I'm sure that's not a coincidence.

Invisible fingers tickle at my neck, prodding me with a creeping sensation. I'm being watched. Possibly even delayed.

"Who do you work for?" My voice is quiet, but clear. He squints at me, his armour slipping bit by bit.

His piercing silver eyes dig into my face, calculating.

Heat rises in my cheeks and ears, a ringing against the mounting panic in my chest. I stamp it down, pretending to ignore the deadly quiet around me and the moving bodies I glimpse beyond the windows in the manor.

Marcellus doesn't answer my question, but I already know the answer. He works for the Elders, but I was hoping he might offer me something else. Of course he wouldn't, though.

I don't ask him the real question I wish to know: *why are you on Amadea's list?*

"You should probably scurry away, little mouse," he says, his deep voice like a caress.

"Do you want me to do that?" I challenge.

He stares at me, nothing in his features giving him away.

I shiver, eyes briefly darting to the Argenti in the hot spring… Empty.

Stars. This doesn't feel right. I let my mask slip an inch when I pull in a shuddering breath. Marcellus notices and his face scrunches a little before he takes a step towards me.

Now, you run.

I back away from him, but he keeps coming, his silver eyes blank.

I take another step back then stop.

Wind kisses my skin, brushing strands of my hair across my cheeks. It ruffles my skirt, yet I stand there, wholly immobile.

Sweat breaks over my forehead and my chest rises and falls rapidly, panic flooding my veins and heating my skin as Marcellus Hart reaches forwards and brushes his thumb against my chin.

"You should've run," he says with a smile.

Run, run, run.

My heart screams in my chest, pounding as nerves slither up and down my body.

I can't move. I try to lift my foot, but it stays securely on the ground. My fingers strain against the invisible bindings, but I can't get them to do more than twitch at my sides.

I think back to the way that Argenti brushed her hand over Marcellus's shoulder. *I don't have my own special Magic—I suck the abilities from others.*

I wouldn't have come out of hiding for anyone other than Marcellus and they predicted as much. So, the Argenti gave him a taste of her Magic.

Helpless, I watch with wide eyes as the rest of the Argenti begin to spill out from the house, their evening clothes swapped for fighting attire. None of them have weapons, but every single one radiates with energy. Silver Magic courses around the manor, crackling in the air as they all stare at me with equally blank faces.

Even if I wasn't frozen, I couldn't raise a hand to them even if I wanted to.

A bead of sweat tickles my brow as a hushed, excited chatter fills the silence.

I swear I hear my name several times and I suddenly want to scream.

No. No, no, no.

My teeth grit together as I try to move my body, muscles quaking under the invisible weight trapping me.

"It's her. It's her!" I hear someone chant.

It's me. I can't see, can't move, can't think, as they all erupt into a flurry behind me.

Stand down, I want to yell. *There's too many of them, they will kill you.*

A group of civilians stand beyond the manor, unable to get in by the Argenti guarding it, disgusted by how close the Commoners are to one of their homes. But the noise only draws more people, and slowly, the crowd of Commoners grows.

The buzz of a Hover whispers towards me, but I can't see it. An Argenti yells at the public to stand back and I try and turn my head to no avail.

My muscles yell at me, craving to *move*.

All I can see is Marcellus and a swarm of guards as they push their way through the crowd outside of the manor, adorned in their silver uniforms.

But inside the manor, the Argenti are grinning, the chaos meaning very little of them.

They are of many nationalities, some with their hair dyed, dipped in streaks, or painted in warm colours. A smaller girl off to the side has her red hair tied up in a bun, with two strands of silver hair tumbling like long curtains past her face.

She wiggles her brows at me.

If I were to guess, they aren't as highly ranked as my mother. Thanks to her, one of the Elders is my grandfather and they're probably both sitting prettily up in the castle while the other Argenti herd me up for them.

I glare at them all, overflowing with rage.

My fingers curve into claws and I notice Marcellus flicking his eyes down to them. He sucks on his lips, then tilts his head down at me, plastering on a smile.

Is he hesitating?

The crowd behind me is going mad.

"Kill her!"

"That's the Promised Queen!"

"Stop the Argenti!"

But when Marcellus inclines his head towards me, I feel my gut drop.

An Argenti reluctantly lets three guards inside the manor, sniffing in disgust at the way they shuffle across their lawn. They saddle their S.P. guns into their holsters and reach for me. I don't even register what they look like as Marcellus takes a step back and then their greedy hands are on me, pivoting my body and twisting my limbs.

I almost want to laugh.

None of the Argenti want to touch me.

Am I really that below them?

I bend at their touch. Feeling enters my limbs with each step they pull me from Marcellus, but it's not enough to defend myself.

As they twist me, my breathing stops. The growing crowd of civilians is endless. Hundreds of them, all here for me.

Some spit at me, claws reaching through the hedge, but others watch me with hands on their hearts and tears welling in their eyes.

They are the future.

I swallow sharply, emotion prickling at my eyes as the guards hoist me onto the nearby Hover. It's a blinding, glistening silver beast, with the Umbran symbol branded in black on the sides.

My teeth chatter as I notice the marble stand with a single post right in the middle of it. A stage to parade me through the village.

My throat seems to close over as they pin my hands above me to the pole. There is nothing in that moment except the pounding of my blood in my heart and the thrumming organ in my chest.

Then I see Marcellus. His face is a careful mask, but he continues to hold my gaze. I know what's going to happen before it does. One of the guards pull out a large nail from somewhere in the machine.

My limp limbs droop against the chilling marble, still utterly useless.

My mind travels back to Elijah and the day we saved him from the safe holds. Raw, helpless agony rips apart my chest.

I can't escape this. I can't feel my legs.

I tear my gaze from Marcellus, my heart dropping like a stone as I see the sun dipping in the sky. The meeting with Tam will happen soon.

One of the guards lifts a hammer into his hand.

Fighting back the tightness in my throat, I close my eyes.

I focus on the weight of my switchblade and Melanie's comm in my pocket and let my mind drift back home as the guards layer my palms on top of each other on the post.

At least I have all the Argenti on me, and not watching my friends.

After today, I will have two armies.

I squeeze my eyes tighter as the guard positions the nail in my palm and don't even scream as he rams it home.

PART THREE

THE SILVER ONES

MELANIE

My heart is pounding in my throat.

Ships pepper the mountain ranges like a flock of silver beasts.

Our army. A small one, but still mighty.

We have one hundred and sixty-five people on this mission and thirty-three ships. A small fleet, but one made for stealth. Chills dance up my arms, my body a tangling mess of nerves.

We are actually doing this.

We found room for them around the flattened, blackened parts of the forest where the bombs have reduced the trees, much to the villagers' dismay. I swallow unsteadily as I watch soldiers mill around the ships and lay claim to whichever ones they fancy, stroking their metal exteriors with awe-filled expressions.

Our people have been training every day. Every. Damn. Day.

Their gazes are hard and determined, still weakened from their time in the safe holds, but remarkably well off thanks to the *Sanitas*. I swallow as they move, muscles etching down across their limbs as they lay claim to their ships.

Samael spots me and turns, a deep grin plastered across his face.

Behind him, the sisters who shadow him are chatting.

The girl with the yellow hair fixes me with a long, hard glare. The passing of time shows her brunette roots, but she sweeps it in an updo to hide it—strong in her ways.

They're fighters. All of them.

I smile at the girl, and she turns back to her sister without acknowledging it. Her sister doesn't notice, too busy tinkering with a med kit.

Some of our people have assumed the roles of healers, helping those from the cells who were on their deathbeds back to recovery. Others picked up a blade and have not stopped swinging it since it was laid in their palm.

Their resilience wakes something in me that has been sleeping for so long—pride, power and, above all, the sweet scent of a life goal, lingering just beyond my grasp.

I take a rattling breath against the cold, stilling my pounding heart.

Generals have been selected. Those with more experience than me have salvaged ships and lumped together fighting units. Every unit has a tech, two fighters, a healer, and a captain to fly the damn thing.

Five people to a ship.

And swarming around it all, are the generals, barking off orders and giving vague nods of approval. I handpicked all three of them, due to their history of leading squadrons on Umbra.

Currently, we are working on rebooting the camouflage mechanisms on the ships so that we can go undetected when we enter the black hole. It's a job for the techs, and I've been up here most days, flitting between helping the squadrons and cracking down on the Umbran security feeds in my office.

I shuffle my feet in the dirt, smiling as a man I do not recognise bombards me with facts about the ships. I stopped listening a while ago, but he seems happy, nonetheless.

Rebooting the ships has been going well. There's nothing the man can tell me that I don't already know.

But I remind myself that one of the most important things for me is to maintain a positive mindset for our mission. For our people, our salvation and for the familiar face walking towards me from their masses.

I survey the man beside me once more, noting the way his beard has caught a few beads of rain that glitter in the sun when it peeks out from behind some clouds. It's a very brown beard for a very old man.

Weird things happen to some Umbrans who stay on Terra for too long. This one hasn't greyed, even though he must be well into his 70's.

He grins at me waiting for an answer. I simply nod at him.

I don't care if it's the appropriate response, because past the squadrons of ships, Elijah is making his way towards me with a brown bag in his hands.

My heart thumps in my chest and all the while that bloody smile stays on my face.

The old man smiles at my answer—Laurence, I think his name is. One of the generals.

"I hope we will be prepared to attack by June. Maybe we should see how many ships we can get if we make a connection to the other bases?"

His voice is low and soothing. I close my eyes, taking a deep breath before I look at him once more. This job doesn't belong to an old man with a brown beard. This job would have been Jesse's. He knows ships better than anyone I know.

If anyone deserves the role of general, it would be him. Granted, he left his training academy before he graduated. Still, his father was the most renowned pilot Umbra had seen in decades. That's all anyone here cares about. We are all the scum of Umbra, in some way or another.

"We don't need the other bases."

"And why not?" a voice cuts in. "It's not a bad idea."

Elijah.

I take him in slowly, squinting my eyes against the sunlight breaking through the trees. I can't help but notice how well his dark fighting leathers fit his body as he hands me a small bag with a sandwich in it.

Samael sees that sandwich. Snickers.

Elijah brings me lunch every damn day.

I fight the war drum beating in my chest as I reach for it, blood heating my body. He doesn't care how much I run myself down so long as I have at least five hours of sleep each night and three meals a day.

"We'll discuss it later." I dismiss the general.

He gives me a small nod and turns back towards the ships.

As if on instinct, Elijah steps forward to fill his place. Samael snickers louder, until the sister with brown hair says something to him to shut him up.

Honestly, I don't really care.

I lean instinctively towards Elijah's warm body. He wrings his hands in front of him as if he's unsure what to do with them now that the bag has left his hands.

I play with the wrapper on the sandwich and study one of the closest ships.

A small squad of guards had been tasked with freeing them while others trained, honing their bodies or learning new crafts. For days, I could see ships roaming the skies in the background of training and hacking, the forest quaking from their engines.

Now, everything feels all too peaceful, like some sort of calm before the storm.

"I've got to return to Mason. I left him alone with the security feeds," I say, turning to Elijah.

His soft eyes never once left my face. I gaze back, devouring the sight of him. We hold each other's eyes for a beat longer than usual, and he swallows.

I keep staring.

Rain starts drizzling down, soft flecks of water breaking through the sunshine in the trees. I watch as it catches in his hair and forms pathways down his black fighting leathers. I don't know what I've done to be blessed with someone as loyal and gentle as Elijah.

We stare at each other until the drizzle passes and the sunshine returns. Then I rip my eyes away.

As I turn back down into the forest back to the Valley, a flutter lifts my chest as I hear him quietly release a breath behind me. I can hear every rise of his chest, every time his boot touches the ground or his leathers rustle.

He follows me into the trees without question. It's not a habit to stand by my side like it was for Jesse. It's a longing.

Every day, I catch him stealing glances at me. I've got to admit, amid the chaos of our lives, it's oddly nice. Not familiar or as easy as breathing like it had been with Jesse, but nice.

I nibble on my lunch, the sound of rustling paper one of few accompanying us as we make our way back to the warehouse. The tension of his gaze on my back is thick as a never-ending fog—so dense it makes me shiver with chills.

I lick some mustard off my gloved fingers and brush my clothes free of crumbs as we near the warehouse.

The villagers acknowledge us as we make our way into my small lab—the refurbished computer room. We're used to seeing Umbrans mingle among them by now.

Elijah swallows deeply from behind me and it takes me a

moment to realise why. Savannah's father. He stands at the entrance to my lab, his face set.

He has not, in any sense of the word, liked that I let Savannah disappear off to Umbra and then proceeded to take his only biological son under my wing to take down the empire.

Everyone has suffered prolonged sidelong glances, muttered curses and general disdain from him.

He hasn't once spoken to me about it. I guess that's just about to change.

"My daughter needs proper help," he says in a gravelly voice. He pushes his lips into a tight line, his gaze hard as I sidestep past him into my lab.

Elijah hesitates, unsure how to deal with the solid form of a man growling at us. Mason snickers from behind the computers, his gangly form bunched up in his chair.

He swings his computer screen around to face me and I take a deep breath just as Savannah's father, Mark, storms back into the room, leaving Elijah reeling by the door.

I've dealt with moody men my entire life in the kingdom. The best thing to do is smile, nod and, ultimately, ignore them.

"Hello? Are you listening to me? My daughter needs help."

The lights of my computer screens reflect on his glasses. The lights from the screens with Savannah's face.

I swallow deeply. The Elders have been watching her since she arrived on Umbra.

But for some reason, they have taken back the feeds. All of the footage I have is a replay of what we have already seen, we know Savannah and Jesse have made to the Kingdom, but nothing after that.

It's almost as if the Elders have sensed me poking around and blocked me out.

I scrunch my brow.

I'd be lying if I told Mark it didn't concern me—the not knowing—but Savannah got my comm and knows the danger. I trust her to handle herself.

I fiddle with my glove, the taste of my lunch resurfacing in my mouth.

"We need to leave, now," Savannah's father says.

I spin towards him slowly, my chest swelling. "We can't. And besides, it might be a good thing that they're off the feeds."

"They're not just *off the feeds*, but there are no feeds to begin with," Mason comments.

"I know," I say hopelessly.

Mason stands and grips the edge of the table, his breath a little shaky. The energy in the room is thick and stifling.

I can feel the erratic rhythm of my pulse even before Mason speaks.

"My plan, Melanie. It's a better way to handle this."

His stupid plan. I don't even know the full extent of it but, whatever it is, we aren't doing it.

"Your sister has been constructing a plan for months, sliding puzzle pieces into play more times than you can count. None of you had any idea—hell, even I didn't until the last minute. We. Must. Follow. Her. Plan. Not anything else."

I didn't mean for my words to chafe, but they do. I watch as Mason flinches, the sentences searing against him. He opens his mouth, words frozen in time.

Mark sucks on his cheek, a muscle in his forehead twitching.

"She is my *daughter*," he says, the words spilling over all of us. "My daughter, whose plans are to keep *us* safe. Not her. She is in danger."

His flaming brown eyes meet my steely gaze in a clash of fire and ice, glasses slipping down his nose.

I stare at him with everything in me, but my resolve feels brittle.

"I've already warned her about the Argenti tracking her, which should have delivered back when she first entered the Kingdom. So she must be staying out of sight now."

Elijah rushes towards me from the doorway. My lab becomes a mess of blurry light as he winds his warm arm around my shoulder.

"Please, Mark, Melanie is doing all she can."

"My daughter is doing more."

Pincers squeeze my heart, making me jerk against Elijah's chest. I all but stop breathing.

Mason is wordless, but Elijah isn't. Not nearly.

"No, you don't get it. You don't get it at all, Mark. We all have a role to play in this war, whether it's as simple as providing food for our troops or as complex as going underground on Umbra. If any one of us sway from our role or cause too big of a wave, it's your daughter's neck on the line. Don't you see that?"

Mark doesn't answer. A muscle ticks in his jaw, his gaze vacant. He probably already knows all this. Knows and doesn't care, because his daughter is clearly in danger and no rational man would be okay with that.

Elijah's arm tightens around my shoulders and something feral twists in my gut, lurching me closer to him. I hadn't even realised I was trembling until he squeezes me in comfort.

Mason moves out from behind my computers, his eyes lit with determination. "Jasmine and I think we should blow up their Dome."

Ice creeps down my body. Had he not listened to anything—

"Before we land," he explains hurriedly. "We land a day earlier than Savannah expects us, blow up their Dome, and then meet up with her when she's expecting us."

The Dome runs because of the volcano and a large plant that converts its energy. It's the main energy source in the Kingdom.

Elijah sucks in a sharp breath. Mark does much the same.

Is this why Mason wanted to learn how to hack? My throat feels thick, my head spinning too damn slow from the lack of sleep.

"We can't," I manage to force out.

Not a single soul in this room should know about the Dome around the Silver Kingdom, not to mention how to blow it up. No one but Jasmine, who obviously provided that wonderful bit of intelligence to Mason.

I grit my teeth at the thought, at the possibility of Jasmine going rouge.

"Get out," I say to Mason, finger jabbing to the door.

Elijah's stiff arm still curls around me and I focus my glare, ignoring the heat cascading down my body. I want to shrug him away to get closer to them, but I don't.

"It will cause a panic. They're used to their Dome and the protection it gives them. If we take it away, it can cover our attack." Mason's eyes are lit up, his body fidgety with excitement.

Mark releases a small breath, his eyes on his son. "It's not a bad idea—"

"Get *out*!" I snap.

They both stare at me. I can tell I'm slashing knives at them with my gaze, but I don't relent until Mason slowly peels himself away from our small group.

Mark takes a depth breath, then tightens his lips as he places a hand gently on his son's back, glaring at me as he follows him out of the room.

"Miss Beckett," he says with a nod before closing the door.

The moment the door clicks shut, I release a heavy breath.

Elijah pulls me into him, crashing my face into his chest. I remain stiff, unsure whether to pull away or stay there until his hand cups my head, twisting into my hair.

His heart is hammering faster than a ship's engine. He doesn't say anything, but he doesn't need to. He's here for me. For Savannah and Jesse.

He may not know how to stop the terrible trio from planning to blow up the Dome, but he will stay by my side the entire time.

"I'm going to spend the night figuring out how to destroy the Dome on Umbra," I say quietly.

His heart skitters even harder against my chest, his hand tightening in my roots.

I think I feel my chest combust with something very close to nerves.

"What?"

I pull away from him, my body wilting now that the tension is gone. He's my comfort. And so I smile at him gently. "If I know every way to blow it up, I know every possible way to stop the Terrible Trio."

He hiccoughs, then his lips quirk. "Terrible Trio?"

I rock on my heels, fighting the urge to smirk back. "Bully me and I'll throw you out on your ass too."

"Never, Miss Beckett," he promises, his words a whisper.

I gently kick his foot. His lips wobble into a wider smile.

I can feel the full weight of his attention as I move around to the desk Mason abandoned, my eyes skirting around him.

A blush stains his cheeks. His neck.

"Okay, good." My words hang heavily in the room, and I'm not sure what to say until I blurt, "Want to evade sleep with me?"

The red in his cheeks deepens and he can barely get the words out as he responds. "Yes, Miss Beckett."

I shouldn't be surprised that he stays.

Elijah Brookes. My comfort.

SAVANNAH

A guard wrestles Melanie's comm and my switchblade out of my pocket.

I watch, my mind feeling separate to my body, as my dress tears under his ridiculously large fingers. It splits up my thigh, exposing my stomach, and I lose focus as a drop of my blood falls and splashes the back of his hand, going with him as he claims my things as his own.

Help me, Melanie. Help me.

He hands the switchblade to Marcellus, who stands at the front of the Hover, his eyes raking blankly over the rowdy crowd lining the street.

The comm doesn't even get that far.

I blink as the guard puts it on the marble between my feet and slams the hammer down onto it. Metal and wire scratch across my shins, pricking my skin. I hardly even feel it. All my awareness has travelled to the agony of the nail in my hands, searing white-hot with every jerk and turn of the Hover. My eyes roll in my head, so I close them.

Goodbye, Melanie.

Around the near-silent Hover, shouts and prayers cascade my ears, battering into the sides of my skull. They get louder by the second as people wander out of their homes and into the street.

From my place at the post, it should be easy to see them around me, but they are a hazy blur. I can barely keep my wits about me, lest I feel every feral whip of pain sucking at my hands. All I can do is hope that Jesse and Lily are far off by the stables, waiting for their friend who will never return. The idea of Jesse being in these crowds, seeing me like this, makes me want to scream.

I stare at his sword, glittering on Marcellus's back. It's better if I just vanish. He doesn't deserve to see me like this.

He should forget about me, build the army, take back Umbra.

I will be here, the distraction.

And soon, it will all be over.

The Hover takes a sudden corner and I vaguely register being pushed back into the post as the vehicle tilts upwards, pulling us up a mountain. The sun has long since left us, but the temperature under the Dome is still warm and comfortable.

I suck in a wobbly breath as the force jolts me back, sending another wave of pain up my arms. I wouldn't mind freezing temperatures right now—at least that would take the feeling out of my body.

One of the guards mutters something, stirring Marcellus. I can sense eyes on me, but it's hard to tell if it's from my companions on the Hover or from the civilians along the road.

A warm hand touches me next, pulling my head forwards. My eyes meet his silver ones, but I don't have strength to pull away. He doesn't say anything. Doesn't need to. His hand drops and he jumps off the Hover.

We have made it onto a cobbled bridge, which turns to gravel on the other side and, beyond that, the entrance to the castle.

I draw in a small mouthful of night air, which helps clear my head slightly. I try not to think about my hands, but everything suddenly hits me with sharp clarity.

The castle is nestled on the peak of the highest mountain, arching up towards the stars. The moon fragments dance around the sky behind it, peppering the night with a jarring moment of history.

People emerge from beyond the fog-shrouded castle, dancing out of it like phantoms. Long silver clocks cover their heads and trail along the gravel at their feet.

Time seems to stretch, their movements lost to me as my lids grow heavy and my head sinks back against the pole. When a figure at the front approaches my little stage on the Hover, a cold, elegant finger lifts my chin and my eyelids peel back enough to drink her in.

"My favourite daughter," she says coolly.

"Your only daughter," I say. My words scrape out of my throat.

She drops her finger, arms poised elegantly besides her cloak. I'm almost glad she doesn't lower her hood. I don't particularly want to see her.

She hums in response. I swear I can almost taste the scent of her humour on the air around us. My head tilts back, eyes locking on the familiar heart constellation she taught me.

Ha. Her daughter has finally made it home.

A guard appears at my side, a large, silver tool in his hands as he lowers towards me.

"Where are your little friends?" my mother asks.

My lips part as I stare at the stars, their pretty lights casting a silver glow onto the pointed peaks of the castle. My heart pounding in my ears is the only sound I hear for a beat before the guard swiftly yanks the nail free of my hands.

A spasm wracks my body, pain lancing down my arms. I lurch forwards until my face touches the cool marble, hard and flat against my cheek.

I lie there, crumpled. Even if I knew where they were, I wouldn't tell her.

"Up," my mother declares. "To the dungeons."

Her footsteps announce her departure, but a gut feeling tells me this is only the beginning. I keep my head high despite it all. At least there's some dignity in that.

ᔐ

I don't know how many hours have passed, but the blood has dried on my hands.

Sleep fights with fear, stopping me from falling into any restful slumber. It's an odd sort of torture, not knowing what to expect or when. I sit still in the dark, waiting to come to my senses before opening my eyes.

A soft drip echoes around me and, somewhere not so far away, a person is softly sobbing, their pleas slowly trickling towards me. Otherwise, it is deathly silent and so cold my bones ache. The images of my family's faces fill my mind. My dad. Mason. Melanie. Jasmine. Eli. Jesse.

My eyes open of their own free will, drinking in the barren sight of my cell. The walls are made of rusted metal, tracked with dust from the grimy floor.

I lift my head towards the light spilling in from behind the bars. Head spinning, I clutch my stomach, only to see the blood on my hands.

My arms begin to shake violently as I raise my palms up to the light. Someone must've given me something to stop the bleeding, but the crusted blood hides the skin on my hands. Even my shoulders and chest are smeared with it. I can't see the incision points beyond the blood, but I don't look very hard for it.

I lightly put my hands together, resting them side by side, my entire body shivering as I place them on my lap.

There's nothing but a long brick wall through the bars before me. All the other cells must be beside mine, trailing down a tunnel. A single strip of lit panels follow the ceiling of the hallway. It's the only source of light in the dungeons, thrumming at a constant brightness, eradicating any sense of day or night.

I stare vacantly through the metal bars for so long that my muscles begin to ache at the upright position of my body. Eventually, the dripping stops, leaving me with the noisiness of blood pounding in my ears and the occasional sob of a prisoner.

My body hurts too much to move to a wall, so I let it slump until my cheek rests on the dusty ground. It stinks like urine, but I can't bring myself to move.

What feels like hours passes. Maybe days. Time doesn't exist here.

Occasionally, when the pain in my hands becomes too much, my mind drifts to Jesse and Lily. They have the map into the Kingdom, the list of names from Amadea and, hopefully, some support from the people.

Even if I die, the world won't stop. My father and Mason might just have a place to live on Umbra yet... Even if I die.

My lip wobbles. A single tear whispers down my cheek and I squeeze my eyes shut, forcing the rest away. I don't yet know if they will feed me or give me water and I need to conserve my strength. Crying is pointless.

What is there to live for? I have no clue. Someone could come in here and kill me within the next hour or, worse, drag it out and make a spectacle of me.

A shiver convulses through my body. If that happens, there is no way to shield my death from Jesse. That image will probably scar him for the rest of his life. He already lived through the loss of Lily and his parents. I can't add myself to the pile.

I open my eyes and take a steady, clearing breath. If I die,

Mason will be left without a sister. That simply can't happen. By any means possible, I need to get through this. For them. For *him*.

My position on the floor begins to numb my left arm, but I don't move. Not until the distant sound of scuffling footsteps fills the dungeon hallway.

I tilt my head to get a better look and, from my spot on the ground, a commanding presence comes before me. The light from the roof plays in his silver hair, making it look blue as I squint at him.

"Rise for the Elders," a guard announces.

I don't move. I just stare.

Elders shouldn't look like the Argenti, yet here he stands.

"Savannah."

His words whisper around me, encasing me in a cold gust that makes me shiver. I want to stand and meet him, but my body feels plastered to the floor.

Instead, I roll onto my back and plaster on a smile. From the corner of my eye, I see him wrap his hands around the bar. Good to know they aren't filled with electricity.

I smile a little more. The movement hurts my face, but I keep it locked there. Perseverance, I suppose.

"Savannah Collins," someone else says. A guard, probably. I hadn't noticed them behind him, but I can hear scuffling on the ground.

"Shaw," I correct, my voice rough with disuse.

A lithe female crosses in front of the Elder, her brows perched high. Her onyx hair is thick and straight, spilling down her back like tar. She looks so stark compared to the silver Elder.

"Good to know," she breathes, her soft voice curious as she tilts her head. If it weren't for the snakeskin armour covering her gown, I'd say she looked like a damsel, but something about this woman tells me she is anything but. She smiles at me, her expressions well-trained and gentle.

She holds a vial of what I immediately recognise as *Velox*, poised like a weapon in front of her silver, snakeskin gown. I devour the sight of it, but after a long beat of me staring at it, I peel my eyes away. They can't see I'm that desperate.

Yet my movements feel sluggish. Everything around me feels like it's been slathered in honey, slow and heavy and bright. I'm sure *every* emotion flashes on my face, so I close my eyes.

"Should we restrain her?" the woman asks, her almond eyes narrowing.

"She's surely not in a state to attack us," the Elder responds.

The corner of my mouth twitches, but he's right. My body is leaden.

The cell door grates against the ground, pushing through the dirt in a wide swing. The woman wanders through the crack, a blackness in the light as she kneels before me.

My eyes meet her dark and imploring gaze as she lifts my arm. Much gentler than I would expect from someone who's friends with an Elder. Or Argenti? I can't decide.

My eyes roll back in my head as the *Velox* surges home through my veins. I hardly feel it as she pulls away from me, her finger brushing over my puncture wound before she stands back in place. Like a well-rehearsed ensemble they stand and watch me, guards carefully stationed at their backs while the liquid courses through my body.

The raw heat in my hands whispers away from my arms, my nerves on fire as it travels back towards the ripped flesh. I don't need to look at myself to know what's happening.

They wouldn't be healing me unless they need something from me—or someone. My blood runs cold as my mind races back to Terra. Without considering how it would look, one of my hands drifts down to my pocket.

My comm. Melanie.

Before, I'd have given the okay via the comm and they would have landed on Umbra with an army to infiltrate and claim the commoners. Now, even without the comm, they will travel to the planet's atmosphere. The comm only existed in case any plans changed or went wrong and we needed them earlier. Which means I just have to hold on until they come. There is no one coming earlier to help me.

A single, stupid tear drips down my cheek, splattering into the dirt beneath me. I smooth my hands through it as motion returns to my limbs.

I rip myself across the floor in one grand movement, foot hooking around the door as one of the guards swings it shut in sudden panic. The movement is too sharp and fast and smacks past my foot, but I didn't have any real hope to escape.

I give them a lazy grin, my body swaying as they gape at me.

"So," I croak, "I assume you're healing me just to torture me further?"

The lithe woman pales. One of her hands grips the empty *Velox* vial. She doesn't seem to have pockets in that pretty little gown.

The guard who slammed the door shut huffs. I roam my eyes over the blood lining his silver uniform. *My blood.* Prick.

"Did you have fun pinning me up like a painting? Or did you just run out of time to shower?" I sing, the words tasting like acid in my mouth.

The duo stare at me until the Elder with the silver hair leans forwards between the bars.

"Go," the lithe woman says to the guards.

They hesitate. Down the hallway, a prisoner begins to sing a sad lament that echoes down the hall.

The Elder taps the bars while the lithe snakeskin woman breathes heavily, her eyes focused as she watches me.

I try and focus on anything besides the Elder whose eyes are boring into mine with such intensity it makes me want to break.

The *Velox* gives me a strange sense of safety, patching up every ache except the resounding panic in my heart. I tamper it down, eyes trailing the guards as they reluctantly disappear from my line of vision, feet pounding up what sounds like stairs.

"Listen, child," The Elder insists.

My eyes stay off to the side of the cell as I answer. "Listening."

The soft *tap, tap* of his fingers echo in my skull.

"They know," he says to me.

"Know what?" I ask vacantly.

My body sways. I can't feel my hands anymore. The contrast of healed hands compared to those in agony has no comparison. I now feel like a ghost.

"That your friends are coming," the woman replies.

"They know more than you think. They have more technology than you think. More weapons," the Elder continues.

He stops tapping the bars on my cell. I whip my gaze to his. "They?"

"We," the woman corrects, her eyes darkening.

Her knuckles are white around the empty *Velox* vial and, despite their traitorous words, I doubt they came here to heal me because they are on my side.

If these dungeons are anything like the Safe Holds back home, they have a segregated area for torture near the entrance. It took several beats for the guards before their feet hit stairs. Anything could be lying around the corner.

I suck in a pained breath. *That your friends are coming.*

But no indication of *when* they're coming, or that I already have some here, building an army behind their backs.

They won't kill me just yet. They need information from me.

The cold war on Umbra has been raging for decades already. Getting their hands on me has nothing to do with me and *everything* to do with stopping what I stand for. I suppose that starts with my friends.

"What do they know?" I implore.

A familiar ache erupts in my stomach. Quite frankly, I don't know the details of what Melanie and the others are up to, nor what Jesse and Lily might decide to do on Umbra with me gone. All I know is that it all boils down to one day, one meeting point, with us conjoining our armies.

But with my comm reduced to shards, we have no way of synchronising that movement. I just have to pray that both parties are ready around the same time.

The woman doesn't respond, her eyes sinking into me. I feel her rip apart my body with her gaze, removing layer by layer.

I turn to the silver Elder. "Are you and your little snake woman just here to torture me?"

"Evaline," the woman says.

I blink. My heart has dropped down to my feet somewhere. "What?"

"My name."

Amadea's list. I plaster on a smile. "Of course. Evaline."

We all gaze at each other, drinking each other in, sizing each other up. It's hard to tell. My eyes fixate on Evaline's dark ones.

She doesn't look like an Argenti—not in the way her companion does—but she radiates a sense of cool power. Which can only mean she's also one of the Elders. But, judging by her companion's silver hair, does that mean he may not be an Elder like her?

Is Evaline the one in charge here?

The footsteps of guards trail back down the stairs and it breaks everyone's concentration. I divert my eyes back onto the wall of my cell, unable to meet the eyes of the guard who's still covered in my blood.

Evaline doesn't say a word, but her silver companion clears his throat.

"Until next time," he mutters.

Both immediately turn their backs on me the moment their guards fall into place.

Until next time.

I swallow sharply, wishing I had some water to wash down the bile rising in my dry throat.

They disappear, taking all sound with them, and I step back shakily into the darkness of my cell, my limbs unsteady as I slide to the floor. The adrenaline washes from my pores as the weight of the situation cascades down on me.

The *Velox* still surges through my body, fixing all the aches, and I ball my hands into fists, unable to look at them. I have the sinking feeling that once the *Velox* has run its course, I will be entirely screwed.

Perhaps they will nail me to the wall again. And again. And again.

Mending and breaking me in search of answers I do not have. With shaking hands, I raise my hands to my face. And in the deathly quiet of my cell, I let myself cry.

MELANIE

It won't be long now, and I will be orbiting around Umbra, seeing it again for the first time in years.

I can already smell it. Not the desert or the metallic fortress of the space centre, but the fruitful air under the Dome.

The Silver Kingdom. My love and my home.

My fingers knot in my shirt, eyes skimming the air around me as dawn splits apart the sleeping quarters at the warehouse.

Last night, after loading all the information I could about the Dome onto the chip in my arm, I lay down in Savannah's old bed, though I could not sleep those remaining few hours until sunrise. Next to me, separated by nothing but a slim curtain, Elijah snores softly.

In a few hours, Mark will be ringing a bell to wake us all up for our first practise drill with the ships. We will fly them off the mountains, into the sky.

Fuel is precious, so we won't quite take them into orbit. Our main purpose is to learn how to work with our teams and to get a feel for the ships.

On a good day, my pilot would have been Jesse. But today, the man captaining my ship is a cranky old fellow called Nico, with skin freckled from sun exposure and blue eyes that are constantly disapproving.

I'm the tech in my team. Elijah is one of our fighters.

I chew on my nails, devouring the sight of him. His soft eyelashes fan his cheeks, the morning sunlight dappling his jaw.

It's Jasmine's ship I'm most worried about. Mason is their tech, Jasmine is one of their fighters, Mark is their healer and Laurence is their pilot. It's a group that can destroy me—destroy us all. But I have no say in it.

Each person on the island has been allocated a role as best as possible, and each of their categories fills me with equal parts dread and annoyance.

Of course they all got different roles and just so casually happened to be on a team together. Naturally, when the roles were announced, I drilled their other guard—the girl with the yellow hair—on the importance of our mission and staying to the plan.

A sick satisfaction swirled in my gut at that. The girl with the yellow hair stared at me when I told her. She didn't speak, but she saw the threat—go rouge with Jasmine and your sister will be in trouble.

Because her sister is on my team as a healer.

It's their pilot, Laurence, who worries me. He isn't so easily swayed and will pick his own battles.

I toss onto my back, take a deep breath, then rip myself from the bed.

No one has woken yet because no one ever wakes this early.

Training takes a lot out of us and we all crash equally exhausted each night.

Not me though. Never me.

I slip on my shoes, roughly throw a jumper over my worn pyjamas, and take my leave from the sleeping quarters.

Behind me, I hear Elijah's bed rustling. He'll follow me shortly and will perhaps find me with a warm cup of coffee and hastily buttered toast.

Three meals a day. Minimum. Our strange little agreement to keep me nourished.

The sky is a soft orange, fog spilling down the mountainside and covering the foliage around the warehouse with dew. This early, the thrum of the beach is louder than ever, singing through the trees as I head down to the stream.

Goats bleat around me, crying out for breakfast.

A man in Umbran clothes carries a bucket of seed from the warehouse, slipping towards a chicken farm. He doesn't see me, but I smile at him anyway.

I climb up onto a fallen log and cross my legs, breathing in the wafting the scent of mandarins and enjoying the ocean breeze through my hair. Elijah clambers down to me several minutes later with steaming cups of citrus tea in his hands and a bag of baked goods under his arm, looking exhausted.

I wrap my arms around myself, fighting the swelling in my chest. In another life, this world would have been perfect, but it's just a blip. I know better than anyone that all things must end—the happy moments most of all.

So I take a deep breath, accept the tea from Elijah, and absorb every damn detail of this moment to remember when I make it to Umbra. It's moments like these that I miss from my planet most—the peace, the homeliness.

I take a scalding sip of tea and curl up into the warm body of the man next to me, shivering against the fog. Together, we watch the stream, time ticking away from us.

⌇

Years of not flying has done nothing to quell the anxiety of boarding a ship.

This small pod is nothing like the cargo ship that ripped me away from Umbra, but it smells the same. Metal. Stale air. Human bodies.

I take a deep breath, fingers wrapped around my metallic arm. My body remembers the movements better than my brain does. Every twitch the captain makes, I mimic. I lean into the ship, trying to absorb it.

My arm is hardwired to a computer panel in the ship by wires that sync with the mechanics in my arm. I'm no expert at flying, but being a human computer has its perks. What most people don't know is that there's a chip in the back of my head connecting the mechanics to my arm. I was forced to live a life without a normal hand, so I made myself a better one.

"Melanie." Elijah's voice pulls me from my trance. "Melanie, are you seeing this?"

His tone is high, fuelled with adrenaline. The ship is running fine, as are the analytics and mainframes. I don't need to be sitting here, cold against the metal floors, feeling the ship with my mind. But it's oddly soothing and I'm more relaxed here than Elijah is by the window.

"*Formation locked, executing take-off,*" the ship hums.

I open my eyes, taking in Elijah with a smile. His hands are white as he grips a railing near the window, his mouth slightly open.

From this vantage point, Silver Island and the endless ocean must be breath-taking.

Anxiety blooms again in my stomach. This ship is not the shuttle that took me from Umbra. It's the one that will take me *back*.

But seeing those blue skies through the windows, troubled with strips of clouds, makes my fingers shake. I feel the ship even out under me, its nose lowering parallel to the ground and its speed evening out.

"*Engaging cruise sequence.*"

A breath of air escapes Elijah. His hands leave the railing, circling around his empty weapons belt. Elijah taking on the role of a fighter is such a juxtaposition to me.

He's good and warm and broken. A part of him died when the bombs swallowed the island, and yet he has been and done anything for everyone else to help get them through their own loss and pain.

He doesn't rip people's throats apart with a blade, he patches people up. People like me. I stand on shaky legs and make my way to him.

Our other fighter and our healer are busy in the back of the ship—the healer looking green in the face while he placidly runs his hand down her back. She fixes her honey eyes on me, bright despite the waxen sheen on her face.

Strong. Queasy from the flight, but ready for action. I immediately like her.

Elijah chews on his lip and holds a hand out for me. Out the window, the sky is alive with ships. Contrails still litter the sky, dispersing into the clouds. We hold rank at the front of our group, Jasmine's ship off towards our right. I can almost taste the excitement in the air, mixing with the anxiety dousing my body.

I swallow sharply, my body rocking beneath me. Elijah isn't looking at the sky anymore. He's looking at me. I let him wrap his hand around my metal fingers and a shiver dances up my spine, as if his touch is short-circuiting my hand.

He tightens his grip and turns back to the sky.

I feel like I'm being burnt alive, but I'm too afraid to move.

"What?" he asks, almost loud enough for our captain to hear, but the pilot is too busy gawking at the sky.

His body is relaxed, a somewhat creepy smile beginning to split apart his face as he takes in the world before us.

He's good with the ship—more calm and in control of himself behind the wheel than he is with his feet on the soil. I can trust him to fly us safely home, even if he has problems with... well, everything else. To him, the rest of our team are simply present. Not a squadron, just his passengers.

He doesn't talk much, if at all, which is a good thing because my head is too overrun with thoughts these days to really partake in prolonged conversation with my peers.

Elijah squeezes my hand. "Mel?"

I hadn't realised I was staring at him—at our hands and the casual way he lets me lean against him. I blink a few times until I begin to truly see his face, the blue sky blurred out behind him.

"You touch my hand as if it's skin and flesh, not wire and metal," I say softly. I swear the metal feels hot, like it's melting into my body. But that's impossible.

His brows furrow. "What do you mean?" His thumb twitches against my prosthetic but he doesn't drop it. "It's just a hand."

My breath rattles in my throat. "That."

His lips part, eyes darting around my face on a quest for answers. "That?"

"That's what I mean. You act like it's..." I swallow.

His face brightens until I withdraw my hand. At the same moment, our other fighter and healer drift up to the window, his arms wrapped around her elbows, leading her to see our world. Her face is tilted to the window, adamant and determined.

She doesn't have eyes for us and the man looks only at her. Still, I feel the weight of a thousand gazes on my wrist as they approach us. Elijah quietly grabs my discarded glove and takes my hand in his. The world slows as he blocks me from them, slipping the material gently over my fingers.

Maybe it's the fact that I haven't been sleeping well for weeks, but for the first time in forever my mind has all but forgotten Umbra and our friends when he slips that dark fabric onto me.

All I can see is his eyes, wide and focused only on me. I feel my chest swell, a whimper threatening to escape my throat as I take him in and truly see him for all that he is to me. And all that I am for him.

My broken man, perhaps a little less so when standing next to me. I give him a new purpose just as he gives me faith and a new way to look at the world.

Together, we have something to fight for.

He drops his hand from mine and gives me a small smile, returning his gaze out the window. The ships still circle around the sky, trying not to drift too close to the mainland. Far off into the ocean, a spec of black separates the mighty blue—a Terran ship. It causes my stomach to flutter and I pull myself closer to Elijah's side.

But then the healer speaks from behind me, and the spell is broken. "This formation is too wide to enter the wormhole at an efficient pace."

I clear my throat, pulling myself towards the cold. My skin feels like it's been submerged into ice.

"This is to protect our fleet from outside forces on either side of the wormhole. It will take several hours to get there, not including travel through the hole itself."

"What outside forces should we prepare for?" the other fighter asks. The man is tall and lean, his blond hair in a ponytail at his nape. I knew his father on Umbra—not well, just a guard's name on a piece of paper—but Reuben Mann had a serious squabble with another guard and both were tried for suspension. The moment his son, Jackson Mann, emerged from the Safe Holds, it was safe to assume there was more to that story. I haven't bothered asking him about it. Every single soul in these ships has a story as unique and bloody as Jackson. It would take forever just to get through them all.

"We are leading up to the journey between planets. It's best to be prepared for encountering other unfriendly vessels."

"They blew up the island," the healer says. She looks younger than Jackson, but not by much. I don't know her name or her story, but I smile and nod at her as if I do.

"They did, but there are two other bases still on Terra. And ultimately, their goal is to cut all ties. Transit between planets will not be safe until that happens."

Behind the steering, Nico grits his teeth and snorts, which I ignore.

"For the record," Elijah says, "we don't *want* them to blow up the Swiss and African bases. No one wants more families to die."

Jackson sucks on his lips, his eyes plastered on me. I give him a sour smile, tilting my head as I turn back to the window. "We will change formation before entering the wormhole, but until then, we travel like this." My words ring around the ship, a pin drop against the sudden quiet.

Nothing but the quiet engine and ventilated air brushes the space around us.

Nico is glaring ahead.

Elijah grabs my hand again.

Jackson says, "You are not our leader, nor are you royalty anymore, Beckett. Lose the superiority, otherwise this unit will *not* work."

I ignore his quip and stare in front of us so intently that my head begins to pound, a dizziness threating to engulf me.

This team is a temporary stepping-stone in a greater journey. His opinion does not matter. But even as I think it, a weight crushes my chest.

It does *not* matter. Arguing does not matter. Nothing matters.

My priority now is Jesse and Savannah and everything we need to do to help them.

Elijah pulls me towards him, but I gently push him away, heading back into the recesses of the ship where I left the power board open earlier. I remove the glove on my left hand and reconnect to the ship. Jackson glances at me, a sullen look on his face. I simply turn my back and lose myself to the wiring.

We're coming soon, Savannah.

I can still see the blue skies in my mind's eye—how it looks like an endless space between our fleet and the planet below us.

I miss the way the Umbran moon peppers the sky like an asteroid shower. I need to be there again, with our future queen. With Savannah.

We're coming.

Elijah is talking to the rest of our unit, but I cannot hear him. He's probably filling in my shoes and trying to get a feel of the people on our team to understand their strengths and weaknesses. He's better with people than I am, so I leave him to it.

I leave him with Terran matters while my mind drifts back to Savannah, one hand drifting to the comm in my pocket. Somewhere, somehow, I imagine Savannah holding her own, thinking of me stuck on this planet.

A part of me is there, on Umbra, right in the comm I made resting in her pocket. Holding my place until I soon take my rightful position at her side.

SAVANNAH

When they finally pull me from my cell, I don't know how much time has passed.

I suppose it doesn't really matter. My stomach churns and gurgles but despite how hungry I am from what has probably been over a day of not eating, I doubt I could keep any food down.

Because that is my mother before me, smiling down at a long tray of knives.

The torture chamber on Umbra is a lot more established than the makeshift one they had in the Safe Holds on Terra. The door leading to the exit by the dungeons is padded so that no noise can travel to the other prisoners.

The guards pull me towards a metal table lit by lights that seem to come from within the fibres of the roof, casting yellow hues onto my dirtied skin.

I clench my fingers into fists. There's no sign of the nails that had punctured my palms, but I swear I can feel the memory of it throbbing down my arms.

My mother's hair glistens in the light, her silver roots a cascading brightness I must squint to look at. I keep my eyes locked on her, but she doesn't raise hers to me once. Though I don't doubt for one second that she doesn't have her other senses trained on me—Silver Magic is hot around the room, crackling in my veins.

Awareness forks out of her, but she makes no move to do anything.

"I have a meeting in an hour, so let's just make this quick," my mother sighs.

Her fingers release a small knife the length of her hand, the sound of it clattering against the tray reverberating through the room.

My heart is hammering wildly in my chest, sweat sheening through the dirt on my skin, but I don't fight. There's no point.

My mother, two guards and a tall man draped in black flank me as one of the guards buckles my limbs to the table. The cold metal bites into my flesh, my once white dress hiked up to my thighs and exposing my skin to them.

I tilt my head up to stare at my mother, blinking rapidly while she avoids looking at me. She sighs again, as if bored, and snaps her fingers.

The other guard touches a panel on the wall between the padding and sound blares around the small room—a crowd, screaming my name among other obscenities. I squint my eyes and train them onto the small holograph floating in the air. Then all the sound vanishes, the echoes dispersing into the room.

I still hear them calling for me in my head. The live footage of the Umbran commoners hangs above me like a threatening cloud. And there, in the middle of them...

My heart plummets as Jesse turns his face, anger lining his jaw.

I hope they don't know he's raising an army.

That's one thing they must never know.

There's no indication to say where he is, but dust kicks up as the crowd swells around him, screaming.

The tall man in black lifts a small, sharp knife. His face is covered in a mask, arms revealing an array of scars. His eyes are blank, his face completely hidden.

My eyes glaze over his features. The last thing I want is for his eyes to haunt my dreams, so I retreat into my mind and blink, erasing his appearance as he stares at me. He's nothing more than a faceless man with no role other than that of hurting others.

The restraints pin me to the cold table, rendering me helpless.

My eyes flicker briefly from Jesse's face on the holo and back to the small knife in the palm of the man in front of me. My pulse flutters and I look back at the screen. Back to the man I need to save.

"*Why are you on Umbra?*" my mother asks.

Her voice shatters the silence, biting into my skull. I can smell her magic on the air, coursing through her words. Her words seem to echo, then vanish completely.

The residual silence is defeating. I twist my fingers, arching them away from the tough leather binding them against the table and, without turning my eyes from the screen I say, "You know why."

The tension in the room is palpable. Or maybe that's the Silver Magic.

It's as hot as coals as the man pulls up my dress, lowering the tip of the blade to my skin. It's angled in warning, ready to slice.

My blood runs cold in my veins. Layer by layer, he intends to remove my flesh if I don't answer them.

"*Why are you on Umbra?*" my mother repeats.

Her words shatter my mind again. It's a pain within itself. When I glance at her, I realise her lips have never moved. *Telepathy.*

That's what her Silver Magic can do and why I can supposedly track people by tapping into their minds myself. We share Mind

Magic, except when I try and use mine, it feels like I'm grasping at air. My Magic is there in theory, but that is all.

My mother, on the other hand, is commonly feared for her ability. The more she speaks into your head, the stronger the connection becomes. A part of me almost wonders that, if I keep letting her in, she will be able to read my thoughts at some point.

Unfortunately for me, I have no choice.

I can't feel my body, too stricken with nerves. I try and focus on the screen, but all my brain can compute is the cold feeling of the knife waiting on my thigh.

You know why I'm here, I want to shout. *You damn well know.*

But she can't read my mind yet, so I say something entirely different. "Home," I say breathlessly. "Umbra is home."

Something moves in my mother's jaw. She flicks her fingers and, without warning, the faceless man's blade slips through my thigh.

I slam my teeth together, refusing to scream. My body tightens against the table, head digging into the hard metal. I think I see a hooked nose peek out from under his hood, but I blink it away.

I forget. I refocus.

These people mean nothing to me. I can do this. I can persevere. My breaths come out strong and sharp and I try to swallow them down.

The room feels sticky around me, the silence howling in my ears even after he finishes. Some inner battle rages within me—the need to lift my head and the need to pull away.

He grips my thigh, coiling his thick hands around the pain. I try and pull myself away, but the restraints grip me.

"Why are you on Umbra?"

Perseverance, Savannah. Just ignore her. Just hold on.

Heat courses up my neck, my teeth grinding as I stare at her. We hold each other's eyes until she snaps again.

The man's knife descends.

Ignore it. Ignore it. Hold on.

This one hurts more because he cuts over the same spot.

Somehow, I can't find my lungs. No sound erupts out of me as my hands squeeze into fists, my nails breaking through flesh. Against my own will, my body bucks even harder on the table. My teeth sink into my cheek. And I glare at my mother.

Her eyes are an endless grey, devoid of all emotion. It's hard to see if it's a wall she's put up herself, or if that's simply how she feels.

A soft sound burbles out of my throat. The man stops cutting, but raw heat still rages up my leg.

"*Why are you on Umbra?*"

I know she sees the liquid pooling in my eyes when I say, "I don't want to be queen."

It's the truth. It's always been the truth. But enough pain and loss builds and creates a path for you—the only path. Tunnel vision had rendered me without option.

I don't want to be queen, but I do want to make Umbra my home. That much is true.

My vision splits as the knife slides back into my thigh. I've answered them honestly, but they're still cutting me. My eyes rip from my mother's and the ceiling of the chamber flickers as I feel my eyes roll in my head. I pull my head back, blood soaking my mouth from where my teeth have clamped into my cheek again.

It doesn't even feel like pain anymore. It feels like I'm floating far away from my body, stretching into oblivion. I feel dirty and raw and hot as the small knife works down my body. All I can do is lie here and take it.

Nothing I tell him will stop this. They hurt me because they can. Because I'm just a toy. I almost don't hear the next words out of my mother's mouth.

"*Tell us the precise location of Jesse Hayes and Melanie Beckett.*"

Their names make my heart flicker in my chest.

A heat, not unlike the one in my thigh, floods my head. It's like I can sense them, far away from me. Both are hurting.

Ignore. It. Hold. On.

Fingers snap. The knife descends.

"Tell us the precise location of Jesse Hayes and Melanie Beckett."

She says it like a chant. Over and over. I fixate my eyes on the faceless man's blood-drenched hand cupping my thigh.

I say nothing, so again he rips into me. My eyes glaze. A soft sound groans out of my throat. I think to myself that it's only a matter of time until I'm screaming for them. But to my surprise, I never do.

I just ride the wave to oblivion.

And try to persevere.

MELANIE

My pulse ticks as I stare down the people who despise me most.

They stare back at me, unwavering.

I've never been one for showdowns, but damn I feel like that's my entire life now. Jasmine hates me. I want to punch that annoying smile off her face, but it's a lose-lose.

Mark scuffles paperwork off his desk. Plans. Maps. Army formations.

We've decided to leave for Umbra early. It makes my heart sing as much as it makes me want to throw up my breakfast. Savannah isn't expecting us yet, but we have developed cloaks for our ships. We will go a week early, in invisibility, to circle Umbra's atmosphere.

Either we wait for the agreed-upon day to meet Savannah or we get a comm to move early. We won't change the plan. Won't blow up the Dome. But I've been forced to compromise.

Contacting Savannah from our end will not happen on my account unless absolutely necessary, but I'm not above hacking into their mainframes and seizing control of their technology before that. Securing knowledge on what's happening below and getting an upper hand does seem practical.

But the final plan is Savannah's. The *only* plan I will allow. Everything we do before then will be subtle and unnoticed.

"As far as Savannah knows—" Jasmine muses from behind me, a faraway look on her face that I damn well know is faked. She twirls her hair, seemingly relaxed as she runs a finger down a map on Mark's desk.

"We made a deal," I say abruptly.

But she ignores me, her arms crossing her chest. "As far as Savannah knows, we are landing an army *blindly* onto Umbra. Sounds like she's planning to take the sharp end of the sword for us," she continues, fixing me with a look. "We only have thirty-three ships and *no plan*. It makes sense to call to action when we arrive. Back her up."

"Jasmine," Elijah warns, "Melanie said we are not blowing up the Dome."

She rolls her eyes. "Waste of an idea, really. Savannah can use our help."

I agree, but I trust she can handle herself. Do you? I want to scream the words at her, but I rein them back. Truth is, no one knows the entire plan expect for Savannah. We just need to trust that and do our part.

I press my fingers into my temples, my mind aching as much as the burning sun hitting our backs. For the first time in weeks, Silver Valley is *hot*. We should be leaving soon, yet Mason, Jasmine, and Mark have decided we should leave even earlier and blow up the Dome.

"Our mission is about stealth. We have thirty-three ships for stars' sake," I say for what has felt like the millionth time.

No one responds. They just stare at me, as if waiting for me to continue.

I can feel Mark's gaze from behind his glasses. His eyes leave the maps, turning towards his son. Mason's focus is locked on the screens at his desk. Security footage plays on them, spiralling in loops. Nothing we haven't already seen.

It's been weeks since any of us have had a good sleep.

"We're leaving early. Can we drop it now? We're ready and it's smart to hang tight around Umbra before landing." My breath huffs in and out rapidly, the sun feeling like it's scorching my throat. "But nothing more. Not without any more information."

The room feels tight. Too many bodies in one space.

"If we get more information when we get there, can we reconsider blowing the Dome up?" Mason quips from behind the computer, his eyes bright.

I've stored all possible information about it the chip in my arm, and all the possible ways to disarm it, and the main thing I've discovered is that we cannot destroy it from the outside—getting rid of the Dome will be an inside job, one that we cannot do until we meet our army up with Savannah.

Because there is *no possible way* to blow up the Dome unless you're within the Kingdom. And I will not allow that to jeopardise our mission.

I meet his gaze, picking at the glove on my wrist as I focus on breathing evenly.

The boy has taken to Umbran attire finely, his tunic polished and his leather shoes glistening in the burning sun. But there are shadows under his eyes from looking at computer screens for hours on end and seeing his sister being tracked throughout the Kingdom.

I glare at him—at the boy pretending to be Umbran.

It's almost as if Umbra is taunting us with the same footage by replaying it over and over.

I say through gritted teeth, "No, Mason."

He grins at me. His innocence fills me with a sense of peace, making me feel separate from the claustrophobic room, if only for a moment.

But I quickly stamp down on the feeling. He will always be on Jasmine's side. He's known her for as long as he can remember and now she wants to save his sister.

He will never fully understand me.

The door behind me creaks upon. For a moment, the noise of the warehouse spins around the room, then Elijah closes the door, coming up to my side.

I gaze at the sun, my vision fractured, as Elijah walks past me to face Jasmine. "Everyone's aware of the new procedure to leave. We're prepping the ships, getting supplies on board."

She ignores him. He's only saying what I already know, but the way he says the words to Jasmine is like a warning.

"You're planning to land a small party of ships onto a planet that knows we are coming. You know that, right?" She sighs, eyes on Mason.

Not once do they leave Mason.

"They don't know we are coming," I say, whipping from the window. "That was the plan."

"That *was* the plan," she reiterates. "Who's to say they haven't been watching us all this time? Hayes turned the generators on the day we saved the prisoners. What if they've always known?"

The wind leaves my lungs and the whole office stills.

And in that moment, when she pins me with those eyes of blue fire, I wonder why she had not been born an Argenti. This girl would be a powerhouse—an absolute wrath to behold—if she were given even the gentlest push of power.

But she is human, so I warn, "Don't push it."

She glares at me. The room heats with tension until Elijah is barely breathing beside me.

"Okay, I'm lost," Mark claims, draining the cold cup of coffee in his grip.

"Of course you're lost," I grunt, harshly spitting the words. "You've been listening to a girl who has been spinning you lies. Fast action is *no* way to win this."

"We're leaving early," Elijah says, placing a shaky hand on my back. "We have preparations to make and talking about this won't change anything. We're going to save Savannah. We will."

Mark wilts. His gaze drops as he turns away from us and takes a step closer to his son. With a deep breath, he nods.

"Savannah has been off the feeds for ages, Dad. It might be a good thing." Mason mutters.

Good, my words have been getting through to him.

A shaky breath cascades out of his father. Jasmine tightens her jaw, but I smile at Mark. He doesn't smile back. He doesn't have eyes for anyone but his son.

"We fly in a few days," Elijah explains, laying it out to the man. "But anything Jasmine says or does from this point will only contribute to Savannah's death. Your daughter has laid a plan deep within more plans. Drift from ours and we disrupt hers."

Yeah, I suppose that's the gist. I tilt my head at him and suck on my lips. His face turns, breaking apart a beam of sunlight that catches on his soft smile.

Elijah will never be the best soldier, but if I could choose anyone to have my back, it would be him. Because maybe, just maybe, I don't need someone with fire in their veins standing next to me. "We get it, Brookes," Jasmine mutters, rolling her eyes.

She looks to Mason for backup, but we've lost him again to the feeds. His shoulders tighten as he takes a deep breath and Mark wraps a hand around his back.

"As we know, the best day to travel to Umbra is the 15th of

June, but traffic will also be at its peak then, it's when Umbra sends most of it's ships between planets. That's what we've been telling the people." My voice moves around the room slowly, methodically. "We leave early, before the travel period starts, in order to avoid detection."

"Did the army buy it?" Jasmine smirks.

"Nothing to buy," Elijah says. "It's the truth."

Mark nods again, his gaze slightly lifting. His back is to Jasmine, so he doesn't see the tension in her jaw as she stares us down.

"Fine, then. That gives me some time to find a better plan," she says sassily.

A muscle ticks in my jaw, but Elijah is right.

Talking about this won't change anything. We leave in a week and that is that.

"Best of luck, then," I hiss.

"Thanks, Beckett."

She doesn't catch the menace.

SAVANNAH

Staying alive is easy. Functioning normally? Now that's hard.

The food they give me tastes like nothing and smells like nothing, but it fills the ache in my stomach. I lift it to my mouth. Lift, eat, swallow. Repeat. I forget that I need water until the food is gone, so I guzzle it, trying to fill the pain in my belly with something solid.

I lay back onto the floor, staring at nothing. It's the same every day. After each session in the padded chamber, they pump me with *Velox* and a guard brings me bread and water. Then I slump in the far corners of my cell and fight the urge to cry. Sometimes, I think I see a figure by the bars before me, swimming in the light. The figure looks to be a girl, but it's a different girl every time.

When I squeeze my eyes shut, she is always gone.

Hallucinations.

My body shakes. I never look at my wounds. It only takes a few minutes until the *Velox* gets rid of them, but even if my body feels fine, my mind stays with that padded room. I've begun to lose track how many times I've been in there. Sometimes it's my mother in there with the faceless man, other times—when breaking me is a greater priority over asking questions—it's a different Argenti.

Not once has it been Marcellus.

I move further back into my cell, far enough from the corner where I relieve myself, but still not far enough to escape the dreadful smell.

My eyes water and I slam my eyes shut and think of them.

Jesse. Melanie. Jasmine. Mason…

Sometimes I forget some of their names, my head struggling. Other times the list feels endless.

Eli. Dad. Lily. Bronson, the baker. Samael, the man I stole my switchblade from…

I'm here for them. I came to Umbra for them. I'm trying.

Perseverance.

My hands shake, the absence of my switchblade a gaping hole. Since that first day, I haven't answered a single question they've asked. And not once have I screamed.

It's my own sort of victory. The only thing I can hold onto.

The ground cuts into my shoulder so I turn on my back, staring at the roof. Outside of my cell, the bustle of footsteps fills the corridor. This is common.

Each day in the padded room my mother plays me footage from a different area of Umbra. Occasionally Jesse is in it. Sometimes he's not. It's all a means to try and get me to speak.

They don't know anything.

Not a single whisper about an army has breached my torture sessions, which can only be a good thing. While I'm here, distracting the Elders and Argenti, my friends are safe to continue our plans.

So I hold my tongue, and I don't utter a single word.

Eventually, to taunt me more, my mother started selecting people from the footage.

After she's done with me in that room, they parade them past my cell, lock them up for a few hours and then bring them out to work on them. All so I can see.

My mother doesn't bother attending these events. They don't take them for answers. They take them to break me and leave the door to the padded room open so I can hear everything. I hide in the far corner of my cell, pretending not to care, but a hefty sob mingles with my breath.

When I get out of here, I will tear the faceless man to shreds and I will make my mother watch.

On days when it hurts to think the names of those I love, I let the feelings ride me. The coppery taste of Silver Magic courses around my cell, but I don't care enough to check if I'm being watched before I do it. Any Argenti could sense the raw energy, but I don't care. Doing this is one of my only happy moments.

I feel my heart pounding in my chest and I think of them—how it feels to be near them, how they smell, how their pulse ticks. And then I'm there.

Jesse is the easiest to find, because he is the closest, but today I try and sense Melanie—because I hadn't yet tried. She's so far away, so impossible to reach without a comm, that I feel my heart shatter slightly. I'm slammed with the scent of metal and citrus when I try and connect.

My hands fist in the torn shards of my dress, prying against the pocket that once held her comm.

Perseverance, Melanie. Persevere—for me.

I wish I could see her. Talk to her. But that's no longer possible without my comm. I didn't think I would use it on Umbra—it was more of a failsafe. But I did need it. I still do.

I should have used it before I got captured. I should have asked her to come earlier. But alas, that was taken from me.

I release the image of her, the smell of citrus evaporating into my cell. Using Silver Magic gets easier every day.

The dragging swathes of time being locked in this cell has made me docile, bored and craving normal human contact. Silver Magic gives me that.

I squirm around in the dust, the nail beds on my thumbs raw from where I've been picking at them. It hurts, but I don't stop.

I miss my switchblade and the comfort of holding it. So instead, I make steady work on picking at my nails. A distraction. A way to release pain. It doesn't matter how gross they look or how much blood spills. Because after the next session in the padded room, they will pump me with more *Velox* and my fingers will be as good as new anyway.

A far away door whispers shut as someone clambers down the stairs. Usually they don't speak among themselves—the only sounds accompanying their footsteps are their next victim blubbering.

But this time, they speak. It's enough to perk my interest.

It takes me a moment to separate and extend my awareness away from this cell. Days of dulling my senses have turned me to stone and the world beyond me aches as I hone into it.

Two pristine Elders come for me, their silk shoes loud on the stone. This time it's not a hallucinated figure.

"—notion that Miss James is alive."

"*Alex,*" a voice hisses. Evaline's voice.

"Hello, Savannah." Alex's voice?

I blink rapidly. They stand right before my cell, closer than I thought they'd be.

"Welcome," my voice croaks, the first time I've used it in... I don't even know how long.

I pull my hands into my lap, fingers picking at the raw flesh around my left thumb. The Elders stand before me, the same two that visited me last time—Evaline, in a soft blue gown with silver iron work around her breasts and shoulders, and Alex with his glistening silver hair and white blouse that plays tricks with my eyes in the harsh lights.

Alex. It's the first time they've used his name. It sounds familiar, but my brain feels thick with honey and I can't remember where from.

He leans towards me, his soft hand coming for me, lean fingers wrapping around the rusted bar. He traps me with his silver eyes. I don't know how he sees me, this far back in my cell washed in shadow, but I hold his gaze. I feel my body swaying, the pressure of sitting upright too much to bother with, so I let myself sink deeper against the wall as he whispers, "Do you know about little Jasmine?"

A chime ticks in my head and I swear I feel a muscle flex in my jaw. His words are near silent, but the walls here have ears, so I don't blame him. Before thinking, I allow him a soft nod.

He holds himself steady, analysing me. I shouldn't have responded. My palms slicken and I pick more frantically at my thumb.

"They may ask you this under a blade, but I urge you not to answer them when they do."

Alright, that I can do. I wasn't planning on ever speaking again. My throat feels too raw and dry, so I nod again.

He presses his lips together, a thin white line, as Evaline grips his hand.

"This coalition is under his thumb, so do not trust anyone. Not the Argenti. Not even us. Promise me this, and you might live."

Evaline's words tumble around me, and suddenly everything clicks.

Evaline, Alexsandre, Roman, Celestine, Marcellus.

Names of people that have my back? Or at least, have it in private.

You should've run—Marcellus's words, moments before they captured me. My throat feels thick, swallowing becoming difficult.

"Whose thumb?" I ask, immediately wishing I hadn't.

Talking is not a sport I enjoy. Stars, my throat hurts.

Evaline purses her lips when I ask this. The Elders rule by votes, mass decisions between them. There's no one ruler who's greater than the other. But, I suppose when power is involved, there are always power plays.

Spies everywhere. Threats in place. People playing both sides.

Trust no one, because no one will trust you.

"Words carry in these walls." Her voice is low. My mind is too hazed to make out what she means by that. "But if you stay alive, you will soon see," Evaline advises. She reaches her hand through the bars, her wrist exposed towards me. There's a satchel of water in her palm, and I scurry for it.

All else becomes irrelevant. My focus hones in on the water, all other senses vanishing. But it isn't the water she wishes me to see. Because on her wrist, shining in the light, is a silver number. The number seven.

The seventh Elder.

Lythia May's mother. Venus Collins' aunt.

This woman is related to me—this gorgeous, olive-skinned person that glimmers like silver and holds herself with beauty and grace is *related to me.*

But I don't really care or even consider what that means, too focused on the water.

My fingers close around the satchel, shaking beyond my control and I stare up at her in total awe. I squeeze the skin into my mouth, making a mess of my shirt. It coats my throat. It fixes everything.

I gasp, choking on the stuff. It's like it brings me back to life and I suddenly begin to realise the implications of her position. She is the mother of the most extraordinary Argenti of all time—Lythia May, the woman who had two ways of harnessing Silver Magic—who predicted my rise to the throne.

She smiles softly at me, nodding her delicate chin towards her companion. The Elder next to her is no Argenti, but his silver hair glistens like one. Suddenly, that doesn't seem so odd after all.

Melanie's distant voice fills my head with a displaced memory.

The first Elders were all scientists and guards. Science is our great-est weapon and feat. She said it to explain why weaponry hadn't advanced so much on Umbra—science had always been their pri-mary progression.

And this man before me is, without a doubt, a scientist. He probably dabbled in Argenti blood and changed his DNA.

I take a shaky sip of the water and remind myself to ask him about it one day.

"Pray this is the last time we meet you in this cell," Evaline says, reaching for Alex's hand.

Translation: we won't return.

Or.

You will be saved soon.

Probably the former. Most of my luck has run out by now.

Alex twists the hand holding the bar, making to grab Evaline's. Knowing what I now know, I roam my eyes over his wrist. And then I stop breathing. Alex gives me a soft smile and nod and they step away from me. The glistening number six on his wrist scorches like a brand in my mind.

I open my mouth to speak, but he shakes his head.

Words carry in these walls.

Liquid soaks my lap and I look down to notice I've dropped the satchel. My mouth is dry again and I won't get any more water until after they torture me. It's their fun little way of rewarding me.

I want to hit myself for being so clumsy, but I can't think of anything beyond the number on his wrist. Which confuses me, because water means more than anything in this cell.

His dull, silver eyes—much like mine—catch my gaze and I tremble. I make insane work on my nails, picking them to pieces.

Evaline squeezes the hand of my grandfather, her brother, Alex-sandre Collins, the Sixth Elder and, together, they disappear up the stairs.

My grandfather.

Blood roaring in my ears, I pull my knees up to my chest, struggling to form any coherent thoughts. One thing does stick with me though: I will never understand how a gentle man like Alex could have ever conceived a woman like Venus Collins.

My body begins to shake.

And it doesn't stop.

SAVANNAH

Within the next few hours, I have realised all of two things.

One—that Alexsandre was the Elder who saved Jasmine from these cells so many years ago. Little does he know that a reunion is probably in the stars for them, if the plans I laid down stay intact.

And two— Alexsandre was the Elder who passed the ban on Terra months ago.

Soon we will no longer affiliate with Terra. My father will pass a ban. Words that my mother spoke months ago, in a different prison, on a different planet, days before Umbran ships blew apart my home.

A part of me wonders if Alexsandre planned the bombing too. Evaline warned me not to trust anyone.

I lower my head into my hands, pulling in long breaths. Two

names on my list have now been ticked off as people I can count to be on my side, but also as people I can never rely on.

Is this my life now? Rotting away in a cell, surrounded by people who support me in secret, yet will just as quickly tie a noose around my neck if given the chance?

My heart aches. I have never missed home more than I do right now.

Not Umbra. Not the base near Silver Valley. Not even Silver Valley itself.

I miss my old, dingy apartment in the city where everything was horrible and nothing ever seemed to matter. I miss not mattering.

Hands shaking and eyes unseeing, I don't realise I have a new visitor until something hits me sharply across the forehead.

What was I hit with? Puzzled, I look around me. My eyes roll in my skull, vaguely making out the silhouette of an exceptionally small human.

"They leave the door unlocked when they enter," they say.

The hallucination looks too real. Way too real. I squeeze my eyes, rub them, and then she is gone. Her small feet patter away from me, but not up the stairs. I try and fool myself that I imagined it, but the pain in my forehead is hard to ignore.

There are people in the padded room right now, the sound of a drill echoing down the corridor and the faint screams of someone following them. I wish the small girl hadn't woken me from my trance. Reality has crept in to allow the high wailing of the drill to break apart my skull. I don't know how to retreat back into my mind now that I'm awake.

My body starts swaying. Blood runs down my fingers as I keep picking at my thumb so hard it stings.

The sound of the girl's footsteps become lost in the sound. It's almost as if she is hiding under the cloak of noise. Who is she?

More screaming.

The drill stops for a small beat. A question is asked, though I'm not sure if the question is answered. I clap my hands over my ears and begin to hum as the raw, human pleading continues back down the hallways.

The drill quickly follows.

My cell is the closest one to the padded room. I can count the steps it takes between here and there—13 steps on a good day, 17 if they are dragging me.

I want them to move me into the darkest depths of the dungeons so I don't hear anything. Maybe if I can't hear what's happening, they will stop it from happening.

The drill increases in tempo, a chime that sings in my skull.

My fingers claw at my hair and I cup my ears with such a force that blood rushes to my cheeks. "*Hmmm mmm hmmm.*"

My humming blends into the drill, coating it like a poorly applied Band-Aid.

"*Mmmmmm.*"

At least it's not Jesse.

"*Hmmm mmmm.*"

Not Melanie. Not my dad.

"*Hmm mmm mmmhmm.*"

Not Mason. *Never* Mason. My precious brother is safe.

My body sways forwards and backwards, and eventually it slides down into the stained dirt. It could be minutes, it could be hours, but the drilling eventually stops.

The person in the padded room never makes it to a cell. I can hear the faceless man leaving. It's utterly quiet.

My fingers shakily move themselves from my ears. The progression takes a while to leave. Perhaps disposing of a body is long, tedious work.

A shadow crosses over my cell. I crack open my eyes to better see it and, there, for the first time since entering the castle, I see him. Marcellus.

He releases a shaky breath upon seeing me. A smirk dances on his face when I lift my head. The lights on the tunnel behind him strike his back, shining against Jesse's sword. Why doesn't he take it off?

I shiver. Drop my gaze. Was he telling the faceless man to drill?

"Hello, little mouse."

I groan. There's no energy left in my body to fight him. He kneels, knees brushing the bars. In his hands, I see my switchblade resting in his large palm.

Mine, I want to shout. *Mine.*

He flashes one word to me. *Perseverance. Perseverance. Perseverance.*

The world around me spins.

His hands gently cup my chin as he stares at me, lifting my gaze to meet his. Silent tears crack down the dust lining my face. I can taste it in my mouth.

"Stay down, little mouse. I'll see you later."

I don't bother clearing my throat before I croak. "Go away."

A muscle flickers in his jaw, the smirk growing wider. My switchblade is gone, but Jesse's sword is still there, shining in the light.

Miraculously, he stands, silver hair a halo on his head as he passes under the light. I don't miss the way he wrings his hands as he leaves, as if his palms are sweating.

MELANIE

Jasmine's declaration to usurp the plan sends waves through the warehouse.

It began as a rumour—*the princess is helpless and alone and we need to help her. Jasmine can help her, just like she helped us.*

It ends with pure rage. Passion overtakes them and common sense vanishes.

Why are we listening to Beckett?

We don't know her.

Jasmine can fix this.

She's always had the Umbran Safe Hold crew tightly wrapped around her little finger. She helped them when no one else did and now that loyalty is finally being rewarded.

What do I—a simple hacker girl with a rich family name—have compared to that? They look at me with disdain. Distrust.

They don't know me and they don't care to. So I turn back to the only thing I know. Computers and, more specifically, hacking.

Terra doesn't have the skin grafting tech to completely fix my arm since the bombing, but it has the people, the knowledge and the abandoned families.

My mediocre office in the Valley is nothing compared to this.

I stand in an old facility on the base, dust coating the desk and my hands as I roam their wondrous screens, a cable attached to my arm and into the beauty that is the Umbraweb. It's a place of infinite knowledge, where quite literally anything is possible and achievable if you know where and how to look.

Umbra is *beautiful*. Complex. A series of screens with images that flash from any angle you stare at. Holograms. Tech. Science.

Mason has corrupted the sanctuary of my self-appointed office in the warehouse. But this? This is *mine*.

"Melanie Beckett," a voice says, snapping me from the depths of the Umbraweb. "Did you really break into Umbran computers to fix your hand, what... three minutes before departure?"

Elijah. Of course.

"I still have three minutes." My focus is entirely locked on the screen and the wires pumping codes into the small incision I fixed into the prosthetic wrist years ago. "And I'm not fixing my hand. I'm adding more data to the chip in it."

Once I leave Terra, there's no certainty I will ever return and I want to carry everything about it with me. The information overwhelms me as I contemplate it. The entirety of the Terran web is being loaded onto a chip on my arm, as it stands, as of today.

One day, when this war is over, I will look back over this life and pine for it. I may even shed a tear. But as I turn to Elijah, all I shed is a part of my soul—the human part—and I refocus on the goal I've always wanted: to go home.

I give him a robotic smile, feeling nothing as he clasps my hand, ready to lead me to the ship that will see my goal through.

The engine is near silent, but I hate the soft hum of it and the way the pod rattles. We repaired it from a near useless state, but it's still partially broken. It has lost the ability to speak right and, instead of giving us updated rundowns of our take-off, it splutters and lurches, spewing out odd words that don't quite make sense. I rub my temples at the sound of it. If it wasn't for Elijah, I'd go insane.

"*We're f-flying s—soon.*"

The caption winces, not knowing why the ship is functioning quite this awfully. Usually, we would have an exact countdown.

"T-minus four minutes, people," I confirm, eyes locked on the small holographic screen floating above us at the front of the ship.

Nico gives me a long, pained look, as if it to say *we can see that.*

This is a different ship to the one we practised in—it's a lot larger, which is nice, but the brokenness more than outweighs that. It's one of few we haven't fully fixed.

Perhaps it's my fault. Jackson grumbles behind me, glaring into my soul. Definitely my fault. Jasmine has the people turning on me or, at the very least, is convincing them to make my life difficult.

"I was told they gave us this ship because you're able to fix things no one else can." It's the first thing Nico has said to me in weeks and I flinch.

I can't fix this. Not mere moments before our mission.

"*We are about to go h-home with our f-flock,*" the ship says unhelpfully.

Apparently, *flock* is the ship's word for squadron. Who was this ship's old captain? A damn bird handler?

Jackson slams his palm into the small dining table propped at the back of the ship. I didn't see him leave the captain's bay, but there he goes, pacing at the back with the healer tapping her fingers on the table as if she's half mad.

I look over at her. Smile. Her sister is Samael's right-hand woman. The same sister that is a guard on Jasmine Spark's ship. And I will not hesitate to follow through on my threats to make her life awful if her sister follows Jasmine's plan to go rouge.

"Andrea, quit it," Jackson snaps.

She keeps tapping, her eyes glazed as she stares out the window in the direction of her sister. She's been doing better since leaving the Safe Holds, but being separated from her sister isn't helping.

Around us, dust swirls and trees bend from the wind of our engines as all thirty-three ships prepare for launch. My fingers are tight as they wrap around the seat belt slashing across my torso, plastering me into my seat behind the captain. Elijah offers me a shaky smile from beside me, but his skin has paled.

Jackson convinces Andrea to move into her seat and, together, they start muttering among themselves. Her nervous energy radiates among our crew and Nico grits his teeth in the captain's seat.

Everyone besides Elijah is purposely ignoring me. I push my head back into my chair, fingers digging into my palm as I stiffen my body.

"We are now flying away from Earth."

Earth. Not Terra. I hadn't heard that word in a while—not until Savannah. But even she adopted the use of the Umbran tongue graciously.

This ship must have spent a lot of time with a captain on Terran soil. The voice speaks in fluent English, not a hint of Latin, French, or any other language that Umbrans may prefer. The ship around us thrusts, engaging take-off.

"Joining—g our f-flock!"

I dissociate as it launches off the ground, joining the swarm of others in the sky. I retreat into myself, thinking of a time and place where there isn't a squadron of people rushing to save their Queen. Where it was just me and Jesse aboard a ship no one wanted to be on—no one except my uncle, who always picks his ambitions over his family.

I haven't heard from Liaison Banks since he fled Silver Valley, and I try not to think of him now. I familiarise myself with the feeling of the ship, the way it hums underneath us, the pounding of my heart as I succumb to it. Then I'm back in my mind's eye, on the floor next to Jesse with shaking fingers and skin aching from the new bruises my uncle had forced onto my skin the night before.

It was the first time I met him. I remember his boyish body as he pulled himself out of the grate the mechanics used to tinker with the ship, smears of black grime on his face and blood around his fingers. I'd never seen anything more endearing in my life.

If I had known him then, I'd have hijacked the engine of the ship from where I had sat against the wall, attaching myself to the wires in the hatch and delaying the engine. It would've taken me seconds. The guards could've left the ship to see what's wrong. Jesse could've strolled right through the main entrance.

None of the prisoners or passengers would've cared. The ship wasn't even that monitored. And yet, he slid onto the floor next to me, panting and covered in grime.

I chuckle to myself, tilting my head back into my seat until the urge to cry pounds behind my eyes.

"Sleep, Melanie," Elijah says beside me.

My entire body has succumbed to my chair. He wipes a finger across my brow and I let myself fall into the dream.

I sleep for around half a day before we are all up and moving around the ship. We activate the communication channels and a constant stream of discussion webs between our squadron arsenals spills through our speakers.

"A1 initiating sequence for admittance. Squad A, fall in line," I command, my fingers wrapped around a small screen as I swish through the numbers of our formation.

My voice travels through the comm on our ship, sending it out to all the others behind us. We are leading the mission, the figurehead entering the wormhole. Going through the entrance between galaxies is our most vulnerable position.

"*Let's go camo, losers.*"

Jasmine's voice grates up through the speaker, as clear as if she's standing next to me. My fingers twitch.

"Does she *know* how to speak formally, for stars' sake?" I say, only broadcasting it to those in our ship. Elijah chuckles and he watches me. With my jaw clenched, I jab the button to broadcast to the other ships. "Squad B fall in line. Squad A, initiate camouflage."

Next to me, I see Jasmine's ship is already semi-transparent. Our invisibility isn't perfect, considering we had to resurrect it with limited availability to Umbran tech, but it's better than nothing.

Nico slides a switch on our ship and the scales on the exterior of our ship shift, a million tiny mirrors that reflect and draw in light, casting us in near invisibility.

"*Hiding now,*" the ship announces.

The rest of Squad A follows our lead, not Jasmine's.

The corner of my lip twitches as I cast an automatic grin towards Jasmine's ship. I swear I can see her outline just past the ship's window, beneath the camouflage, sticking her tongue out at me.

"Squad B, initiating camouflage sequence," a person from ship B1 announces.

I focus on our vessel and the looming wormhole splitting apart the galaxy before us. As we enter it, the stars begin to stretch. I've only seen this in person once, but I know the theories, having read about it in our histories a great many times.

Learning the stars and the science of the world is fundamental in the upbringing of any noble child on Umbra. But the reality of seeing it in person is just that much more awe-inspiring.

In the grand scheme of the galaxy, little things like my love for Jesse, my confusion over Elijah and my hatred for Jasmine mean nothing.

My finger slips on the screen as I reach for Elijah. He hesitates, unsure if he should touch my gloved hand. With a shuddering breath, I slip off the glove and grip him with the metal gleaming out of my arm. It does more than prove a point.

When he pulls his attention from the stars and onto the glove at our feet, my heart flutters.

The universe is a ricochet of light as space moves around us, twisting and dancing, compressing into the portal.

I nod at the stars, urging Elijah to look. Even for me—a girl made of stardust and planets—the anomaly of space is mind-bending. Seeing the stars and planets existing in an endless maze around us is one thing, but seeing it warp into a passageway is a sight no one should miss.

Our ships move as a unit, merging into formation like a well-oiled machine. I take a deep, steadying breath as we approach the end of the tunnel, which yawns open into something glittering and peaceful.

"Reposition all units upon entrance," I instruct into the speaker before me, sending my voice over to all other ships. Like a wave, they ripple out of the wormhole and return to a better position for long-term exposure among the stars.

Jasmine's ship fans out from us, still invisible, but the stars reflect just a fragment too brightly off the exterior of her vessel, pinpointing them to me.

Elijah releases a heavy breath as Andrea gasps, muttering a name over and over.

"Cass, Cass, Cass." Her sister. "CASSIDY!"

She plasters her face on the window, grinning as her sister's ship comes beside us. I see the girl's yellow hair shining as she waves at her sibling.

"Just over a day left until we approach the atmosphere on Umbra," Nico states, twisting around in his chair to survey me. I don't respond, not deigning to move the muscles in my face.

"You know the plan," Elijah says on my behalf. "We orbit Umbra until the 15th."

"And hover in the skies like sitting ducks," Jackson grumbles from his seat.

"And hover in the skies to *prepare ourselves*," I exclaim, my tone dark.

Silence envelops the cabin as ships fan out around us, expanding our reach. Stars blip by our window like swirling infernos that wink at us from across the cosmos.

And there, far beyond the swirling lights, I swear I can see the Umbran galaxy.

Jasmine must have the same thought because her voice screams over the speakers. "*Let's screw 'em up, gang! Full steam ahead!*"

My fingers are shaking with the need to jab the button on the speaker. Jackson snorts from behind me and, when the chorus of replies from other ships sound in, I feel the need to physically remove myself from the front of the ship.

"*Let's get them!*"

"*Whooo!*"

"*Rot in the stars, Umbra!*"

"*Grab your weapons, I think I saw an Umbran ship!*"

They scream at each other, fraying at the seams. Voices clash and tangle over the speakers, an eruption of stupidity. Jackson rises, spinning a blade around his fingers with a thirsty expression.

A few ships drift away from formation. A screen blinks in front of Nico, informing us that we are breaking apart and the formation is shredding.

Andrea gasps, stepping back from the window, shaking her head. Jackson reaches for her. And through the comm, Jasmine's voice spreads to our ship. *Only* our ship.

"Happy arrival. Do you really expect me to hang around, waiting for something to happen?"

No. No no no no.

Elijah's face is white as he rips his way to the front of the ship and yells into the speaker. "Jasmine! Hold your ground!"

"No!" I gasp, legs unsteady and body shaking as I take a step backwards. Nico looks at the wires in my prosthetic. Jackson looks ready to abandon ship. And Andrea is pacing, her eyes wide. "She has the army. She's going to do something."

"Cassidy is on our side," Andrea assures me. "She won't get herself killed."

I locate my seat, sinking deep within it and forcing myself to just breathe.

"Make me," Jasmine's voice clashes back over the speakers, taunting.

Andrea gasps. I can feel Jasmine's smirk reaching my ship, just as Elijah slams his hand beside the intercom.

"*Let's go down now!*"

"*Umbra isn't expecting us.*"

"*Let's destroy those silver pricks!*"

Elijah's face flushes red and a tear slides down his cheek. He speaks without hesitation, his jaw taut as he says what I cannot.

"Do you all *want* to die? Do you *want* to lose your families? We are in their territory now. They will kill us. We are only thirty-three ships! HOLD YOUR POSITIONS."

Silence drifts around our ship. All the talking stops, turning to static.

My heart vanishes somewhere, falling to my feet as I lean towards Elijah. His eyes are glazed and red. I'd bet anything a cloud of memory has taken him, his eyes unseeing as he deflates next to me.

Pain, loss, fire, bombs…It all dances in his eyes, catching up to him. For months, he's been repressing the grief.

In my own mind, I relive the bombing. I see them fall from the sky—see the eyes of his dead parents. What he doesn't realise is how right his words were.

He pushes past me, heading to the back of the ship, his breathing shallow. I reach out to brush his sleeve, but he doesn't turn around or look at me. He just beelines straight to the sleeping quarters.

I can barely breathe. I can barely think.

My hands shake, the metal of my prosthetic glinting in the lights dancing from the roof of the ship.

Fire took everything from me just as it took everything from Elijah.

Umbra fights with fire, just as Jasmine fights with passion.

I plan to fight with my common sense. "Nico, lead our squadrons. I'll be right back," I breathe.

Elijah's the only goddamn soul in the universe on my side and I plan to keep him with me. I almost fall to my knees when I pull apart the curtains to the sleeping quarters and see him sobbing on the floor, his head in his hands.

The weak lights of the ship swallow him, making him a dark phantom on the floor. Cots line the walls, compressing the room. His form is shadowed, hidden from me, but I feel it screaming for me like a beacon of light.

I make it to his side before I finally collapse, grab his head in my arms and hold him to my chest. The sounds of his sobs pull apart my body. He doesn't speak, but I didn't expect him to. Months of pain catches up to him, exploding from him in waves. I finally watch him unfold and I decide to break my promise to Nico.

Silently, the ship waits for my return, but I don't go back. I don't plan to return without Elijah next to me.

We stay here, leaning against the metal bunks with the flat mattresses, until we get to Umbra. Until the next day dawns.

But all I can think about is Elijah. Always defending me. Always defending common sense.

I try my hardest not to fall apart with him.

SAVANNAH

I listen to Marcellus and stay down in my cell, the dust from the ground choking me. Mostly because I haven't the strength to move, but I do wonder what he meant.

To save me? Probably not. But I'll take any change of scenery at this point. And, to my surprise, he does in fact come back later.

He's donned in fighting leathers and it's the first time I've seen him look inexplicably angry. His fingers twitch as he stands before me, his pale cheeks flushed scarlet. Behind him, the faceless man doesn't say a word. He just watches us in quiet trepidation.

I strain my ears. Something is dripping again, some cellmates are groaning and the faceless man is scuffling his feet.

But it's the soft padding of shoes whispering by the stairs that makes a muscle twitch in Marcellus's jaw. I hold my gaze on his, noticing that he masks it with a smile.

I swallow deeply. *They leave the door unlocked when they enter.*

"Get up, Savannah."

I do not. Instead, I wonder what has happened to my mother and why she hasn't bothered to show. Perhaps she's done with her questions. Perhaps they just plan to break me now.

Why kill your enemy if you can rip them apart, limbs, mind, heart and soul? There will be no one left to fight for if they are broken. Just a hollow corpse of a girl.

My eyes drift closed. Crust has formed around the edges of my eyes and my tongue sits dry like sandpaper in my mouth.

"Get up." His voice slams into me, deep and rough.

I take a shuddering breath that rattles all the way down my body. The faceless man behind Marcellus clears his throat.

I hear Marcellus turn. "Get her water."

"That's against protocol."

It's the first time I hear the man speak and I almost jump at the sound. He sounds so… squeaky.

"It's been two days since you last touched her, fed her and watered her—do you *want* her to die?" Marcellus's words bite into the empty corridor, sharper than any blade my torturer could whip up. "Water. Now."

The man grinds his teeth, but pushes aside his long black garb to hand Marcellus a water skin. Humour glitters in Marcellus's eyes as he wraps his fingers around it and throws it at me. It slams into the side of my head.

The harsh gesture causes me to sit up. I rub my eyes and stare at him blankly. The water tumbles onto the dirt next to me and I blink, the stinging pain tickling my cheek.

With shaking fingers, I grab the water skin.

This man tracked me down in the desert. He is a powerful Argenti, able to suck all Silver Magic out of the pores of his friends and rivals.

He'll never leave the shelter of the Elders. The castle is his fortress. And yet, he is giving me water.

I open my mouth and pour the precious liquid onto my face. It makes it into my mouth, down my neck, onto my chest. I suck it in like air, forcing it into my hollow stomach. The muscles cramp, squeezing against the sudden onslaught, but I don't stop.

It soaks my clothes, my face, and I gasp for breath. Marcellus watches me intently, the corner of his mouth quirking. I stare back, my heart beating erratically.

Around me, the world is a mess of darkness and agony, but the water feels like the brightest thing in the entire universe.

He gestures to the torturer and I hardly notice them enter my cell until the awful stench of the faceless man's breath hits my cheek as he hoists me up from the floor.

My body feels like liquid as they carry me. The water skin slips from my fingers. Mostly empty. Through a haze, I follow Marcellus's fingers as he lifts it from the dirt.

My chest tightens. Water sloshes in my stomach until nausea creeps up on me and bile courses up my throat.

I unleash the water I just drank all over the faceless man's shoes.

The world spins as his fingers tighten on me, the stark lights above our heads drilling into my eyes as I roll in his arms, stomach acid ripping through my throat.

I heave, chest constricting. Tears blur my vision as I tilt towards the ground in his grip. The dark grey stone floor swims below me, splattered with my bile.

With trembling lips, I swallow deeply.

The faceless man is seething, his nails clipping into my arm. "If you hadn't let her drink my entire water skin so fast—"

"If you had actually provided her with sufficient nutrition," Marcellus interrupts, "she would not have reacted to the water."

"She gets it after I'm done with her."

My entire body feels damp—from water, bile, and other things

I'd rather not think about. But Marcellus helps steady me, as if touching me is not such an awful thing. At least, until I turn my pounding head to see his face crumpled.

Wonderful.

I try and pull away from them, but the man tightens his hold, leading me to the padded room. Even more wonderful.

I flutter my eyes closed, not wanting to see. It doesn't matter though. I know every step by heart and the image of the dungeon fills my mind.

My bare feet bump into a crack in the stone floor and I know we are halfway. To my right are the stairs out of here. They're long, spiralling, and made of stone. One way goes up, the other descends to more cells. It takes exactly 20 steps to go up to the exit until there's a large door.

The door is wooden, thick and almost red in colour. When it's open, the outside light smears over the crevices people have dented into the smooth texture over the years.

They leave the door unlocked when they enter.

My chest flutters, body yearning towards the door. But I'm immediately torn away. The entrance to the padded room yawns open instead, light pooling at my feet. My legs buckle slightly, but the faceless man's death grip keeps me from falling.

Marcellus's silver eyes pierce me. He frowns at me, his skin so smooth and ageless that the motion is almost impossible to detect.

"Savannah?" he asks, as if I spoke his name aloud.

I squeeze my eyes shut as the table comes into view.

It would be glorious to have him be my lifeline—to have him capture me in his gaze and pull me through. But the world hurts too much to be present, so I let myself sink into oblivion. My consciousness goes down, down, deep into my chest.

I detach myself from the world as the faceless man attaches me to the table.

It's more durable this way.

A saw. An arm. My breath wobbles past my lips, bubbling like a stream. Is that bone?

Fear drenches me. Somewhere, there's wire.

I sink deep into myself. And then Marcellus touches my hand. I feel myself grip it like a lifeline. But the world is lost on me.

Red. Hot. Pain.

And there's my arm again, with warm liquid trickling down onto the table I lay on.

~

Water touches my lips. The darkness of my cell envelops me.

I've fallen into a place no one can reach me, but there's still pressure in my hand, wrapping around my fingers.

I didn't let him go. He doesn't give me any pity or any comforting words, as Melanie would have. He doesn't even stand beside me, like Jesse would have.

He is from this world. Perhaps he has even been in my place before. But he shakes his hand from mine to go and stand with the faceless man.

I let the water coat my throat. It feels odd, drinking when the world is so shattered. My chest heaves and one sob escapes.

Marcellus leaves me to rest, but the water stays. Bread and water.

"Until next time." He says the words, his voice swirling above my head.

I cannot do this anymore. There's nothing left in me I want to save, so I sob, my face in the dirt of my cell.

Until next time.

~

It's difficult to know tell how much time passes in this cell.

My skin has not felt sunlight in so long. The dungeons under the castle have become my world. It's even worse to tell time in the padded room—there it elongates, stretching for so long that I want to scream. And in this the cell, time races, passing over me in a blur. Nothing makes sense anymore.

"Hello." The soft voice flutters around me, so pleasant in a place so vile.

Lightning strikes in my veins. Heart hammering, I force myself to sit upright.

It's the young girl who has been slipping in and out of the dungeons. It has been her a great many times, only she looks absolutely nothing like I remember.

Her dark skin glistens in the light overhead, beautifully complemented with her deep maroon dress, glittering off her small frame like a ruby. Her brown eyes are wide and bright, like she's about to giggle at any moment.

I blink profusely, sinking back into the dirt.

"Eyes can be tricked," she whispers. And then she actually giggles.

I rub my eyes as she leans towards me, a familiar look in her eye as she grips the bars of my cell and sways on the balls of her feet. Her ebony, voluminous hair is pulled into two short ponytails, secured by a silver ribbon that matches the silver treading in her silken ruby dress.

Do I know her? I get the tickling sensation that I do.

I squeeze the balls of my hands against my temples, head pounding as she stares at me. My blood feels thick in my veins, sluggish as I try and come to.

She tilts her head, waiting. And it's at that precise moment that I sense the thick, honey coat of Silver Magic pouring throughout my cell. It sure as hell isn't coming from me.

"What are you doing?" I feel the warm coat of Silver Magic vanish as Marcellus's voice reverberates down the hall.

The girl tenses, her eyes darting as if she's debating running or confronting him. He eliminates her choices when he comes towards her and grasps her arm. He takes a deep breath when their skin meets.

What can this girl do?

Marcellus turns to me slowly, his expression bored. But my eyes catch his like static. It's easy to read a person, if you know where to look. And right now, Marcellus is pissed. His gaze sears into mine, but flickers away quickly. It's not me he's mad with.

"Come on." His voice is gruff, but she doesn't immediately budge.

She smiles at me softly. There's something sad about that smile, but my vision spins and I blink to regain my focus until suddenly, it's gone.

I need to build my strength. But I just… I don't care anymore.

She wrestles with him and purses her round lips at me.

I know this isn't a place for a young girl to be, but I almost want to tell him to leave her be. Almost. The feeling is deep in my gut, a swirling of old feelings. She looks at me like Mason does, all hope and smiles.

But this girl is not Mason.

I squeeze my eyes.

The girl huffs as Marcellus tears her away. "It's okay," she declares, as if trying to assure me. "My family isn't all bad. I promise."

My eyes snap open. A trickling cold sensation spreads over me. Their footsteps vanish. The heavy door opens and closes. And I know exactly why she was familiar to me.

Eyes can be tricked.

Despite how she looks, I've met this girl before—Amadea, the small redheaded Argenti girl who played that piano for Lucille. The girl that gave me the list of names.

Silver Magic swarms around me like hellfire. My magic was the reason I recognised her. The reason I sensed her so many times in the dungeons. I clung to her like a bee to honey.

Amadea.

My head spirals, heart singing.

The question is, do Lucille and Tamaz know she is here? Do they know about who she is and what her list means?

My head ticks through the names like clockwork.

Evaline
Alexsandre
Roman
Celestine
Marcellus

And I realise something with sharp clarity—she might be the key to everything.

The key to my freedom.

MELANIE

Play-acting Savannah's role as leader in this mission was stupid. I just want to stay here, huddled in the back of this small, dark room with Elijah and let the world take me.

We fell asleep like that, huddled on the floor, until slowly Elijah rustles me and I lurch awake, my eyes frantically scanning his face.

"Melanie. I'm okay, I'm okay…" Elijah rises.

The ship utters some nonsense about seeing Umbra, but I stay on the floor, balled into myself. Then I breathe. In. Out. Let my mind wake up.

From beyond the curtain, I can hear footsteps, followed by Jackson's voice spluttering something.

"You're not okay," I finally say, clearing my throat. "You haven't had time to heal since the fire."

Elijah's brown eyes rise to my face, ringed in red from lost tears.

I reach for him, muscles twitching, and hold him when he leans into me. My fingers knot around his arms, unable to really let go. He doesn't once flinch at the feel of my prosthetic hand on his warm skin, but I do—however briefly.

He notices and slowly pulls away again.

"The fire didn't touch me," he murmurs. "I'm okay. I'm still here."

"It did. And you need to let yourself feel that pain sometimes, so it doesn't destroy you."

The fire killed Eli and it gave me Elijah Brookes.

"Is that how you rationalise your uncle? His years of physical abuse?"

I wince. I never speak about that, but it is one of the worst things that came out of the fire that killed my parents. It made me shed a part of myself—the sweet courtier's daughter— replacing her with someone tougher and with a purpose. No matter how many times my uncle physically hurt me at home, I always had a place I could retreat to. Computers. Knowledge. A mission. And then Jesse.

"Occasionally."

Elijah straightens.

My body feels stiff from staying on the floor so long. My stomach rumbles. My mouth feels dry. And I need to use the bathroom.

He struggles to meet my gaze, but Jackson's footsteps increase in pitch and soon he has another thing to latch his eyes on. The fighter's flustered face appears around the corner, his eyes wide.

"I hate to interrupt," he says.

My gut sinks.

Sweat glistens on his brow from the outside light and he steps aside swiftly as I rise from my feet and scramble from the room.

"What happened?" I ask from ahead of him.

Jackson follows close behind me, as eloquent as Jesse in his role as a guard.

"Umbran pilot. Doing a test drill."

I can see the front window by the time he answers. Umbra is a swirling mass in the abyss of space. Its ring splinters the sky, arching through the blackness, alight from the glow of the stars and sun.

Elijah misses a step behind me at the sight of it.

Nico is pounding buttons before him, his hands shaking, nerves coating every ligament of his body. It's enough to make my whole body run cold.

"Our invisible shields worked," Andrea starts, hunched over at the front of the window, her eyes locked on the stars. Her hair is twisted into a braid like her sister always wears it, but long tendrils of her brown hair have escaped and sit plastered against the sweat on her neck. "Until Jasmine made contact."

"She did *what?*" I answer. I ball my hands against the window, breath pooling against the glass.

"My sister, Cassidy, is on that ship." Andrea's voice breaks.

And sure enough, Jasmine's ship has lost its invisibility, silver and grand and shining, as the Umbran pilot's ship docks theirs. I see it all in slow motion, air gushing in my ears as the others chatter behind me. The ship is positioning itself under theirs, a locking mechanism reaching its prongs out.

Minutes. We have *minutes* until it attaches. Until Jasmine lets the pilot on their ship and the cover of our entire squadron could be blown.

I push away from the window so abruptly my head spins. "Get me a space suit," I tell Jackson, as I move towards the exit.

Andrea breathes deep. She turns and looks at me, tearing her gaze from the window. Jackson just stares at me, his eyes glazed.

"Space suit!" I repeat.

If the Elders get us, we lose everything. Months of planning. Over a hundred fighters.

Jackson understands that. He doesn't so much as nod at me, just steps back into the ship, his back straight and gaze hard.

"No," Elijah says, gripping the guard's arm.

"Let me go, Brookes."

"You aren't sending her out there," he declares.

Jackson fixes him with an empty stare.

"She needs to help them," Andrea says.

"Keep an eye on their ship, on your sister," Nico snaps at her, busy working on getting the exit seals ready.

Jackson rips himself free from Elijah's stare, his hand hovering by his sword. Elijah does the same, reaching for his knife.

"It's her, or it's all of us," Jackson says.

My heart pings as I watch Elijah's hard mask drop for a mere second.

Elijah gives me a teary stare, emotion cresting in his eyes. "Anyone but Mel."

I swallow. Take a deep breath. I turn my back to him, twisting my hair into a knot on my head and reaching for the cupboard with spare thermals. It will be bloody freezing in space.

"Jackson, *suit*!" I yell.

Elijah swallows deeply, his eyes locked on me. "Melanie."

"Elijah. Don't."

If he looks at me like that, I will stay. And I can't. I just *can't*.

Jackson finally goes for the suit. We don't have much time.

Hopefully Mason is smart enough to cut the comms to their ship before the pilot boards—unless Umbrans now carry pocket-sized comms like Savannah and me, he will have to return to his ship to alert the Elders.

Savannah will *kill* me for putting her brother in this position. He should have been on my team, not Jasmine's.

Thermals tumble out of a small cupboard and I reach for the first one my hand touches, shoving the slightly large shirt over my head.

"*Jackson!*"

There is a hiss from the exit of the ship—the airlock pressurising with oxygen. The airlock acts as a decompression chamber, allowing me to enter and be released safely into space. Once the process completes, I shove the door open, throwing a pair of heavy boots into the chamber before heading in myself.

Jackson skids by the entrance, tossing the suit into the air towards me.

I catch it in my prosthetic hand, swiftly swinging it around to my front and slipping my legs through it.

"I'm going with her," Elijah declares from behind me.

I trip over the leg of the black suit. It clings to my body, tough as leather, and I hiss. "You are *not*. Cover me from in here. Keep the ship running."

"You're our tech—*you* keep the ship running," he challenges.

He stands in front of me, his body crowding the entrance to the airlock, his chest falling and rising deeply. From behind me, space is spiralling, just a door away.

I shake my head at him. My body shakes a little too.

"I can't lose you too," he whispers.

I force the tears from my eyes. "You aren't losing me, you're letting me save Savannah's brother. Andrea's sister. Your friends."

I yank my suit closed, slipping the helmet made of translucent Umbran fibre over my head. It does nothing to cloud my vision, but he swims before me.

Jackson grips a fist around the back of Elijah's shirt, yanking him back into the ship just as Nico lets the compression door hiss shut.

Against the wall, there's a long round of wire, half as thick as my wrist. The metal fuses into my suit, my lifeline to the ship. In my haste, I activate a switch on my boots, the magnets attaching me to the floor as the door opens.

My world spins as air rushes out of the chamber, cold and biting. I close my eyes. I take a deep breath. My feet stay planted against the floor, holding me in place as the air around me connects to space.

Elijah stares at me from inside the ship, his gaze burning brighter than the pounding in my heart, but I don't look too long as I step out into the stars.

I'll be fine. Mason will be fine. We'll all be fine.

I deactivate the magnets on my boots and push myself further from the chamber, flying away from the ship. There is no up or down, just blackness peppered with light.

I centre myself, eyes scanning my target.

The pilot has latched onto their ship. My muscles harden, breathing hard, as I pin my eyes onto the entrance hatch on his small vessel.

My suit activates and I sail towards the very person I hate most in this world. The suit has a jetpack embedded to it—small, fast rockets that allow me to tailor the speed I use to zip through space. I reach for the controls on my right forearm and push to full speed.

If I save Jasmine's damned ass, I will let Jackson beat her senseless for her stupidity. The image follows me through space and it's that which gives me the greatest push forwards, not Elijah.

It sits in my gut wrong, twisting the same as I spin around the endless black.

My breath gets lodged in my throat and I hiccough. I'm only vaguely aware of the eyes of our entire fleet on me before I slow my speed, still banging into the pilot's ship. Metal reverberates.

Below me, there's a handle on the edge of the ship for the main exit doors. My fingers clasp it with near desperation. I hang in space, hand on the ship, body dangling.

I gasp shakily, sucking in the air pumping through my suit, and give my heart several beats to settle. And then I locate the control panel box keeping the door held into place. The box is several metres away from the door and I push myself off the handle, sailing towards it, arms reaching.

This entrance into the ship is only accessible when on the ground, as there isn't an airlock. But I pry open the shaft and reveal my prosthetic arm. The suit around my elbow compresses, moulding to my skin as I reveal my fingers, preventing the vacuum of space sucking all the oxygen from my suit.

I look towards the topside exiting shaft where it's connected to Jasmine's ship. Pilots are taught to close the hatch after disembarking to another ship, in case of the need for quick detachment. By overriding the main exit, I shouldn't jeopardise the people in Jasmine's ship. At least, I hope I won't.

I slide my fingers around some exposed wires in my left arm, opening an access to reach for the appropriate fuse I need. No one else can override the main entrance doors because no one else has an arm like mine.

I attach a wire from my arm into the shaft on the ship and hear a mechanical release, followed by a rush of wind—the air pressure releasing. It takes less time than it does for me to take a deep breath.

Sirens wail from inside in the ship.

I wrap my arms through the handles of the ship and lock my muscles. The wire in my arm pops loose from where it was attached. The door to the ship slides open.

I know I'm already in a safe zone, but one is never truly safe in space. My breath clouds within my mask, a steady throb pounding behind my eyes.

Anything that was loose inside the ship slams out into the blackness, bumping and clashing around each other, whirring among the stars. A photo frame with smiling children ricochets off the door and spins past me.

I grit my teeth, holding on with every damn muscle in my body until it's over and the space around me settles. Without waiting for my heart to relax, I make haste towards the entrance. Loose items spiral behind me, a soft green blanket wistfully trailing in the zero gravity, like a aurora in the sky.

I haul myself into the ship, fingers skimming the control panel by the exit, shakily searching for a button to activate the doors. My hands tremble as I find it, the doors sliding closed and sealing. No one else can enter until I activate pressurisation, yet my pulse is ticking like a time bomb.

My body hangs mid-air in the ship and I spin myself around, scanning for the pilot's seat. The ship is much smaller than any back on Terra—made for speed and a maximum of two people. I push against the wall behind me, shooting towards the front and skirting around the ladder centring the room. It leads to a circular hatch which has been sealed closed. The entrance to Jasmine.

I grip onto the pilot's seat to slow down and hold myself in place.

The controls on the screen are flashing bright orange.

Pulling myself in front of the control panel, barely hovering above the seat, I run my fingers over a series of screens until the sirens quieten.

This ship has synced its biometrics to the pilot. But since the pilot left the ship running…

I flick my hands over a transparent screen, pulling it up before me. Blue lights swirl around it, like a hovering holograph. I release a shaky breath, warmth flooding my veins. Oh, how I've missed Umbran tech.

I flick through numbers and swirling patterns, settling on a flashing silver light that runs the pressurisation. In small Umbran ships, this feature is always accessible in case it's needed, though it's hardly ever used. I dig my way to it, running through numbers and lights. The mechanics feel like a part of my soul.

"*Pressurisation, activated.*" The ship speaks in French, but I understand it.

There is a slight hiss as the ship pressurises and I feel the air move around me. I take stabilising breaths, the air in the suit beginning to make my throat feel raw.

With my heart pounding, I search through the control screen for the anti-gravity activation. It takes me seconds to locate it and, moments after activating the gravity, I sink into the seat, the weight of the world resting on me as gravity takes hold.

"*Completed*," the computer announces when the oxygen levels read 100%.

Without a moment's hesitation, I pull my suit off. It slithers to the floor, catching on my feet. I kick off the boots, hating how heavy they suddenly feel.

The moment they're off, I go back to the screen to check the communication log, to see if we should be expecting any more company. News highlights dance up on the screen. Blood rushes from my face, down my neck, a thump pounding in my forehead. I squeeze the back of the seat.

My vision glazes. I watch, but don't quite take in the images of Savannah nailed to a post on top of a Hover as they flash from screen to screen.

Argenti pulling her immobile body onto a marble plate. *Flash.* A close-up as they nail her body against a post. *Flash.* Her blood on the marble. *Flash.* A crowd going wild. *Flash.* Her head lolling as they parade her through the village. *Flash.*

Crack. My fist goes into the screen. It clatters into a million pieces before softening into a crystalline gel at my feet, winking and spurting light. My hand should hurt, but it doesn't. The metal in my fist breaks through most everything.

But everything else hurts. The world around me hurts.

Where was Jesse when they were parading Savannah through the street?

And, more importantly, how long ago was this? *Have they built an army there yet, to save her?*

I dissociate, the world around me blurring as my body acts on its own command. I move away, hands latching onto metal rungs. The hatch to Jasmine's ship is right before my face and, pushing against the heavy weight of gravity, muscles straining, I swing the hatch open. And then I hear Mason's voice.

"Mel?"

My mind clears slightly as I clamber up into their ship. It looks the same as my own, but everything about it is different. Every light is on, a halo of clattering colour. It blinds me. Screens display old news—not the news I need them to see—and screams at me like a riot. Mason is stuck to the chair in front of me as if frozen, his fingers shaking.

The world slows when I see the yellow hair. Cassidy, sprawled on the ground, blood on her face. Her long hair is in a braid, identical to Andrea's, spooling in her own blood, brushing the edges of Mason's boots.

Dead.

My heart slows. She stood up to Jasmine. She actually did it.

All for her sister, who she thought I would kill if she didn't.

That girl is dead because of you. Andrea will never recover.

Bile coats my tongue.

I rip my eyes away from her, seeing stars. If only I got here faster. If only.

I make to move towards them—towards that silver pilot uniform and halo of dark hair that has his back to me—but am slammed backwards in Laurence's grip.

He catches my abdomen, holding me firmly.

"It's gone south," he mutters quietly into my ear. Which is precisely the moment I realise the pilot is holding a pretty little blade against Jasmine's throat.

A blade that is still covered in blood. Cassidy's blood.

Jasmine's blue eyes flicker to mine, fear drenching her face. The news channel in front of Mason flickers to a different scene and the air before me slows. Not a single person breathes.

What did you expect to happen, Jasmine? I want to say.

But instead, I feel the blood drain from my face as she groans, "Melanie, help."

Just as the pilot moves to slash her throat.

MELANIE

T he world before me is a riot of sound and colour.

I can't stop seeing Savannah being nailed to a post as a faceless fighter pilot before me runs his blade past Jasmine's neck. I can't, even if I wanted to, because it's spilling all over the news feeds behind Mason.

I release a clattered breath. And then I do something I never thought I would do. I save Jasmine's life.

Laurence doesn't have his weapons belt anymore. But he is Umbran and he knows how to hide his blades. The moment Jasmine flashes her eyes to me, I feel his fingers slip a weapon into my metal palm. A blade. Small and dexterous.

I'm no fighter, but this arm is pure tech. It never misses. I lunge forwards, aiming for the pilot's back.

"MELANIE," Mason squalls.

Mark hesitates, lost between lunging for his son and saving Jasmine.

The pilot turns at the sound of my name. As Jasmine pulls back, he slashes the side of her neck, thankfully not deep enough to kill her.

The pilot side steps.

And the entire force of my mechanic arms thrusts the blade into her Jasmine's spine as she turns.

I watch as if the world is moving through water, not quite feeling my body. I step back from the wound with shaking hands.

"Jasmine," I breathe.

She cries out, her back arching from impact. Blood drips from the side of Jasmine's neck as she crumples. It's all I see as she crashes to the floor, the knife from my hand in her back and blood dripping onto her shoulder.

Her hands falls right by Cassidy's head, fingers brushing red.

I stare at the blood on her neck. At the blood on the floor. It's hard to know which body it belongs too. It mingles. Moves. Claims the panelled floor of the ship.

"Melanie, watch out!" Mark yells.

I hear Laurence lurch behind me, trying to hold me back. Just as I move, the pilot comes for me—amber eyes lit like an inferno of flame.

My breath stops.

Laurence grabs my cyborg arm and uses it to thrust deep into the pilot's stomach. Deeper. Deeper.

I growl. Flesh rips around my fingers until I feel all of it. Organs. Blood. Warmth. It spills around my glove, soaking it. The pilot falls to the ground groaning. I intended to incapacitate him with the knife, but his death is coming. I scramble to take my glove off, hands shaking at the feeling of it stuck to my skin, red and glistening.

It lands on the floor with a wet slap.

I take a trembling breath.

All eyes are on me, including the pilot's. He grabs his chest when our eyes meet, a familiar stone glinting beneath his fingers.

Jasmine had one too—one of Lythia May's power stones.

With his blood still coating my arm, I press down on him, fingers circling around his throat. Behind me, Mark fusses over Jasmine. I don't question why Mason hasn't gone to her. Perhaps he is startled.

"What power is in that stone?" I ask.

Probably not the most important question, but the one at the forefront of my mind. He gapes like a fish, blood dripping from his mouth. Weak, shaking hands come to grip my arm. On the wrist of his uniform, a number is counting down—89, 88, 87…

"It slowed us down," Laurence says, "like walking through water. Mason can barely move. Cassidy tried but the pilot got her first."

I don't look at Andrea's sister. My eyes flicker to the news screen behind Mason, a swirling holograph of colour. On it, Savannah is being pulled onto the marble platform again. She, too, is immobile.

I swallow. "Cassidy's sister is on my ship."

I squeeze the pilot's throat a little, not quite having it in me to kill him, but letting the rage cascade through my fingers, nonetheless. If he notices the way my hands shake, he doesn't mention it. Hell, he can't really speak around the blood washing out of his mouth.

"We saw her through the window," Mason responds.

I don't look at him. I glare at the pilot, pinning him with every ouch of rage in my body.

60, 59, 58…

"What is the countdown for?" I press, knowing he doesn't really have it in him to answer. But thankfully, I have Laurence.

"Backup. Umbran military," Laurence says. "Got to be."

My hands lift from the pilot's neck, shaking in the air before him. The world around us goes quiet. Mason finally moves close enough to the news feeds to shut them up. Lights blink out, then darkness coats us, licking our bodies.

Not only does Mason take away the news feeds, but most of the electricity in the ship. I feel it shudder beneath me.

My eyes meet Mark's while he holds Jasmine's head. She's breathing. She doesn't move, but she's breathing.

"We are the only people the Elders know about. We're Savannah's family," I say slowly.

42, 41, 40…

The pilot slumps as the light leaves his eyes. No one else moves.

35, 34, 33…

"I don't know what you mean by that," Mark says, his lip trembling as he takes me in. His glasses are skewed, hair mussed. Pure, innocent, father-figure human. He doesn't know how much danger he is in.

"If we go, others will be safe," Mason says with a small gasp.

"And before you ask, this isn't debatable," I say softly. "Sorry."

Laurence takes a long pull of air.

Jasmine groans. Loudly. She lets her head fall back onto the ground, her blonde curls dancing around her head. Her legs twist at a weird angle, but she doesn't move, seemingly defeated.

"Mark, you're the healer on this ship. Get Jasmine some *Velox*," I urge.

He peers up at me, his hands shaking, and furrows his brow. He blinks away the confusion, just as Mason swings the med kit we equipped each ship with from out of a cupboard and tosses it to his father. It glides across the floor, crashing into Mark's hands.

Hands still shaking, he locates a vial of *Velox* from within, then turns to remove the knife from out of Jasmine's back.

I slowly rise from the floor and avoid everyone's eyes as I stand over the controls, pulling the ship's comm towards me.

19, 18, 17…

I don't look at the pilot's numbers anymore, but they tick in my head. I count every damn second.

My eyes stay glued out the window on Umbra swirling before me. In the distance, specs become small ships soaring up from its atmosphere. With a shuddering pulse, I open my mouth to speak to our infantry.

"Hold your ground. No one is to remove their invisibility. An Umbran fleet is arriving to take Squad A2 down to Umbran soil—if we do not return in five days, follow the protocols from Jackson in Squad A1." My voice cracks. I pause. Take a deep breath. "Let's not allow this to ruin our mission. Thank you all for your service."

I drop the comm so it bounces against my feet. Static buzzes through the ship.

"I'm so sorry," I mumble, staring out ahead of me.

No one says anything. Even the other ships remain silent as they process my command. Thank the stars.

Jasmine groans as Mark frees the knife from her back and immediately stabs a vial of *Velox* into her body. I tune them out as I scan the window, my teeth slightly chattering. What must be 100 ships cloud the view before us, soaring through space from Umbra. So many. More than we could dream to take.

I quickly locate the main power frame from the ship and disable all communications. I damage the connection. I damage all of it.

Static resumes.

Mark finally rises, his eyes wide as stars. With shaking fingers, he helps Mason to his feet, the Magic from the stone still making them partially sluggish.

I suck in a shaky breath, knotting my fingers together to still them. It isn't until Mark places a soft hand on my back that I breathe evenly.

"Jasmine, come stand with us," I say, as Laurence walks forwards and takes his captain's seat, head still high despite the shaking in his shoulders.

And then Mark's hand on my back is trying to get me to turn.

"I can't," Jasmine says, gasping.

Mason lets loose a hiccough.

"I can't!"

A boom resounds outside.

"Jasmine!" I urge. The *Velox* has had ample time to begin healing her, unless…

My body stills all at once. *Velox* can regrow tissue, muscle, bone, cartilage, but if I severed some nerves in her spine…

Jasmine's face is waxen. Shock dances over her features until a silent tear leaks from her eye. "I can't. *I can't.*" Tears muffle her words.

I whip around, unable to believe the possibility. "Just stand up."

Her mouth is open, wobbling. Her hands are shaking. "*I can't.*"

My ears ring as I stare at her, helpless, on the ground.

I shake, rubbing my quaking hands over my face. Ships surround us.

Bang. Bang. Thick arms of metal lash out to our ship, connecting us with theirs. It crunches as it moulds to the metal. Trapping us. *Bang.*

"Melanie," Jasmine pleads. "Melanie, help. Help me."

I feel separate from my body as I stare at her. Everything has gone cold.

"Jasmine, please stand up," I beg.

I cannot be the reason she becomes paralysed. This is a joke.

Everything moves through water. Tears trail down Jasmine's face. Her legs are still twisted in that awful angle. Mark looks up at me, his eyes blinking, face pale.

"You hit my spine," Jasmine gasps.

I hit her spine.

"Please stand up," I repeat.

Bang. Our ship sways. I almost lose my footing. Jasmine's body slides across the floor a little.

"You hit my spine," she repeats. "You hit my spine!"

"No." I shake my head.

"She's paralysed from the waist down, the *Velox* didn't seem to heal her severed nerves," Mark murmurs, fingers drifting over her.

"Melanie," she cries, her voice cracking. "Help me." Her hand wobbles, hanging in the air above her torso. She drops it, dragging her nails down her legs. "Melanie, I can't feel anything!"

Radios stir from the dead pilot's ship below us. Voices scream. They'll be inside our ship within minutes.

Mason heaves a spluttering sob. He falls to his knees, gripping the shoulders of his father, eyes focused on Jasmine.

"I can't stand. I can't stand." Her chanting is a haunting whisper and, all the while, she digs her nails into her legs so hard, welts form.

We stare at each other, as if willing it to change. Neither of us break our gaze, even when the hatch to the pilot's ship swings open and Umbran military fan out around us. Her lip wobbles. I've never seen her skin so pale, so void of life, as she lowers her head back to the floor.

Guards file into our small quarters, adorned in silver from head to toe and wearing masks. There are six of them, all pointing weaponry that looks like a gun up to our faces.

"Stand down," the first one demands, his voice muffled by his helmet.

Comms chime from their belts, voices filling the quiet space. I barely hear them or myself as I say, "Welcome to Umbra."

I hold out my hands, expecting restraints. The one closest to us grabs me, pinning my front against a wall.

"No! No!" Mason cries as they pull him away from his father. Mark grunts and reaches for his son. Jasmine doesn't move.

They plant one of their guns to my temple. I bang my forehead against the wall, squeezing my eyes.

"So much for Umbra being a peaceful planet of science," Laurence sighs.

It's the last thing any of us say.

SAVANNAH

Nothing really seems to matter anymore.

I lay on that metal table far too often now, what feels like multiple times a day. They're getting desperate, but still I do not speak. They break me, over and over.

Sometimes I scream. Occasionally I sob.

But I never speak.

It helps now that my mind is one with the small Argenti girl's. I am not like my mother—I can't speak into people's minds or look through their eyes. But I can follow Amadea's mind everywhere.

Today, she is on the far side of the castle. I can sense her impatient, but excited energy. I could be selfish enough to say it's because she finally made progress with me, but I try not to think like that.

Hope is contagious though. I cling to her like it's the only goddamn thing left in the universe.

"Your allies from Terra have been accessing our security feeds again. Do you know how they broke the firewall?"

My mother is back as the interrogator.

Marcellus wasn't one for asking questions. He was simply there to watch me break. The only time they ask me questions is when my mother is present, because of her ability.

Her fingers motion for the faceless man to lower something to my forearm. I didn't catch what tool he favours today, but it doesn't matter. All I know is that it hurts.

My vision fissures as he works on me, my focus on Amadea slipping. I cling to her mind, urging her optimism to wash over me.

Above us, the continuous roll of security footage flickers, the image swaying on the thin screen. My mother gestures for the torturer to stop, giving me a breath to collect myself.

On a good day, I would have tried to figure out why the security feeds are shaking. But today, I'm too far gone in Amadea's mind.

She is moving. Her thoughts seem to be short-circuiting, buzzing as she tries to find someone.

The castle is massive, filled with many layers and alleyways. Amadea navigates them like it's an extension of herself, the same way her mind is an extension of mine. I can feel her drifting, moving about the giant stone beast above our heads like a mouse.

No one stops her. Her mind is too focused on whatever she is doing.

Perhaps it's because people give her leeway as an Argenti, or maybe it's simply because people do not pay attention to, nor care about, children.

"Your friend—who trained her?"

My mother's words disjoint me. I miss a breath, blinking up at her as she leans over my table. Her fingers wrap around my wrist, nails scraping into the leather that binds me. Unblinking, I stare at her, drinking her in.

Her silver hair, long and tipped in brown dye, cascades across my arm. Her breath smells like berries and coffee, mingling around my face.

The torturer makes a move on me, but my mother snaps at him. "Hart!"

I stop breathing, my lungs compressing for a moment as her actual voice presses around us, pounding out of the open door.

I focus on stilling my heartbeat and try to understand what she is asking.

Who trained my friend? *What* friend? *What* training?

Thoughts drip away from me like honey and I brush my eyes closed. My mother rips herself away from me, her hair whipping my arm like a lash.

Dea is still dashing through the castle. She is so close to us now. Her mind is vibrant, a chorus of singsong emotions as I feel her approach me.

And then Marcellus is at our door—all silver and shining in a long robe, Jesse's sword still slung across his back. "The Third Elder requests you."

His voice shows no hint of feeling. No insinuation of where his head is at. He grips my mother's hand for a moment. Then lets it go.

"*Hello, little mouse. Having a good nap?*"

He's drinking in her Magic, apparently. I try not to let my glare towards him be too obvious.

The scent of Silver Magic is always thick in this room, but right now it's at an all-time high. I lean into the advantage of my Magic getting lost in the thick of it all and extend my senses out to him.

His presence feels comforting and cold all at once. I shiver, but fold into it. I wish my Magic allowed me to read emotions beyond the surface, because all I feel from him is an overwhelming sense of annoyance. And that can mean anything.

"What does he want?" my mother snaps, pulling back from him.

On better days, she would have schooled her emotions in front of so many witnesses. She would have asked him this question mind-to-mind. And he, with her Magic in his veins, would have responded.

I open my eyes, drinking in the sight of them. My mother's face is impassive and Marcellus's is blank as paper. Both gaze at each other with what seems like open distaste. I blink my eyes rapidly, unable to tell the difference from the obvious and from my Magic.

"You," Marcellus says, his voice low and brazen.

I can see a heat rising in my mother as she crosses her arms.

Above her head, the security feeds are flat. The light in the room dances, as if it's being tampered with. Beyond the door to the padded room, I can hear cellmates chattering. They know something is up. They're getting rowdy.

I take a deep breath.

Ice pours through my veins, heightening the world into clarity. The happy haze I have trapped myself into for days vanishes for a moment. I lose sense of Amadea, who's somewhere near the dungeons. I detach from my mother and Marcellus, and stare blankly at the dead feeds.

All of a sudden, I know exactly why my mother is questioning me today.

Melanie.

Was she able to finally break through Umbra's security from galaxies away? Why else would my mother question me about it?

I dart my eyes to Marcellus, but he doesn't meet my gaze. He and my mother are locked in a heated confrontation, both glaring at each other. Whatever she is saying to him mind-to-mind, neither of them is being kind about it.

Melanie.

I drift my eyes across the ceiling. There's a strip of metal lining the corners of the roof, thrumming in beat to the sounds in the room. It records everything that has been said.

Has Melanie heard? Does she know I'm here? A shiver puckers my skin and I pull against the restraints. In response, a blazing inferno ricochets up my arms.

My heart begins to pound erratically and the faceless man tilts his head towards me. I don't want to know what he has done to my arms, but I look anyway.

I immediately wish I hadn't.

Nails have been hammered along my forearm in a line. My right arm is better off, as it is the one he was still working on, with only two nails near my wrist. The left one is a mess.

I squeeze my eyes shut, tears swelling around my eyes. I wish Melanie had not seen nor heard what goes down in this room. She doesn't deserve that.

My torturer sighs loudly behind me. I try and focus on what he is looking at and notice that my mother and Marcellus are both still staring at each other. At the sound, my mother snaps free, her mouth in a hard line.

"Get her into her cell. Lock all the entrances and tell the guards that if they leave their posts, I will pin them to this torture bed. Got that?"

He lowers his head to my mother, hood draping.

Before he has the chance to rise, she storms out of the door, almost pushing Marcellus out of the way. He steps calmly aside, hands in his pockets.

He clicks his tongue and shakes his head. "You've done horrible work on her arms. Clean her up, would you? I could do without seeing those nails. It makes me feel faint."

Marcellus's voice sounds detached as he speaks. I reach for his mind, but he turns and gives me a deadpanned look. The thick taste of my Magic hangs in the air, so I immediately reel it back. But not before I sense Dea's mind outside the room.

The faceless man makes quick work on me, popping free each nail without a care for how it tugs at my skin. I blink away the tears, trying to recede back into that spot in my mind that offers oblivion. But no matter how I try, I can't quite reach it.

Melanie has hacked the Umbran main frame.

A wet sound escapes my throat as the nail closest to my shoulder slides free, breaking the overwhelming quiet of the room. I hate the way this room muffles sound—how the sound of my moaning seems to press around my skull.

I tilt my head for the door, nose flaring as I inhale the sickly-sweet smell of decay and urine wafting from beyond. Nothing could be more appealing right now.

This room smells like heavy bleach when the tang of Silver Magic leaves the air. It makes me sick.

"*Velox*," Marcellus orders, his hand extended.

I groan as the last two nails slowly come free from my other arm. Marcellus doesn't bat an eyelid—his palm raised above my body, waiting for the small vial of heaven—but he does sigh. Exasperated.

"Chin up, little mouse. Your nap is over."

The sound of Marcellus's voice encases me as he pinches the *Velox* into my arm. I think I moan, because he chuckles at me.

"I will see her back to her cell," squeaks the torturer.

"You will clean the blood up from the floor," Marcellus corrects.

The faceless man glares at him.

Marcellus places the empty vial of *Velox* on the table and my head spins as the chemicals surge their way through my body, wrapping honey around the puncture wounds in my arms.

Then two things happen at once.

The faceless man steps around my table, a scalpel shaking in his hand. Just as Dea appears in the doorway.

Marcellus freezes.

The faceless man swallows.

My body sighs as the Silver Magic surges out of my pores, wrapping around her, scenting the familiar perfume of her mind. It's her, even if it doesn't look like her.

She looks like Marcellus, only younger and female. In the same silver robe with the same thoughtful expression. Silver hair, striking eyes, her features sharp yet soft all at once. Her brow scrunches on her forehead.

I know her. But I don't.

"Amadea Hart," the faceless man says, his head tilting to the side. And because my attention is piqued, I can see the exact moment a shadow crosses Marcellus's face. A beat passes, long enough for my heart to echo in my ears. And then he's across the room. His long fingers grab the scalpel in the torturer's hand and twist it around and into his throat.

I gasp. My torturer isn't a fighter. I suppose those who relish in pain rely on others to bring their victims to them.

Amadea hiccups.

I sink down on the table, eyes rolling in my head as the faceless man gapes, blood leaking past his lips and splattering on the floor at his feet.

Marcellus releases him and steps backwards, face impassive as he watches the man grapple for the scalpel in his throat.

I hold my breath as he folds over the torture table. Over me. His back catches my legs, dangling him across the table.

The hood slips and eyes as black as night pierce my own. Unwillingly, I see his face for the first time. The world around me feels sharp. The haze is gone. His vacant eyes stare at me and he enters my soul, his features branding my mind.

A hooked nose. Pale face. Small mouth. He looks young and old at the same time.

I squirm, trying not to scream as his skin meets mine. I squeeze my eyes closed, breathe. It's so hard not to scream.

Get him off, get him off, get him off.

"Now I need to find someone else to clean up the blood," Marcellus grunts. "I didn't wear this pretty silver robe just to ruin it. We have a fun occasion to get to this evening. Don't we, Dea?"

Get him off me, goddammit.

I turn to Marcellus, but my torturer's face follows me in my mind, branding me.

He deserved a worse death. I would have done it slow.

Blood blooms in my mouth from where I clamp my jaw shut, causing teeth to dig into my gums.

Heat rises in my chest and I thrash against the bindings holding me to the table. The *Velox* works quickly down my arms, bringing strength back to my body.

But I'm still here. On this table. Touching him.

Amadea—sweet, silver-haired Amadea—balls her hands before her heart and walks slowly across the room to me. Remarkably, she doesn't bat an eye at the dead man. She just rakes her hands down my bindings.

Get him off me.

I scratch at the palms of my hands, heat and pain screaming in my head as I pick at my skin. I want out. I *need* to get out.

I glare at the small girl with the heat of a million suns and, with shaking hands, she finally releases me. She works on my leg restraints first, then moves to my hands.

The first binding on my arm slides free and I lash my hand forwards, shoving the dead man until he slumps away.

The second pops free and I roll off the table, hands slapping on the ground.

Marcellus doesn't move a muscle. He stares at the dead security footage above with a vacant expression. "Get her out, Dea. Now."

I'm panting on the floor, chest swelling as I force myself to my feet. My legs struggle to hold me as the world sways.

Amadea steps back, her hands shaking. The silver in her robe ripples under the light. Neither of them do anything as I cross the room, my bare foot slamming with all my strength into the jaw of the faceless man. Bone crunches under the force.

I don't want to see his face.

I need him gone.

My chest heaves as anger pounds through my veins.

Finally, I dash for the exit. Marcellus calmly steps aside, Jesse's sword flashing as he moves. It is that motion that causes me to still.

Amadea lifts a small knife off the table in her shaking hands, then drops it as if she's repulsed.

"The door that's always unlocked is not safe today." I flick my eyes to her. She averts her own, looking past me. "Take the back tunnel?" she suggests.

"Back tunnel?" I rasp.

Marcellus smiles. "Behind the tapestry."

A tapestry in a dungeon?

I click my tongue, eyes pinned on the girl. Her silver eyes dance to my hands. I look down, seeing myself pick the edges of my fingers so dynamically that fresh blood bursts through the skin.

Marcellus comes to the entrance, leaning against the door to the padded room. Blood stains everything behind him. No one and nothing could make me want to ever step foot in that room again.

Amadea peers around her brother, wrapping her fingers around his arm.

I take a deep breath, then hold my hand out to Marcellus. I owe this man everything, but he still has my switchblade.

He takes my hand and clamps it steady. A small smirk crosses his features.

"No," I gasp, trying to pull my hand back, eyes on Jesse's sword. My mind is on my switchblade.

"You'll get it back. I'll take care of your blade, little mouse. Unfortunately, your mother knows I have it and I'd rather not die when you leave."

I squirm to shake off his hand, frowning at him. Is this a game to him? He holds me so tight it's almost painful.

And then a warmth seeps up my arms, the same time as the

thick scent of Silver Magic plasters the air around us. Amadea clears her throat as if in pain, her breathing laboured.

Not pain. *Magic.* I can feel her, as if she's wrapped perfectly around my mind.

Then my pores shift.

"We should go blonde. I'm curious to see how you'd look blonde. And green eyes—we don't see enough of them on Umbra and I would love to say I've seen something beautiful in these dungeons. No offense, you're not disgusting, but—" he cuts off, just as I feel my body ripple under his grip. He releases my hand, still smirking. "Excellent."

I raise my hands to my face. It's still mine, but when Amadea's hair ripples blonde for a moment, then flashes back to silver, I wonder if perhaps the rest of my features changed as well.

My heart pounds in my head and I lower my shaky hands. I hesitate, looking at a section of the floor, just above Marcellus's feet.

Savannah is gone. I'm new. The padded room has stolen the girl that was.

"She doesn't talk much," Dea comments.

Marcellus tilts his head. "You doing good, little mouse? Hmm. You'll live. You survived the worst we have to offer. Congrats, you're a part of the big game now. The fight for the crown will appease you soon. I'll be waiting."

I stare blankly at him then blink and breathe deeply.

I don't respond.

His lip twitches, but straightens as a voice echoes down the corridor. From far away, I can sense someone—a guard. No, several guards.

Marcellus hears it too.

My pulse skitters, joining the pounding in my head. On top of the stairs leading out of the dungeon, the exit looms.

I feel every fragment of my body lean towards it. Towards freedom.

But I don't run for it. Good god, I don't.

My head turns back towards the dungeons, following the grey tunnel of stone and metal that's covered in faeces and urine.

My body feels weak and my mind still dips in and out of reality, swaying against any movement like a tide. I take a step away from Marcellus, feeling unsteady.

If only I stayed long enough for water and food. My mouth is dry, my stomach empty. I keep making work on my nails, peeling the skin.

"Go get 'em, little mouse." Marcellus's voice swirls around my head.

He stays still by the padded room, as at ease as someone would be when safe at home. Amadea smiles at me.

They receive nothing but a blank stare from me as I attempt to collect figments of my thoughts. Could I be... leaving?

My friends are waiting for me. They have armies. They can protect me.

I squeeze my eyes shut and take a step away from them with stars in my eyes.

No one says another word as I turn back to the dungeons in search of a tapestry.

MELANIE

I'm home.

I can't stop my teeth from chattering or my smile from widening since the ship docked in Sector 2, otherwise known as the military hub. It's located on a different continent than Silver Kingdom, right by the ocean's edge instead of the sprawling river that slashes the main city. But Umbra is so small, land is visible in the distance. It won't take long to reach the other side.

I swallow sharply, my mouth dry. I wish I could stop moving long enough to go the bathroom or get something to eat or drink.

Even though I prayed for it, a part of me was never certain I'd return and yet...

The Sector is red and silver, black and white, harsh and rough.

All civilians who live in this Sector are allocated quarters so small and barren, you could toss an apple and hit the farthest wall.

Families sleep in bunks. Guards, pilots, and military technicians start their day at the crack of dawn, go back to their chambers for five hours for recovery, then continue until nightfall.

This is the place where Jesse grew up.

I hate it. I hate how it reminds me of him.

They parade us through the Sector, making sure to keep us from seeing too much. But I stumble with every door we pass. I know exactly where the mess hall is, where the pilots train and how to get to the hangar.

Mason takes it in with wide eyes, oblivious to the metal cuffs binding his hands. Laurence and Mark look like they want to vomit. Jasmine looks like she's about to cry.

They cart her on a metal plate that hovers above the ground at waist height, shackling her so she can't move. Not that she could. What do they expect? For her to roll off the metal and land in a heap at their feet?

I squint as they lead us to a large rolling door as wide as seven Hovers and as tall as the ceiling. Daylight streams in from behind, fusing with the lights spilling from the metal walls and ceiling.

My hands are bound, preventing me from shielding my eyes, so I close my lids and keep them shut. I don't open them until I can smell brine and feel the biting sun clapping my shoulders. It's only morning, but it's still hot outside.

My eyes well when I open them. Red sand meets blue ocean, bright and clear. The water is a swirling riot of life and a long metal bridge travels over it, high enough above the water that ships can travel below.

As a child, I wanted my father to take me to this bridge. I wanted to jump off it, like I heard the military children do. I wanted to feel the ocean hugging me as I pounded through the surface.

I never did.

We aren't allowed to dwindle in the military sector. I still don't know if it was truth or tale that military kids did that. It could've been something they just raved about at school.

The guards shove us across it and into the Ocean Train, or so it's nicknamed—20 carriages long, used to transport goods, people, and armies across.

I shiver when the shade hits me.

Of course, it isn't common knowledge that the Elders are building an army. Calling Sector 2 military is like nicknaming Sector 1 the Kingdom. It's nothing more than a turn of the phrase, for lack of a better word. Our planet is peaceful. But even science, I realise, bends to the curiosity of warfare. The gun prodding at my back tells me everything.

They've been inventing new weapons. As a precaution, they might say. A fail-safe, Jesse would contradict.

Laurence doesn't take his eyes off the weapon. If I asked, he would probably scoff at any statement of defence, just like Jesse. He's from this sector, after all.

Wind tosses my hair. It brushes my cheeks, warm from the sun. At some point in the flight down to Umbra, it fell around my face.

The door to Ocean Train clatters shut. The wind stills. They place us on hard wooden benches and magnetically attach our cuffs to the wall behind us. On the wall opposite, the guards stand in a line, their eyes hard.

The room is barely lit, without any windows. I wish I could feel the ocean on my skin. Jump off the bridge. Swim home.

Mason is shivering beside me as he trails his eyes over the metal carriage. My apprentice. Savannah's brother. Mark's son.

If it weren't for him, I'd be gone already. Slipped through the cracks. Sweet-talked my way out of capture. *Anything.*

But the idea of leaving him alone is too repulsive to imagine.

"What are those?" he enquires, eyes on their guns.

It's half the length of his forearm, all looping metals and swirls, the Umbran crest stamped just above the firing end so that the thought of the Elders would be the last thing that crosses your mind before you die.

The guards don't answer. Nobody in our party knows.

Jasmine groans from her perch on the wooden bench. Dried blood speckles her legs.

"It's alright, Mason." Mark's words jump around the carriage.

Mason swallows, tipping his head onto his father's shoulder. I cast a look at Mark. His breath shudders as he glances back at me. I'm the only one who notices the way he holds his body, trying to shield his son from the guards. Protecting him.

He pulls his eyes away from me, unsaid words spiralling in both our heads.

It only takes 12 minutes on the Ocean Train to get to the docks near Sector 1. I know this from memory, yet I still let my eyes drift shut.

The pounding in my head is relentless and I need to use the bathroom, but having a moment to close my eyes feels nice.

The train slows. Enters the Dome. It happens all too fast.

Both Laurence and Jasmine hold their breath, knowing what the slowing speed means.

I bunch my hands into fists, fighting the urge to scream as they load us off the carriage almost as quickly as they boarded us. Outside, the wind is no longer as harsh. Instead, a fruit-scented breeze whispers across my skin. The Dome distils everything, even the wind.

I shudder as I lift my head, strands of hair grazing my cheeks. *Home.*

They tumble us out and I don't miss the way Jasmine's face contorts at the image of the Dome behind us, slashing through the sky.

But I don't care. Her plans won't happen anymore and besides, *I'm home.*

Warmth spreads in my chest.

Mason's plan to blow it up seems like an ancient threat. He

pushes back his shoulders as he walks off the carriage, a guard lugging him forward. He doesn't even see the Dome. His eyes are all for Umbra, because he's home too.

I watch the way the stars twinkle in his eyes and turn to the world I once knew so well. It feels like I'm seeing it for the first time. The Ocean Train bridge ends inland, a whisper away from where the Kingdom river meets the ocean, trees tumbling down from hills around it. Fruit trees that are both Terran and Umbran scatter the countryside—a smattering of oaks, palm trees holding coconuts, peach trees hanging low with ripe fruit, apples littering the ground—everything that shouldn't live near each other, living in harmony. All manufactured and tailored to perfection. Birds flutter in the sky. Butterflies hum around flowers. The world is set in an eternal spring.

It's so beautiful, it hurts.

They parade us from the bridge down stone stairs to where the ground is flat with dirt. A large array of guards stand in wait. They line the stairs, making a path for us to walk through. Some have guns. Others have swords. All are expressionless.

Beyond them, a line of Hovers wait to take us up to the castle.

The sound of my feet hitting stone feels infinite. My pulse is ticking by the time we touch the ground and I face our welcome party. My eyes trail them, hitting each of their faces. Some are Argenti, others aren't.

My gut twists as I slam my foot on the ground. It's stupid and my face goes sour at the thought of it, but it shocks me that my uncle isn't here. That he doesn't care enough to see his niece.

I lower my eyes the moment I notice he isn't present and I take a long breath.

Mark blanches. He must have stopped walking, because guards bustle around him. "Keep moving!"

It only takes me a moment to realise why. My eyes flicker up and I see her. The one person worse than my uncle.

Standing metres away, among a guard of Argenti I do not know, is Venus Collins. Savannah's mother.

She looks winded, her gaze like steel, as if she rushed to meet us. She doesn't look at her son or her husband, but the moment I lift my head, her eyes capture me. They burn into my skull.

She has Magic here. She has access to your head.

The world before me slows as what feels like ants dance over my skin. My breathing grows laboured. I barely even notice the way Mark is gasping beside me.

I can feel her in my head. Battering her way in.

And so, I do what I do best on Umbra.

I drop my mask. I drop all feeling and show them the person they want.

I show them the helpless girl I was.

My eyes stay void of expression, but a small smile adorns my lips as I stare at her.

"Your friend awaits you."

I wince at the intrusion in my head. Bloody mind speaker. My brain throbs and I tighten my jaw, staring at those soulless eyes, letting her see me. Then the gentle smile returns to my face and my shoulders loosen. I am nothing more than Winston Beckett's daughter. The gentle soul. The courtier. The Liaison's niece.

She isn't fooled for a second.

"But you already know that, don't you, little hacker?"

This time, my mask doesn't slip.

I twirl my hair casually, taking the win as a moment's frustration crashes over her face. When she turns, I try not to blanch.

With her back to us, Venus beckons a finger. The wind bristles against us, singing and swaying as the Argenti swarm towards us, all of them on beat.

They don't have a Hover with a marble platform and a pole to nail us to. I guess we aren't that important. Instead, they have a Hover carrying a cage that looks entirely too small to fit us all.

A cage. For animals.

My breathing quickens and the world slows.

I exchange a look with Laurence, who looks ready to hit someone at the sight of the thing.

"Mum? Mum, it's me." Mason's voice travels softly, hitting Venus's back.

I freeze, eyes still on Laurence. The whole damn world pauses as the Umbran breeze dances down my spine, igniting my nerves.

Venus doesn't turn. Each one of her footsteps seems louder than the bustle around us, nailing a hammer into my heart. Here, she has the power to sense the minds of those she is closest to. She probably knew her son and father were on this planet the moment we breached the atmosphere.

But she doesn't care. She never did.

Neither of them is Savannah.

"Mum?" Mason gasps. "Mum!"

Mark attempts to move towards his son, but a guard yanks him back.

"Mason, don't." He turns to his wife. "Venus…" His words are faint, as if spoken in a trance.

An Argenti breaks free from the crowd, her silver hair cropped and glittering in the sun. She places her hand on Mark's shoulder, almost reassuringly, and then lightning strikes from her veins. I watch as they seep from her skin, travel down her arm and into Mark's flesh. His whole body tightens, bending forwards, and then he collapses to the soil.

He's the first person they throw into the small cage.

Mason opens his mouth to scream, his eyes darting from me to his father, to his mother. I turn, reaching for him, but I barely get another glimpse of his brown curls before a guard snaps my head back.

"No—" I start.

The guard's fingers dig into my shoulders and I spin in his grip, vision spotting.

Venus disappears, holing up into a Hover. A few other Argenti follow her. I force my body to spin back to Mason, desperate to reassure him.

When someone lays a soft hand on my back, pain forks through me. My body burns, aching. I open my mouth to scream, images of a house fire speeding through my mind. Fire. Pain. My home—a place I loved so much, lost to the flames. Eli, lost to the flames.

Now me...

I scream until I see the sky. The broken moon above our heads. I don't even get a proper glimpse of the Argenti girl's face before her lightning takes me.

The world goes white. Everything vanishes.

I float away.

SAVANNAH

T he tapestry is a depiction of the Moon Blitz, black and grey and glistening silver as it maps out the shards around the planet with thread.

I lift it with shaking fingers. And then I notice the stench.

My foot misses a step. Dead bodies have been dumped in the back tunnel. I don't see them in the dark, but I can *smell* them. The silver plastic they were left in shines into my eyes. I don't remember details of the tunnel, except for the feel of stone under my hands as I run them along the walls.

My hands are coated in moisture by the time I leave the castle. The daylight is blinding. Everything is white—even my hair is brighter than usual.

It swings into my eyes, doing little to shield me from the pain of seeing the sun for the first time in so long.

People turn to look at me. Nobles in fancy gowns having fancy conversations. They give me dirty looks and turn to their friends, gossiping about me.

No one takes much notice. I'm blonde, which means I'm boring to them. Just a commoner. A nobody.

I guess I stopped being Savannah weeks ago.

I grab my head and squint, sinking down to the stone. My skin is black with grime, matching the dirt. I want to close my eyes and not see the pain blinding me, but I hold on. Everything around me blurs. I'm not sure how much time passes before I centre myself.

And then I start to walk. And walk. And walk.

I stride past the nobles and their flashy clothes, milling in the gardens outside the castle. My strange, small feet carry me. My too-long fingers grasp for handholds.

The castle goes from a looming giant behind me to a blip on top of a mountain.

Grass turns to stone. Stone turns to dirt. Dirt turns to flowers.

Not a single guard stops me.

I'm *alone*.

I rotate in the summer breeze, eyes latching on fruit hanging from trees. My fingers strain for them. There isn't a single soul on the castle road. Just me, the fruit, and the screaming sun. It's not as hot as I remember the desert being. I suppose it's not meant to be.

The glittering Dome above my head, solid and grand, protects us.

My arms prickle and I run my fingers over my skin, calming the way my heart pounds. Small, quaint, and quiet houses greet me along the road, but the people aren't here. If anyone is, they keep to themselves.

The nearest house has an arching tree in the garden, its limbs casting shade on the neat array of flowers some Umbran must have spent years tending.

I reach for a plump fruit.

"Ahhh," I moan.

Juices run down my arms, the soft flesh of a nectarine touching my tongue. I barely chew. It's gone in moments. Another one hangs right by my face, and I reach for it before I drop the pit of my last one. The remains of the old nectarine land by my feet just as I sink my teeth into the fresh flesh.

Something squeezes in my stomach, but I keep chewing. Another fruit. Then another, until a fist wraps its tendons around my gut.

Feet slipping on the grass, I crumble to the ground just as the fruit surges back up my throat, splattering all over someone's flower bed.

No one comes out of the house. No one is on this street.

A stark comparison to the mobs they showed me on the news feeds.

I rub my palm against my temple and force myself to stand, practically feeling my body yell at me as I move onwards.

Where is Jesse? The castle is far away, but still near. Has he built an army with Tam? Have they tried to free me?

Stars, I *feel* dead. I don't even wipe the dirt off my knees before taking the next road. My eyes don't catch onto the Umbrans' perfectly primed houses.

I don't see anything as I walk and walk.

I keep going until my feet crack and I drift down to my knees. The breeze tries to play with my hair, but it's so greasy and matted that it barely moves. Along the road, trees dance in the wind.

Something begins to prickle behind my eyes. It travels up my chest, clogging my throat. I stumble, then fist my fingers in the grass below me.

The trees look like they're from home.

They're magnificent, tall, and imposing—a terrifying beauty.

I keep waiting for mist to surge from their limbs, cascading down from the mountain where the castle sits. But it's the middle of the day and the sun chases away the haze.

I clutch my head and still, not a single soul bothers me.

I fist my matted hair. And then, a tree stirs. It takes me a beat to respond, my eyes slowly trailing up to meet the leaves. Something loudly huffs. No, some*one*.

"Jesse?" I breathe.

It's Lily's cat, Cerberus, that pops out. His coat gleams in the sunlight. He sniffs as he sees me, but doesn't leave the trees. If the snow cat is here, Lily must be too.

We never took him with us across the lake. They must have gone back for him.

Lily must have decided to stay.

I raise my hand, dirt-stained skin straining for its snout. My hand almost looks like mine again. Cerberus just stares at me.

"Where are they?" I croak.

I'm far away from the Argenti houses. Even farther away from the common houses. Somehow, I've found my way back to a forest, a dense pocket of normality under the Dome.

It's exactly the sort of place Jesse and Lily would be, hiding undercover.

"Please."

The cat opens its maw, revealing some teeth.

I lower my hand, slapping it down onto the ground. Veins of grass toss and sway in the wind, tickling my exposed skin.

"Where are they?" My voice cracks. I breathe loudly, staring at the damned thing. It gives me another warning growl and then huffs deeply.

Resigned, it lowers itself to the grass, head tilted towards the breeze. His thick white coat flutters and moves like the leaves above us. He must feel so warm, being this far south and away from the snow. He wouldn't be here without Lily.

"Where are they?" I whisper. He closes his eyes. "Answer!" I pound my fist into the ground, ripping up dirt. "Answer me!"

Sobs wrack my body, tearing apart the serenity of the forest.

I howl, letting the twisting in my heart guide me, shattering me completely. My head pounds. My body loosens. I tilt and fall to the grass.

"Where are they, where are they, *where are they?*" I cry. Over and over.

Cerberus slowly falls asleep, but I can't.

I don't think I'll ever be able to sleep again.

I drag my fists against my head and wail into the dirt.

And that freaking cat just lies there.

He. Just. Lies. There.

I'm so alone.

MELANIE

T he cage is wet and smells like decay, and each time we hit a
rock in the road, Mark's arm rams into the soft flesh at my
stomach. *Thunk.*

I squeeze my eyes shut, letting the darkness hold me for a
moment longer.

Mark is breathing heavily. It's difficult to say whether he's
awake, but based on the way Mason keeps gasping and squirming
nearby, he must be.

Even with my eyes closed, I can imagine the way Mason is
pointing things out for us. I can nearly see them in my mind—swelling hills, dirt tracks bordering on the edges of hills and swooping
between homes, flourishing vegetable gardens, flocks of wildflowers
straining for us as we whisk by.

The side of my head slams into the metal bars and I choke back a sob. What I wouldn't give to run my fingers through the wildflowers, to pluck fresh fruit and gallivant through the village without a care except for what I'm going to have for lunch.

Only, I have no home to return to, no maid to bring me food, no father to sit down at the table and tell me about his latest challenge at work.

It'd just be me and the flowers. And this stupid cage holding me back.

"Where are we going?" Mason asks.

No one answers, but as the Hover moves uphill towards the mountain, I already know. I always knew.

We're going to the goddamn castle.

My eyes flash open and I suddenly spasm at the thought.

Jasmine startles, her head whacking on the cage as I lurch into movement.

"What—what the hell?"

My heart aches from the sudden movement and I attempt to catch my breath.

Ahead of us, the back of our driver's head—dark with long brown hair, meaning he's a guard not an Argenti—bobs as he swerves along the path. They carry us in an old Hover and it bounces all over the place.

"What was *that*?" Mark exclaims, rubbing his eyes.

Jasmine grumbles, sinking back down into the cage as if I'm boring her. I distinctly notice how her eyes are glazed over. Unseeing. I turn to look anywhere else and sigh softly. Memories flood back to me, expanding my chest.

"'Morning," I mutter.

They're taking us to the castle, just as they took Savannah. I taste bile in my throat as I twist my body and reach for my comm.

Savannah doesn't have hers anymore, they smashed it when they were parading her down the street. The images dart through my mind, each one tasting like poison, and I swallow more bile stirring in my throat as I hold the comm in my shaky palm.

In one fluid motion, I let it go.

It falls between the bars of our cage, thumping to the ground.

Mason watches me, tears welling behind his eyes. He sniffs and hastily brushes them away. His gangling limbs clutter the cage as he fumbles to turn, twisting around us to look at something, anything else.

"Oh!" he exclaims.

I blink, slowly lifting my head.

And there it is.

"Jasmine, Dad, look. Up there. You see it, Jasmine? Can you see it?"

The castle glitters in the sun, almost white above the trees. It would be hard not to see it, but Jasmine doesn't respond.

Her foot is nearly on my lap, jerking with every bump in the road. Her eyes vacantly track trees ahead of us. She practically flinches when I glance at her.

I clumsily push her feet off me. She notices and a small tear wells in her eye.

I tense my jaw, turning my head.

Laurence has his head tilted to the sky, squinting against the sun. The cage flickers as we move past each branch. I wouldn't have taken an old pilot to be so damn sentimental.

Mason, noticing I'm awake, reaches over to tug my sleeve. "The castle, Melanie."

And he's right. At the tallest mountain peak, surrounded by a halo of sunshine, sits the grand stone monument. The figurehead of the Silver Kingdom and home to the strongest Argenti and their founding parents—the seven Elders responsible for ending my parents' life, for sending me to live with my uncle who has since forgotten about me, and destroying all my friends' lives.

It's beautiful. Proud. No one can conquer it.

I flick my eyes to Mason, hold his gaze, and slowly loosen the tension in my jaw.

"You're finally home, Melanie."

Home.

I suck on the insides of my lips. Everyone inside the cage is looking at me, and yet the ones most important to me aren't here. Where are the people who promised to bring me home?

"Mhmm," I murmur, tilting my head back onto the metal bars.

Laurence hisses, turning his head from where he's still looking above us.

"Melanie?" Mason asks.

"Ignore her, she's obviously suffering," Jasmine mutters, turning her cheek onto the dank wooden floor.

"Oh, am I?" I snark back.

"Poor Melanie, she's in a cage. Poor Melanie, she had to leave her lover in space. Whatever will Eli do?"

I whip my head up. "Take his name out of your mouth."

"Why? He's my friend, too."

"He stopped being your friend the moment you invited that pilot onto your ship and *set us up to die.*"

She blinks at me and awkwardly hoists herself up. Her legs drag, as limp against the floor as her curls are against her neck, swaying in the cage.

The Hover moves up the mountain towards the castle, giving her the angle to support herself.

"I don't know about that last part," she says. "Why would I want you to die?"

I glare at her with every ounce of my anger.

Her eyes glaze over, but she holds herself upright. She fixes her blue eyes on a spot over my shoulder, where the sun hits the path behind the Hover.

"Never thought I'd be back here. You?"

More emotion crests up my chest, but I don't respond. Mason turns his head towards me. I don't meet his eyes and, thankfully,

Mark reaches out to pull him from the discussion, enveloping his son in a side hug he only vaguely seems to want.

It's hard not to smile at the way he protects his son, but I keep my face as expressionless as I can.

I shrug at Jasmine, not bothering to reply.

"The scenery here is nice," she says quietly. "Look at those pretty, purple flowers. I'm happy I got to see them again."

My head tilts on its own volition. It's not something I would have ever expected her to say.

"Huh?" I mutter.

No bitterness reaches her face when she speaks again. "I welcomed the pilot into our ship because, when I lived in Sector 2, most pilots had family on Terra. Silver Island in particular. Figured they'd be pretty unhappy about the bombing."

A soft breath escapes my lips. "You lived in Sector 2?"

She's not military. Her parents were alive during the Moon Blitz and went through hell because of it. Their lucky break was when her mother worked for Lythia May many years after. That all screams Sector 1 to me, or at the very least Sector 3—which is in the desert with the wild folk, far away from this continent.

Maybe her parents are so old, they experienced all three Sectors. Who knows? Who really cares?

"For a time," is all she says, still staring at the purple flowers behind me. She's right; they are quite pretty, flocking up and down the road towards the castle.

I squirm, all too willing to shove them down her throat if it helps her get her damn words out. Stars, does she ever answer a question straight?

Mason reaches over his father, eyes imploring. "We wanted to use the pilot's ship to hack into Umbra and see how to remove the Dome. We thought he would work with us." He says it so quietly, I barely hear him. His head is lowered to his feet when I meet his eyes, for once not looking in awe at the world around him.

"It was all my idea," Jasmine says bluntly. "There's no 'we' in that plan."

My eyebrows raise a fraction of an inch. Mason stiffens his jaw.

Only Laurence and I see her words for what they mean. He takes a deep breath, then turns back to the trees as if he wants no part in it.

Jasmine protecting the little boy by admitting the fact she's been manipulating him. Admitting *blame*.

There must be a catch.

I take a long, drawn-out breath.

"For the record," I explain, "I didn't mean to stab you in the back.

Jasmine doesn't meet my gaze. "I never liked my legs anyway."

I give her a long look. "Yes, you did."

She winces. "Yeah, I did."

The Hover stops abruptly. Laurence clutches onto the bars, stopping himself from toppling over, as though expecting it. Or maybe it's just the fact that he's trained to expect it.

The rest of us cascade over Jasmine.

"What—why?" Mark says.

The road crosses over from gravel to stone, indicating our proximity to the castle. I stare at them with my cheek against the bars, legs around Jasmine's feet.

Mark pushes my torso, clearing Mason out from under us. I let him move me, distracted by the throngs of guards clouding the view ahead. They stamp down towards us in two long lines, trailing down either side of our carriage. The electric-shocking Argenti at the front of our Hover hisses, then throws out veins of lightning into the trees.

"No way," I mutter, fingers gripping the bars as I strain to see. "No way in hell."

"What?" Mason asks. "Melanie, what?" I squeeze my face right up against the metal, scratching my cheek. "Melanie, *what?*"

A gasp shudders out from me. Jasmine starts hitting my foot, batting it off from her. I yank it forwards and kick her in the jaw.

Accidentally, of course.

"OW—" she starts.

"Shut it, something's happening ahead. Maybe it's Savannah." I don't even feel myself talking.

Venus is calling out something far ahead. A few Argenti fan out off the path, scaling down the stone bridge and castle walls, then disappearing into the forest.

"Savannah?" Mark breathes. "She's here?"

"Where?" Mason exclaims. "Where is she?"

"Someone's in the trees," Laurence whispers, head dipping upwards. "They've been following us this whole way."

Ah. That's why he's been watching the sky.

"And you only tell us this now?" I ask.

He gives me a long look. What happened to the guy who planned battle strategies with me? Ugh.

I cram around them all, standing as high as the cage allows me. And then I see it. I see *him*.

Jesse. *Jesse, Jesse, Jesse.*

He's here.

I feel my heart lurching. An involuntary smile crashes over my face because I see him. I stop breathing.

Jesse. My Jesse.

He sits in a tree, his body angled, a smirk on his face.

No one sees him but me.

I look at him and he looks at me, as if we're sharing the sweetest secret in the world.

He whips his head towards the castle, reluctantly dropping my gaze to take in the Argenti. Someone else is out there. Yelling meets my ears, but I don't turn my gaze away from him.

My heart is a mess. An erratic, pounding mess. I don't care who hears it or who sees me grinning.

Jesse is here.

Stars, why is he in a tree?

I don't ask him. I don't reach up to him. I don't dare spoil his position.

But my face must give it away. Jasmine sees my expression and turns her head to the sky. She groans deeply.

"Oh, for heaven's sake…"

Laurence clicks his lips, turning to Mark with an amused expression. It's like *he* was the one to discover Jesse. I roll my eyes, but it's hard to stay bitter.

Jesse's here to save us.

I wring my hands around the bars. The metal plating covering the exposed wires in my prosthetic hand is revealed to everyone. I notice Jesse's eyes flick to it before he slides down from the tree, swinging from the branches. He timed it while the guards weren't looking.

I finally reach for him, my hands gripping his ankles through the bars over our heads. He stumbles as I do so, slipping, but I need to touch him. Need to feel him.

He immediately winces.

It causes my heart to shudder when I notice why. Bruised face. Torn clothes. Rings under the eyes.

He's *exhausted*. Beaten, perhaps by guards.

I squeeze his ankles tighter.

"Jesse. Jesse!"

Jesse's sapphire eyes melt on my face, his body shuddering. His skin feels warm as he reaches down to touch me, as though starved.

I close my eyes. *Jesse is home.*

"I saw you," he whispers. "I saw the ships."

An Argenti screeches. Jasmine tugs my leg at the same time.

"Jesse…"

"I saw you, Mel."

I open my eyes. His face is near mine, full of bruises and old cuts. He'll have a scar there, above his cheek…

How much have I missed? What has this man been up to? I dig

my nails into the skin at his ankles, taking a deep, steadying breath. He doesn't wince, even as I nearly break his flesh.

"Jesse, where's Savannah?"

Mark lets out a long, shaky breath. I hear Mason move towards me, eyes imploring as his face nearly meets mine.

Jesse doesn't answer.

The driver fumbles from the front of the Hover, rocking our cage. His head turns to look at us, just as Jesse ducks out of view, squatting down to the ground.

I don't turn to him, but my gaze stays firm on him, aware of how his eyes tracking the movement ahead. Why does he keep looking over there? What's happening? A bead of sweat spills out from his dark hair, curling gently near his forehead.

"Jesse," I whisper, pulling myself as close to the bars as I can get to hiss the words, "*Savannah*?"

He doesn't look me in the eyes. Mark pulls himself higher, gripping his large hand around the bars.

"Gone, Mel. She's gone," Jesse mutters from where he kneels. His posture is solid. Not a single emotion crosses his face.

"What do you mean, *gone*? Where's my daughter?" Mark interrupts.

I don't believe the words, either. I shake my head. "No."

Jesse slowly meets Mark's eyes. "They took her to the castle. She sacrificed herself, so that we could build an army. But we haven't been able to free her."

Mason turns to look at the way it swoops up from the trees. We're less than a hundred metres away. So close to his sister.

Savannah's there! Mason's eyes seem to say. And when he turns to me, he doesn't have to. Hope crescendos out of him. Everyone sees it. I'm not strong enough to be the person to crush it.

"You have an army, but still couldn't get to her?" Mark demands, fixated on all the wrong things.

"We've been trying, all of us," Jesse says, flinching from a bruise on his arm as he leans on it. "It's been too long."

Blood covers him, old and new. He looks at me, all but given up. Savannah is gone.

"How many people is 'we'?" Jasmine murmurs from the ground.

To no one's surprise, Jesse doesn't answer her.

The driver jumps out of his seat and makes his way towards us, hands shaking around a sword.

Jesse jumps off the cage, feet pounding on the stones below. I watch as he slips out a knife from his pocket and jumps to the front of the Hover.

The driver is there. And then he isn't.

We all watch as the man rolls soundlessly to the ground, blood pooling around his neck. Jesse pulls the keys from his pocket and tosses them in the air languidly as he strides back to the cage. I watch the keyring as it rises up and down from his hand to the sky, over and over, as he strolls towards us.

The sounds of the bustle ahead of us has quietened.

Jesse's allies. Savannah's followers.

We have an army on Umbra and an army in the sky. We still have a chance. We just need to escape and get Savannah out.

Jesse puts the key into the lock on our cage, just us the cage roof bangs.

I startle, falling backwards. Mason nearly screams. But it's only a person.

Female. Wild hair. Eyes flickering around us like a cat watching for prey. Her feline gaze rests on me, and it all clicks into place immediately. The reason he kept looking ahead of us. The reason for the distraction.

And stars, she looks just like Jesse.

She gracefully pulls herself off the cage, sliding down the bars in one effortless movement and resting just before Jasmine's head on the other side. She crouches, partially hiding from the guards before us, and takes us in with a predatory gaze.

"Hello," she says, tilting her face.

Her eyes capture Jasmine's, who stares back.

"Everyone, meet my dead sister," Jesse announces, throwing open our cage.

The bars groan against the hinges and Laurence lunges immediately, hands reaching for the open air. He twists his back, eyes instantly darting for the treeline.

I follow him and brush his elbow.

"Go," I nod.

He turns to me, blinking. The rest of our group clambers out of the cage, fixing themselves up. All but Jasmine.

Laurence darts his eyes to me, to them, then back to the forest.

Jesse is on my side immediately and it's he who makes the decision for Laurence. "Take this with you," he says, offering up his knife. "You'll find the resistance in the trees. Tell them I sent you."

Laurence grabs it before I have the chance to collect my breath. The two stand face-to-face, soldier to soldier, and nod. But he doesn't move. He waits.

"It's my only one, but Tam will recognise it. Ask for Tam," Jesse adds.

Laurence frowns. "You're giving me your only weapon? Against over a hundred Argenti?"

He stays, waiting. Checking to see if we'll be okay. It's enough for me to admit we can trust him. He'll return for us.

"A hundred very confused Argenti following a very false lead," Lily purrs, her eyes twinkling from where she still stays near Jasmine's head.

"Jesse, your idiotic nature isn't a secret, but seriously? We'll need weapons," Jasmine mutters. She tilts her head to Lily. "You're the brains of this operation, huh?"

Lily grins. Winks. A light crosses Jasmine's face.

Jesse explains, "I have Melanie now. She's my biggest weapon."

I blink, heart pounding. "Will you stay, then?" I whisper, my voice barely cresting above a breath.

His eyes lower to mine, lashes brushing the bruises under his vibrant eyes.

My heart explodes. Raptures. *Breaks.* I all but stop feeling.

To prevent myself from doing something stupid, I twist my hands into my pocket, squeezing my fingers into fists.

"I'm not leaving your side. Never again, Mel. Never again."

I let out a shaky breath.

Stars dance in my head and I want to reach for him, but don't. I take a step back and nod, keeping the emotion away from my face.

"Should we go with Laurence to the trees? Is that safe?" Mason asks softly.

His father holds him steady under his arms while Laurence smiles, takes a deep breath and then scales over the edge of the stone bridge. The way he hesitates before dropping down screams about his desire to get us to follow him.

But none of us move, we all stand shakily as we hear him land below. It isn't a far fall. We could all follow him if it wasn't for Jasmine's injury.

Mark makes a move to the edge of the wall, his mind only on his son.

"Jasmine is paralysed," I tell Jesse. "She won't be able to climb the trees or scale the wall for that matter."

Jesse releases a breath. Hopefully, Laurence will return for us.

Lily swallows sharply. "The world often scars the most beautiful creatures."

"Well, we need to find a way," Mark says, body angled towards escape.

All Argenti are occupied, but from the way Jasmine is twisting her head back, I have a feeling it won't be long.

She sees something we don't as she peers through the bars of the cage.

"Oh, honey. You were always a little slow," Venus Collins announces, staring at her husband.

Mark stills. Pushes his son behind him. And now, our choices narrow to zero.

My heart slams in my chest. Jesse grabs me, fingers twisting around my prosthetic arm as if trying to hide it out of habit. I use the contact as an excuse to pull him closer.

Lily protects Jasmine—likely knowing the broken girl is our greatest weakness.

And then, just like that, I realise we all made a great fatal flaw.

My heart drops and I all but stop breathing.

In one single swoop, Venus Collins now knows each of our greatest weaknesses. We all stepped closer to the one we wish to protect. I take a brash step away from Jesse, as if the damage can be erased.

"*We have your friend in the castle. Your princess. I can take you to her.*"

Her words slice through all our heads. Every single one of us flinches. Even Mason squints, clenching his forehead.

"Do we have a choice?" Mark splutters.

"We don't," Jesse says. But his eyes twinkle as he stares at her. Venus grins.

But she has no idea how many people we have hiding in the trees.

Hell, I don't even know.

"They have Savannah," Mark says.

The rest of the Argenti are still in the forest or far ahead on the road. We can still run. Nerves dance down my spine, my feet shuffling on the ground. *We can still run.*

My eyes flicker to Jasmine's broken legs. Jesse notices, shooting me a look. Neither of us are particularly fond of her, but Savannah will hate it if we abandon her.

I shake my head softly, answering his unsaid question.

He takes a deep breath.

"Take me to our daughter," Mark demands.

Venus smiles slightly and must say something in his head because his strong stance buckles a fraction as she pins her eyes on his. Mason pops his mouth open, taking in his parents as if unsure what to make of anything anymore.

"Oh, hell to the no." Jasmine groans.

Lily clicks her tongue. Jasmine looks at her. Lily looks back. Then red creeps up Jasmine's neck.

Interesting.

"Alright," I announce, sighing.

Jesse nods. With me, always.

I'm not leaving your side. Never again, Mel. Never again.

We all stand strong, staring each other down until it's hard to breathe.

Venus turns to the closest guards, preparing to call for them. Lily takes the distraction as an excuse to climb into the cage towards Jasmine, pulling her out towards us.

Seconds. We have seconds left to run. Everything in me wants to jump over that wall and even Jesse is shaking as he grabs my hand again.

Savannah is gone. She's dead. We're chasing a ghost.

The world glazes over, as if I'm looking through water. Tears threaten to spill as I gaze up at him.

My teeth involuntarily chatter. A well of pain crests up my chest as Jesse pulls me to him. "It's okay," he purrs. "It will be okay."

It absolutely will not. But at least I have Jesse.

"We'll find a way out, and get back to our people," he murmurs into my hair. I shudder, breathing in his comforting scent of linen and metal.

"What do you say, legless girl?" Lily declares loudly to Jasmine.

They sit on the edge of the open cage, Jasmine's legs hanging limply over the edge as Lily holds her by the shoulder.

I blink at them, watching as Jasmine holds out a hand for Lily. Jasmine takes a deep breath. Pain lashes over her eyes—and not the physical kind. I watch as a girl so used to running finally straightens her back, eyes hardening.

Something like pride crosses my chest. How odd.

"Let's go to the castle and give them hell."

Everyone watches as Lily's hand crashes down into Jasmine's, high-fiving her palm in approval.

I can feel Jesse's heartbeat. Mine mingles with his, racing.

Guards swarm out behind the cage—eight at most, all sporting those weird new guns. Lily turns around, sees them propped towards her and flinches.

"Put them down," Lily hisses, voice shaking.

They do not.

Jesse squeezes my hand.

"Well, shall we continue?" Venus says, a small smile breaking apart her face.

"You know what our answer is," Jasmine snarls.

Mason coughs.

"I'm with the pretty one," Lily declares, winking at Jasmine.

Jesse pulls in a long breath.

I pull him closer. Nod at Venus.

I hope if they kill us, they at least do it quickly.

SAVANNAH

I see my friends. *All of them.*

Jesse. Melanie. Jasmine. My brother. My father.

I see them enter the castle, and my world spins again.

Cerberus bumps into me. The damn cat followed me the whole way around the village for only the stars know how long.

That must be what his job is—babysitting. But if that's the case, why did my friends not come for me? If Lily knows I'm out of the castle, why is she following my friends back inside?

I crouch on the stone entrance, hands gripping my skull. A tree is near my back, its leaves brushing the wall of stones.

Anyone can find me here, but no one does.

I'm alone. Always alone.

I rip my hair out, strands drifting to my feet. It's brown again, back to good old Savannah. It makes me feel even more distant to the world, as if I'm back *there*. Back in hell.

A choke escapes me. Breathing increasing, I scramble my mind and push every thought down until I gradually stop feeling. Until only emptiness resides.

I stare at it unseeing. I never left the padded room. It follows me everywhere.

I try and reach the minds of my friends, but I just don't have the energy too. My breathing grows laboured, and in my search, I accidentally stumble back upon Amadea. Searching for her mind is too much of a habit, and it makes me vaguely nauseous.

I quickly release her, but not before getting a taste of someone else.

Marcellus is still with her, in the castle.

I lick my lips, mind crashing back to the water sachet he gave me a while ago. I don't know when I last had water. They usually fed me after the padded room.

Cerberus rests his head on my lap, purring as I stretch out my legs. He licks his maw, as if reading my mind, so I instinctively pull away from him.

All the guards, the Argenti, and even my mother have abandoned the front of the castle. The winds around me whistles, filling the empty space.

Tracking Marcellus, I explore the castle. His mind thrums in a pleasant way, full of complexity and satisfaction. The mind of a schemer. It swarms in my gut, filling the empty parts of me.

I wish I knew precisely what he was thinking. Especially when his mind suddenly connects with my mother.

I know the moment it happens. It splits his head like it splits mine.

Fear crashes through him, drenching his thoughts.

I clasp onto him, wondering if he knows I am near. But it's not him who senses me.

"*Savannah.*" Her words. Filling me. "*Savannah?*"

I rip myself out of Marcellus's mind. My hands slap on the stone, dirty nails raking them as I pant. Breathing becomes hard. The world speeds up around me.

Breathe, just breathe.

The sun breaks through some clouds, smiling down at me as I clutch at myself, hands gripping the dirty seams of my once beautiful dress. My skin feels hot from the sun, the proximity of Venus's mind, or maybe even from my own demons.

Cerberus stands and hisses at the castle. I turn my head slowly, trailing my eyes over the hackles raised on the large cat's back.

My mother knows I am here.

Without thinking, I stand, making the choice before my mother makes it for me.

I walk towards hell.

Time slows as I move forwards. Cerberus hisses at my back, growling and causing a fuss, but he doesn't follow me.

I walk alone into the castle.

MELANIE

They take us to the throne room, which is the tallest, grandest place in the castle. The desire to grab Jesse and run sits heavy on my shoulders, going unanswered.

Heart pounding, I take a deep breath.

I came here once when I was 13. My father had a meeting with the First Elder and some other courtiers. I don't recall the purpose of it, but I do remember the stars and the Umbran crest.

A large Dome filled with glittering specs of silver and dark blue cover the roof. The material is transparent and the way the sun moves through the clouds outside makes it look like the ceiling is swirling. Whorls of silver pepper our skin in starlight, painting a cosmic sea on everyone's pale skin.

Everything is silver. The ornate windows around the room. The thrones. The veins in the marble at our feet.

The difference between then and now is how many people are present. Argenti of every age and status line the edges of the Dome. Girls, boys, men, and women. All of them wear long silver gowns that brush against the marble floor.

Guards stand back by the doors, as if afraid to approach the glittering beings before them.

Mason takes a shaky breath, eyes trailing the sight from behind his father. His doe eyes hardly blink as he spreads his palms before him, touching the stars. Only he is oblivious to the threats before him.

Jasmine notices too, glaring at him from the silver chair they wheeled her into the room in.

"Ahh, so nice to see you, Miss Beckett."

My head spins, following the echo of my name. Situated on a dais covered in a plush navy rug, stands the coalition of the Elders. Behind them, the familiar Umbran symbol—the upside-down crescent moon with a sword dipping down into it—shines in my eyes. I squint at them, heart pounding.

Their genders and races vary, and all are adorned in clothing ranging from battle armour to gowns to casual linens.

The only thing they have in common is their youthful appearance and how they lean on their silver thrones with casual authority. My gaze settles on a man with a spark of auburn hair and tanned skin. The one who spoke brushes his hand down the length of his throne, the silver rings on his hand clinking.

The Third Elder. His throne situated third from the left.

Soft afternoon light spills from one of the ornate windows next to their thrones, battling on their skin against the stars reflecting from the sky.

"Wish I could say the pleasure is all mine."

Beside me, Jesse hides a soft chuckle. The door moans behind us, but I don't turn.

Jasmine squirms in her seat—a silver chair held aloft by magnets, much like a Hover. The floor beneath us is scattered with minerals, making the magnetic attraction possible. She hangs her head, sighing deeply.

A medic pokes her head into the room, white linens covering her body with a silver cross stamped to her chest. An Argenti closest to the door ushers her over and immediately, the medic homes in on Jasmine.

A long vial of *Velox* appears in her hand.

Jasmine sees it, rolls her eyes. "I'm paralysed, moron," she exclaims. The medic frowns, then stabs a long needle into her back. "FOR THE LOVE OF— OUCH."

I swallow sharply, eyes raking over all the Argenti lining the walls of the circular throne room. My back faces Venus Collins as she comes towards the front of the door, positioning herself between the Argenti.

"Looks as if the weapon that hit you struck the spine and slipped between a vertebra," the medic muses, a deep frown on her face. "It's a shame that *Velox* doesn't reconnect severed nerves."

At that, Jasmine fixes me with a long look.

I wince, but my heart misses a beat when she rolls her eyes and winks at me. What? Does she forgive me? I frown at her.

"We are working on a medicine to aid in this type of healing, it will help with paralysis—" the medic starts.

"Enough!" The First Elder on the dais calls out, stilling the room. Lights dance on his dark complexion, making a constellation.

Lily hovers as close as she can to the doors, as if planning a quick exit. But a guard grips her by the elbow and yanks her towards us. She spits at him in response.

The medic makes a quick exit, the wooden doors slamming shut after her, ringing around the room.

No one else makes a sound.

Lily is baring her teeth.

My skin puckers with nerves, as Mark takes an uneasy step forward.

"Where is my daughter?" he says loudly.

Fear cascades down my arms. *No, Mark. No. Leave it alone.*

"Your plaything?" the First Elder asks, his black eyes flashing to Venus. "Care to explain?"

Venus takes an uneasy step forward. She shrugs past us, her gown billowing as she sails towards them, her head dipped. In one easy stride, she kneels before the dais.

"He's yours to do whatever you please with." The words couldn't come to her fast enough.

Mark clears his throat. "Um, *hello?*"

The question sounds weak and helpless against the intense gaze of Venus. I listen with my heart in my chest as it spirals around the room.

No one says anything, but Venus does raise her head. No one has his back as he blinks at his wife.

With a hefty puff, Mason steps forward. His face is burning red and, for the first time since coming to Umbra, Mason looks scared. Above all, though, he is furious.

My whole body freezes, as does everyone else, while we all collectively turn to watch the way he grasps his father's hand. Solidarity screams from his chest as he holds his chin up to the Elders. He stares them down as if he brings their reckoning.

"And what of the boy that clings to his arms?" the Third Elder demands, eyes blankly passing over him.

Venus softly raises her head.

Every damn soul in the room has their gazes on the Third Elder. All except Mason and Mark, who stare at the Argenti on her knees. I swear I even see the Fourth Elder wring his small hands, his glasses sliding down his nose as he dips his head towards the Third Elder.

It's enough to get me to turn my attention away from Mason.

The Third Elder doesn't look like much—he's far less imposing than the First and frailer than the Seventh—yet a cool power oozes from him.

Chills claw down my back.

Venus clears her throat and I swear the world slows.

Mason detaches himself from his father, fighting Mark's prying gaze. He rests his hopeful eyes before him, face red, eyes blazing. I could not be any more damned proud.

"He is nothing," Venus mutters.

Lights play on Mason's skin, lining up his freckles, distorting him as he rests his gaze on his mother. Cool and upset. Red now covers his chest, making his freckles burn with fire.

She doesn't turn to him. Even if she cared for him—even if that could be true—this is not the place for it.

He doesn't see that. He doesn't understand.

My chest split as Mason opens his mouth to speak, but his mother beats him to it, adding an extra punch.

"He was a harmless experiment. I'm happy to pass the question of his future onto you."

Mason closes his mouth. Pain crashes over his face, his eyes losing their eternal spark. Fire lashes through my chest, but I don't reach for him like I wish I could.

Savannah would kill me for not trying. But I stand my ground.

The Third Elder looks like he sucked on something sour, but he holds his gaze. None of the other Elders speak.

I shiver as Jesse's hand touches my back. He bundles the fabric of my shirt into his fist, hands slightly shaking.

My chest rises and falls rapidly as I watch Mason. They're unlikely to let us go.

The First Elder clears his throat for Venus to stand. He nods his head and she retreats quickly back into the fray, standing out like a halo among the crowd.

A quirky smile stands on her face, glittering like the silver of her hair. She tilts her chin to the thrones, hands behind her back. Still, the Elders don't speak.

"Do you have my sister?" Mason asks shakily, blinking the moisture from his eyes. His echoes around the throne room, as gentle as a piano.

The Seventh Elder—Lythia May's mother—all soft in a navy gown with silver decals, turns her gaze away. The Third Elder quirks his lip, mimicking Venus's sneer, but says nothing.

My pocket feels like it's burning, the absence of the comm mocking me, an aching hole, waiting for Savannah. *She is not here. They must not have her anymore.*

Behind my back, I whack Jesse.

He grunts quietly, his gaze landing on mine for a beat. He realises too.

Swallowing sharply, he turns away, eyes on the sky. His posture is foreboding. Strained. He wants to run. To grapple a gun from a guard and hold it to everyone's heads. I can feel it in the tense veins rippling down his arms.

Gone, Mel. She's gone.

I wring my hand around his belt, latching myself to him. If Savannah was dead, we wouldn't be here. They're procrastinating. Holding us. *Using* us.

"Are you or are you not using us as bait to draw her to the castle?" I announce, my voice slamming through the throne room.

Every damn pair of eyes lands on me.

I stare at The Third Elder, my face hard, void of all expression. This may be a democracy, but he clearly has everyone under his grip. If any one of these Georgian scientists were to wear a crown, it would be on his head.

He turns away from me, as if he doesn't know what I am talking about. He must look to a guard, because I feel people pressing up behind me, ready to swoop down.

Jesse swallows sharply, but all the blood has already left my face.

Any chance of us leaving this castle left the moment we stepped through the gates.

My body tenses. What we say now doesn't matter.

The Fourth Elder stands. He doesn't look a day over 20, so dainty and petite, with freckles adorning his face. He clears his throat, glasses bobbing.

"We apologise for any ill doing on our part, truly. But you must know that we will take any action against anyone threatening harm and destruction upon our home. We understand that you're here to retrieve your friend and, believe us when we say we'd love to let you go free, but we're terrified of what that might mean for our home."

The words ping around the room. I take another step forwards.

"You bombed innocent people. You took *their* homes. Ripped their lives from them. You really expect us not to be upset about that?" I demand.

The Fourth Elder touches his glasses, head dipping. "We mourn those losses every day. But we gave them a choice and they chose Terra."

Mark glares at him, his hands shaking. "This isn't about Umbra versus Earth. This is a matter of right and wrong. You killed many of our people—people who didn't know your planet existed," he pitches in.

I watch the way his throat bobs up and down, flabbergasted. I flex my prosthetic fingers together, feeling the way the wires course through my hands, sparking them with a strength I would not have had years before.

They destroyed everything we hold dear, but at least I became stronger for it. Even Mark, with his shaking hands, stands proud.

"We thought long and hard about it—for centuries, in fact. Eventually we concluded that we cannot attach ourselves to Terra. We would love nothing more than to share our lovely home with the people of our home planet, but humans are a greedy, vicious unit. They will swarm our planet. Destroy it. It's much better for them to never know this place exists—that immortality doesn't exist. What they don't know won't hurt them. We must cut all ties."

I rub my temples.

Behind me, Lily sways from foot to foot. Her gaze continues to dart back to the door behind her, fighting the overwhelming urge to flee.

I don't blame her.

The Fourth Elder purses his lips. When he does, wrinkles form at the edges.

Starlight touches the faces of the Elders, casting them in ribbons of silver. They look ethereal, looking down at us from the dais, but they are only human.

Humans, who once walked a different planet.

An Argenti man steps forward from the crowd. His hair is a shock of silver, his eyes ringed with cool flame. His palm falls from another Argenti besides him, as if he is sucking the Magic from her. He rests his gaze nonchalantly upon me and smiles.

No, not me. Jesse.

He tenses, his body going so subtly rigid only I could notice.

I twist my fingers through his, trying to pry into the confines of his mind. My blood runs cold when he pushes me away.

"Father," the Argenti man says, turning dead eyes onto the Third Elder.

The men hardly blink at each other. Stone-cold nothingness spreads between them, casting a chill across the room.

Jesse swallows sharply.

"Someone's here," the son says.

His father nods. And the whole world slows down.

Mason furrows his brows.

Mark begins to breathe rapidly.

The massive wooden doors behind us creak open. The Argenti goes back to his position, re-joining a young girl who holds her ground, but has eyes that flash with fear.

I can hardly breathe.

The guards move aside, pulling a small figure into the space. Their silver garbs hide who it is, reflecting the starlight from the ceiling as they ease her into our space.

Beside me, Jasmine gags.

The guards move aside. And there is Savannah.

A sob forces its way up my chest, splintering my heart. The guards wrestle her into the throne room. She doesn't fight. Doesn't hold her ground. And when she meets my eyes, I barely recognise her.

Her hair hangs in wisps past her shoulders, weeks of dirt and blood clotting her face and clothing. Dirtied hands bound in restraints hang limply at her side.

Argenti move, their bodies brushing one another. I swear I hear the young, frightened girl yelp and immediately, Savannah's silver eyes travel past mine and land on the girl. They hold each other's gaze until Savannah's eyes track to the Argenti man next to her, the one that announced her arrival.

A guard pushes Savannah forwards, forcing her to the ground ahead of us.

Beside me, Jasmine is barely breathing. Her father and brother can only gape. Lily looks like she's about to bolt through the splitting doors—and she almost does, her body moving, until Jasmine grapples her hand.

Tears trail down Mason's cheeks.

I want to reach for him, knowing this is what Savannah would want. But the girl before us isn't Savannah. She kneels on the reflective marble floor, her feet black and her head lowered. She isn't Savannah at all.

Jesse mutters quietly next to me, as if in a trance. "She's gone, Mel. She's gone."

I want to scream. I want to run. Instead, I just stare.

I stare at the deflated person that was once my friend.

SAVANNAH

Marcellus has his eyes on me, Amadea at his side.

I'm both inside his head and inside the throne room all at once.

Returning to the castle wasn't a difficult feat. Most Argenti had been in this room and only a small rotation of guards had been set to man the castle.

They wanted me to come back.

I walked their gilded halls, tracking my filth all the way with me. I scaled stairs, heard my breath reverberate off the stone walls. I wish I could say I saw the castle for the first time with beauty and a full heart, but the truth is I hardly saw anything at all.

I pulled the thread in my mind towards Marcellus, knowing he'd likely be with my friends. Eventually, I was found by Melanie's uncle.

Liaison Banks was wringing his hands in a hallway close to the throne room. Not important enough to be there, but with enough ego to be pissed about it.

The way he smiled didn't bother me. He grappled my arm and lugged me towards the throne room. I swear I could hear his heart pounding in ecstasy.

And then I was there. *Here.*

The throne room is blinding. My body buckles and I fall to my knees before the Elders. The marble floor feels cool under my hands, their gazes hot on my back.

I can hear Mason gasping, but I don't turn to him. I don't have the energy to turn to my brother.

Melanie stares at me and I can practically feel her screaming inside.

My dad has tears in his eyes.

Jasmine sits in a weird chair with her legs all tangled and Lily stands behind her, staring at the open doors like she's starving for freedom.

I let them drift from my mind. Acknowledge them. See them, then let them go.

It's my mother that steals my attention against my wishes. "*If we kill all the people in this room, this revolution ends.*"

A lick of Silver Magic courses through me. I taste it on my tongue, devouring it. I can feel her mind, needle-sharp and impartial. My mother isn't evil, she's ambitious. Cruelty is what's needed to get where she wishes to be.

I suppose that's why Melanie's uncle likes her so much.

I lift my head to her, trapping her in a prolonged gaze as I try and spell out her expression. Every few moments, her eyes dart towards the Third Elder. The leader, I suppose—if unofficially. The world can be democratic and still have someone in power with the most strings to pull.

I hold her gaze and eventually she stops flicking her eyes away. I say out loud, hoping she hears. "What revolution?"

No one speaks. My voice sounds wrong. Gravelly.

It's no longer mine, too broken from disuse.

My mother's face sours and behind me, I feel my friends squirming, desperate to come to me.

"Savannah Shaw, daughter of Venus Collins and Argenti offspring. Your hair speaks of the common people, yet the silver in your gaze speaks in homage to our soldiers." Words, words, words. The Fourth Elder spills them into the room.

"Your little mission to attack our people is, and always will be, a ruse. Prophecies don't need to become true. But they can be the start of something else."

I drag my eyes past Alexsandre and Evaline, the Sixth and Seventh, as they stare with detached expressions to where I kneel. Alexsandre's silver hair gleams as bright as the Argenti bordering the room.

I latch my mind back to Marcellus. Noise greets me as I search for him.

"Perhaps we can come to an understanding," the Fourth Elder continues. "All we ever wanted from you were answers, yet you remain quiet. Why don't you speak?"

"Because you're taking up all the air," I mutter.

So many minds. So much space. I still have Celestine and Roman left to find.

Amadea's list rang true, but my assumptions of it rang false. They are trapped in a game they don't want to play. They are like me.

Everyone stares and holds their breath.

I wonder if my words shocked them. I wonder if they care.

"If you don't let my friends and family go, I will kill myself," I announce.

Let's get this over with. In and out. Get myself in. Get them out.

I say the words to cut to the point. I test them, as they have been testing me, and gently lift my head to see their reactions.

They don't disappoint.

Static pings in Marcellus's head.

The Elders furrow their brows.

No one says a word nor moves, until they do.

"As you wish," my mother says and snatches an S.P. gun off a guard.

The Elders stand. Alexsandre calls out for her to stop at the same time as Mason does.

"Venus, return to your post!" he yells, the same time my brother shouts, "No!"

I vaguely hear feet tumbling towards me.

Our mother raises the S.P. gun.

The warm arms of my brother wrap around my neck until his soft cheek lands on my shoulder.

"Get him back!" Venus snaps.

I turn to face Mason, who has tears leaking down his face. "You're not going to die," he is saying. "I won't let it happen. I have a plan to—"

"Get him *back*!"

A blinding light cracks through the room. The tang of Silver Magic thickens on my tongue. Guards swell for me, but they won't kill me.

Someone released their Magic to startle us which, of course, panics everyone.

I watch as my father reaches for one of the guards, tearing an S.P. gun out of their grip. Some of the Argenti without fighting abilities do the same, in a much kinder way.

I shudder as someone reaches for Melanie. She catches my eyes again, her fingers digging into her pocket as if out of habit. A comm. *Our* comm. Does she still have it?

She pulls her fingers out empty, in shock, just as Jesse lunges forwards.

There's too much movement in the room. Too many bodies.

He goes temporarily unnoticed as people try to regain awareness of their surroundings. Then an Argenti on the dais fires an S.P. gun at him, narrowly missing.

I groan, my heart quickening. He reaches for me, all pleas and hopelessness.

I don't know what they see behind me, but chaos ensues and I feel a cold barrel of a weapon find its way to my temple, warning me not to move.

Guards press forwards, catching my friends. More Argenti break formation.

Amadea takes a step back, hands on her temples.

Inside my head, all I feel is panic. My body feels hot and sick with it.

Jesse reaches for me, his beautiful sapphire eyes full of fear and desperation. His weapons belt hangs barren. His hands slash at air. My heart surges to him, encapsulating him, wanting to be near him again.

I hold my hand in the air, fingers mere inches away from touching his.

Dad screams a warning. I hardly notice my father as an Argenti moves from her position against the edge of the room, lightning sparking down her arms.

Melanie screams for me, but the barrel of the S.P. gun still winks by my face, the Umbran crest glinting.

"Savannah," Mason cries, trying to get my attention. "Savannah!"

I blink the stars out of my eyes, just as the Argenti with the lightning slaps her hand down on Jesse and the S.P. gun behind me redirects onto him too.

Lightning forks up his body, wrapping him in light.

The Argenti behind me steps forward, prepared to end him entirely. Prepared to *shoot* him.

Jesse arches in the air and I lunge towards him on instinct.

Mason reaches for me. The last thing I feel is my brother's

palms crashing against my shoulders, his voice yelling, "Get out of the way!" before the Argenti holding the S.P. gun hisses and pulls the trigger.

I watch with a vacant expression as it misses me, misses Jesse, and sends my brother up in red smoke.

MELANIE

I scream until my throat is raw. Until I can't feel my face.

Red partials drift across the marble surface. The remains of Mason Shaw.

They land on my face. On my skin.

Jesse is on the ground, alive but unconscious.

I hardly feel him as I land on my knees near his head. I hardly feel it as a guard yanks me up from the floor.

Savannah lies in front of me, so close I can smell the weeks of dried sweat on her skin. Next to her, S.P. gun hanging from her hand, is Venus Collins. I stop screaming, and I finally hear Mark.

"YOU KILLED OUR SON. YOU KILLED OUR SON." He is fighting off four Argenti men holding him back as he pushes himself towards his wife.

"YOU KILLED OUR SON."

Silver light skitters across him, highlighting the snot and tears leaking from his face as he spits at the woman before him.

His glasses fall to the floor, shattering under an Argenti's boot.

The girl with the lightning touch finally reaches Mark and knocks him flat. His back arches as he continues to blubber through the pain, "My son. My son…"

Darkness takes him.

Savannah holds her hands out before her, analysing the red particles on her skin.

White spots cloud my vision and I free myself from the guard restraining me to make it back to Jesse.

It could have been him. It *was* meant to be him.

My fingers scramble to touch Jesse, unable to part myself with him.

"You killed the one person who loved you," Savannah croaks towards her mother, her mouth the only part of her that moves. She doesn't seem to know how to act. How to react.

And then her eyes scan the dais, latching onto the eyes of the Sixth Elder. The man has kind eyes, yet looks troubled as he fumbles behind him for his seat.

Most of them are standing.

"Everyone, quiet!" the First Elder says. His brown eyes are on fire as he scans the room, landing on Venus.

"It was nothing. He was nobody, it was—it was nothing." She steps backwards. Drops the S.P. gun.

"He wasn't yours to kill."

For the first time, Venus looks afraid.

The Third Elder clears his throat. "The council will deliberate what to do. For the time being, we will hold the rest of Savannah's party in the dungeons."

Savannah lunges for the S.P. gun My world slows as she holds it in shaky hands, turns it around and rests it against her temple.

"No," she breathes. Her finger twitches on the trigger.

Behind me, Jasmine squirms. She can't rise from her seat, but I can hear her muttering. And when I turn to look at her, she doesn't look herself. She looks like a ghost.

Love and pain and hatred mingle her features. She's white with it. Fingers shaking. Breathing rapid.

I sure as hell don't blame her.

"We'll go," I announce.

Savannah flashes her eyes on me. "No."

Silver fire slices me as she stares me down, her anger breaking through the vacant mould she's been broken into. Her shoulders stand back. Her face is hard.

I press a firm hand to Jesse's chest, searching for the pattering of his heart to ground me.

"Send them away, and I'll join you in the castle. Send them away, and I'm yours," Savannah says.

I shake my head, unable to form coherent thoughts.

Jasmine rustles in her chair, causing a fuss. "We won't—" she begins.

"Be grateful that we're sparing you," the First Elder announces.

Savannah releases a soft breath. The S.P. gun shakes in her grip.

My heart whacks a painful rhythm in my head—a hard and fast headache spreading down my neck as I stare the coalition of Elders down.

Nothing, and I mean *nothing*, could have prepared me for his next words.

"Send them to Liaison Banks to return them to Terra."

SAVANNAH

I lower their stupid gun to the ground and pant as I stare at their stupid leaders.

Melanie's entire world implodes before her, but all I can feel is the red dust on my fingers. At the brother I killed.

He came for me. I let him.

He defended me. I let him.

He died. *And I let him.*

The sun begins to set through their stupidly ornate windows. A sunset my brother will never see.

My hands shake as I stare at the S.P. gun. The Umbran crest on it screams at me.

It rolls near Jesse, nearly touching his dark hair from where he lies on the ground, Melanie shaking above him.

I could have saved my brother, I realise with a jolt, *if I hadn't moved for Jesse instead.*

Melanie turns her back to me, her fingers stretching over his chest. It makes me recoil.

Jesse killed my brother.

I can't even stand to look at him.

From beyond the doors, Banks, the Terran Liaison, and Stone, the Umbran Liaison, smile at us in greeting.

A nerve pings through my body.

Ass kissers. Go home. Go away.

I stare at Liaison Banks and my body goes cold. He abandoned us in Silver Valley. He's part of the reason Mason is gone.

Melanie spins to face her uncle, her mouth opening and closing. Her gaze lands on mine and I hold her eyes one last time.

Goodbye, Melanie. Go home. Please.

Instead of sharing the sentiment, she turns her gaze to the guards, glaring. Something stirs in my chest. Pride? Excitement?

All the Argenti soldiers stand still in the throne room, but their guards shuffle.

No, Melanie won't be going home. She won't even make it to the hangars. Not with her anger, Jasmine's inability to flee and Lily's fear of the people restraining them all. They will escape, re-join our people, and come back for me.

The first smile I've felt in weeks blooms on my cheeks, then falls away.

My gaze lands on Jesse and I dart my eyes away. I try and hide my face from the Elders on the dais and the Argenti before me. But Marcellus sees the emotion spreading there. He sees me and I feel his mind wavering.

Uncertainty breaches the depths of his thoughts, crashing to the surface as I lick the emotion away from him. I haven't seen him touch another Argenti since entering the throne room, but that doesn't mean he doesn't have any power licking in his veins.

My heart is pounding like a furnace in my chest, ready to combust. I turn back to the dais, pointedly keeping my eyes away from the red powder at my feet.

Not my brother. Not Mason. He's alive and well.

The Umbran symbol burns in my brain, flashing above the heads of the Elders. The same symbol that ended my brother's life.

He would have loved Umbra—loved the village.

I'll never get to show him.

My chest threatens to split open entirely, but I hold my thoughts. My consciousness escapes to a deep, far away part of my mind where nothing matters and my brother is still alive.

"If I hear of any disruption to their travels back to Terra, Banks, I will end every single one of your lives. Do not disappoint us."

The Third Elder's words meet me, breaking the darkness in my head. I look up at the way he stands ahead of all the rest, the silver decals in his clothing shimmering.

"There is always one person who wears the crown," I mumble to myself, staring at them all before me, displaying a unit of Georgian power. They all seem to blur, to fade away into the light.

"What was that?" Alexsandre asks. His breathing is shallow, long, and drawn, as he tilts his head to me.

I stare at the setting sun that casts a silver glow on the throne room, splashing at the feet of those who play at royalty.

The crown is not a thing. It is not a king, nor a queen. And it most definitely is not the usurper of a girl standing before them to steal it.

It's Umbra. She's the vision, the real prize.

The crown is Umbra.

And it belongs to the person who knows best how to play her. The person who has the most power, the smartest in the room, the one with the most tricks.

It's not a jewelled headband. It's not a throne. The crown is a *game*.

The Elders know it and now I know it, too.

Melanie stares at me, oblivious to the truth, tears cresting in her eyes as they try and move her out of the throne room. Her comm sits abandoned on the floor, her fingers twitching as she leans for me.

She always wanted me to carry this burden, yet she never understood it.

But now I do.

"Father, you are aware that the Liaison is her uncle. How can you be certain we can trust him?" Marcellus asks.

I turn to look at him—at the way the light shifts in his silver hair. He looks the same as the Argenti around him, yet he stands out like a beacon. He doesn't look at me, so I turn away.

I turn back to my friends.

Jasmine is staring at me, her curls hanging limp. They still have her in that odd chair, her legs splayed out before her.

She touches a spot on her heart gently and I do the same.

This isn't the end for us.

Melanie moves towards Jasmine, her hands resting on her chair.

This isn't the end for any of us.

"Never underestimate the ambitions of men."

The Third Elder's words make Liaison Banks flinch, but a soft smile flutters on Melanie's face. Her uncle grapples for her and a guard quickly stops him. The Liaison bites his lip, his face red as the guards bind my friends' hands.

Even my father's and Jesse's, who they carry in their arms, still knocked out.

"Certainly, Father," Marcellus mutters.

Amadea wrings her hands as her brother steps back to join her.

"Not yet, Marcellus," The Third Elder says.

I blink at the doors as they swing shut. At the way they swallow my friends.

The moment they leave the room, the air gets sucked out of me.

I turn to the Elders and stare the Third Elder down.

Silver Magic coats my arms, my back, my head. All the Argenti in the room would be able to taste it, but I simply don't care.

Satisfaction leaks from the Elder's mind. To him, the great game is only beginning.

The fight for Umbra is one he intends to win. I just need to last long enough to figure him out, learn about his strengths and assets and, even more importantly, his blind spots and weaknesses.

"Take her to the annex room for me. We need a moment to speak with her mother," the Elder decides.

I swear I notice Marcellus's shoulders loosen, but from within the throng of Argenti, my mother's face goes pale. Marcellus nods.

All at once, the Argenti move. Guards swing open the grand doors, trailing out of the throne room in unison as they take their leave.

Amadea crosses close to me, her stance matching those of the others. Her silver robe ripples, moving around her small body as she departs the space.

Through the windows, a gentle, warm light breaks through the silver, spilling over the red particles at my feet. I stare down the sun, letting it burn my eyes.

It splashes colours across the horizon, lighting up all the trees across the village.

The room is mostly empty as Marcellus nods at the Argenti and leads me back through the castle.

"Caught in another trap, aren't you, little mouse?"

He smiles softly, his cold mask gently slipping as he beckons for me to turn right down the stairs. I don't smile. Not as my heart bleeds.

Outside the throne room, the world is cast in shadows that stream through the castle, gold sunlight splashing against stone.

Silver light fans my back, dispersing as I take their tunnels, their shadows drawing me home. Guards fall in line around us and Marcellus lowers his hand.

I breathe slowly, my breathing uneven, but I keep my shoulders back. I let them lead me—but it's almost as if I'm leading them, dancing all the right steps and playing all the right games.

They have yet to see it.

In the shadows, I let loose a long breath.

May the most powerful player win.

And may they get the crown.

ACKNOWLEDGEMENTS

Going on the journey curating *Silver Kingdom*, book 2 of the *Silver Valley Trilogy*, has been nothing short of special. The world of Silver Kingdom is exactly what I dreamt this universe to be like, and I cannot be any more proud of my characters and to have bared witness in the development of their world.

From the bottom of my heart, thank you to everyone who made this book possible yet again. Sailing the stars would have been a lonely place without you.

To my friends, Georgia Franck and Melissa Picone, who have stuck by me through thick and thin. Finally, we get to see Marcellus Hart's grand 'peach scene' entrance on the page! The night we sat around and brainstormed that scene, huddled in blankets, has become a permanent memory in my mind. Both of your love and willingness to help me sail through the tricky waters of the publishing world has meant everything to me. Thank you.

To my BETA readers, who went above and beyond! Not only did you give me conceptual feedback that increased any expectations, but you even combed through and pointed out my tragic typos, prior to official editing! You guys are the best.

To my family, who will always whisper in anyone's ear that their daughter has written a book! To my mother who's always there by my side, my father who will listen to me talk about the stars for hours, and my brother who single-handedly came up with some of the coolest concepts for Umbra—I mean, powering the Dome around the Kingdom via volcano is brilliant!

To my social media manager, Kaya Thackary, who will always stop and listen to me chat incessantly about my story even when he has no idea about the context. The enthusiasm you have for this book is unparalleled and I'm so grateful to have you along for the journey.

And of course, how could I forget my wonderful creative team? A massive thank you to my brilliant cover artist, Gabby, my exceptional editor, Chloe, and the whole team at Author Services Australia for your outstanding formatting! I couldn't have brought this book to life quite so beautifully if it weren't for you all.

Which brings me to my readers on TikTok/Instagram! You guys are the Melanie to my Savannah, the stars to my Umbra. Thank you for being there, for reading my books, for *enjoying* my books. It makes me smile every time I see a comment from one of you or when an online review pings through my phone. I can't wait to take on the world with you, and I wish I could give you all the biggest hug.

I hope you all enjoy and love *Silver Kingdom*, I'll be there through every laugh, every smile, every shed tear. *Silver Valley* is my baby, my heart, my wildest fantasy, and I am eternally grateful for each and every single person who has taken the time to sit down and read the *Silver Valley Trilogy*. I love and appreciate you all, thank you for everything.

ABOUT THE AUTHOR

Arabella Rosier is a 24 year old bibliophile from NSW, Australia. Books have always been a part of her heart since the moment she learnt how to read. When she was 14 years old, she read her first big fantasy novel and dream of writing her own. And now, 10 years later, *Silver Valley* has come to life. Hopefully it enraptures your soul as much as it has hers.

www.ingramcontent.com/pod-product-compliance
Lightning Source LLC
Chambersburg PA
CBHW050105120726
47904CB00004B/1222